THE PENGUIN POETS

GERMAN VERSE

THE PENGUIN BOOK OF

GERMAN VERSE

INTRODUCED AND EDITED BY

LEONARD FORSTER

*

WITH PLAIN PROSE TRANSLATIONS
OF EACH POEM

PENGUIN BOOKS

Penguin Books Ltd, Harmondsworth, Middlesex, England
Penguin Books Inc., 7110 Ambassador Road, Baltimore, Maryland 21207, U.S.A.
Penguin Books Australia Ltd, Ringwood, Victoria, Australia

—

This selection first published 1957
Reprinted with revisions 1959
Reprinted 1961, 1963, 1965, 1966, 1967, 1969, 1972

—

Copyright © Leonard Forster, 1957, 1959

—

Made and printed in Great Britain
by Richard Clay (The Chaucer Press) Ltd,
Bungay, Suffolk
Set in Monotype Fournier

TABLE OF CONTENTS

indicates extract or abridgement

v

TABLE OF CONTENTS

JOHANN KLAJ (1616–56), a Saxon, the principal figure of a
   circle of poets at Nürnberg. His stylistic virtuosity can be seen
   in this oratorio-like piece.

CHRISTIAN   HOFMANN   VON   HOFMANNS-
   WALDAU (1618–79), a Silesian official, master of a jewelled
   and elaborate style which conceals intense passion.

ANGELUS SILESIUS, the name taken by the Silesian
   JOHANNES SCHEFFLER (1624–77), on his conversion
   to Catholicism in 1653. His epigrams embody mystical doctrine
   in concentrated form; his hymns are known to Catholic and
   Protestant alike.

JOHANN WOLFGANG VON GOETHE (1749–1832)
was the first writer in German since Luther whose work compelled the attention of a European public. His great lyric poetry begins with his studies at Strasbourg in 1770 and his meeting with J. G. Herder there, and continues unbroken until his death. His guiding principle that all being was an organic whole informs his poetry and ensures a basic strictness of form despite apparent irregularities. He progressed from the immediacy of the Strasbourg period to a controlled style in his Weimar period (after 1775) which was heightened after his journey to Italy (1786–88); the 'Olympian serenity' of his later work was achieved only by a balance of opposing forces which he maintained – often precariously – to the end of his life. Despite the high quality of his dramas, novels, and critical and

scientific writings, it is, above all, by virtue of his *Faust* and his lyrics that he occupies the dominating place in German literature.

FRIEDRICH, called MALER, MÜLLER (1749–1825), a painter active in Mannheim and later in Rome, wrote poems, plays, and idylls.

TABLE OF CONTENTS

JOHANN CHRISTIAN FRIEDRICH HÖLDERLIN
(1770–1843), a Swabian, who started as an admirer of Schiller
but developed his own highly personal style in which to ex-
press his vision of Hellenic perfection; this vision he found
incarnated in Susette Gontard, the wife of a Frankfurt banker.
In 1802 he became insane and in 1806 proved to be incurable.
Besides his lyrics he wrote a novel, *Hyperion*, from which
'Hyperions Schicksalslied' is taken.

NOVALIS, the pseudonym of FRIEDRICH LEOPOLD
VON HARDENBERG (1772–1801), mining engineer,
novelist, and the only truly lyric talent of the first generation
of German Romantics. He created the Blue Flower as the sym-
bol of romantic longing. His *Hymnen an die Nacht* (1800) ex-
pressed a mystical death-wish soon to be granted; he died of
consumption.

CLEMENS MARIA BRENTANO (1778–1842) wrote, be-
side voluminous dramas and devotional works, highly melo-
dious and powerful poetry often in the folk-song style.

LUDWIG UHLAND (1787–1862), university professor and
liberal politician, successfully cultivated the narrative ballad
and the simple (often too simple) lyric in the style of the folk-
song.

JOSEPH VON EICHENDORFF (1788–1857), a Catholic
Silesian nobleman, whose serene and melodious lyrics reflect
an inner life securely founded in faith and delight in the ex-
ternal world as God's creation. He expresses essentially roman-
tic themes without strain or 'Weltschmerz'.

FRIEDRICH RÜCKERT (1788–1866), a professor of Orien-
tal languages, whose translations from Arabic and Sanskrit
were important. His lyric poetry, with one or two exceptions,
lives only by virtue of the settings by Brahms, Schubert, and
Mahler.

AUGUST GRAF VON PLATEN-HALLERMÜNDE
(1796–1835), a Bavarian nobleman, whose austere pessimism
combined with a cult of classical beauty made him a bitter
enemy of the Romantics.

ANNETTE VON DROSTE-HÜLSHOFF (1797–1848)
came of a family of Westphalian nobility. Her Catholicism and
her experience of nature are less serene but more passionate
than Eichendorff's, and her expression is more astringent. She
is Germany's greatest woman writer.

THEODOR STORM (1817–88), a Holsteiner, was primarily a
   writer of short stories, but a few of his short concentrated
   lyrics still 'speak to the heart', as he intended they should.

KLAUS GROTH (1819–99), also a Holsteiner, initiated a re-
   vival of Low German literature with his lyrics and stories; his
   hard-shell, soft-hearted sentiment is sometimes reminiscent of
   A Shropshire Lad.

TABLE OF CONTENTS

TABLE OF CONTENTS

STEFAN GEORGE (1868–1933), a Rhinelander, who brought about a reform of poetic diction by his own example and through his exclusive journal *Blätter für die Kunst* (1892–1919) after the fashion of the French Parnassians and Symbolists. A prophet of the greatness of the human personality in a European tradition, his influence has been profound and extensive. The spelling and punctuation of these poems is the poet's own.

CHRISTIAN MORGENSTERN (1871–1914), whose anthroposophical and mystical writings are largely forgotten, lives by his almost untranslatable burlesque and nonsense poetry, in which Herr von Korf, who has no physical existence, Palmström, the Nasobēm, and many other figures lead a Lewis Carroll life in the amiable realms of a higher absurdity with serious undertones.

AUGUST STRAMM (1874–1915), a Westphalian post-office official, killed on the Russian front. His intensely concentrated poetry is characteristic of expressionism, and was not appreciated until after his death. It is the fashion to belittle his 'wild experiments', but he becomes more intelligible when he is compared with abstract artists like Klee and Kandinsky.

TABLE OF CONTENTS

HUGO VON HOFMANNSTHAL (1874–1929), a Viennese, most of whose few but flawless lyric poems were written between the ages of seventeen and twenty-five, after which he turned to drama and criticism. Rooted in the great Viennese cultural tradition, which may be said to have come to an end with him, he is one of the great figures of modern German literature.

RAINER MARIA RILKE (1875–1926), a native of Prague; his 'existential' poetry and highly personal abstract–concrete style, with its combination of complexity and simplicity, has had a wide influence on European literature. He found his true vein in 1907, but his great achievement was the cycles of *Sonette an Orpheus* (1923) and *Duineser Elegien* (1911–22). The shorter poems since then are now more appreciated than his earlier work.

HANS CAROSSA (1878–1956), a Bavarian doctor whose chief work is a series of largely autobiographical writings in which the events of his time are seen through the eyes of a wise, cultivated, and gentle person, whose Goethean faith in life as an organic whole is the keynote of his work. *Abendländische Elegie* was first published in Switzerland in 1945.

RUDOLF ALEXANDER SCHRÖDER (1878–), from Bremen, in his poems, essays, and translations a representative of the European classical and Christian tradition. His recent work, from which the poems below are taken, shows him as the outstanding Christian poet of the present time in Germany in the protestant tradition; he has brought new life to a variety of poetic forms, among them the German hymn.

WILHELM LEHMANN (1882–), a friend of Oskar Loerke, and close to him in his perception of nature and his 'orphic' lyricism. He is an important influence on younger poets of the post-war generation.

ERNST STADLER (1883–1914), an Alsatian, was a Rhodes scholar at Oxford and a lecturer at the Universities of Strasbourg and Brussels before he was killed in Flanders. He belongs with Heym and Trakl to the early expressionists.

OSKAR LOERKE (1884–1941), a West Prussian, whose quiet incantatory poetry invokes the natural forces of growth and decay, is an important influence on post-war German writing.

GOTTFRIED BENN (1886–1956), a Berlin doctor, began as an expressionist, which he essentially remained. He is the outstanding literary figure in post-war Germany, a poet of nihilism and isolation for whom art is the only permanence in a chaotic world. His ejaculatory poems, often without verbs or even syntax, make concise and concentrated intellectual statements in melodious and disturbing rhythms sometimes reminiscent of Swinburne.

GEORG TRAKL (1887–1914), an Austrian, deeply conscious of the evil in the world, by which he felt himself particularly menaced (he was a drug addict); his creative work was his principal hold upon life. Died by his own hand on the Galician front after the battle of Grodek.

GEORG HEYM (1887–1912), a Silesian; his early death in a skating accident saved him from the fulfilment of his startling prophecies of the violent break-up of the world he was born into.

FRANZ WERFEL (1890–1945), a Jew from Prague, one of the prominent figures of expressionism in the lyric, drama, and novel. His later poetry, written in exile, is more sober. He attained world fame with his novel *The Song of Bernadette* (1941).

BERTOLD BRECHT (1898–1956) from Augsburg, lived in East Berlin and is the most gifted literary figure of Eastern Germany since the war, a tireless experimenter in the theatre, writer of short stories and ballads, informed with a deep sympathy for the underdog; at first a radical nihilist, later a Marxist.

ACKNOWLEDGEMENTS

THE extent to which I have pillaged earlier translators for renderings of individual passages will be clear to the discerning, but I must mention my special debt to Mr Michael Hamburger's masterly verse translations of Hölderlin. I am further indebted to many friends, colleagues and other well-disposed persons, including my own family, who have helped me with this book in a variety of ways. I am specially grateful to the late Dr Hans Carossa, who cleared up some points in his *Abendländische Elegie*, but also to Hermann Boeschenstein, J. M. Cohen, W. E. Delp, Barker Fairley, Irene Galewski, Lillian Haddakin, A. T. Hatto, Clemens Heselhaus, Trevor Jones, W. Niekerken, Brian Rowley, Emil Staiger, S. H. Steinberg, Ann Toulmin, J. L. M. Trim, M. O'C. Walshe, D. B. Welbourne, Elizabeth M. Wilkinson, and Marianne Winder. Dr Delp and Miss Winder checked the typescript for the press, Mr Cohen and Dr Steinberg gave invaluable assistance in proof, Professor Hatto helped me with the Middle Ages, and Dr Haddakin was most helpful throughout the compilation and translation. The responsibility for disregarding expert advice, and for any other errors and infelicities, is entirely mine.

I am glad to acknowledge permission given by publishers of copyright material as follows: Arche Verlag, Zürich, for Gottfried Benn's *Statische Gedichte*; Heinrich Ellermann, Hamburg, for Ernst Stadler and Georg Heym; S. Fischer, Frankfurt am Main, for Hugo von Hofmannsthal, Oskar Loerke, Franz Werfel, and Carl Zuckmayer; Matthias Grünewald Verlag, Mainz, for Elizabeth Langgässer; Hogarth Press, London, who hold the rights for English translations of R. M. Rilke; Insel Verlag, Wiesbaden, for Hans Carossa and R. M. Rilke; Vittorio Klostermann, Frankfurt am Main, for F. G. Jünger; Limes Verlag, Wiesbaden, for Gottfried Benn; Otto Müller Verlag, Salzburg, for Georg Trakl; Lambert Schneider Verlag, Heidelberg, for Wilhelm Lehmann; Suhrkamp Verlag, Berlin and Frankfurt am Main, for Bertolt Brecht and Rudolf Alexander Schröder; Verlag Helmut Küpper vormals Georg Bondi, Düsseldorf, for Stefan George.

INTRODUCTION

GERMAN poetry is generally known in this country through German music. By a fortunate combination of circumstances, one of the great epochs of German lyric poetry overlapped a great period in German music, and we know the work of Klopstock, Goethe, Schiller, Heine, Mörike, and Eichendorff mainly through the international language written by Beethoven, Schubert, Schumann, Brahms, and Wolf. It was a period in which composers were in close touch with literature, and they usually showed admirable taste in the choice of the poems they set. A small but acceptable anthology of German verse could be compiled from them. In many cases the words have become virtually inseparable from the music, so that the task of assessing them by purely literary standards is often very difficult.

Music also brought us another strand of German poetry, which is so interwoven with our experience that we do not normally recognize its origin: the protestant hymn. 'A safe stronghold our God is still', 'O sacred head surrounded', 'The duteous day now closeth', 'O Love who formedst me to wear', 'Now thank we all our God' (all of which will be found in this book[1]), have become an unquestioned part of our heritage. Here, too, the texts are for most of us inextricably associated with the tunes, some of them dignified by Bach.

So it comes about that even those who know no German are in fact often acquainted with a good deal of German poetry of a high order, but in a form which distracts attention from the poetry itself. Moreover, the translations in which it is known were not made with the intention of communicating poetry: the English versions of German '*lieder*' were made for the convenience of the singer, and renderings of hymns are usually made for the edification of the devout.

This anthology aims at presenting German poems able to stand on their own without the aid of music; no poem has been included merely because there is a good setting of it. The

[1] On pages 65, 117, 115, 147, and 99 respectively.

translations are intended simply as aids to the understanding of the German; their presence has rendered a much wider selection possible than previous anthologists of German poetry in this country have been able to make. Poems whose language is so archaic or so local that the average reader cannot cope with them unaided, can thus be made accessible for the first time. In particular, the Middle Ages can take their rightful place in an anthology of German verse.

The beginnings of German literature become visible earlier than French, but later than English. In the Romance-speaking countries Latin could remain a sufficient vehicle of Christian culture as long as it was felt to be a heightened and dignified form of the popular speech. In Celtic and Teutonic lands, where Latin was a completely foreign tongue, the Church naturally began to cultivate the language of the people very much earlier. A political document, the 'Strasbourg Oaths' of 842, was recorded in parallel contemporary French and German versions, but whereas the French text is the first surviving piece of writing in a language recognizable as French, the German text is in a language with nearly a hundred years of literary culture behind it. This culture was to a notable extent derived from England and Ireland, whose missionaries had played an important part in converting the Teutonic tribes in what is now Germany. The pre-Christian oral literature of these tribes is preserved largely in English and Scandinavian; German has only one early monument of heroic poetry, the stark tragic *Lay of Hildebrand*. Despite its fragmentary and often corrupt state and the chaotic mixture of dialects in which the unique text we have of it is written, it remains an essential part of German literature and is recognized as such by Germans in a way *Beowulf*, for instance, is not accepted by most Englishmen. Apart from this solitary fragment and some heathen charms, German literature of the early Middle Ages is mainly missionary and devotional, consisting very largely of translation. The Teutonic alliterative verse, which survived in England until the fourteenth century, was superseded in Germany in the ninth century by rhyme, but not before it had been put to church use; the Bavarian poem *Muspilli* is one example. There followed a break due to political and religious developments, which coincided with important linguistic changes.

In the meantime the literatures of France had come to their flowering, and French became the dominant literature of Europe after Medieval Latin. It is with the rise of chivalry in the twelfth century that truly lyric poetry appears in Germany. A group of poets in Austria and South Germany, among them the knight of Kürenberg, had produced some charmingly simple (though by no means unsophisticated) love lyrics in which requited love is celebrated and the lady often expresses her longing for the man. The ballad of *Kerenstein* probably originated at this period. With Heinrich von Veldeke and Fridrich von Hûsen the French and Provençal convention of unrequited love is adopted, with the knight longing for the favour of the (married) lady. The paradox of a love which must remain secret yet must be publicly celebrated in verse is the basis of the convention, and the ability to write this sort of verse is part of the ordinary accomplishments of a gentleman; *er sanc vil wol von minnen* ('he composed admirable love poetry') is the crowning touch in the portrait of a perfect knight. The art is known as 'Minnesang'. Requited love was treated in a highly stylized genre, the 'Tagelied', dealing with the parting of lovers at dawn in which secrecy was essential.[1] Later poets tried to escape from the rigour of the convention and treated fulfilled love with nobly born or – more usually – less nobly born women. Artificial though it undoubtedly was, the chivalric ethic at its best was an ennobling and refining thing, leading the devotee eventually to the supreme good of God's grace; Walther von der Vogelweide's poem *Ich saz ûf eime steine* indicates some of its bases. Within a relatively short space of time a poetry of great intensity and sophistication developed, which later generations imitated, elaborated (Der Mîsnaere), or parodied (Steinmar). In

[1] Examples will be found below by Dietmar von Aist, Heinrich von Morungen, Wolfram von Eschenbach, and Steinmar.

this way the Germans shared in the movement of European culture at the highest literary level and, unlike the English, were able to express it in their own language. Comparable poetry in England was mostly written in French until the middle of the thirteenth century. We had to wait until the fourteenth century for Chaucer, by which time the great period of German medieval secular literature was long past. The idea of chivalry which we gain from English literature is determined for us by Sir Thomas Malory in the fifteenth century, who was looking backward, already half romantic; that is one of the reasons why our romantically-minded Victorians found the age of chivalry so congenial.

By the mid-thirteenth century the aristocratic chivalric ideal of life had ceased to be viable in practice; Neidhart, the impoverished nobleman, satirizes chivalry and peasantry alike, and commoners write reflective and didactic verse, often using bold imagery but going off into allegory and moralizing. Lyrics become sermons and increase correspondingly in length. Mysticism becomes the dominant religious force. The townsmen who are the carriers of later medieval literature developed the complicated 'Meistergesang', a closed art of technical elaboration. Its beginnings may be seen in the poems of Der Mîsnaere, which are akin to the florid intensity of later gothic architecture. The picture of the Mastersingers presented by Wagner is highly romanticized; except to the specialist, the literature of 'Meistergesang' is of an appalling dullness.[1] Only one late derived example of it is included here, relatively simple and enlivened by real emotion – Zwingli's *Gebetslied*. Alongside this rather esoteric art there flourished the anonymous narrative ballad, some of the finest examples of which are in the Low German dialects of North Germany, which the Hanseatic League had made the business language of northern Europe from London to Riga. The lyric was mainly represented by the anonymous popular song, in which chivalric conventions were transformed to meet the needs of a new public, and which received impulses

[1] The Wagnerian will, however, not be disappointed in the ballad of *Danhauser*.

from renaissance Italy in the course of the sixteenth century. Renaissance lyric was written in Latin; Germany had no Wyatt or Surrey and no Pléiade, for the Reformation absorbed the best minds, and even the lyric could become the vehicle of propaganda, as Ulrich von Hutten was quick to see. Here Martin Luther, by his translation of the Bible, laid the foundation of a unified literary language – a thing Germany had never had, even in the thirteenth century. His reorganization of the liturgy brought with it the creation of the protestant hymn which is Germany's great poetic contribution to European literature in the sixteenth and seventeenth centuries.

During the sixteenth century the importance of courts as cultural centres had been growing; but the lack of a central power with a central court materially assisted the cultural fragmentation of Germany, which the Reformation helped to perpetuate. In these circumstances it was natural that German poets should look to the international public which read Latin. The reform of poetry, which the Pléiade in France had brought about from 1550 onwards and Spenser and his followers in England by the end of the sixteenth century, was not attempted in Germany until after the first decade of the seventeenth. Shakespeare was dead, and Malherbe had virtually accomplished his work when Opitz, building largely on the work of Ronsard and contemporary Dutchmen, began the reform of German poetry in 1624. His essential achievement was in the field of poetic craftsmanship – the insistence that word accent and metrical stress must coincide, and that there must be a regular alternation of stressed and unstressed syllables in verse. This restricted the type of verse used to trochees and iambics, and it was some time before dactyls and anapaests were considered suitable. The free stress rhythm which Weckherlin and Spee employed was, however, still used by popular poets, and can be seen as late as 1669 in the work of Grimmelshausen. The metrical reform enabled various French and Italian stanzaic forms like the sonnet and the ode to be taken over easily into German, and the alexandrine became the dominant verse line of the century. Its amplitude, combined with the strict rules governing its structure, made for an effect of majestic and rhetorical dignity which was fully exploited by the greatest lyric poet between Walther von der Vogelweide and Goethe – Andreas Gryphius. The agonies and doubts of a religious man in the turmoil of the Thirty Years War and the hardly less turbulent period which succeeded it are the essential themes of seventeenth-century poetry, in which passion and existential distress express themselves through rhetoric and intellectual conceits; in this Gryphius stands between Donne and Milton. In a time of war and chaos poets took refuge in attention to form, in an ideal pastoral world of beauty and harmony, and in an intense religious inner life.

The Reformation and the Thirty Years War and their consequences had thrust German literature into a provincial position among the literatures of Europe, despite the remarkable achievements of individual poets. Germany had no Elizabethan flowering, no *grand siècle*, no Augustan age contemporary with developments in England and France.

The lyric of the early part of the eighteenth century is gracious, rococo, playful, and rationalist on the one hand, and on the other it sentimentalizes the religious strain of the preceding century, notably in the writing of hymns, many of which have found their way into English church use. So far poetry had had a social function of instructing and entertaining; both in the 'Minnesang' and in the seventeenth century direct expression of emotion had been possible only within a framework of convention, in which what the poet himself actually felt was not immediately relevant. Günther had been the first to break through this convention and write personal poetry. The middle of the eighteenth century saw the rise of a new confessional poetry, 'the true voice of feeling', 'the unaffected language of the heart'. In Germany it was rooted in pietist religiosity, in which self-analysis had been combined with outpourings of religious emotion. It was in this tradition that Klopstock grew up; starting from a sentimental pietism he infused language with feeling and created a new poetic diction of which younger writers quickly took advantage – e.g. Hölty, Bürger, Tiedge, Lenz, and the young Goethe. A quiet idyllic strain, the product of happy and integrated domesticity and an uncomplicated religious life, finds its most perfect representative in Matthias Claudius, but there were other, less successful, practitioners too. In the early nineteenth century it comes to the fore again, but the great disturbances of the French Revolution and the Napoleonic wars, the shattering of a traditional society and a deep feeling of insecurity lie between Claudius and the poetry of Hebel and Mörike, which sometimes seems at first sight so like his.

A new immediacy and force of utterance appears with the early poetry of Goethe. It was closely connected with the discovery of the folk-song, and especially the ballad, for German literature by Johann Gottfried Herder. Over the years Goethe made himself one of the great European masters of the short lyric. As from a central point–'Seelenwärme, Mittelpunkt', as he says in an early poem – he radiates outward in all directions, with amazing versatility and appropriateness of style, ranging from what seem like 'plain statements of unvarnished fact' (*Mailied, Gretchen am Spinnrade, Wanderers Nachtlied, Dämmrung senkte sich von oben*) to poems of great complexity (*Selige Sehnsucht, Urworte Orphisch*). His long creative life embraced the most exciting period in the history of German literature, which in the short space of a generation ceased to be the provincial affair it had been since the Middle Ages and caught up with literary developments in other countries so quickly that before Goethe's death in 1832 it had taken its place in the centre of European interest. Goethe himself had been very largely instrumental in bringing this about. He had drawn the attention of Europe to German literature with *Werther*, and he participated in all stages of it, from the immediacy of *Mailied* through the classicism of the *Römische Elegien* and *Iphigenie*, through the philosophical lyrics of his later years to the Romantic affinities of the *Westöstlicher Divan* and the second part of *Faust*. His friendship with Schiller was of abiding importance for them both, as men and as creative artists, and their literary alliance

was one of the vital elements in the moulding of German litera-
ture. Weimar, where he and Schiller lived, became a literary
centre of a kind Germany had never had before. Both Goethe
and Schiller incorporated in a characteristically German form the
lofty ideal of the human personality which is one of the major
contributions of the eighteenth century to European civilization.
Schiller's dramas, essays, and philosophical poems, admirable as
they are of their kind, with their nobility, their splendid rhetoric,
and their acuteness of thought, now seem more 'of their time'
than Goethe's combination of introspection and objectivity in
striking but discreet symbolism. Schiller's *Das Lied von der
Glocke* surveys and casts into lasting poetic form an ordered and
humane way of life, but one menaced by forces from within and
without and preserved only by wise self-discipline; the whole an
achievement of the integrated human personality as the bell is
the achievement of human craftsmanship and art.

Friedrich Hölderlin stands aside both from the classicism of
Goethe and Schiller and from the romanticism of Novalis, to
whose generation he belonged; he was isolated in his lifetime
and little known until he was rediscovered by Stefan George,
A maker of myths like Blake and Yeats, he combined the wis-
dom and simplicity of a child with a rarely equalled power of
symbolic expression.

Early romanticism in Germany was theoretical and intellec-
tual, despite its insistence on intuition and emotion. The only
true lyric poet of the first generation of romantics was Novalis,
whose novel *Heinrich von Ofterdingen* was a storehouse of
romantic themes, and whose *Hymnen an die Nacht* pointed the
way into an 'Innerlichkeit' as a refuge from the political frustra-
tion of Napoleonic Europe. His vision of an integrated Chris-
tian Europe in the Middle Ages was a potent influence on later
writers, and is still active today. A younger group exploited folk
literature; *Des Knaben Wunderhorn*, the folk-song collection
which Clemens Brentano and his brother-in-law Achim von
Arnim produced between 1805 and 1808, determined the style
of German poetry for a generation. (Several of the folk-song

and ballad texts in this book are taken from it.) The combination of 'folksy' diction and romantic introspection created a poetic idiom which was soon as stereotyped as the most rigid 'classical' style and became fatally easy to write. Despite attacks by Heine and Platen, it had its practitioners until the eighteen-eighties. German romanticism made available a multitude of themes for poetry – nature, longing, the Middle Ages, the occult, wandering, night, and death – and revitalized a number of genres, such as the ballad and the fairy tale; a great outburst of lyric writing was the result. Most of it has not stood the test of time; the immense production of romantic and post-romantic ballads, despite individual high points, has an average level of 'Good King Wenceslas looked out' or 'The boy stood on the burning deck'. Only Brentano and Eichendorff seem now to have more than a local or historical importance as lyric poets. The romantic attempt to transcend in the realm of the mind those limitations which could not be transcended in real life was succeeded by a disposition to accept them – sometimes fearfully, sometimes gladly, sometimes devoutly, sometimes resignedly, but always consciously. This is the spirit of the work of Droste-Hülshoff, Mörike, Keller, Storm; in Heine it is an ironical, angry, rebellious acceptance, and it is the astringent and mocking resignation of the later Heine which appeals to us today, rather than the sentimental 'Weltschmerz' of his early poems which our Victorian great-grandparents preferred. (For that reason it seemed best to translate the *Lorelei* in the spirit in which it was most probably meant, rather than in the spirit in which it has usually been taken.)

Meanwhile a new field of poetic endeavour had been discovered, and the resources of the German dialects began to be explored. 'Wo aber ist dann die Nation zu finden?' asked Hofmannsthal in 1927, and answered his own question: 'Einzig in den hohen Sprachdenkmälern und in den Volksdialekten'. The linguistic taboos which exist in England are not valid in Germany, where dialect is spoken very much farther up the social scale than here; in Switzerland it is the normal language of conversation in all classes. There was therefore nothing quaint about Johann Peter Hebel's dialect poems, and in them he achieved an effect of immediacy and simplicity without the strain which so often accompanied the romantics' striving after the same qualities. His *Die Vergänglichkeit*, with its powerful evocation of natural and supernatural scenes in everyday terms, is one of the minor masterpieces of German literature. In the north, the Low German speech which had been the family language of Matthias Claudius was made the vehicle of lyric poetry a generation later by Klaus Groth, but where Hebel is naïve and natural Groth is often forced and self-consciously 'countrified'. These two poets stand at the beginning of a flourishing dialect literature; both of them are still read.

Conrad Ferdinand Meyer, a Swiss whose contacts with French culture were close, produced some quiet restrained lyrics of great formal beauty in which the personal content is crystallized in an image rather than explicitly stated. It was some time before this means of expression was taken up again and fully explored by the three great lyric poets of the turn of the century, George, Hofmannsthal, and Rilke. Between Meyer and George lies a period in which the poetic diction fashioned by Goethe and after him by the Romantics had become commonplace and served purposes of decoration rather than of expression. In this period also falls the passionate protest of Nietzsche against the hollowness of society which the current language of poetry reflected. His own verse was without influence, but his thought profoundly affected all who came after him, particularly Arno Holz and Stefan George who, in two totally different ways, brought about a reform of the language of poetry. George sought a return to a stricter tradition coupled with the service of an austere ideal, much as some of our own Pre-Raphaelites had done; he admired Rossetti and translated his sonnets. Holz, like Whitman, sought a natural speech rhythm for poetry and exploited the expressive word-building resources of the German language in ways the later expressionists were to re-discover; he had a good deal of influence on the writing of prose, but little on poetry. Hofmannsthal and Rilke stood closer to George in this matter, but both of them found their own highly personal solutions. The nearest to Holz in that generation was perhaps August Stramm. Rilke and Hofmannsthal, and – to a much lesser extent – George are still living forces in German literature; Stramm is now influencing younger men.

The years before 1914 saw the rise of the early expressionists who, like the Imagists in this country and in America, concentrated on the juxtaposition of images, presented without comment. As in England, it was a period of intense individualism and reaction against the constricting social conventions of the nineteenth century, and the isolation of the creative artist in society becomes one of the dominant themes of poetry, even where it is not given direct expression. Heym, Trakl, Benn, and Stramm are the chief figures here. The years following the First World War saw a reaction among a younger generation of expressionists (for instance Brecht and Werfel) towards a hectic proclamation of human brotherhood to overcome the barriers between man and man and thus also between the poet and society. These hopes were disappointed by the political developments after 1933 and true poets, whether they emigrated or not, were more isolated than ever. The end of the Second World War was the signal for an outburst of lyric poetry; much of it was worthless, but the public suddenly became aware of the poetry of an older generation which had been silent or neglected, and Benn, Trakl, Loerke, and Lehmann stood out as an inspiration to younger men. Hans Carossa in his quiet, unobtrusive way had steadily continued writing; his *Abendländische Elegie* is a dignified summing up of the destruction and the hopes of recovery of the early forties. In Eastern Germany Brecht seems to have been the only lyric poet of consequence; he, too, made his name in the twenties. The difficulty of selection from contemporaries for an anthology of this kind has not been solved, and the circumstance that the most discussed authors in Germany today are over sixty years of age is reflected in the compiler's decision to include no author born after 1900.

There is a certain abruptness about the progress of German literature; at intervals traditions seem to be lost and have to be re-created, or something new has to be started from unpromising beginnings. The movements of 'Sturm und Drang' in the 1770s, Young Germany in the 1830s, Naturalism in the 1880s, post-war Expressionism in the 1920s, all represent breaks with the past and fresh starts of a kind rare in English and French literature; poets like Weckherlin, Opitz, Klopstock, Goethe, Hölderlin, Rilke, Trakl, start from scratch in a way no English poet has done since Chaucer. And so an anthology of German poetry gives a rather disjointed impression. But its underlying unity is that of the German mind itself. Readers of this anthology will see that the chief themes on which German lyric poetry of high quality has been written are dusk, night, peace of mind, death, and God; nature and love occupy a much less important place than in English or French poetry. But any selection falsifies the picture to some extent; perhaps Clemens Brentano summed up the themes of German lyric poetry best in his ecstatic cry:[1]

O Stern und Blume, Geist und Kleid,
Lieb, Leid und Zeit und Ewigkeit!

THE TEXTS

TEXTS earlier than the sixteenth century have not been modernized. Texts from the time of Luther onwards have been modernized in spelling but not in language. One or two sixteenth-century poems have resisted all attempts at normalization and have been left as they were, as the translation seemed a sufficient guide to comprehension.

Some poems have been abridged. They are marked by an asterisk in the list of contents, and the passages omitted are indicated in the texts by three dots between square brackets, thus: [...]. In medieval poems gaps in the text due to faulty transmission down the ages are indicated by dots without

[1] Below, page 307.

brackets (e.g. in the *Hildebrandslied*). Where this device is employed in later poems it is part of the author's own punctuation (as in the poem by Arno Holz).

Pronunciation of Medieval German: vowels and consonants as in modern German except:

1. The circumflex accent ˆ is the sign of a long vowel; all vowels not so marked are short, except *æ* and *œ* and diphthongs, which are always long. Thus *haben* is pronounced with a short vowel, =*habben* (not like modern German *haben*, which has a long vowel).

   æ is a long *ä* (as in modern German *gähnen*)

   œ is a long *ö* (as in modern German *höhnen*)

   iu is a long *ü* (as in modern German *sühnen* except in the first three poems in this book, where it is pronounced as written [approximately as in English *new*])

   ou may be pronounced like modern German *au*

   öi, öu may be pronounced like modern German *eu*

   ie is a diphthong, sounding approximately as in English *pier* (not a long *i* as in modern German *Biene*)

   uo and *üe* are diphthongs in which the first element has the stress: thus *uo* approximates to the sound in English *poor*.

   It may be helpful to remember that –

   medieval *î* generally corresponds to modern ei: *mîn* = mein

   û generally corresponds to modern au: *hûs* = Haus

   iu generally corresponds to modern eu: *hiute* = heute

   uo generally corresponds to modern u: *guot* = gut

   ue generally corresponds to modern ü: *güete* = Güte

2. The sign ʒ is pronounced like -*ss*-. ð is pronounced like *th* in English *this*.

   h is pronounced like modern German *ch* in all positions except at the beginnings of words and in the combination *th* (pronounced as *t* except in the first poem, where it = *th* in English *this*) and *ph* (pronounced as *pf*)

   w is pronounced as in English

   st and *sp* at the beginnings of words are pronounced as in English, not as in modern German.

In medieval German texts nouns are written without capital letters.

Poems in dialect. The original spelling of these poems has been retained, inconsistent though it is, as there seemed no workable alternative except phonetic transcription. If read as ordinary German they should not present insuperable difficulties, but some hints may be welcome.

Low German pieces (some ballads and folk-songs, the poems by Heinrich von Veldeke and Klaus Groth, and one poem by Storm) will be intelligible if pronounced as standard German; the consonant system is often closer to English (*dat* = that, *ik mak* = I make, *ik slaap* = I sleep), the vowel system to medieval German (*Maanschin* = Mondschein, medieval *des mânen schîn*; *Hus* = Haus, medieval *hûs*). In Klaus Groth's poems *æ* is pronounced as an open *ö* (like the vowel in English *fur*). Doubled vowels are long; *st* and *sp* are pronounced as in English.

Swiss pieces (some folk-songs, Zwingli's and Hebel's poems) will also be intelligible if pronounced as standard German; the vowel system is that of medieval German, though the spelling conventions are different. *ie* and *ue* are diphthongs (like earlier *ie*, *uo*); *y* stands for medieval long *î* and is so pronounced; long *o* often corresponds to standard German long *a* (e.g. *Schof* = Schaf). Doubled vowels are long. Final *-n* and *-e* are often dropped; *ch* often corresponds to standard German *k* (e.g. *Chatz* = Katze) and is always pronounced as in standard German *ach*, never as in *ich*; *st* and *sp* are pronounced *scht* and *schp* in all positions.

Swabian, Bavarian, and Austrian pieces (folk-songs) are in general closer to standard German than the Low German and Swiss poems. *oa* corresponds to standard German *ei* (*koan* = kein); final *-n* and *-e* are frequently dropped.

In the English translations the mark / indicates the point at which the corresponding German text on the page concerned begins or ends.

THE PENGUIN BOOK OF
GERMAN VERSE

THE TRANSLATOR TO THE READER

SEH ich die Werke der Meister an,
So seh ich das, was sie getan;
Betracht ich meine Siebensachen,
Seh ich, was ich hätt' sollen machen.

GOETHE

WHEN I look at the works of the masters, I see what they have done. When I consider my own trifles, I see what I ought to have done.

HILDEBRANDSLIED

Ik gihôrta ðat seggen,
ðat sih urhêttun · ænon muotîn,
Hiltibrant enti Haðubrant · untar heriun tuêm,
sunufatarungo; · iro saro rihtun,
garutun se iro gûðhamun, · gurtun sih iro suert ana,
helidos, ubar hringâ, · dô sie tô dero hiltiu ritun.
Hiltibrant gimahalta, Heribrantes sunu: · her uuas hêrôro
    man,
ferahes frôtôro; · her frâgên gistuont
fôhêm uuortum, · hwer sîn fater wâri
fireo in folche, · ....
.... · «eddo hwelîhhes cnuosles dû sîs.
Ibu dû mî ênan sagês, · ik mî dê ôdre uuêt;
chind, in chunincrîche · chûd ist mir al irmindeot.»
Hadubrant gimahalta, · Hiltibrantes sunu:
«dat sagêtun mî · ûsere liuti,
alte anti frôte, · dea êrhina wârun,
dat Hiltibrant hætti mîn fater: · ih heittu Hadubrant.
Forn her ôstar giweit, · flôh her Ôtachres nîd,
hina miti Theotrîhhe · enti sînero degano filu.

The Lay of Hildebrand

I have heard tell that two picked men, Hildebrand and Hadu-
brand, met in single combat between two armies, the father and the
son. The champions tested their equipment, prepared their armour,
and buckled on their swords over their chain mail before they rode
to the encounter.

Hildebrand, the son of Heribrand – he was the older and more
experienced man – began to ask in a few words who his father was
among the warriors, 'or of what family you are. If you tell me one,
I shall know the rest; young man, I know all worshipful men in the
kingdom.' Hadubrant, Hildebrand's son, said: 'Old and wise men
of our people, who lived long ago, told me that my father's name
was Hildebrand. My name is Hadubrand. A long time ago he, with
many of his warriors, was driven out by the wrath of Odoacer; he
fled to the east with Theodoric. / He left behind him in misery a

3

Her furlæt in lante · luttila sitten
prût in bûre · barn unwahsan,
arbeo laosa: · her raet ôstar hina.
Sîd Dêtrihhe · darbâ gistuontun
fateres mînes: · dat uuas sô friuntlaos man.
Her was Ôtachre · ummet tirri,
Degano dechisto · miti Deotrîchhe.
Her was eo folches at ente: · imo was eo fehta ti leop:
chûd was her ..... · chônnêm mannum.
Ni wâniu ih iû lîb habbe» .....,.
«Wêttu irmingot» quad Hiltibrant · «obana ab hevane,
dat dû neo dana halt · mit sus sippan man
dinc ni gileitôs» .....
Want her dô ar arme · wuntane baugâ,
cheisuringu gitân, · sô imo se der chuning gap,
Hûneo truhtîn: · «dat ih dir it nû bi huldî gibu.»
Hadubrant gimahalta, · Hiltibrantes sunu
«Mit gêru scal man · geba infâhan,
ort widar orte. · ....
Dû bist dir, altêr Hûn, ummet spâhêr,
spenis mih mit dînêm wortun, · wili mih dînu speru
werpan.
Pist alsô gialtêt man, · sô dû êwîn inwit fôrtôs.

young wife in the bower and an infant child without inheritance;
he rode away eastwards. Theodoric, who was without allies, badly
needed my father after that. He was very angry with Odoacer; he
was the best-loved of Theodoric's men. He was always in the fore-
front of the army and he always enjoyed fighting. Brave men knew
him well. I do not suppose he is still alive.'

'Now God bear witness from Heaven,' said Hildebrand, 'may you
never fight with a man who is so closely related to you.' He took
from his arm twisted torcs set with gold besants, which the King,
the lord of the Huns, had given him. 'I give you this out of friend-
ship.'

Hadubrand, Hildebrand's son, said: 'The way to take gifts is
with spears, point against point. Old Hun, you are very cunning,
you are leading me on with your words, and you mean to throw
your spear at me. You have only grown to be so old because you

4

Dat sagêtun mî · sêolîdante
westar ubar wentilsêo · dat inan wîc furnam:
tôt ist Hiltibrant, · Heribrantes suno.»
Hiltibrant gimahalta, · Heribrantes suno:
«Wela gisihu ih · in dînêm hrustim,
dat dû habês hême · hêrron gôten,
dat dû noh bî desemo rîche · reccheo ni wurti.
Welaga nû, waltant got» quad Hiltibrant, · «wêwurt
    skihit.
Ih wallôta sumaro enti wintro · sehstic ur lante,
dâr man mih eo scerita · in folc sceotantero:
sô man mir at burc ênîgeru · banun ni gifasta,
nû scal mih suâsat chind · suertu hauwan,
bretôn mit sînu billiu, · eddo ih imo ti banin werdan.
Doh maht dû nû aodlîhho, · ibu dir dîn ellen taoc,
in sus hêremo man · hrusti giwinnan,
rauba birahanen, · ibu dû dâr ênîc reht habês.
Der sî doh nû argôsto» quad Hiltibrant · «ôstarliuto,
der dir nû wîges warne, · nû dih es sô wel lustit,
gûdea gimeinûn: · niuse dê môtti
hwerdar sih hiutu · dero hregilo rûmen muotti,

have always practised treachery. / Sailors plying west over the Medi-
terranean told me that he was killed in battle: Hildebrand, the son
of Heribrand, is dead.'

Hildebrand, the son of Heribrand, said: 'I can see from your
equipment that you have a generous master at home and that
you have never been exiled under his rule. Alas, Lord God', said
Hildebrand, 'an evil destiny is working itself out. I have wandered
for thirty summers and thirty winters away from my country, and
all this time I was enrolled among the shock troops, without anyone
having brought me to my death before any fortified place. Now my
own son is to strike me with his sword and batter me with his
brand or else I must bring him to his death. But if you have enough
courage you may easily win the armour from an old man like me
and carry away the spoils, if you have any right to them. Not even
the most cowardly of the Eastern men,' said Hildebrand, 'could
refuse you battle now you are so anxious for single combat. Let us

erdo desero brunnôno · bêdero uualtan.»
Dô lêttun se ærist · asckim scrîtan,
scarpên scûrim: · dat in dêm sciltim stônt.
Dô stôptun tô samane · staimbort chludun,
heuwun harmlicco · huîtte scilti,
unti im iro lintûn · luttilo wurtun,
giwigan miti wabnum · ....

From: MUSPILLI

[...] Daʒ hôrt ih rahhôn · dia weroltrehtwîson,
daʒ sculi der antichristo · mit Eliase pâgan.
Der warch ist kiwâfanit, · denne wirdit untar in wîc
arhapan.
Khenfun sint sô kreftîc, · diu kôsa ist sô mihhil.
Elias strîtit · pi den êwîgon lîp,
wili dên rehtkernôn · daʒ rîhhi kistarkan:
pidiu scal imo helfan · der himiles kiwaltit.
Der antichristo · stêt pi demo altfîante,
stêt pi demo Satanase, · .... der inan varsenkan scal:

see which of us will have to give up his equipment / and which of
us is to own both these coats of mail.'
    Then they hurled their ashen spears in deadly showers; they
stuck in the shields. Then they closed on foot and struck at the
[battle-] shields, hewed fiercely at the bright shields until the
[wooden] shields were shattered, hacked to pieces with their weapons.

The End of the World

I heard it said by pious men in the world that Antichrist would
fight with Elias. The evil one is armed; then the battle begins. The
champions are strong, the stakes are very great. Elias fights for
eternal life, to make the Kingdom safe for the righteous, and so the
Ruler of Heaven will help him. The Antichrist is on the side of the
old enemy, on the side of Satan, [some lines missing] who will de-
stroy him, / and so he will fall wounded on the battlefield and find

6

pidiu scal er in deru wîcsteti · wunt pivallan
enti in demo sinde · sigalôs werdan.
Doh wânit des vilo ..... · gotmanno,
daʒ Elias in demo wîge · arwartit werde.
Sô daʒ Eliases pluot · in erda kitriufit,
sô inprinnant die pergâ, · poum ni kistentit
ênîc in erdu, · ahâ artruknênt,
muor varswilhit sih, · swilizôt lougiu der himil,
mâno vallit, · prinnit mittilagart,
stên ni kistentit. · verit denne stûatago in lant,
verit mit diu vuiru · viriho wîsôn:
dâr ni mac denne mâk andremo · helfan vora demo
    mûspille.
Denne daʒ preita wasal · allaʒ varprinnit,
enti vuir enti luft · iʒ allaʒ arfurpit,
wâr ist denne diu marha, · dâr man dâr eo mit sînên
    mâgon piec?
Diu marha ist farprunnan, · diu sêla stêt pidungan,
ni weiʒ mit wiu puaʒe: · sô verit si za wîʒe [...]

his defeat on that expedition. But many godly men believe that
Elias will be wounded in that battle.

    When Elias' blood falls on the ground the mountains will catch
fire, not a tree will stand on earth, the rivers will dry up, the marshes
disappear, the sky will smoulder in the fire, the moon will fall, the
habitation of men will burn, not a stone will stand upon another.
Then the Judgement Day will come upon the land with fire to seek
men out.

    Then no one will be able to help his kinsman, for the end of the
world will have come. When the broad fertile land is burning and
fire and wind sweeps it all away, where is the landmark about
which man fought beside his kinsmen? The boundary is burnt,
the soul stands oppressed, it does not know how to make amends;
and so it goes to its punishment.

WEINGARTNER REISESEGEN

Ic dir nâch sihe · ic dir nâch sendi
mit mînin funf fingirin · funvi undi funfzic engili.
Got mit gisundi · heim dich gisendi.
Offin sî dir diz sigidor · sami sî dir diz sældidor,
bislozin sî dir diz wâgidor · sami sî dir diz wâfindor. [...]

DER VON KÜRENBERG

Ich zôch mir einen valken · mêre danne ein jâr.
Dô ich in gezamete · als ich in wolte hân
und ich im sîn gevidere · mit golde wol bewant,
er huop sich ûf vil hôhe · und floug in anderiu lant.

Sît sach ich den valken · schône fliegen:
er fuorte an sînem fuoze · sîdîne riemen,
und was im sîn gevidere · alrôt guldîn.
Got sende si zesamene · die gerne geliep wellen sîn!

A Blessing on One Going on a Journey

I watch you as you go, with my five fingers I send after you five
and fifty angels. May God bring you safe home. May the gate of
success be open to you, and the gate of fortune too; may the gate
of the waters be closed to you, and the gate of weapons too.

I trained a falcon for more than a year. When I had trained him
as I wished to have him, and had bound his feathers well with gold,
he took wing, rose very high, and flew into foreign lands.
Since then I have seen the falcon flying freely; he was wearing
silken jesses on his feet, and his feathers were red gold. May God
bring them together who love and desire one another!

8

Dᴇʀ tunkele sterne · der birget sich.
Als tuo du, frouwe schœne, · sô du sehest mich,
sô lâ du dîniu ougen gên · an einen andern man.
Son weiz doch lützel ieman · wiez undr uns zwein ist
    getân.

Jô stuont ich nechtint spâte · vor dînem bette:
do getorste ich dich, frouwe · niwet wecken.
«Des gehazze iemer · got den dînen lîp!
jo enwas ich kein eber wilde» · so sprach daz [wætlîch]
    wîp.

DIETMAR VON AIST

«Uꜰ der linden obene · dâ sanc ein kleinez vogellîn.
Vor dem walde wart ez lût: · dô huop sich aber daz herze
    mîn
an eine stat da'z ê dâ was. · Ich sach die rôsebluomen
    stân:
die manent mich der gedanke vil · die ich hin zeiner
    frouwen hân.»

Tʜᴇ dim star hides himself, and you, fair lady, must do the same
when you see me: let your eyes rest on some other man, then no
one will know how it is between us two.

Tʜᴏᴜɢʜ I stood at your bedside late last night, lady, I did not
dare to wake you. 'God's curse on you for ever! Why, I was not a
wild boar!' That is what that splendid woman said.

[*Knight*:] 'ᴜᴘ ᴛʜᴇʀᴇ on the lime-tree a little bird was singing; its
song could be heard at the edge of the forest. Then my heart again
sped to a place where it had been before. I saw the roses blooming:
they remind me of the many thoughts I have about a certain lady.'

9

«Eʒ dunket mich wol tûsent jâr · daʒ ich an liebes arme
    lac.
Sunder âne mîne schulde · fremedet er mich manegen tac.
Sît ich bluomen niht ensach · noch hôrte kleiner vogele
    sanc,
sît was mir mîn fröide kurz · und ouch der jâmer alze-
    lanc.»

      Eʒ stuont ein frouwe alleine
      und warte uber heide
      und warte ir liebes,
      so gesach sie valken fliegen.
      «Sô wol dir, valke, daʒ du bist!
      Du fliugest swar dir liep ist:
      du erkiusest dir in dem walde
      einen boum der dir gevalle.
      Alsô hân ouch ich getân:
      ich erkôs mir selbe einen man,
      den erwelton mîniu ougen.
      Daʒ nîdent schœne vrouwen.
      Owe wan lânt si mir mîn liep?
      Joh engerte ich ir dekeiner trûtes niet.»

[*Lady*:] 'It seems like a thousand years since I lay in my love's arms; he has kept away from me for many days through no fault of mine. Since there have been no flowers to see or song of small birds to hear my joy has been short-lived but my sorrow far too long.'

A LADY was standing by herself and looking out over the heath to see if she could see her lover, when she saw falcons flying. 'How lucky you are, falcon! You can fly wherever you like; in the forest you can choose any tree that pleases you. That is what I have done too: I chose a man for myself, my eyes made the choice. Now beautiful women are jealous of it. Oh, why don't they leave me my lover? After all, I have never wanted any lover of theirs!'

«Slâfest du, friedel ziere?
Man wecket uns leider schiere:
ein vogellîn sô wol getân
daz ist der linden an daz zwî gegân.»

«Ich was vil sanfte entslâfen:
nu rüefestu kint Wâfen.
Liep âne leit mac niht gesîn.
Swaz du gebiutest, daz leiste ich friundin mîn.»

Diu frouwe begunde weinen.
«Du rîtest und lâst mich einen.
Wenne wilt du wider her zuo mir?
Owê du füerest mîn fröide sament dir!»

ANONYMOUS

Dû bist mîn, ich bin dîn:
des solt dû gewis sîn.
Dû bist beslozzen
in mînem herzen;
verlorn ist daz slüzzelîn:
dû muost immer drinne sîn.

[*Lady*:] 'ARE YOU still asleep, my handsome lover? Alas, in a moment they will be waking us! A neat little bird has perched on the branch of the lime-tree.'

[*Knight*:] 'I had fallen peacefully asleep, and now you, sweet, give the alarm. There is no such thing as love without sorrow. Sweetheart, I will do anything you say.'

The lady began to weep. 'You are going to ride off and leave me alone. When will you come back to me again? Alas, you will take all my joy with you.'

You are mine, I am yours, you may be sure of that. You are locked in my heart; the key is lost; you will have to stay inside it for always.

Wær diu werlt alliu mîn
von dem mere unz an den Rîn,
des wolt ih mih darben,
daz diu künegîn von Engellant
læge an mînem arme.

HEINRICH VON VELDEKE

Tristrant mûste âne sînen danc
stâde sîn der koninginnen,
want poisûn heme dâ tû dwanc
mêre dan dî cracht der minnen.
Des sal mich dî gûde danc
weten dat ich nîne gedranc
sulic pîment ende ich sî minne
bat dan hê, ende mach dat sîn.
Wale gedâne,
valsches âne,
lât mich wesen dîn
ende wis dû mîn.

If the whole world belonged to me, from the ocean to the Rhine,
I would gladly give it up if I could have the Queen of England
lying in my arms.

Tristan had to be faithful to the queen, whether he would or no,
because it was a philtre that forced him to do so rather than the
power of love. My lady ought to be grateful to me that I never
drank such a brew and yet my love for her surpasses his, if that be
possible. Fair one, sincere one, let me be yours and be you mine.

FRIDRICH VON HÛSEN

Mîn herze und mîn lîp diu wellent scheiden,
diu mit ein ander varnt nu mange zît.
Der lîp wil gerne vehten an die heiden:
sô hât iedoch daz herze erwelt ein wîp
vor al der werlt. Daz müet mich iemer sît,
daz si ein ander niene volgent beide.
Mir habent diu ougen vil getân ze leide.
Got eine mücze scheiden noch den strît.

Ich wânde ledic sîn von solher swære,
dô ich daz kriuze in gotes êre nam.
Ez wære ouch reht deiz herze als ich dâ wære,
wan daz sîn stætekeit im sîn verban.
Ich solte sîn ze rehte ein lebendic man,
ob ez den tumben willen sîn verbære.
Nu sihe ich wol daz im ist gar unmære
wie ez mir an dem ende süle ergân.

Sît ich dich, herze, niht wol mac erwenden,
dun wellest mich vil trûreclîchen lân,
sô bite ich got daz er dich ruoche senden
an eine stat dâ man dich wol enpfâ.

My heart and my body, who have journeyed together for a long time now, wish to part. My body wants to fight against the heathen, but my heart has chosen a lady for its own above all the world. Ever since, I have been distressed that the two will not stay together. My eyes have brought much trouble upon me. Only God can settle this dispute.

I thought I had escaped from this predicament when I went on a crusade to the glory of God. My heart's duty would have been to stay with me, but its own constancy prevented it. If only it would give up its foolish intention I should be a right-living man. Now I see that it does not care what finally becomes of me.

As I cannot prevent you, heart, from leaving me in great distress, I pray God that it may please him to send you to a place where you will be well received.

Owê wie sol eʒ armen dir ergân!
Wie torstest eine an solhe nôt ernenden?
Wer sol dir dîne sorge helfen enden
mit solhen triuwen als ich hân getân?

Ich denke under wîlen,
ob ich ir nâher wære,
waʒ ich ir wolte sagen.
Daʒ kürzet mir die mîlen,
swenn ich ir mîne swære
sô mit gedanken klage.
Mich sehent mange tage
die liute in der gebære
als ich niht sorgen habe,
wan ichs alsô vertrage.

Het ich sô hôher minne
mich nie underwunden,
mîn möhte werden rât.
Ich tet eʒ âne sinne:
des lîde ich zallen stunden
nôt diu mir nâhe gât.

But oh, what will happen to you? How could you dare to go alone into such danger? Who is to bring your troubles to an end as faithfully as I have done?

I OFTEN think what I would say to her if I were nearer her. It shortens the miles for me to imagine myself complaining of my sorrows to her. And so people see me behaving for days together as though I had not a care in the world, because I get over it like this.

If I had never taken such lofty devotion upon myself there might be some help for me. I did it without thinking, and so now all the time I have to bear distress which touches me closely. / My own con-

Mîn stæte mir nu hât
daz herze alsô gebunden,
daz siz niht scheiden lât
von ir als ez nu stât.

Ez ist ein grôzez wunder:
diech aller sêrest minne,
diu was mir ie gevê.
Nu müeze solhen kumber
niemer man bevinden,
der alsô nâhe gê.
Erkennen wânde i'n ê,
nu hân i'n baz befunden:
mir was dâ heime wê,
und hie wol drîstunt mê.

Swie kleine ez mich vervâhe,
sô vröwe ich mich doch sêre
daz mir niemen kan
erwern, ichn denke ir nâhe
swar ich landes kêre.
Den trôst sol si mir lân.
Wil siz für guot enpfân,
daz fröut mich iemer mêre,
wan ich für alle man
ir ie was undertân.

stancy has bound my heart so fast that, as things are now, she will
not let it go.

It is a very strange thing: she whom I now love more than any-
one has always been hostile to me. May no one ever know a sorrow
which touches so closely; I thought I knew it already, but now I
realize it fully. I was sad enough at home, but now I am three times
as sad.

However little good it may do me, I am glad that no one can
prevent my thoughts from being near her wherever I may be. This
consolation at least she must let me have, and if she takes it in good
part it will always give me delight, for I have always been more at
her service than any other man.

HEINRICH VON MORUNGEN

«O wê, sol aber mir iemer mê
geliuhten dur die naht
noch wîzer danne ein snê
ir lîp vil wol geslaht?
Der trouc diu ougen mîn:
ich wânde, eʒ solde sîn
des liehten mânen schîn,
   dô taget eʒ.»

«Owê, sol aber er iemer mê
den morgen hie betagen?
Als uns diu naht engê,
daʒ wir niht durfen klagen:
‹owê, nu ist eʒ tac›,
als er mit klage pflac
do er jungest bî mir lac.
   Dô taget eʒ.»

«Owê, si kuste âne zal
in deme slâfe mich.
Dô vielen hin ze tal
ir trêne nider sich,
iedoch getrôste ich sî,
daʒ si ir weinen lî
und mich al ummevî.
   Dô taget eʒ.»

[*Knight*:] 'Alas, and will her shapely body, whiter even than a
fall of snow, no longer gleam for me through the night? It deceived
my eyes; I thought it must be the light of the bright moon, then the
day dawned.'

[*Lady*:] 'Alas, will he ever again stay here in the morning? that
when the night fades we may no longer need to lament: "Alas, it is
day now", as he lamented the last time he lay with me; then the day
dawned.'

[*Knight*:] 'Alas, she kissed me countless times in her sleep. Her
tears fell down and down, but I comforted her, so that she stopped
crying and threw her arms round me. Then the day dawned.'

«Owê, daz er sô dicke sich
bî mir ersehen hât!
Als er endahte mich,
sô wolte er sunder wât
mich armen schouwen blôz.
Ez was ein wunder grôz
daz in des nie verdrôz.
    Dô taget ez.»

Iсн hôrt ûf der heide
lûte stimme und süezen klanc.
Dâ von wart ich beide
fröiden rîch und trûrens kranc.
Nâch der mîn gedanc · sêre ranc · unde swanc,
die vant ich ze tanze dâ si sanc.
Ane leide · ich dô spranc.

Ich vant si verborgen
eine und ir wengel naz,
dô si an dem morgen
mînes tôdes sich vermaz.
Der vil lieben haz · tuot mir baz · danne daz
dô ich vor ir kniete dâ si saz
und ir sorgen · gar vergaz.

[*Lady*:] 'Alas, that he has so often feasted his eyes on me! When
he drew back the bedclothes, he wanted to see my poor self without
any covering. It was a wonderful thing that he never grew tired of
it. Then the day dawned.'

Out in the country I heard the sound of voices and sweet music.
This made me rich in joy and poor in sorrow. Her to whom my
thoughts had been sorely striving and flying, I found her singing as
she danced. Full of joy, I danced there too.
    I found her withdrawn and alone, with wet cheeks, on the mor-
row of the day on which she had thought I was dead. Even her dis-
like pleases me better than what happened when I knelt down be-
fore her as she sat and forgot her sorrow.

Ich vants an der zinnen,
eine, und ich was zir besant.
Dâ moht ichs ir minnen
wol mit fuoge hân gepfant.
Dô wând ich diu lant · hân verbrant · sâ zehant,
wan daz mich ir süezen minne bant
an den sinnen · hât erblant.

REINMAR VON HAGENAU

Ich wil allez gâhen
zuo der liebe die ich hân.
So ist ez niender nâhen
daz sich ende noch mîn wân.
Doch versuoche ichz alle tage
und diene ir sô dazs âne ir danc
  mit fröiden muoz erwenden kumber den ich trage.

Mich betwanc ein mære
daz ich von ir hôrte sagen,
wies ein vrouwe wære
diu sich schône kunde tragen.
Daz versuochte ich unde ist wâr.
Ir kunde nie kein wîp geschaden
  (daz ist wol kleine) alsô grôz als umbe ein hâr.

I found her alone on the castle wall and she had sent for me. I could have exacted a pledge of love from her then. It seemed to me that I could have set the world afire on the spot, if the bonds of her sweet love had not blindfolded my senses.

I WILL hurry away to my beloved, though a happy end to my yearning is still far off. Even so, I try every day and I serve her so that she will have to change the sorrow I bear into joy whether she wants to or not.

I was struck by something I heard said about her, that she was a lady of upright life. I put it to the test, and it is true. No [comparison with any] woman could harm her by as much as a hair's breadth, and that is little enough.

Swaz in allen landen
mir ze liebe mac geschehen,
daz stât in ir handen:
anders niemen wil ichs jehen.
Si ist mîn ôsterlîcher tac,
und hâns in mînem herzen liep:
    daz weiz er wol dem nieman niht geliegen mac.

WALTHER VON DER VOGELWEIDE

Sô die bluomen ûz dem grase dringent,
same si lachen gegen der spilden sunnen,
in einem meien an dem morgen fruo,
und diu kleinen vogellîn wol singent
in ir besten wîse, die si kunnen,
waz wünne mac sich dâ gelîchen zuo?
Ez ist wol halb ein himelrîche.
Suln wir sprechen, waz sich deme gelîche,
sô sage ich, waz mir dicke baz
in mînen ougen hât getân,
    und tæte ouch noch, gesæhe ich daz.

Whatever pleasure comes to me, wherever it may be, depends on her: I will not say this of anyone else. She is my Easter day, I love her from the bottom of my heart: He knows that well, to whom no man can lie.

EARLY on a May morning when the flowers push up through the grass, as though they are smiling at the dazzling sun, and the little birds skilfully sing the best tunes they know, what joy can compare with this? It is half heaven. But if it comes to saying what equals it. I will tell you what has often given my eyes more pleasure, and would now, if I could only see it.

Swâ ein edeliu schœne frouwe reine,
wol gekleidet unde wol gebunden,
dur kurzewîle zuo vil liuten gât,
hovelîchen hôhgemuot, niht eine,
umbe sehende ein wênic under stunden,
alsam der sunne gegen den sternen stât, –
der meie bringe uns al sîn wunder,
waz ist dâ sô wünneclîches under,
als ir vil minneclîcher lîp?
wir lâzen alle bluomen stân
    und kapfen an daz werde wîp.

Nû wol dan, welt ir die wârheit schouwen!
Gân wir zuo des meien hôhgezîte!
Der ist mit aller sîner krefte komen.
Seht an in und seht an schœne frouwen,
wederz dâ daz ander überstrîte:
daz bezzer spil, ob ich daz hân genomen.
Owê der mich dâ welen hieze,
deich daz eine dur daz ander lieze,
wie rehte schiere ich danne kür!
Hêr Meie, ir müeset merze sîn,
    ê ich mîn frouwen dâ verlür!

Where a nobly-born, beautiful, and chaste lady, well turned out
from head to foot, her spirits high but controlled, goes for pleasure
into a gathering of people with her like the sun among the stars,
and glances round from time to time – even if May offers all his
marvels, which of them is as attractive as her delightful presence?
We let all the flowers be and gaze in admiration at the splendid
woman.

Well, if you want to see the real thing, let us go to the festival of
May! He has come in all his profusion. Look at him, and look at
beautiful ladies, and see which surpasses the other, and whether I
have not chosen the better part! Oh, if anyone were to give me the
choice between them, even if by choosing the one I had to forego
the other, how quickly my choice would be made! Sir May, you
would have to be March before I would give up my lady for you!

In einem zwîvellîchen wân
was ich gesezzen und gedâhte
ich wolte von ir dienste gân,
wan daz ein trôst mich wider brâhte.
Trôst mag ez rehte niht geheizen, ouwê des!
Ez ist vil kûme ein kleinez trœstelîn,
sô kleine, swenne ichz iu gesage, ir spottet mîn.
Doch fröwet sich lützel iemen, er enwizze wes.

Mich hât ein halm gemachet frô:
er giht ich sül genâde vinden.
Ich maz daz selbe kleine strô,
als ich hie vore sach von kinden.
Nû hœret unde merket, ob siz denne tuo:
«Si tuot, si entuot, si tuot, si entuot, si tuot.»
Swie dicke ichz tete, sô was ie daz ende guot.
Daz trœstet mich: dâ hœret ouch geloube zuo.

I was sitting in a dejected frame of mind and thinking that I would
leave her service, but a comforting thought made me change my
mind. It cannot be called a comfort, no indeed, hardly even a little
grain of comfort: it is so small that you will laugh at me if I tell
you. But no one is pleased without knowing why.

It is a stalk of grass that has cheered me up: it says that I shall
find favour. I measured off that little stalk as I have seen children
do. Now listen and see whether she will or not: 'She loves me, she
loves me not, she loves me, she loves me not, she loves me!' No
matter how often I did it, it always came out right. This comforts
me, but of course one has to believe in it [if it is to work].

Ich saʒ ûf eime steine
und dahte bein mit beine:
dar ûf sazt ich den ellenbogen:
ich hâte in mîne hant gesmogen
mîn kinne und ein mîn wange.
Dô dâhte ich mir vil ange,
wie man zer werlte solte leben.
Dekeinen rât kond ich gegeben,
wie man driu dinc erwurbe,
der keines nicht verdurbe.
Diu zwei sint êre und varnde guot,
daʒ dicke ein ander schaden tuot:
daʒ dritte ist gotes hulde,
der zweier übergulde.
Die wolde ich gerne in einen schrîn.
Jâ leider desn mac niht gesîn,
daʒ guot und werltlich êre
und gotes hulde mêre
zesamene in ein herze komen.
Stîg unde wege sint in benomen:
untriuwe ist in der sâʒe,
gewalt vert ûf der strâʒe,
frid unde reht sint sêre wunt:
diu driu enhabent geleites niht, · diu zwei
enwerden ê gesunt.

I SAT down on a stone, and crossed my legs and set my elbows on
them; I rested my chin and cheek in my hand. Then I pondered
very earnestly how one ought to live one's life on earth. I could not
find any solution to the problem of how to gain three things with-
out one or other of them spoiling. Two of the three are good repute
and worldly possessions, which often work against one another;
the third is God's grace, the crown of both of them. I would like to
keep them all locked away together in a safe. But unfortunately it
is not possible for possessions, and reputation in the world, and the
favour of God as well, to meet in one heart. There are no paths for
them to get there. Treachery lies in ambush, brute force roams the
roads, peace and justice are in a sad state. If these two last do not
recover, the other three will have no escort on their way.

«Under der linden
an der heide,
dâ unser zweier bette was,
dâ muget ir vinden
schône beide
gebrochen bluomen unde gras.
Vor dem walde in einem tal
tandaradei!
    schône sanc diu nahtegal.

Ich kam gegangen
zuo der ouwe:
dô was mîn vriedel komen ê.
Dâ wart ich enpfangen,
hêre frouwe,
daჳ ich bin sælic iemer mê.
Kust er mich? Wol tûsentstunt!
tandaradei!
    seht wie rôt mir ist der munt.

Dô hâte er gemachet
alsô rîche
von bluomen eine bettestat.

Under the lime-tree by the common, where we two had our bed, you can find flowers and grass both neatly picked; at the edge of the forest in the dell, tandaradei, the nightingale sang so sweetly.

'I came to the meadow, to find my sweetheart was already there. There I was received with the words "Noble lady!" I shall always be happy to think of it. Did he kiss me? I should think about a thousand times! Tandaradei! See how red my mouth is!

'I saw that he had made a lovely bed out of flowers./Anybody

Des wirt noch gelachet
inneclîche,
kumt iemen an daʒ selbe pfat.
Bî den rôsen er wol mac,
tandaradei!
    merken wâ mirʒ houbet lac.

Daʒ er bî mir læge,
wesseʒ iemen,
(nu enwelle got!), sô schamte ich mich.
Wes er mit mir pflæge,
niemer niemen
bevinde daʒ wan er und ich,
und ein kleineʒ vogellîn,
tandaradei!
    daʒ mac wol getriuwe sîn.»

Mit sælden müeʒe ich hiute ûf stên,
got hêrre, in dîner huote gên
und rîten, swar ich in dem lande kêre.

Krist hêrre, lâʒ an mir werden schîn
die grôʒen kraft der güete dîn
und pflic mîn wol durch dîner muoter êre.

who comes by that way will give a knowing smile; he can see from
the roses where my head lay.
   'If anyone were to know – God forbid they should – that he lay
with me, I would be ashamed. I hope no one will ever find out what
he did to me, except us two and a little bird – tandaradei – but then
it can keep a secret!'

May God's blessing be upon my up-rising today; Lord God, let
me walk and ride in Thy charge wherever I go. Lord Christ, let the
great power of Thy loving-kindness be apparent in me, and keep
me for Thy Mother's sake. / And just as the holy angel cared for her

Als ir der heilig engel pflæge,
und dîn, dô du in der kripfen læge,
junger mensch und alter got,
dêmüetic vor dem esel und vor dem rinde,
und doch mit sældenrîcher huote
pflac dîn Gabriêl der guote
wol mit triuwen sunder spot:
als pflig ouch mîn, daz an mir iht erwinde
daz dîn vil götelîch gebot.

O wê war sint verswunden · alliu mîniu jâr?
Ist mir mîn leben getroumet · oder ist ez wâr?
Daz ich ie wânde daz · iht wære, was daz iht?
Dar nâch hân ich geslâfen · und enweiz es niht.
Nû bin ich erwachet, · und ist mir unbekant
daz mir hie vor was kündic · als mîn ander hant.
Liut unde lant, dâ ich · von kinde bin erzogen,
die sint mir frömde worden, · reht als ez sî gelogen.
Die mîne gespilen wâren, · die sint træge unt alt:
vereitet ist daz velt, · verhouwen ist der walt.

and Thee when Thou wert lying in the manger, an infant man and ancient God, humbly before the ass and the ox (and yet kind Gabriel kept Thee in his blessed charge faithfully in good earnest), so mayest Thou care for me so that Thy most divine law may not cease to be active in me.

ALAS, where have all my years gone to? Has my life been just a dream, or is it real? And all those things that I used to think stood for something, did they really stand for anything? It seems as though I have been asleep without knowing it. Now I have woken up, and all the things I used to know like the palm of my hand look strange to me. The place where I was brought up and the people there have become as foreign to me as if it were not true that I had ever known them. The people who used to be my companions are now old and slow, the fields are scorched, the woods cut down. / If

Wan daz daz wazzer vliuzet · als ez wîlent flôz,
für wâr ich wânde mîn · unglücke wurde grôz.
Mich grüezet maniger trâge, · der mich bekande ê wol.
Diu werlt ist allenthalben · ungenâden vol.
Als ich gedenke an manigen · wünneclîchen tac,
die mir sint enpfallen gar · als in daz mer ein slac,
iemer mêre ouwê.

Owê wie jæmerlîche · junge liute tuont!
Den unvil riuweclîche · ir gemüete stuont,
Die kunnen niuwan sorgen: ouwê wie tuont si sô?
swar ich zer werlte kêre, · dâ ist nieman frô;
tanzen, lachen, singen · zergât mit sorgen gar,
nie kein kristenman gesach · sô jæmerlîche schar.
Nu merket, wie den frouwen · ir gebende stât;
die stolzen ritter tragent · dörperlîche wât.
Uns sint unsenfte brieve · her von Rôme komen:
uns ist erloubet trûren · und freude gar benomen.
Daz müet mich inneclîchen · (wir lebten ie vil wol),
daz ich nû für mîn lachen · weinen kiesen sol.
Die wilden vogele · betrüebet unser klage:
waz wunders ist, ob ich · dâ von vil gar verzage?

it were not that the water still flows as it used to do, my depression
would be great indeed. Many people now greet me distantly who
used to know me well. The world is full of ill-grace everywhere: so
many happy days that I can think of have disappeared like the
ripples when you throw something into the water. Alas, for ever
alas!

  Oh, how miserably young people behave nowadays! Those who
always used to be so gay can now do nothing but worry; oh, how
can they be so miserable! Wherever I go, no one is happy. Dancing,
laughing, singing are all being superseded by worry, no Christian
man ever saw such a miserable lot! Look at the hats women wear
these days! And stylish gentlemen dress like farm labourers! Dis-
turbing dispatches have arrived from Rome. We are only allowed
to be sad, and gaiety is altogether taken away from us. It distresses
me very much – after all, we used to live so graciously – that I have
to indulge in weeping instead of laughter. Even the wild birds
mourn with us, so is it surprising that I lose heart? / But how foolish

Waz spriche ich tumber man · durch mînen bœsen zorn?
Swer dirre wünne volget, der · hât jene dort verlorn,
iemer mêre, ouwê!

Owê wie uns mit süezen · dingen ist vergeben!
Ich sihe die gallen mitten · in dem honege sweben.
Diu werlt ist ûzen schœne · wîz, grüen unde rôt
und innân swarzer varwe, · vinster sam der tôt.
Swen si nû habe verleitet, · der schouwe sînen trôst:
er wirt mit swacher buoze · grôzer sünde erlôst.
Dar an gedenket, ritter, · ez ist iuwer dinc:
ir traget die liehten helme · und mangen herten rinc,
dar zuo die vesten schilte · und diu gewihten swert!
Wolte got, wær' ich · der sigenünfte wert!
So wolte ich nôtic man · verdienen rîchen solt.
Joch meine ich niht die huoben · noch der hêrren golt;
ich wolte sælden krône · êweclîchen tragen,
die möhte ein soldenære · mit sîme sper bejagen.
Möht ich die lieben reise · gevaren über sê,
sô wolte ich denne singen «wol» · und niemer mêre
    «ouwê»,
niemer mêre ouwê!

I am to be saying this just because I am angry; the man who seeks
after pleasure here will have already lost the joys to come, for ever,
alas!

Alas, how the sweet things of life poison us! I can see the gall
lurking in the honey. The world is lovely from the outside, white,
green, and red, but within it is all black and dark as death. I will
show where comfort lies for those whom it has led astray: an easy
penance can save them from great sin. Knights, bear this in mind,
for it is your affair; you wear gleaming helmets and hard rings of
mail, carry strong shields and consecrated swords! I wish to God
I were fit to take part in this victorious crusade; I am a poor man,
and it would bring me rich reward. Of course I do not mean acres
of land and gold from lords; I mean that I would wear the crown of
bliss eternally, which even a mercenary can earn with his spear. If I
were able to complete that longed-for expedition overseas I would
sing 'Hurray' and not 'Alas' any more, not 'Alas' any more.

WOLFRAM VON ESCHENBACH

«Sîne klâwen · durh die wolken sint geslagen,
er stîget ûf mit grôȝer kraft;
ich sih in grâwen · tägelîch als er wil tagen,
den tac, der im geselleschaft
erwenden wil, dem werden man,
den ich mit sorgen în verlieȝ.
Ich bringe in hinnen, ob ich kan:
sîn manegiu tugent mich daȝ leisten hieȝ.»

«Wahter, du singest · daȝ mir manege freude nimt
unde mêret mîne klage.
Mære du bringest, · der mich leider niht gezimt,
iemer morgens gegen dem tage.
Die solt du mir verswîgen gar:
daȝ biute ih den triwen dîn;
des lôn ich dir als ich getar
sô blîbet hie der trûtgeselle mîn.»

«Er muoȝ et hinnen · balde und âne sûmen sich:
nu gib im urloup, süeȝeȝ wîp.
Lâȝe in minnen · her nâch sô verholne dich,
daȝ er behalte êr und den lîp.

'Its claws have struck through the clouds, it rises up with great power, I see it turning the sky grey, day-like, as it is about to break – the day that will deprive him of his companion, that noble man whom I let in at such risk. I will get him away if I can; his many admirable qualities have induced me to do him this service.'

'Watchman, what you sing takes many joys away from me and increases my lament. Every morning at daybreak you bring news I do not, alas, wish to hear. You must keep it from me, I order you to do it. If my companion can remain here, I will reward you as I may.'

'He must leave here quickly and without delay. Now give him your parting favour, sweet lady, let him love you afterwards so secretly that he may keep safe both reputation and life. / He entrusted

Er gab sich mîner triwe alsô
daz ih in bræhte ouch wider dan.
Ez ist nu tac: naht was ez dô
mit drucke an brust dîn kus mirn an gewan.»

«Swaz dir gevalle, · wahter, sinc und lâ den hie,
der minne brâht und minne enphienc.
Von dînem schalle · ist er und ich erschrocken ie,
sô ninder morgenstern ûf gienc
ûf in, der her nâch minne ist komen,
noch ninder lûhte tages lieht:
du hâst in dicke mir benomen
von blanken armen, und ûz herzen nieht.»

Von den blicken, · die der tac tet durh diu glas,
und dô der wahter warnen sanc,
sie muose erschricken · durch den der dâ bî ir was.
Ir brüstelîn an brust sie dwanc.
Der rîter ellens niht vergaz
(des wold in wenden wahters dôn):
urloup nâh unde nâher baz
mit kusse und anders gab in minne lôn.

himself to my faithful care so that I should get him away again. It
is day now; it was night then, when you pressed your breast to his
and your kiss received him from me.'

'Sing as you please, watchman, and leave him here, who has
brought love and received love. He and I have always taken alarm
at your song. Even when the morning-star had not risen upon him
who came here for love, and when no daylight had shone at all, you
have often taken him from me, out of my white arms but not out
of my heart.'

Because of the gleam the day sent through the panes, and as the
watchman sang his warning song, she was afraid for the knight
who was with her. She pressed her little breasts against his chest.
The knight did not forget his courage (which the watchman's song
was meant to take from him). A tender and yet tenderer leave-
taking with kissing and much else besides gave them love's reward.

NEIDHART VON REUENTAL

D ER walt
aber mit maneger kleiner süeʒer stimme erhillet:
diu vogelîn sint ir sanges ungestillet;
diu habent ir trûren ûf gegeben.
Mit vreuden leben
den meien!
Ir megede, ir sult iuch zweien.

Sô hebet
sich aber an der strâʒe vreude von den kinden.
Wir suln den sumer kiesen bî der linden.
Diu ist niuwes loubes rîch,
gar wunneclîch
ir tolden.
Ir habt den meien holden!

Daʒ tou
an der wise den bluomen in ir ougen vellet.
Ir stolze megde, belîbt niht ungesellet:
ir zieret wol den iuwern lîp!
Ir jungiu wîp
sult reien
gein disem süeʒen meien.

T HE sound of many sweet small voices is heard again in the woods,
the birds never stop singing, they have cast off their sadness; they
greet May with joy! Girls, you must pair off!

And so there is excitement once more among the girls on the
village street. We can tell whether it is summer yet by the lime-
tree; it is covered with fresh leaves, its crown is beautiful. Gracious
May is here!

The dew falls into the eyes of the flowers in the meadow. You
fine girls must find partners; I expect you are dressing yourselves
up. You young women, you must dance to welcome sweet May in!

«Wie holt
im daȝ herze mîn vor allen mannen wære»
sprach Uodelhilt, ein magt unwandelbære,
«der mir lôste mîniu bant!
An sîner hant
ich sprunge,
daȝ im sîn helze erklunge.

Mîn hâr
an dem reien sol mit sîden sîn bewunden
durch des willen der mîn zallen stunden
wünschet hin ze Riuwental.
Des winders zâl
hât ende.
Ich minne in, deist unwende.»

«Nu ist der küele winder gar zergangen;
diu naht ist kurz, der tac beginnet langen;
sich hebet ein wunneclîchiu zît,
diu al der werlde vreude gît;
baȝ gesungen nie die vogele ê noch sît.

'How I would love him in my heart, more than any other man,'
said Udelhild, no foolish virgin she, 'the man who unlaces me! If I
was dancing hand in hand with him, I would make his swordhilt
jingle!
'At that dance my hair will be bound with silk for the sake of the
man [= Neidhart] who is always wanting me to go to Reuental.
The dull time of winter is over; he's the one I love, that's certain.'

'Now the chill winter has quite gone, the nights are short, the
days are beginning to draw out, and that pleasant season is begin-
ning again which gives joy to all the world. The birds have never
sung so sweetly before or since.

Komen ist uns ein liehtiu ougenweide:
man siht der rôsen wunder ûf der heide;
die bluomen dringent durch daz gras.
Wie schône ein wise getouwet was,
dâ mir mîn geselle zeinem kranze las!

Der walt hât sîner grîse gar vergezzen;
der meie ist ûf ein grüenez zwî gesezzen;
er hât gewunnen loubes vil.
Bint dir balde, trûtgespil:
dû weist wol daz ich mit einem ritter wil.»

Daz gehôrte der mägde muoter tougen.
Sî sprach «Behalte hinne vür dîn lougen.
Dîn wankelmuot ist offenbâr.
Wint ein hüetel um dîn hâr.
Dû muost âne dîne wât, wilt an die schar.»

«Muoter mîn, wer gap iu daz ze lêhen,
daz ich iuch mîner wæte solde vlêhen?
Dern gespunnet ir nie vadem.
Lâzet ruowen solhen kradem.
Wâ nû slüzzel? Sliuz ûf balde mir daz gadem.»

'What a bright and lovely sight it is; you can see roses in plenty
on the common; the flowers are sprouting in the grass. How thick
with dew that meadow was when my sweetheart picked flowers to
make me a garland!
'The wood has quite forgotten its greyness; May has settled on
a green branch; he has put out plenty of leaves. Put on your hat,
my dear, you know I am going out with a knight!'
Meanwhile the girl's mother had been secretly listening. She said:
'Don't try to deny it, anyone can see what a flirt you are. A scarf is
what you should be putting round your head! If you want to join
the others you will have to go without your party dress!'
'Mother, what right have you to make me beg my own dress
from you? You never spun a single thread of it! Give over your
scolding! Where's the key? Just you open the cupboard for me,
quick!'

Diu wât diu was in einem schrîne versperret.
Daz wart bî einem staffel ûf gezerret.
Diu alte ir leider nie gesach.
Dô daz kint ir kisten brach,
dô gesweic ir zunge, daz sî niht ensprach.

Dar ûz nam sî daz röckel alsô balde.
Daz was gelegen in maneger kleinen valde.
Ir gürtel was ein rieme smal.
In des hant von Riuwental
warf diu stolze maget ir gickelvêhen bal.

Diu alte diu begreif ein rocken grôzen.
Si begunde ir tohter bliuwen unde stôzen.
«Daz habe dir des von Riuwental.
Rûch ist im sîn überval.
Nû var hin, daz hiute der tievel ûz dir kal.»

STEINMAR

Ein kneht der lac verborgen,
bî einer dirne er slief
unz ûf den liehten morgen:

The dress was locked up in a chest – that was soon forced open
with a chair-leg. Never had the old woman seen anything so morti-
fying; words failed her while her daughter was breaking open the
chest and she could not speak at all.

[The girl] quickly took out the dress; it had been put away neatly
folded; her girdle was a narrow band. It was into the hand of the
knight of Reuental [= Neidhart] that the handsome girl threw her
many-coloured ball.

[When she came back] the old woman seized a large distaff and
began to beat and bash her daughter. 'That's for your Knight of
Reuental, with his fur collar! Now be off, and the sooner the devil
takes you the better!'

A labourer was lying hidden, he had been sleeping with a farm
girl until the bright morning. / The herdsman called out loudly,

33

der hirte lûte rief
«Wol ûf, lâ₃ û₃ die hert!»
Des erschrac diu dirne · und ir geselle wert.

Da₃ strou da₃ muost er rûmen
und von der lieben varn.
Er torste sich niht sûmen,
er nam si an den arn.
Da₃ höi da₃ ob im lac
da₃ ersach diu reine · ûf fliegen in den tac.

Dâ von si muoste erlachen,
ir sigen diu ougen zuo.
Sô suo₃e kunde er machen
in deme morgen fruo
mit ir da₃ bettespil;
wer sach ân geræte · ie fröiden mê sô vil!

Sî t si mir niht lônen wil
der ich hân gesungen vil,
seht sô wil ich prîsen
den der mir tuot sorgen rât,
herbest der des meien wât
vellet von den rîsen.
Ich wei₃ wol, e₃ ist ein alte₃ mære

'Get up, let out the herd.' This startled the girl and her precious
companion.

He had to leave the straw and go away from his darling. He dared
not delay. He took her in his arms. The pure young maiden saw the
hay that covered him fly up into the light.

This made her laugh aloud; her eyes closed. So sweetly could he
play the bed-game with her in the early morning! Whoever saw so
much pleasure with so few resources?

As she to whom I have sung so often will not reward me, you see,
I will praise the one who takes away my sorrows, the autumn who
strips the garment of May from the branches. I know it is an old

daz ein armez minnerlîn ist rehte ein marteræere.
Seht, zuo den was ich geweten:
wâfen! Die wil ich lân und wil inz luoder treten. [...]

Wirt, durh mich ein strâze gât:
dar ûf schaffe uns allen rât,
manger hande spîse.
Wînes der wol tribe ein rat
hœret ûf der strâze pfat.
Mînen slunt ich prîse:
mich würget niht ein grôziu gans so ichs slinde.
Herbest, trûtgeselle mîn, noch nim mich zingesinde.
Min sêle ûf eime rippe stât,
wâfen! diu von dem wîne drûf gehüppet hât!

ANONYMOUS

KRÂMER, gip die varwe mir
diu mîn wengel rœte,
dâ mit ich die jungen man
ân ir dank der minnenliebe nœte.
Seht mich an,
jungen man!
Lât mich eu gevallen!

story / that a poor lover is a martyr indeed. You see I used to be har-
nessed to that team but hurray now! I shall leave them and turn to
eating and swilling.
  Landlord, a highroad runs through me, give us provisions of all
sorts of food for it. Enough wine to drive a mill-wheel is needed for
the carriage way of this road. I have a fine gullet: if I swallowed a
large goose it would not choke me! Autumn, my dear companion,
take me as your retainer! My soul is sitting on one of my ribs
(hurray now!), where it had to hop up to get out of the wine!

Mary Magdalene's Song

PEDLAR, let me have the paint to redden my cheeks, to compel
young men willy-nilly to love. Look at me, young men, take your
pleasure in me!

Minnet, tugentlîche man,
minneklîche vrauwen!
Minne tuet eu hôch gemüt,
unde lât euch in hôhen êren schauwen.
 Seht mich an,
 jungen man!
 Lât mich eu gevallen!

Wol dir werlt, daz du bist
also vreudenrîche!
Ich wil dir sîn undertân
durch dîn liebe immer sicherlîche.
 Seht mich an
 jungen man!
 Lât mich eu gevallen!

DER WILDE ALEXANDER

Hie vor dô wir kinder wâren
und diu zît was in dên jâren
daz wir liefen ûf die wisen,
her von jenen wider ze disen:
dâ wir under stunden
vîol funden,
dâ siht man nu rinder bisen.

Gentle men, love lovely women! Love raises your spirits and shows you off to good advantage. Look at me, young men, take your pleasure in me!

Hail to you, World, for you are so full of delight. For the joy you give I will always serve you truly. Look at me, young men, take your pleasure in me!

Years ago when we were children and at the stage when we used to run about in the meadows, from one to the other, in the places where we sometimes used to find violets you can now see cattle gadding about.

36

Ich gedenk wol daʒ wir sâʒen
in den bluomen unde mâʒen
welch diu schœnest möhte sîn.
Dô schein unser kintlich schîn
mit dem niuwen kranze
zuo dem tanze.
Alsus gât diu zît von hin.

Seht, dô lief wir ertber suochen
von der tannen zuo der buochen
über stoc und über stein
der wîle daʒ diu sunne schein.
Dô rief ein waltwîser
durch diu rîser
«wol dan, kinder, und gêt hein.»

Wir enpfiengen alle mâsen
gestern dô wir ertber lâsen:
daʒ was uns ein kintlich spil.
Dô erhôrten wir sô vil
unsern hirte rüefen
unde wüefen
«kinder, hie gêt slangen vil.»

I remember how we used to sit among the flowers and compare
them to see which flower was the prettiest. Our childishness was
apparent as we danced bedecked with freshly made wreaths. So
time passes.

Look, that is where we used to go to look for strawberries, from
the pines to the beeches, over hedges and stiles as long as the sun
shone. A gamekeeper would call through the bushes: 'Come on,
children, go home.'

We all used to come out in spots in those yesterdays when we
gathered strawberries; it was just a childish game to us. We often
used to hear our herdsman's warning shout: 'Children, there are a
lot of snakes here.'

Ez gienc ein kint in dem krûte:
daz erschrac und rief vil lûte
«kinder, hie lief ein slang în,
der beiz unser pherdelîn:
daz ne heilet nimmer.
Er müez immer
sûren unde unsælic sîn!»

«Wol dan, gêt hin ûz dem walde!
Unde enîlet ir niht balde,
iu geschiht als ich iu sage:
werbet ir niht bî dem tage
daz ir den walt rûmet,
ir versûmet
iuch und wirt iur vröude ein klage.

Wizzet ir daz vünf juncvrouwen
sich versûmten in den ouwen
unz der künc den sal beslôz?
Ir klag und ir schade was grôz,
wande die stocwarten
von in zarten
daz si stuonden kleider blôz.»

A child was walking in the long grass; it started and shouted 'I
say, a snake went in here – it has bitten our pony so that it will never
get well again. Curse that beastly snake!'

'Come now, children, away from the wood! If you do not hurry
I will tell you what will happen to you; if you do not make sure to
get out of the wood while it is still light you will lose your way and
your pleasure will end in tears.

'Do you know that Five Virgins dallied in the meadows until
the King shut the door of the hall? Their misfortune and their
lamentation was great, for the gaolers tore everything off them, so
that they stood there without any clothes.'

DER GUOTÆRE

HIE vor ein werder ritter lac
tôtsiech dâ an dem bette sîn.
Sô schœne eine vrouwe vür in gie
daz er sô hô ir schœne wac:
sî het vor allen wîben schîn,
ern sach ouch schœner vrowen nie.
Sî stuont vor im und sprach «nu sage,
guot ritter, wie ich dir behage:
du hâst gedienet vlîzic mir
gar dîne tage: nu bin ich komen und wil nâch tôde lônen
    dir.»

    Von golde ir krône, wol geberlt
ir wât ir gürtel ir vürspan:
dô sprach er «vrouwe, wer sît ir?»
Sî sprach zuo zim «ich binz diu Werlt,
du solt mich hinden schouwen an:
sich, den lôn den bringe ich dir.»
Ir was der rucke vleisches hol,
er was gar kroten würme vol
und stanc alsam ein vûler hunt.
Dô weinet er und sprach «owê daz dir wart ie mîn dienest
    kunt!» [...]

ONCE a noble knight lay mortally ill in his bed. A beautiful lady
appeared before him, so beautiful that he thought her brighter than
all other women and that he had never seen a lovelier woman.
She stood before him and said 'Tell me now, good knight, how do
you like me? You have served me diligently all your days; now I
have come to reward you after your death.'

    Her crown was of gold, her dress, her belt, her waist-buckle were
ornamented with pearls. Then he said, 'Lady, who are you?' She
said to him, 'I am the World, you must see me from behind; look,
this is the reward I bring you.' Her back was fleshless and hollow,
it was full of toads and worms and stank like a dead dog. Then he
wept and said, 'Alas that I ever gave you my service.'

DER MÎSNAERE

GOT ist gewaltic,
manicvaltic
sint sîniu werc, sîn name ist gedrîet;
er ist der erste unde ouch der leste, Got sîn leben ist ân'
    ende.
Obe im ist keiner,
er ist einer,
der allen creatiuren lên verlîet;
er ist almehtic; wer vermac daz, daz er vermac? Uns
    macheten sîne hende.
Er meistert allez, daz dâ lebet;
er ne vürhtet künic, noch keiser niht: in vürhtent alle
    schepfenunge,
swaz swimmet oder in lüften swebet,
swaz ie gewart, daz lobet der megede kint unde die Gotes
    barmunge.
Hêr aller wunder,
oben und under,
mit sîner kraft al eine mac betwingen:
der ist gemant, unt helf' uns dar, dâr wir sîn lob mit allen
    engeln singen.

GOD is mighty, manifold are His works, His name is triple; He is
the first and the last, God's life is without end. There is none above
Him, He alone gives fiefs to all created things; He is almighty.
Who can do what He can do? His hands made us. He controls
everything that lives, He fears neither king nor emperor, all crea-
tures fear Him, whatever swims or flies in the air, everything made
praises the Virgin's child and the mercy of God. Lord of all
miracles above and below, He can conquer everything with His
power alone: He has become man, and may He help us to go there
where we shall sing His praises with all the angels.

HEILIGER geist, nu geiste uns hie mit dîme geiste;
unser geist dem vleische lît ze nâhe, dîn geist mac uns den
  geist entzünden wol.
Heiliger geist, dîner pfliht ger ich allermeiste;
drîvaldic stric, die drî ein Got, vater sun heiliger geist,
  tugende vol;
almehtic Got, dîn kint barmunge rîch, heiliger geist, uns
  riuwe lîe.
Sin unde witze, unser geloube, die drîe,
an bete einigen Got, der unser geist ze sîme geiste haben
  sol.

ÂN anevanc unde ende hôher künic, Got, schepfer aller
  dinge,
wie wazzer obe den himelen sî,
waran der himel unt wolken hangen, daz ist ein wunder;
wie sunne, und mân', gestirne stê, wie wâc erden umb-
  ringe,
wie diz halten Gotes vinger drî,
wîsheit, gewalt, barmunge, dort obene unt hie under.
An wîsheit hat Got alliu dinc

HOLY GHOST now inspire us with Thy Spirit! Our spirit is too
close to the flesh, Thy spirit can easily inflame our spirits. Holy
Ghost, I desire Thy protection above all; threefold rope, the three
one God, Father, Son, and Holy Ghost, full of virtue, Almighty
God, Thy child full of mercy, Holy Ghost, give us penitence!
Sense, intellect, and our faith, these three, worship the one God,
who shall take our spirit into His spirit!

WITHOUT beginning and without end, high King, God, creator of
all things, it is a miracle indeed that water is above the firmament
from which the sky and clouds hang; that sun and moon and stars
have their places, that waters surround the earth, and that God's
three fingers, wisdom, power, and mercy, hold all these things both
above and below. In His wisdom God has made all things, / nothing

gemachet, im ist niht verborgen,
sîn gewalt überringet allen rinc,
die naht unde ouch den morgen;
er ist der barmunge ein ursprinc,
da mite er nert, swaʒ dâ lebet gar âne sorgen.

ANONYMOUS

Maria stuont in grôʒen nœten,
do siu ir liebeʒ kint sach tœten;
ein swerte ir durch die sêle sneit.
Daʒ lô dir, sünder, wesen leit.
   Des hilf uns, lieber herre got;
   des biten wir dich durch dinen tôt.

Ihesus riefe in himmelrîche
sînen engeln alle gelîche;
er sprach zu in vil senedeclîchen:
«Die cristenheit wil mir entwîchen.
Des wil ich lôn
die welt zergôn;
daʒ wiʒʒent sicher ône wân!»
   Dô vor behüet uns, herre got:
   des biten wir dich durch dînen tôt.

is hidden from Him, His power outcircles all circles, night and morning; He is a fountain of mercy, with which He keeps safe everything that lives without a thought [of Him].

A Flagellants' Song

Mary stood in great grief when she saw her dear son killed; a sword pierced through her soul. Sinner, let this distress you. – So help us, dear Lord God, we pray Thee by Thy death!

Jesus in heaven cried to all his angels, full of sorrow he said to them: 'Christendom is about to forsake me, so I will cause the world to come to an end; know this for certain and without doubt!' – Preserve us Lord God, we pray Thee by Thy death!

Maria bat irn sun, den süeʒen:
«Liebeʒ kint, lô siu dir büeʒen;
So wil ich schicken, daʒ siu müeʒen
bekêren sich.
Des bit ich dich,
  vil liebeʒ kint, des gewer du mich!»
    Des biten wir sünder ouch alle gelîch.

Die erde bidemet, eʒ klungent die steine:
ir herten hertzen, ir sullent weinen.
Weinent tougen
mit den ougen!
Schlâhent iuch sêre
durch Cristus êre!
Durch in vergieʒen wir unser bluot:
daʒ sî uns für die sünde guot.
    Daʒ hilf uns lieber herre got;
    daʒ biten wir dich durch dînen tôt.

JOHANNES TAULER

Es kumpt ein schiff geladen
recht ûff sin höchstes port,
es bringt uns den sune des vatters,
das êwig wôre wort.

Mary prayed her sweet son: 'Dear child, let them do penance!
If you will, then I will cause them to be converted. I beg you,
dearest child, grant me my prayer!' – We sinners all pray for this
too.

The earth trembled, the rocks resounded; you hard hearts, you
must weep. Weep secretly with your eyes! Scourge yourselves
sorely for the honour of Christ! For His sake we shed our blood,
may it be good for our sin! – So help us, dear Lord God, we pray
Thee by Thy death!

A ship is coming, laden right up to the gunwale; it brings us the
Son of the Father, the eternal true Word.

Ûff ainem stillen wâge
kumpt uns das schiffelîn,
es bringt uns rîche gâbe,
die hêren künigîn.

Maria, du edler rôse,
aller sælden ain zwî,
du schöner zîtenlôse,
mach uns von sünden frî.

Das schifflîn das gât stille
und bringt uns rîchen last,
der segel ist die minne,
der hailig gaist der mast.

ANONYMOUS

Kerenstein

«Ich bin durch frauen willen · geritten in fremdeu land,
mich hât ein edler ritter · zuo poten her gesant.
Der enpeut euch, schöne fraue, · sein vil werden gruoß.
Nuen enpiet im, was ir wellet! · Von eu so hat er freden
  genuog.»

The ship is coming towards us over a calm sea; it brings us a
rich gift, the noble Queen.

Mary, you precious rose, branch of every bliss, you lovely crocus
flower, cleanse us from our sins.

The ship is sailing quietly and brings us rich cargo. Love is its
sail, its mast the Holy Ghost.

The Ballad of Kerenstein

'I have ridden into foreign parts for a lady's sake; a noble knight
has sent me to you as a messenger. He sends you his kindest greet-
ings, fair lady. Now send him what message you think fit; he has
great joy in you.'

«Was söl ich im enpieten?» · redt als das magedein:
«sech ich den helt mit augen, · des erfreuet sich das hertze
  mein.
Und sichstu dört die linden · wol vor der purge stan?
Do haiß den deinen heren · des aubendtz spät darunder
  gân!»

Da der edel ritter · da under die linden kam,
was fand er under der linden? · Ein maget die was wol
  getan.
Ab zoch er den mantel sein, · er warft in in das gras.
Da lagen die zway die langen nacht · pis an den liechten
  tag.

«Nuon ist dein wille ergangen», · redt als das magedein:
«sô tuost du woll den geleichen, · sam du von mir welst
  sein,
und kêrst mir woll den ruocken · und reitst dahin von
  mir,
sô tuo ich als ein kleines kind · und wain auch, edler her,
  nach dir.»

'What can I send him?' the maiden replied. 'If I could see the
knight with my own eyes, my heart would be full of delight. Do
you see the lime-tree which stands outside the castle gate? Tell
your master to wait under it late this evening.'
    When the noble knight arrived under the lime-tree, what did he
find under the tree? A beautiful maiden. He took off his cloak and
threw it down on the grass, and there the two lay the long night
through until the bright day came.
    'Now you have had your desire,' the maiden said. 'If it seems as
though you want to go from me, and if you turn your back on me
and ride away from me, then I shall do as a little child does and cry
for you, noble lord.'

«So verpüt ich euren augen, · ir wunderschônes weib,
daß si nach mir nit waine, · ich kum herwider in kurzer
zeit.
Und sichst du dört den voln · an der heffte haben?
Der sol dich, allerliebstes lieb, aus grôßen nöten tragen.»

Da hueb sich in der purge · wol wundergrôßer schall,
der wachter an der zinnen · der sang: «die burg ist
aufgetôn!
Hat ymant hie verloren, · der sol sein nemen war.»
Da sprach der edel von Kerenstain: · «ich hab meine
schöne dochter verloren.»

«Nuen waiß es Crist von himel wol, · das ich unschuldig
pin.
Und ist mein schône juncfrau · mit ainem anderen dôhin,
das was ir bayder wille, · si waren einander lieb.»
Der wachter an der zinnen · der sang so wol ein tagelied.

'Then, you very lovely woman, I forbid your eyes to weep for
me; I shall come back in a short time. Do you see the young horse
tied up there? He will carry you, dearest sweetheart, away from
great distress.'
Then a great noise was heard in the castle. The watchman on the
castle walls sang out, 'The castle gates are open! Let each man look
to see if he has lost anything.' Then the Lord of Kerenstein said,
'I have lost my beautiful daughter.'
[The watchman said:] 'Now Christ in Heaven knows that I am
free from blame, and if my young mistress has gone away with
another, it was because they both desired it: they loved one
another.' The watchman on the battlements sweetly sang a morning
song.

Brunenberch

[...] D E valschen kleffer schloten einen rat
dat Brunenberch gefangen wart,
gefangen up frîer strâten,
in ein torn wart he gelâten.

Darin satt he wol söven jâr,
sîn kop wart witt, sîn bart wart grauw,
sin môt begund em to breken,
nên wort konde he mer spreken.

Se lêden Brunenberch up einen disch,
se rêten en recht wo einen visch,
se nêmen em ût sîn herte,
dat dêde dem helde grôt schmerte.

Se nêmen em ût sîn junge herte fîn,
recht so einem wildenschwîn,
vorweldent in einem peper,
se gevent der schönsten to eten.

«Wat isset dat ick gegeten hebb,
dat mi so wol geschmecket hefft?»
«Dat is Brunenberges herte,
dat dêde dem helde grôt schmerte.»

The Ballad of Brunenberg

THE treacherous slanderers planned it so that Brunenberg was cap-
tured, captured on the open road; he was put away in a dungeon.

He lay there for seven years, his head grew white, his beard grew
grey, his spirit began to break, he could no longer speak a word.

They laid Brunenberg on a table and they split him just like a
fish; they took out his heart; this gave the brave man great pain.

They took out his brave young heart as if he were a wild boar,
they disguised it in a stew and gave it to the lady to eat.

'What is this that I have been eating that tasted so good?' 'That
is Brunenberg's heart, that gave the brave man great pain.'

«Is dat Brunenberges junge herte fîn,
sô schenket mi den kôlen wîn,
schenket in unde gevet mi drinken!
Mîn herte wil mi vorsinken.

So neme ick dit up mîne leste henfart
dat ick Brunenberges sîn nicht schüldich wart
denn reine küsche lêve,
dat konde uns nêmant vorbêden.»

Den ersten drâpen den se drank,
er herte in dûsent stücke sprank:
berât, herr Christ, de reine
mit dîner gnâd alleine!

Totenamt

«I t daget in dat osten,
de maen schînt averall;
wo weinich wêt mîn lêveken,
wor ick benachten schal.

'If that is Brunenberg's brave young heart, pour me out the cool wine, pour it out and let me drink it! My heart fails me.

'I take this thought on my last journey: that there was never anything between Brunenberg and me but pure chaste love, which no one could forbid us.'

The first drop she drank, her heart broke into a thousand pieces. Grant the pure lady, Lord Christ, thy grace alone!

Mass for the Dead

'The day is breaking in the east, the moon shines everywhere; little does my sweetheart know where I shall pass the night.

Weren dat alle mîne fründe,
dat nu mîne vîende sîn,
ick förde se ût dem lande,
min lêf und minnekîn.»

«All wor hen scholde gi mi vören,
stolt rüter wolgemeit?
Ick ligge in lêves armen
in sô grôter werdicheit.»

«Ligge gi in juwes lêves armen?
Bî lo! gi segget nicht wâr;
gât hen to der linden gröne,
vorschlagen licht he dar!»

Dat mêdeken nam ere mantel
unde se gink einen gank
all to der linden gröne,
dar se den dôden vant.

«Wo ligge gi hir vorschlagen,
vorschmort in juwem blôt!
Dat hefft gedân juw röment,
darto juwe hôge môt.

'If all those who are now my enemies were my friends, I would
leave the country with her, my sweetheart and my darling.'
'Where would you take me, bold joyful knight? I lie in my love's
arms in great comfort.'
'You are lying in your love's arms, are you? By God, you are
not speaking the truth. Go to the green lime-tree, he is lying there
killed.'
The girl took her cloak and went away to the green lime-tree,
where she found the dead man.
'So you lie there killed, all drenched in your blood. That is the
result of your boasting and your exultant spirits.

Wo ligge gi hir vorschlagen,
de mi to trösten plach!
Wat hebbe gi mi nâgelâten?
So mengen bedröveden dach!»

Dat megdeken nam ere mantel
und se gink einen gank
all nâ eres vaders porten,
de se togeschlâten vant.

«Got gröte juw heren alle,
mînen vader mit im talle!
Unde is hir ein here
effte ein edel man,
de mi dissen dôden
begraven helpen kan?»

De heren schwêgen stille,
se makeden nên gelût;
dat megdeken kêrde sick umme
unde se gink wênent ût.

Mit eren schnêwitten henden
se de erde upgroef,
mit eren schnêwitten armen
se en to grave droech.

'So you who used to comfort me lie here killed! What have you left me? Many days of sadness.'

The girl took her cloak and went away to her father's gate, which she found locked.

'Good day to all you gentlemen and to my father too! Is there a lord or a gentleman here who can help me bury this dead man?'

The lords kept silent, they did not make a sound. The girl turned and went out, weeping.

She turned up the earth with her snow-white hands, with her snow-white arms she carried him to the grave.

«Nu wil ick mi begeven
in ein klein klösterlîn
und dragen schwarte klêder
und werden ein nünnekîn.»

Mit erem hellen stemmen
se em de misse sank,
mit eren schnêwitten henden
se em de schellen klank.

Danhauser

Nun will ichs aber heben an
Von dem Danhauser zu singen,
Und was er Wunders hat getan
Mit seiner Frau Venusinne.

Danhauser war ein Ritter gut
Wann er wollt Wunder schauen,
Er wollt hin zu Frau Venus Berg
Zu andern schönen Frauen.

«Herr Danhauser, ihr seid mir lieb,
Daran sollt ihr gedenken!
Ihr habt mir einen Eid geschworn:
Ihr wöllet von mir nicht wenken.»

'Now I will go into a convent and wear black clothes and become a nun.'

With her clear voice she sang the mass for him, with her snow-white hands she rang the handbell for him.

The Ballad of Tannhäuser

Now I will begin to sing of Tannhäuser and what marvels he has done with his Dame Venus.

Tannhäuser was an honest knight, except that in quest of marvels he wanted to go into Dame Venus' mountain, to find other pretty ladies.

'Sir Tannhäuser, I love you dearly, and you must not forget it. You have sworn me an oath not to leave me.'

«Frau Venus! Das enhab ich nit,
Ich will es widersprechen,
Und redt das jemand mehr dann ihr,
Gott helf mirs an ihm rächen!»

«Herr Danhauser, wie redt ihr also?
Ihr sollt bei mir beleiben,
Wann ich will euch mein Gespiele geben
Zu einem steten Weibe.»

«Und nähm ich nun ein anders Weib,
Noch hab ich in meim Sinne:
So müßt ich in der Höllen Glut
Auch ewiglich verbrinnen.»

«Ihr sagt mir viel von der Höllen Glut
Und ihr habts nie befunden:
Gedenkt an meinen roten Mund!
Der lacht zu allen Stunden.»

«Was hilft mich dann eur roter Mund?
Der ist mir ganz unmäre;
Nun gebt mir Urlaub, mein Fräulein zart,
Durch aller Frauen Ehre!»

'Dame Venus, I have done nothing of the kind, I deny it, and
if it is anyone but you that says it, may God help me to avenge it.'
'Sir Tannhäuser, what things you say! You must stay with me
and I will give you my companion to be your constant wife.'
'And if I take another wife than the one who is in my mind [i.e.
the Virgin Mary], I would have to burn eternally in hell fire.'
'You talk a lot about hell fire, but you have never felt it. Think
of my red mouth which is always smiling [for you].'
'What use is your red mouth to me? It revolts me. Now let me
take my leave, gentle lady, for the honour of all women.'

«Herr Danhauser! Wollt ihr Urlaub han,
Ich will euch keinen geben;
Nun bleibet, edler Danhauser,
Und fristet euer Leben!»

«Mein Leben, das ist worden krank,
Ich mag nicht länger bleiben;
Nun gebt mir Urlaub, Fräulein zart,
Von eurem stolzen Leibe!»

«Herr Danhauser, redt nit also!
Ihr seid nit wohl bei Sinne;
So gehn wir in ein Kämmerlein
Und spielen der edlen Minne!»

«Gebraucht ich nun ein fremdes Weib,
Ich hab in meinem Sinne:
Frau Venus, edle Fraue zart!
Ihr seid ein Teufelinne!»

«Herr Danhauser, wie redt ihr nun,
Daß ihr mich begunnt zu schelten?
Sollt ihr länger hie innen sein,
Ihr müßt sein oft entgelten.»

'Sir Tannhäuser, if you want to take your leave I will not let you
do so. Stay now, noble Tannhäuser, and spend your life here.'

'My life has become wretched, I cannot stay any longer. Now
let me take my leave, gentle lady, from your fair self.'

'Sir Tannhäuser, do not say such things, you have taken leave
of your senses. Let us go into a bedroom and play the gentle
game of love.'

'If I were to have to do with any other woman than the one who
is in my mind – Dame Venus, noble gentle lady, you are a very
devil!'

'Sir Tannhäuser, what is this? now you begin to abuse me; if
you stay here any longer you will pay for it many times over.'

«Frau Venus, und das will ich nicht,
Ich mag nicht länger bleiben.
Maria Mutter, reine Magd,
Nun hilf mir von dem Weibe!»

«Danhauser, ihr sollt Urlaub han,
Mein Lob, das sollt ihr preisen,
Wo ihr nun in dem Land umfahren;
Nehmt Urlaub von dem Greisen!»

Da schied er wieder aus dem Berg
In Jammer und in Reuen:
«Ich will gen Rom wohl in die Stadt
Auf eines Papstes Treuen.

Nun fahr ich fröhlich auf die Bahn,
Gott müss sein immer walten!
Zu einem Papst, der heißt Urban,
Ob er mich möcht behalten. –

Ach Papst, viel lieber Herre mein!
Ich klag euch meine Sünde,
Die ich mein Tag begangen hab,
Als ich euch will verkünden.

'Dame Venus, I will not do that, I will not stay any longer. Mary Mother, pure Maid, help me to escape from this woman!'

'Tannhäuser, I give you leave to go, and you shall sing my praises wherever you go all over the country; take leave of the old man too.'

Thereupon he went away from the mountain in sorrow and repentance. 'I will go to the city of Rome, and trust to the Pope.

'Now I set out joyfully on my journey, may God watch over it, to a Pope called Urban, to see if he can save me.

'O Pope, my dear lord, I lament the sin to you which I have committed in my life, as I will explain.

Ich bin gewesen auch ein Jahr
Bei Venus, einer Frauen;
So wollt ich Beicht und Buß empfahn,
Ob ich Gott möcht anschauen.»

Er hätt ein Stab in seiner Hand
Und der was aller dürre:
«Als wenig der da grünen mag,
Kommst du zu Gottes Hulden.»

«Und sollt ich leben nur ein Jahr,
Ein Jahr auf dieser Erden,
So wollt ich Beicht und Buß empfahn
Und Gottes Huld erwerben.»

Da zog er wieder aus der Stadt
In Jammer und in Leide:
«Maria Mutter, reine Magd!
Muß ich mich von dir scheiden.»

Da zog er wieder in den Berg
Und ewiglich ohn Ende:
«Ich will zu Venus der Frauen zart,
Wo mich Gott hin will senden.»

'Moreover I have spent a year with Venus, a fair lady, and I wish
to confess and do penance, so that I may be able to see God.'
[The Pope] had a staff in his hand and it was dry as could be.
'You can not attain the favour of God any more than this can
put out leaves.'
'Even if I had only had a year to live on this earth, I would have
wanted to confess and do penance and gain God's favour.'
Then he went out of the city in pain and sorrow: 'Mary Mother,
pure Maid, so I must part from you!'
Then he went back into the mountain for ever without end: 'I
will go back to Venus the gentle lady, for it is there that God sends
me.'

«Seid Gott-willkumm, Herr Danhauser!
Ich hab eur lang emboren;
Seid willkummen, mein lieber Herr,
Zu einem Buhlen auserkoren!»

Das währt bis an den dritten Tag,
Der Stab hub an zu grünen;
Der Papst schickt aus in alle Land:
Wo der Danhauser wär hinkommen?

Da war er wieder in dem Berg
Und hätt sein Lieb erkoren,
Da mußt der vierde Papst Urban
Auch ewig sein verloren.

Herr von Falkenstein

Es reit der Herr von Falkenstein
Wohl über ein breite Heide.
Was sieht er an dem Wege stehn?
Ein Mädel mit weißem Kleide.

'Welcome, Sir Tannhäuser, I have missed you for such a long time. Welcome, dear lord, to be a chosen lover.'

That lasted until the third day the staff began to put out leaves. The Pope sent messengers into every country to find out what had happened to Tannhäuser.

But by that time he was back in the mountain and had chosen his lover. For this Pope Urban the fourth was eternally damned too.

The Ballad of Lord Falkenstein

THE Lord of Falkenstein rides over a wide heath. What does he see standing at the side of the path? A girl in a white dress.

«Wohin, wohinaus, du schöne Magd?
Was machet ihr hier alleine?
Wollt ihr die Nacht mein Schlafbuhle sein,
So reitet ihr mit mir heime.»

«Mit euch heimreiten, das tu ich nicht,
Kann euch doch nicht erkennen.»
«Ich bin der Herr von Falkenstein,
Und tu mich selber nennen.»

«Seid ihr der Herr von Falkenstein,
Derselbe edle Herre,
So will ich euch bitten um'n Gefang'n mein,
Den will ich haben zur Ehe.»

«Den Gefangnen mein, den geb ich dir nicht,
Im Turm muß er vertrauern.
Zu Falkenstein steht ein tiefer Turm,
Wohl zwischen zwei hohen Mauern.»

«Steht zu Falkenstein ein tiefer Turm,
Wohl zwischen zwei hohen Mauern,
So will ich an den Mauern stehn,
Und will ihm helfen trauern.»

'Where are you going, pretty girl? What are you doing alone here? If you will be my lover tonight, ride home with me.'

'What, ride home with you? I won't do that, I don't even know you.' 'I am the Lord of Falkenstein, I have no cause to conceal my name.'

'If you are the Lord of Falkenstein, that noble gentleman, I will beg you for my love who is a prisoner; I wish to marry him.'

'I will not give you my prisoner, he must languish in the dungeon. There is a deep dungeon at Falkenstein, between two high walls.'

'If there is a deep dungeon at Falkenstein between two high walls, I will stand by the walls and help him to lament.'

Sie ging den Turm wohl um und wieder um:
«Feinslieb, bist du darinnen?
Und wenn ich dich nicht sehen kann,
So komm ich von meinen Sinnen.»

Sie ging den Turm wohl um und wieder um,
Den Turm wollt sie aufschließen:
«Und wenn die Nacht ein Jahr lang wär,
Keine Stund tät mich verdrießen!

Ei, dürft ich scharfe Messer tragen,
Wie unsers Herrn sein Knechte,
Ich tät mit'm Herrn von Falkenstein
Um meinen Herzliebsten fechten!»

«Mit einer Jungfrau fecht ich nicht,
Das wär mir immer ein Schande!
Ich will dir deinen Gefangnen geben;
Zieh mit ihm aus dem Lande!»

«Wohl aus dem Lande, da zieh ich nicht,
Hab niemand was gestohlen;
Und wenn ich was hab liegen lan,
So darf ich's wieder holen.»

She went round and round the dungeon: 'Sweetheart, are you inside there? If I cannot see you I shall go out of my mind.'

She went round and round the dungeon, she tried to open the dungeon. 'And if the night was as long as a year, I would not count an hour wasted.

'Why, if I were allowed to wear sharp knives, as our master's servants do, I would fight the Lord of Falkenstein for my sweetheart!'

'I will not fight with a girl, that would bring shame on me for ever. I will give you your prisoner, leave the country with him!'

'I will not leave the country, I have not stolen anything from anybody, and if I have left anything behind I can come and fetch it back.'

Schondilie

ALS Schondilie noch ein klein Kind war,
Da starb ihr Vater und Mutter ab.

Schondilie wuchs auf und sie ward groß,
Sie wuchs einem Reiter in seinen Schooß.

«Schondilie, willst du mein Hausfrau sein?
Zehn Tonnen Gold sollen dein eigen sein.»

Schondilie gedacht in ihrem Mut,
Zehn Tonnen Gold, die wären gut.

Schondilie gedacht in ihrem Sinn,
Zehn Tonnen Gold macht eine Kaiserin.

Was trug Schondilie über den blanken Leib?
Ein Hemdchen wie der Schnee so weiß.

Was trug Schondilie über ihr Hemdchen weiß?
Einen Rock, der war von dem Gold so steif.

The Ballad of Schondilie

WHEN Schondilie was a little child her father and her mother died.

Schondilie grew up and became a big girl, she grew into a knight's lap.

'Schondilie, will you be my wife? You shall have ten tons of gold for your own.'

Schondilie thought to herself that ten tons of gold would be a good thing.

Schondilie thought to herself that she could be an empress with ten tons of gold.

What did Schondilie wear over her bare body? A shift as white as snow.

What did Schondilie wear over her white shift? A dress that was stiff with gold.

Was trug Schondilie über ihr gehl kraus Haar?
Eine Krone, die war von Gold so klar.

Da sah Schondilie zum Fenster heraus:
«Nun komm stolz Reiter und hol deine Braut.»

Die Jungfrau war ihm lieb und wert,
Er schwenkt sie hinter sich wohl auf sein Pferd.

Sie reiten den Tag dreißig Meilen lang,
Eh sie weder Essen noch Trinken fand.

«Ach Reiter, steh herab, es ist Mittag:
Wo sollen wir Essen und Trinken han?»

«Wohl in dem breiten Lindenbreit,
Da wirst du finden dein Essen bereit.»

«Ach Reiter, steh herab, es ist schon Nacht,
Wo sollen wir diesen Abend schlafen gahn?»

«Wohl in dem breiten Lindenbreit,
Da wirst du finden dein Bettchen gespreit.»

What did Schondilie wear over her curly yellow hair? A crown
that was bright with gold.

Then Schondilie looked out of the window: 'Now, bold knight,
come and fetch your bride.'

The girl was dear and precious to him: he lifted her on to the
crupper of his horse.

They rode thirty miles that day before they got anything to eat
or drink.

'Oh, knight, dismount, it is midday, where shall we get any-
thing to eat and drink?'

'Under the broad lime-tree you will find your meal made ready
for you.'

'Oh, knight, dismount, it is midnight, where are we going to
sleep this evening?'

'Under the broad lime-tree you will find your bed made ready
for you.'

Wie sie wohl an den Lindenbaum kamm,
Dan hingen sieben Jungfrauen daran.

«Hier siehst du sieben Jungfräulein,
Schondilie, willst du die achte sein?

Willst du hangen den hohen Baum,
Oder willst du fließen den Wasserstrom,
Oder willst du küssen das blanke Schwert?»

«Ich will nicht hangen den hohen Baum,
Ich will nicht schwimmen den Wasserstrom,
Ich will lieber küssen das blanke Schwert.

Ach Reiter, zieh aus dein Oberkleid,
Jungfrauenblut spritzt weit und breit.»

Schondilie, sie packt das Schwert mit dem Knopf,
Sie hieb dem Ritter ab den Kopf.

Da lacht die falsche Zung und sprach:
«In meiner Tasche, da ist ein Horn,
Da blas du ein, so kommst du fort.»

And when they came to the lime-tree, seven maidens were hang-
ing on it.
'You see seven maidens here, Schondilie, will you be the
eighth?
'Will you hang on the tall tree, or will you float in the watery
stream, or will you kiss the naked sword?'
'I will not hang on the tall tree, I will not swim in the watery
stream, I had rather kiss the naked sword.
'Oh, knight, take off your outer garment, maiden's blood spurts
out far and wide.'
Schöndilie seized the sword by the pommel, and she cut off the
knight's head.
Its false tongue laughed and said, 'There is a horn in my satchel,
if you blow it you will get away from here.'

Schondilie gedacht in ihrem Mut,
Viel Tuten und Blasen wär nicht gut.

Schondilie saß auf sein apfelbraun Ross
Und ritt zum grünen Wald hinaus.

Als sie wohl vor den grünen Wald kam,
Da begegnen ihr auch seiner Brüder drei.

«Schondilie, wo ist mein Bruder fein,
Daß du jetzt reitest ganz allein?»

«In dem breiten Lindenbreit,
Da spielt er mit sieben Jungfräulein fein.»

«Schondilie, wie sind deine Schühlein so rot?»
«Drei Täubchen hab ich geschossen tot.»

Es waren zwei Königskinder,
Die hatten einander so lieb;
Sie konnten beisammen nicht kommen,
Das Wasser war viel zu tief.

Schondilie thought to herself that it would not be a good thing
to do much tooting and blowing.
Schondilie got on his dappled horse, and rode out of the green
wood.
As she came to the edge of the green wood she met his three
brothers.
'Schondilie, where is my fair brother and why are you travelling
all by yourself?'
'Under the broad lime-tree, he is playing with seven fair maidens
there.'
'Schondilie, why are your shoes so red?' 'I have shot down three
pigeons.'

There were two royal children, who loved one another so dearly;
they could not come together, the water was much too deep.

«Ach Schätzchen, ach könntest du schwimmen,
So schwimm doch herüber zu mir!
Drei Kerzchen will ich anzünden,
Und die solln leuchten zu dir.»

Das hört ein falsches Nönnchen,
Die tat, als wenn sie schlief;
Sie tät die Kerzlein auslöschen,
Der Jüngling ertrank so tief. —

«Ach Fischer, lieber Fischer,
Willst dir verdienen Lohn,
So senk deine Netze ins Wasser,
Fisch' mir den Königssohn!»

Sie faßt ihn in ihre Arme
Und küßt seinen roten Mund:
«Ach Mündlein, könntest du sprechen,
So wär mein jung Herze gesund.»

Sie schwang sich um ihren Mantel
Und sprang wohl in die See:
«Gut Nacht, mein Vater und Mutter,
Ihr seht mich nimmermeh!»

'Oh, sweetheart, if you can swim, swim across to me! I will light
three candles and they will give you light!'
    A false nun heard this, who pretended to be asleep. She put out
the candles, the young man was drowned so deep.
    'Oh, fisherman, dear fisherman, if you want to earn a reward,
cast your nets into the water, fish up the king's son for me.'
    She took him in her arms and kissed his red mouth. 'Oh, mouth,
if you could speak my young heart would be well again.'
    She wrapped herself in her cloak and jumped straight into the
sea. 'Good night, my father and mother, you will never see me
again.'

Da hört man Glockenläuten,
Da hört man Jammer und Not:
Hier liegen zwei Königskinder,
Die sind alle beide tot.

MARTIN LUTHER

Nunc dimittis

MIT Fried und Freud ich fahr dahin
In Gotts Wille,
Getrost ist mir mein Herz und Sinn,
Sanft und stille.
Wie Gott mir verheißen hat:
Der Tod ist mein Schlaf worden.

Das macht Christus, wahr Gottes Sohn,
Der treu Heiland,
Den du mich, Herr, hast sehen lon
Und gmacht bekannt,
Daß er sei das Leben mein
Und Heil in Not und Sterben.

Then the tolling of bells was heard and distress and mourning was heard too. Here lie two royal children, and both of them are dead.

Nunc dimittis

I DEPART in peace and joy according to God's will. My heart and mind are at peace, quiet and tranquil. As God promised me, now death is but a sleep for me.

Christ has done this, the true Son of God, the faithful Saviour, whom Thou, Lord, hast allowed me to see and revealed to me so that He may be my life and my salvation in distress and death;

Den hast du allen fürgestellt
Mit groß Gnaden,
Zu seinem Reich die ganze Welt
Heißen laden,
Durch dein teur heilsams Wort,
An allem Ort erschollen.

Er ist das hell und selig Licht
Für die Heiden,
Zu 'rleuchten, die dich kennen nicht,
Und zu weiden.
Er ist deins Volks Israel
Der Preis, Ehr, Freud und Wonne.

Ein' feste Burg ist unser Gott,
Ein gute Wehr und Waffen.
Er hilft uns frei aus aller Not,
Die uns jetzt hat betroffen.
Der alt böse Feind,
Mit Ernst ers jetzt meint,
Groß Macht und viel List,
Sein grausam Rüstung ist,
Auf Erd ist nicht seins gleichen.

Whom Thou hast with great grace put before all others, hast
invited the whole world to His Kingdom through Thy precious
saving word which is gone out into all places.

He is the bright and blessed light to the Gentiles to lighten and
feed those who do not know Thee. He is the glory, honour, joy and
delight of Thy people Israel.

Our God is a firm stronghold, a good shield and weapon. He will
quickly help us out of all the distress which has come upon us
now. The old evil enemy is making a serious effort now, his dread-
ful armament consists of great power and much cunning. There is
nothing equal to him on earth.

Mit unser Macht ist nichts getan
Wir sind gar bald verloren.
Es streit für uns der rechte Mann,
Den Gott hat selbst erkoren.
Fragst du, wer der ist?
Er heißt Jesu Christ,
Der Herr Zebaoth,
Und ist kein ander Gott,
Das Feld muß er behalten.

Und wenn die Welt voll Teufel wär
Und wollt uns gar verschlingen,
So fürchten wir uns nicht zu sehr,
Es soll uns doch gelingen.
Der Fürst dieser Welt,
Wie saur er sich stellt,
Tut er uns doch nicht,
Das macht, er ist gericht,
Ein Wörtlein kann ihn fällen.

Das Wort sie sollen lassen stahn
Und kein Dank dazu haben.
Er ist bei uns wohl auf dem Plan
Mit seinem Geist und Gaben.
Nehmen sie den Leib,
Gut, Ehr, Kind und Weib:

Our own strength is of no use, we are quickly lost. The true
Man fights for us whom God has chosen. If you ask who he is, his
name is Jesus Christ, the Lord of Hosts, there is no other God. He
will hold the field.

And even though the world were full of devils and threatened to
devour us, we do not lose heart, we shall be successful. The Prince
of this world, however angry he may seem, can do nothing to us,
because he is already judged; a mere word can send him toppling.

They must let the Word be whether they will or no. He is in the
field on our side with His spirit and His gifts. If they take our bodies,
possessions, reputation, children, wives, / let them all go, they will

Laß fahren dahin,
Sie haben's kein Gewinn,
Das Reich muß uns doch bleiben.

HULDRYCH ZWINGLI

Gebetslied in der Pest

1. *Im anfang der krankheit*

HILF, herr got, hilf
in diser not!
Ich mein, der tod
si an der tür.
Stand, Christe, für,
dann du in überwunden hast!

Zuo dir ich gilf:
Ist es din will,
züch uß den pfil,
der mich verwunt,
nit laßt ein stund
mich haben weder ruow noch rast!

have no profit from it, in spite of them the kingdom will still be ours.

Prayer during the Plague

1. At the beginning of his sickness

HELP, Lord God, help me in this extremity! I think death is at the door. Stand forth, O Christ, for Thou has overcome him!

I cry to Thee: if it is Thy will, draw out the dart which has wounded me and which leaves me not a moment's peace nor rest.

Wilt du dann glich
tod haben mich
in mits der tagen min,
so sol es willig sin.
Tuo, wie du wilt!
Mich nüt bevilt.
Din haf bin ich:
Mach ganz ald brich!
Dann, nimpst du hin
den geiste min
von diser erd,
tuost dus, daß er nit böser werd
ald andren nit
befleck ir leben from und sit.

2. *In mitten der krankheit*

Tröst, herr got, tröst!
Die krankheit wachst
We und angst faßt
min sel und lib.
Darumb dich schib
gen mir, einiger trost, mit gnad,
   die gewüß erlöst
ein ieden, der
sin herzlich bger

But if Thou wishest to have me dead in the middle of my days, I am content. Do as Thou wilt, nothing shall be too much for me. I am Thy vessel, mend me or break me! When Thou takest my spirit from this earth, do it so that it shall not grow more evil and not disgrace other people's pious way of life.

2. During his sickness

Comfort me, Lord God, comfort me! the sickness grows, pain and fear seize upon my soul and body. So come to me my only

und hoffnung setzt
in dich, verschetzt
darzuo dis zits all nutz und schad.

Nun ist es umb.
Min zung ist stumb,
mag sprechen nit ein wort;
min sinn sind all verdort.
Darumb ist zit,
daß du min strit
füerist fürhin,
so ich nit bin
so starch, daß ich
mög dapferlich
tuon widerstand
des tüfels fecht und frevner hand.
Doch wirt min gmüet
stät bliben dir, wie er joch wüet.

3. *In der besserung*

Gsund, herr got, gsund!
Ich mein, ich ker
schon widrumb her.

solace, with grace which assuredly saves any man who sets his
heart's desire / and hope in Thee and despises for its sake all the good
and ill of this temporal world.

Now it is all over with me, my tongue is dumb, it cannot speak
a word; my senses are all dried up. So now the time has come when
Thou must fight my battle henceforward, if I am not strong enough
boldly to resist the devil's enmity and his evil hand. But my soul
will always remain true to Thee, however he may rage.

3. While recovering

Health, Lord God, health! I seem to be returning unharmed. / Yes,
if Thou thinkest that the spark of sin will not rule me any more on

Ja, wenn dich dunk,
der sünden funk
werd nit mer bherrschen mich uf erd,

so muoß min mund
din lob und ler
ußsprechen mer
dann vormals je,
wie es joch ge,
einfaltiglich on alle gfärd.

Wiewol ich muoß
des todes buoß
erliden zwar ein mal
villicht mit größerm qual,
dann iezund wär
geschehen, herr,
so ich sust bin
nach gfaren hin:
so wil ich doch
den trutz und boch
in diser welt
tragen frölich umb widergelt
mit hilfe din,
on den nüt mag volkumen sin.

earth, then my mouth must utter Thy praise and glory more than
ever before, however things may turn out, in perfect simplicity of
heart.

Although I must sooner or later suffer the pain of death, perhaps
with greater suffering than I would have undergone this time, Lord,
when I nearly passed away, I will joyfully endure the spiteful blows
of this world, sure of my reward, with Thy help, without which
nothing can be perfect.

ULRICH VON HUTTEN

Ich habs gewagt mit Sinnen
Und trag des noch kein Reu;
Mag ich nit dran gewinnen,
Noch muß man spüren Treu,
Darmit ich mein:
Nit eim allein,
Wenn man es wollt erkennen,
Dem Land zu gut,
Wiewohl man tut
Ein Pfaffenfeind mich nennen.

Da laß ich jeden lügen
Und reden, was er will.
Hätt Wahrheit ich geschwiegen,
Mir wären Hulder viel.
Nun hab ichs gsagt,
Bin drumb verjagt
Das klag ich allen Frummen.
Wiewohl noch ich
Nit weiter flich,
Vielleicht werd wiederkummen. [...]

I meant to do what I dared to do and I still do not regret it. Even though I may gain nothing from it, my honesty must be plain in what I believe: if you look at it closely, you must serve the commonweal and not one man alone, even though they do call me a priest-hater.

I will leave everyone to lie and say what they like. If I had concealed the truth I should have many admirers. Now I have spoken out and have been banished for it; I appeal to all honest men. Though I shall flee no further and may yet come back.

Nun ist oft diesergleichen
Geschehen auch hievor,
Daß einer von den Reichen
Ein gutes Spiel verlor.
Oft großer Flamm
Von Fünklein kam;
Wer weiß, ob ichs werd rächen!
Staht schon im Lauf,
So setz ich drauf:
Muß gahn oder brechen! [...]

Ob dann mir nach tut denken
Der Kurtisanen List:
Ein Herz laßt sich nit kränken,
Das rechter Meinung ist!
Ich weiß noch viel,
Wölln auch ins Spiel,
Und solltens drüber sterben:
Auf, Landsknecht gut
Und Reuters Mut,
Laß Hutten nit verderben!

But this sort of thing has often happened before, that people in authority have lost what seemed a certain game. A small spark has often started a big fire; I may get my own back yet, who knows? When things begin to move I shall stake what I have on it, to win or lose everything!

Though the benefice-hunters are after me with their cunning, a man who does what his heart tells him is right cannot be put off. I know many others who want to take part in this game, even at the risk of their lives. Up, stout spearman and gallant knight, don't let Hutten down!

JOHANN HESSE

Von dem christlichen Abschied dieser Welt

O WELT, ich muß dich lassen,
Ich fahr dahin mein Straßen
Ins ewig Vaterland;
Mein Geist will ich aufgeben,
Darzu mein Leib und Leben
Setzen gnädig in Gottes Hand.

Mein Zeit ist nun vollendet,
Der Tod das Leben schändet,
Sterben ist mein Gewinn:
Kein Bleiben ist auf Erden,
Das Ewig muß mir werden,
Mit Fried und Freud ich fahr dahin. [...]

Ich bin ein unnütz Knechte,
Mein Tun ist viel zu schlechte,
Dan daß ich ihm bezahl
Darmit das ewig Leben:
Umsonst will er mirs geben
Und nicht nach meim Verdienst und Wahl. [...]

A Christian Farewell to the World

O WORLD, I have to leave you, I am going on my way to the eternal home. I will give up my spirit, and lay my body and my life humbly in the hand of God.

My time is completed, death makes a mock of life, dying is my profit: there is no permanency on earth, I must obtain eternal life; I depart in peace and joy.

I am an unprofitable servant, my deeds are much too lowly for me to earn eternal life from Him with them; He gives it me for nothing and not according to my deserts and choice.

Damit fahr ich von hinnen:
O Welt, tu dich besinnen,
Wann du mußt auch hernach;
Tu dich zu Gott bekehren
Und von ihm Gnad begehren,
Im Glauben sei du auch nicht schwach. [...]

Das schenk ich dir am Ende.
Ade! Zu Gott ich wende,
Zu ihm steht auch mein Be'gehr;
Hüt dich vor Pein und Schmerzen,
Nimm mein Abschied zu Herzen,
Meins Bleibens ist jetzt hie nicht mehr.

ANONYMOUS

In dulci jubilo
Nun singet und seid froh!
Unsers Herzens Wonne
Leit in *praesepio*,
Leuchtet vor die Sonne
Matris in gremio.
Alpha es et O.

And so I depart from here: O World, consider, for in time you
must do so too. Turn to God and ask for grace from Him and do
not be weak in faith.

That is my last gift to you. Farewell, I turn towards God, my
desire is fixed on Him; protect yourself from pain and sorrow, take
my farewell to heart, my habitation is no longer here.

In sweet rejoicing now sing and be merry; the joy of our hearts is
lying in the manger and gleams brighter than the sun in His
mother's lap. Thou art Alpha and Omega.

O Jesu parvule,
Nach dir ist mir so weh,
Tröst mir mein Gemüte,
O puer optime,
Durch aller Jungfraun Güte,
O princeps gloriae!
Trahe me post te!

Ubi sunt gaudia?
Niendert mehr denn da,
Da die Engel singen
Nova cantica
Und die Schellen klingen
In Regis curia.
Eia, wärn wir da!

Mater et filia
Ist Jungfrau Maria.
Wir waren gar verdorben
Per nostra crimina;
Nu hat sie uns erworben
Coelorum gaudia!
Quanta gratia!

O little Jesus, I long for Thee; console my spirit, O best of
children, for the sake of all virgins, O prince of glory! Draw me
after Thee!

Where are the joys? Where else but there, where the angels sing
new songs and the bells ring in the King's court! Ah, if only we
were there!

Mary the Virgin is mother and maid; we were damned because
of our sins, now she has gained for us the joys of Heaven, and by
what great grace!

Innsbruck, ich muß dich lassen,
ich fahr dahin mein Straßen,
in fremde Land dahin.
Mein Freud ist mir genommen,
die ich nit weiß bekommen,
wo ich im Elend bin.

Groß Leid muß ich jetzt tragen,
das ich allein tu klagen
dem liebsten Buhlen mein.
Ach Lieb, nun laß mich Armen
im Herzen dein erbarmen,
daß ich muß dannen sein.

Mein Trost ob allen Weiben,
dein tu ich ewig bleiben,
stät, treu, der Ehren frumm.
Nun müß dich Gott bewahren,
in aller Tugend sparen,
biß daß ich wiederkumm.

Ich gib mich gantz ze wellen dir,
Ob allen menschen liebst du mir;
Hett ich gewalt nach meiner gir,
Alles guten must du sein gewert.

Innsbruck, I have to leave you, I am going on my way into
foreign lands. My joy has been taken away from me and I cannot
have it now I am away from home.

I have to bear great sorrow which I can only complain about to
my own dearest love. Oh, love, take pity in your heart upon my
misery because I have to go away.

My comfort above all women, I shall always be yours, constant,
true, and honest. Now God preserve you and keep you in all virtue
until I come back again.

I surrender myself entirely to you; you please me above all
others. If I had power as I would like, you should be supplied with
all good things.

Nymm hin von mir die triue mein,
Nach meiner gir bin ich der dein;
Entschliusse dein hertz, nymm mich darein,
So bin ich gantz von dir ernert.

Sich an mein dienst vnd nymm der war,
Ich leb dir ze willen gar;
Schick mir ze diesem Newen Jar
Dein gunst, nicht mer mein hertz begert.

Iсн saß und war einmal allein
In einem Stübelein,
Da sah ich zu der Tür hinein
Die Allerliebste mein.

Von Herzen war ich nie so froh,
Wußt selber nit wie mir war;
Ich ging zu meinem feinen Buhlen,
Ich nahm sie in meinen Arm.

Grüß dich Gott, mein feines Lieb!
Wie steht unser Sach?
Ich seh's an deinem Mündelein,
Dein Herz leidt Ungemach.

Accept from me the pledge of my faith, I desire to be yours; un-
lock your heart, take me into it, and you will be my salvation
entirely.

Look on my devotion and take note of it. I live only for you.
Send me a sign of your favour this New Year; there is nothing else
my heart desires.

I was sitting by myself for a while in a room when I saw my sweet
love coming through the door.

I was glad as never before, I could not describe how I felt; I went
up to my sweetheart and took her in my arms.

Good day to you, my darling, how are things between us? I
see from your dear mouth that your heart is disturbed.

Dein Mündlein ist verblichen,
Ist nimmer als rot als vor,
Da ich dich zum ersten mal liebgewann,
Ist länger dann ein Jahr.

Und wer mir trauren helfen will,
Der heb ein Finger auf! –
Ich seh viel Finger und wenig Treu,
Drum so hör ich das Singen auf.

Ich send dir, liebes Lieb, ein'n Gruß
Auf einer Nachtigallen Fuß,
Auf jeglichem Klauen
Einen gülden Pfauen.
Als mannich gut Jahr geh dich an
Als ein geleiterter Wagen
Gefüllter Rosen mag getragen,
Jegliches Blatt in neun gespalten.
Gott müsse deines jungen Leibes walten.

Your dear mouth has grown pale, it is not so red as it used to be
when I first fell in love with you more than a year ago.
Now let anyone who will mourn with me put up a finger. – I see
a lot of fingers and little fidelity, so I will stop my singing.

I send you a greeting, sweetheart, by a nightingale's foot, and on
every claw a golden peacock. May you have as many prosperous
years as a piled-up hay-wain can carry roses, and every petal divided
into nine! May God protect your dear young self!

WEIN, Wein von dem Rhein,
Lauter, klar und fein,
Dein Farb gibt gar lichten Schein,
Als Kristall und Rubein.
Du gibst Medizein
Für Trauren. Schenk du ein!
Trink, gut Kätterlein,
Mach rote Wängelein!
Du söhnst die allzeit pflegen Feind zu sein,
Den Augustein
Und die Begein;
Ihnen beiden · scheiden · kannst du Sorg und Pein,
Daß sie vergessen Deutsch und auch Latein! [...]

WIE schön blüht uns der Maien,
der Sommer fährt dahin.
Mir ist ein schöns Jungfräulein
gefallen in meinen Sinn.
Bei ihr ja wär mir wohl;
wann ich nur an sie denke,
mein Herz ist freudenvoll.

WINE, wine from the Rhine, pure, clear, and delicate, your colour
shines brilliantly like crystal and ruby. You are a medicine against
depression. Pour it out and drink, good Kate, and make your
cheeks red! Wine, you make peace between those who are always
at odds with one another, the Augustinians and the Beguines, and
you can drive away all sorrow from both of them so that they forget
both German and Latin!

HOW fine the blossom is in May! the summer is on its way. My
thoughts have turned to a beautiful maiden. If I were with her, I
should be happy; whenever I think of her my heart is filled with
joy.

Bei ihr, da wär ich gerne,
bei ihr, da wär mirs wohl;
sie ist mein Morgensterne,
strahlt mir ins Herz so voll.
Sie hat ein roten Mund –
sollt ich sie darauf küssen,
mein Herz würd mir gesund.

Wollt Gott, ich fänd im Garten
drei Rosen auf einem Zweig;
ich wollte auf sie warten,
ein Zeichen wär mirs gleich.
Das Morgenrot ist weit,
es streut schon seine Rosen:
ade, du schöne Maid!

Ich hört ein Sichelein rauschen,
wohl rauschen durch das Korn,
ich hört ein feine Magd klagen,
sie hätt ihr Lieb verlorn.

«Laß rauschen, Lieb, laß rauschen,
ich acht nit, wie es geh;
ich hab mir ein Buhlen erworben
in Veiel und grünem Klee.»

I wish I were with her; if I were with her I would be happy. She is my morning star and shines right into my heart. She has a red mouth; if I could kiss her on it my heart would be sound again.

Would to God I might find in the garden three roses on one branch; I would wait for her, it would be a sign for me. The dawn is far off, it casts its roses already. Farewell you fair maiden.

I heard a reaping-hook rustle, rustle through the corn, I heard a fair maid lamenting that she had lost her lover.

'Let it rustle, my dear, let it rustle, I do not care how it is; I have got myself a sweetheart, among the violets and the green clover.'

«Hast du einen Buhlen erworben
in Veiel und grünem Klee,
so steh ich hier alleine,
tut meinem Herzen weh.»

Es ist ein Ros entsprungen
aus einer Wurzel zart,
als uns die Alten sungen,
aus Jesse kam die Art,
und hat ein Blümlein bracht,
mitten in kaltem Winter,
wohl zu der halben Nacht.

Das Röslein, das ich meine,
darvon Esaias sagt,
hat uns gebracht alleine
Marie die reine Magd;
aus Gottes ewgem Rat
hat sie ein Kind geboren
wohl zu der halben Nacht.

'Though you have got yourself a sweetheart among the violets
and the green clover, I stand here alone, with pain in my heart.'

A ROSE has sprouted from a tender root, as the prophets sang, the
strain came from Jesse, and it has given us a flower in the middle of
cold winter, at midnight.

The Rose I mean, of which Isaiah spoke, has been given us by
Mary the pure maid herself; according to God's eternal will she has
born a child at midnight.

«O BAUERNKNECHT, laß die Röslein stahn,
Sie sein nit dein,
Du trägst noch wohl von Nesselnkraut
Ein Kränzelein.»

Das Nesselkraut ist bitter und saur
Und brennet mich.
Verlorn hab ich mein schönes Lieb,
Das reuet mich.

Es reut mich sehr und tut mir
Im Herzen weh.
Gesegen dich Gott, mein holder Buhl,
Ich sehe dich nimmermehr.

Es geht eine dunkle Wolk herein;
mich deucht, es wird ein Regen sein,
ein Regen aus den Wolken
wohl in das grüne Gras.

Und kommst du, liebe Sonn, nit bald
so weset alls im grünen Wald,
und all die müden Blumen,
die haben müden Tod.

'O FARM lad, let the roses be, they are not yours, [or else] you will wear a wreath of nettle leaves.'

The nettle leaves are bitter and sharp and they sting me. I have lost my sweetheart; that makes me sad.

It makes me sad and cuts me to the heart. God bless you, my dear love, I shall never see you any more.

A DARK cloud is coming up, I think it will bring rain, rain from the clouds on to the green grass.

Dear sun, if you do not come soon everything in the green wood will spoil and all the weary flowers will find a weary death.

Es geht eine dunkle Wolk herein,
es soll und muß geschieden sein;
ade, Feinslieb, dein Scheiden
macht mir das Herze schwer.

Es ist ein Schnitter, heißt der Tod,
hat Gwalt vom großen Gott.
Heut wetzt er das Messer,
es schneidt schon viel besser,
bald wird er drein schneiden,
wir müssens nur leiden:
hüt dich, schöns Blümelein!

Was heut noch grün und frisch dasteht,
wird morgen weggemäht:
die edel Narzissel,
die englische Schlüssel,
die schön Hyazinthen,
die türkische Binden:
hüt dich, schöns Blümelein!

A dark cloud is coming up, we must part, we must. Good-bye,
dear love, it makes my heart heavy that you must part from me.

THERE is a reaper, his name is death, he has power from almighty
God. Today he is sharpening his scythe, already it cuts much better,
soon he will reap away, we shall have to endure it. Take care, fair
little flower!
     What is green today and stands up fresh will be mown away to-
morrow. The stately daffodil, the primrose, the lovely hyacinth,
the martagon lily. Take care, fair little flower!

Viel hunderttausend ungezählt,
da unter die Sichel hinfällt;
rot Rosen, weiß Lilgen,
beid wird er austilgen,
ihr Kaiserkronen,
man wird euch nicht schonen:
hüt dich, schöns Blümelein! [...]

Trutz Tod! Komm her, ich fürcht dich nit!
Trutz, komm und tu ein Schnitt!
Wenn er mich verletzet,
so werd ich versetzet,
ich will es erwarten,
in himmlischen Garten:
freu dich, schöns Blümelein!

Du mein einzig Licht,
die Lilg' und Ros' hat nicht,
was an Farb' und Schein
dir möcht ähnlich sein;
nur daß dein stolzer Mut,
der Schönheit Unrecht tut.

Countless hundreds of thousands fall beneath his sickle, red roses, white lilies, he will destroy them both, you crown-imperials, too, will not be spared. Take care, fair little flower!

Death, do your worst! come on, I am not afraid of you! Come, do your worst and cut me down! If he harms me I shall be transported, as I trust, into the heavenly garden: rejoice, fair little flower!

You my only light, lily and rose have nothing that can be compared with you for colour and brightness; but your proud mind does your beauty wrong.

Meine Heimat du,
von solcher Lust und Ruh
ist der Himmel gar
wie die Erde bar;
nur daß dein strenges Wort
mich wehrt vom süßen Port.

WENN ich ein Vöglein wär
und auch zwei Flüglein hätt,
flög ich zu dir.
Weils aber nicht kann sein,
bleib ich allhier.

Bin ich gleich weit von dir,
bin doch im Schlaf bei dir
und red mit dir.
Wenn ich erwachen tu,
bin ich allein.

Es vergeht kein Stund in der Nacht,
daß mein Herz nicht erwacht
und an dich denkt,
daß du mir vieltausendmal
dein Herz geschenkt.

You, my home where I belong, earth and even heaven offer no
such joy and pleasure; but your stern word keeps me away from
that sweet haven.

IF I were a bird and had two wings I would fly to you. As that can-
not be, I have to stay here.
   Even though I am far from you, in my sleep I am with you and
speak to you. When I wake up I am alone.
   Not an hour passes in the night but my heart wakes and thinks
of you, and that you have given me your heart so many thousand
times.

KEIN Feuer, keine Kohle
Kann brennen so heiß
Als heimliche Liebe,
Von der niemand nichts weiß.

Keine Rose, keine Nelke
Kann blühen so schön,
Als wenn zwei verliebte Seelen
Beieinander tun stehn.

Setz du mir einen Spiegel
Ins Herze hinein,
Damit du kannst sehen,
Wie so treu ich es mein'!

DA droben auf jenem Berge,
Da steht ein hohes Haus,
Da schauen alle Frühmorgen
Drei schöne Jungfrauen heraus.

Die eine, die heißt Susanne,
Die andre Annemarei,
Die dritte, die darf ich nicht nennen,
Die soll mein eigen sein.

No fire, no coal, can burn so hot as secret love that no one knows
about.
No rose, no carnation can bloom so beautifully as when two
people in love are together.
Set a glass in my heart so that you can see how true my love is.

UP there on the hill there is a big house, and every morning early
three fair maidens look out.
The first is called Susanna, the second Annemarie, I must not
name the third one, she's the one I want.

Da drunten in jenem Tale,
Da treibt das Wasser ein Rad,
Das mahlet nichts als Liebe
Von morgens bis abends spat.

Das Mühlrad ist zerbrochen,
Die Liebe hat ein End,
Wo zwei Verliebte sich scheiden,
Sie geben einander die Händ.

Ach Scheiden, immer Scheiden,
Wer hat dich doch erdacht!
Du hast mein junges Herze
Aus Freuden in Trauern gebracht.

Emmentaler Hochzeitstanz

Die Braut:

Bin alben e wärti Tächter gsi;
Bin us em Hus, cha nümme dri,
Eh! nümme dri mir Läbelang.
Dr Ätti, ds Müeti, Brueder u Schwester u wän i ha,

Down there in the valley the water drives a wheel; it grinds
nothing but love from morning to evening.

The millwheel is broken, love comes to an end. When two lovers
part they take each other by the hand.

Oh, parting, always parting, whoever invented you! You have
brought my young heart from joy into sorrow.

Emmental Bridal Dance

The Bride:

I HAVE always been a cherished daughter. I have left the house, I
can't come in any more, oh, never again as long as I live. Father,
mother, brother, and sister and all who are mine, /I must leave them

87

Die mueß ig alli jitz verlah,
Mueß luege, wie mer's dusse gang.
O du mi trüli wärte Schatz
Jez chumen-i, hesch mer Platz?

Der Bräutigam:

Bisch frili e wärti Tächter gsi;
Muest äbe so ne wärti si,
E wärti si dir Läbelang.
Dr Ätti, ds Müeti, Brueder u Schwester u wän i ha,
Hätt' längist di gärn bi 'ne gha;
Un i ha beitet scho gar lang.
O du mi trüli wärte Schatz,
Chunst ändlig? I ha der Platz. [...]

Mɪ Schatz, we du tuesch z'Chilche gah,
Lueg nume nit gäng mi a!
Sust säge die fule Chlapperlüt,
Mir müeßen enandere ha.

Mi Schatz, we du i ds Wirtshus tuesch gah,
Bring mir nit gäng so dis Glas!
Bring's nume den andere Meitschene oh,
Däich nüsti, du gönnist mir's bas.

all now, I must see how I get on outside. O my true cherished
sweetheart, I am coming now, have you room for me?
The Bridegroom:
Yes, you have been a cherished daughter, now you will be just
as cherished, just as cherished as long as you live. Father, mother,
brother, and sister, and all who are mine, have been looking for-
ward to having you with them, and I have been waiting a very long
time. O my true cherished sweetheart, are you coming at last? I
have room for you.

[*Girl:*] Sᴡᴇᴇᴛʜᴇᴀʀᴛ, when you go to church don't always look
at me, otherwise the idle gossips will say that we *have* to get married.
Sweetheart, when you go to the pub don't always raise your glass
to me; drink to other girls too; I shall know just the same that it's
really meant for me.

Mi Schatz, we du zum Tanz tuesch gah,
Tanz nume nit gäng mit mir!
Tanz og no mit andere Meitschene,
Z'Nacht chunsch-de de notti zu mir.

Mi Schatz, we du tuesch z'Märit gah,
Chram nume nit gäng so viel!
We du dis Gältli verchrämerlet hesch,
Was soll i de tue mit dir!

«Ha dir no nüt verchrämerlet,
Ha dir no nüt verta.
Du bist mer no niene so lubi gsi,
Wie-n-i dergliche ha ta.»

Ich hab die Nacht geträumet
wohl einen schweren Traum;
es wuchs in meinem Garten
ein Rosmarienbaum.

Sweetheart, when you go dancing, don't always dance with me;
dance with other girls too, at night you can come to me just the
same.

Sweetheart, when you go to market don't buy so many fairings
for me; what am I to do with you when you've thrown away all
your bit of money on that sort of thing?

[*Man:*] I've never wasted *our* money on fairings, I have never
thrown *our* money away; I've never been so set on you as I made
out.

I DREAMT an oppressive dream last night: a rosemary tree was
growing in my garden;

Ein Kirchhof war der Garten,
das Blumenbeet ein Grab,
und von dem grünen Baume
fiel Kron und Blüten ab.

Die Blüten tät ich sammeln
in einen goldnen Krug,
der fiel mir aus den Händen,
daß er in Stücken schlug.

Draus sah ich Perlen rinnen
und Tröpflein rosenrot.
Was mag der Traum bedeuten?
– Herzliebster, bist du tot?

DAT du min Leevsten büst,
dat du woll weest.
Kumm bi de Nacht, kumm bi de Nacht,
segg, wo du heest.

Kumm du üm Middernacht,
kumm du Klock een;
Vader slöppt, Moder slöppt,
ick slaap alleen.

The garden was a churchyard, the bed of flowers a grave, and the
topmost leaves and the blossoms fell from the green tree.
I gathered up the blossoms in a golden jug, it slipped from my
hands so that it smashed to pieces.
I saw pearls run from it and rosy red drops. What can the dream
mean? Sweetheart, are you dead?

You know very well you are my sweetheart; come at night, come
at night, say who you are.
Come at midnight, come at one o'clock. Father will be asleep,
mother will be asleep, I sleep by myself.

Klopp an de Kamerdör,
  klopp an de Klink;
Vader meent, Moder meent,
  dat deit de Wind.

MEI Mutter mag mi net,
und koin Schatz han i net,
ei, warum stirb i net?
Was tu i do?

Gestern ischt Kirchweih gwe,
mich hat mer gewiß net gseh;
denn mir ischt gar so weh.
I tanz jo net.

Laß die drei Rösle stehn,
die dort am Kreuzle blühn!
Hent ihr des Mädle kennt,
das drunter leit?

Tap at the door of the room, tap on the latch; father will think, mother will think it is the wind does that.

My mother doesn't love me and I haven't got a sweetheart. Oh, why don't I die? What's left for me to do?

It was the fair yesterday; of course nobody saw me there, I am so miserable. I can't dance.

Let those three roses be, that bloom there by the cross. Did you know the girl that lies below them?

Wär ich ein wilder Falke,
ich wollt mich schwingen auf
und wollt mich niederlassen
vor eines Grafen Haus.

Und wollt mit starkem Flügel
da schlagen an Liebchens Tür,
daß springen sollt der Riegel,
mein Liebchen trät herfür.

«Hörst du die Schlüssel klingen?
Dein Mutter ist nicht weit;
so zieh mit mir von hinnen
wohl über die Heide breit!»

Und wollt in ihrem Nacken
die goldnen Flechten schön
mit wildem Schnabel packen,
sie tragen zu dieser Höhn.

Ja wohl zu dieser Höhen,
hier wär ein schönes Nest! –
Wie ist mir doch geschehen,
daß ich gesetzet fest!

If I were a wild falcon I would take wing and alight in front of a
nobleman's house,
     And I would strike with my strong wing against my love's door
that the bolt should snap and my love should come out.
     'Do you hear the keys rattle? Your mother is not far off; then
come away with me over the hills and far away.'
     And I would seize the golden plaits at her neck with my fierce
beak and carry her to this high place.
     Yes, up to this high place, it would be fine for a nest. What has
happened to me that I am pinned down!

Ja, trüg ich sie im Fluge,
mich schöß der Graf nicht tot,
sein Töchterlein, zum Fluche,
das fiele sich ja tot.

So aber sind die Schwingen
mir allesamt gelähmt,
wie hell ich ihr auch singe,
mein Lieb sich meiner schämt.

Jetz gang i ans Brünnele, trink aber net;
do such i mein herztausige Schatz, findn aber net.

Do laß i mein Äugele um und um gehn,
Do siehn i mein herztausige Schatz bei men andre stehn.

Und bei men andre stehn sehn, ach, das tut weh!
Jetz b'hüt di Gott, herztausiger Schatz, di b'siehn i
      nimmemeh.

Jetz kauf i mir Tinten und Fedr und Papier
And schreib meim herztausige Schatz einen Abschieds-
      brief.

Yes, if I were to fly away with her, the nobleman would not
shoot me dead; his little daughter would fall dead, for a curse upon
him.
   But as it is, my wings are paralysed; however clearly I sing to
her, my love is ashamed of me.

I go to the fountain, but I do not drink, I look for my own true
love but I cannot find her.
   I cast my eyes all round, then I see my true love going with
someone else.
   And, oh, it hurts to see her going with someone else! Now good-
bye, my true love, I shall never see you again.
   Now I'll buy ink and pen and paper and write my true love a
farewell letter.

Jetz leg i mi nieder aufs Heu und aufs Moos,
Do falle drei Rösele mir in den Schoß.

Und diese drei Rösele sind blutigrot:
Jetz weiß i net, lebt mei Schatz oder ist er tot.

Moosburger Weihnachtslied

HEUNT Nacht wàch i im Feld
Und schlag mir auf ein Zelt
Bei meinen Schafen:
Hab mi glögt wohl zur Rue,
Gdruckt meine Augen zue,
Könnt doch nit schlafen.

Ja dort in meiner Hütt
Könnt i heunt schlafen nit,
Hört i schen singen.
I woaß das noch nit wie,
Mein Lebtag hab i nie
So schen ghert klingen.

Now I lie down in the hay and the moss, and three roses fall into my lap.
And these three roses are red as blood; now I don't know whether my love is alive or dead.

Christmas Carol from Moosburg (Carinthia)

TONIGHT I am on watch in the field and put up a tent near my sheep; I lay down to sleep and shut my eyes, but I could not sleep.
There in my shelter I have not been able to sleep tonight. I heard lovely singing; I don't know that I have ever heard such a lovely sound in my life.

Glei kimmt ein Engel her
Und spricht freundli zue mir,
I sollt gschwind gehen
Dorthin nach Wethlachem,
Wo Rind und Esel stehn,
Würd eppas sehen.

Dort wo der Steren brinnt,
Sollt sein ein kleines Kind,
Hab i vernommen;
Das solt Messias sein,
Ligt in eim Krippelein,
Vom Himmel kommen.

I dacht, was ligst im Stall,
Ein Gott vom Himmelssaal?
Wer ist dann größer?
Kehrst du nit ein in d' Stadt,
Die schene Zimmer hat?
Wär ja vül bößer.

Dies hat die Liebe gmacht,
Hat dich vom Himmel bracht
Zu uns auf Erden.
Nit in ein Königssaal,
Nur in eim kalten Stall,
Wüllst gboren werden.

Soon an angel comes along and tells me in a friendly way to go
quickly over to Bethlehem where ox and ass stand, and I would see
something.

Over there where the star is burning, he said there was supposed
to be a little child, as I heard; he said it was the Messiah come from
heaven, lying in a crib.

I thought, 'Why are you lying in a stable, a God from the
heavenly palace? Who is greater than you? Why don't you call at the
town, where they've got lovely rooms? That would be much better.'

Love has done this, it has brought you down from heaven to us
on earth. You do not wish to be born in a royal hall but only in a
cold stable.

Herzliebstes Jesulein
Englisches Kindelein,
Wüll dirs Herz schenken.
Wann wir in letzten Zügn
Im Todbett werden liegn,
Wöllst auf uns denken.

DEANDL, geh ans Fenster her,
  alloa is mirs load;
wannst's Kitterl net findst
  geh nur her in da Pfoad.

«Geh weg von meim Fensta,
  was hast denn im Sinn,
wannst a rechter Bua waarst
  waarst lang scho herinn.»

WANN'S bumbert im Kammerl
schimpft d'Mutter auf mi,
und sag i: «Dös war d'Katz!»
Sagt s': «So? G'stiefelt is die?»

Dearest Jesus, angelic child, I will give you my heart. When we
are lying on our death-beds at our last gasp, think of us.

DEAR, come to the window, it's no fun here alone. If you can't find
your dress just come in your shift.
  'Go away from my window, what are you thinking of? If you
were a real man you would have been in here long ago.'

IF there is a noise in my bedroom my mother scolds me, and if I
say, 'That was the cat!' she says, 'Puss in Boots, I suppose?'

Für d' Flöh gibts a Pulver
für d' Schuach gibts a Wix,
für'n Durst gibts a Wasser –
bloß für d' Dummheit gibts nix.

G. R. WECKHERLIN

Bestätigung seiner Treue

Ach, was betrübt ihr mich so sehr,
Daß ihr mich wankelmütig nennet?
Ich weiß, daß Amor mich viel mehr
Dann euch – so schön – standhaft bekennet.

Wie euers Leibs Vollkommenheit
Mit keiner anderen zu vergleichen,
So meiner Lieb Beständigkeit
Weiß keiner Lieb und Treu zu weichen.

Da ich euch meine Treu versprach,
Hab ich mir selbst nichts vorbehalten;
Darum wär es ein große Schmach,
Wann euer Glaub nu sollt verkalten.

There's Keatings for fleas and polish for shoes and water for
thirst, but there's no cure for half-wittedness.

Assurance of his Fidelity

Oh, how can you distress me so much, and call me flighty? I know
that Love confesses me constant rather than you, beautiful as you
are!

Just as the perfection of your person is not to be compared with
any other, so the constancy of my love cannot give way before
anyone's love and fidelity.

When I promised you to be true I made no reservations, and so
it would be a great injustice if your faith in me were to cool.

In euch ist mein Herz, Geist und Sinn;
Zu lieben euch bin ich bei Leben;
Ach, wann ich nicht mehr euer bin,
So sagt mir, wem ihr mich gegeben!

Traum: von dem H. von B.

ICH sah in meinem Schlaf ein Bild gleich einem Gott,
Auf einem reichen Thron ganz prächtiglich erhaben,
Auf dessen Dienst und Schutz, zugleich aus Lust und
Not,
Sich die törichte Leut stets haufenweis begaben.
Ich sah, wie dieses Bild, dem wahren Gott zu Spott,
Empfing – zwar niemal satt – Gelübd, Lob, Opfergaben
Und gab auch wem es wollt das Leben und den Tod
Und pflag sich mit Rach, Straf und Bosheit zu erlaben.
Und ob der Himmel schon oftmal, des Bilds Undank
Zu strafen, seine Stern versammlete mit Wunder,
So war doch des Bilds Stimm noch lauter dann der
Dunder,

My heart, spirit, and mind are in you; I live to love you; oh, if I
am not yours any longer, then tell me to whom you have given me!

Vision: of the D[uke] of B[uckingham]

I SAW in my sleep an image like a god, exalted most magnificently
on a rich throne, into whose service and protection, both out of
inclination and necessity, the foolish people continually thronged.
I saw how this image, in mockery of the true God, received –
though never sated – vows, praise, and sacrifices, and gave life and
death to whom it would, and took pleasure in vengeance, punish-
ment, and wickedness. And though heaven often marshalled its
stars in signs and wonders to punish the image's ungratefulness, the
image's voice nonetheless was louder even than the thunder,/until

Bis endlich, als sein Stolz war in dem höchsten Schwang,
Da schlug ein schneller Blitz das schöne Bild herunder,
Verkehrend seinen Pracht in Kot, Würm und Gestank.

MARTIN RINCKART

Neujahr-, Monat-, Wochen-, und Tage-Segen

Nun danket alle Gott
Mit Herzen, Mund und Händen,
Der große Dinge tut
An uns und allen Enden,
Der uns von Mutterleib
Und Kindesbeinen an
Unzählig viel zu gut
Und noch jetzund getan.

Der ewig reiche Gott
Woll uns bei unserm Leben
Ein immer fröhlich Herz
Und edlen Frieden geben
Und uns in seiner Gnad
Erhalten fort und fort
Und uns aus aller Not
Erlösen hier und dort.

at last, when its pride was at its zenith, a swift lightning flash struck
the fair image down, converting its splendour into filth, worms, and
stench.

Blessing for the New Year, and for each Month, Week, and Day

Now all thank God with heart and mouth and hands, who does
great things in us and everywhere, who from our mother's womb
and from our childhood has given us countless benefits and still
does so now.

May the ever-mighty God give us during our lives always joyful
hearts and precious peace and keep us in his grace continually and
save us from all danger here and hereafter.

Lob, Ehr und Preis sei Gott,
Dem Vater und dem Sohne
Und dem, der beiden gleich,
Im höchsten Himmelsthrone,
Dem ewig-höchsten Gott,
Als er anfänglich war
Und ist und bleiben wird
Jetzund und immerdar.

FRIEDRICH VON SPEE

Die Gespons Jesu klaget ihren Herzenbrand

GLEICH früh wann sich entzündet
Der silberweiße Tag,
Und uns die Sonn verkündet,
Was nachts verborgen lag:
Die Lieb in meinem Herzen
Ein Flämmlein stecket an;
Das brinnt gleich einer Kerzen,
So niemand leschen kann.

Wann schon ichs trag in Winden
Gen Ost- und Nordenbraus;
Doch Ruh noch Rast mag finden,
Laßt nie sich blasen aus.

Praise, honour, and glory to God the Father and the Son and Him, who is co-equal with them on the highest throne of Heaven, the ever highest God, as He was in the beginning, is now and ever shall be.

Jesus' Spouse Complains of the Flame in her Heart

As soon as silvery-white dawn lights up in the early morning and the sun reveals what lay hidden during the night, love lights a flame in my heart; it burns like a candle which no one can put out.

Though I carry it in the wind, against the fury of the east and the north, I can find no peace nor rest, it cannot be blown out./Oh,

O weh der Qual und Peinen!
Wo soll mich wenden hin?
Ich immerdar muß weinen,
Weil stets in Schmerzen bin.

Wann wieder dann entflogen
Der Tag zur Nacht hinein,
Und nunder sich gebogen
Die Sonn und Sonnenschein;
Das Flämmlein, so mich quälet
Noch bleibt in voller Glut;
All Stund, so viel man zählet,
Michs je noch brennen tut.

Das Flämmlein, das ich meine,
Ist Jesu süßer Nam;
Es zehrt Mark und Beine,
Frißt ein sich wundersam.
O Süßigkeit in Schmerzen!
O Schmerz in Süßigkeit!
Ach bleibe noch im Herzen,
Noch bleib in Ewigkeit.

Ob schon in Pein und Qualen
Mein Leben schwindet hin,
Wann Jesu Pfeil und Strahlen

alas for the pain and torment! Where shall I turn? I must always be
weeping because I am in continual pain.

And when day has returned to night, the sun and its light have
taken their downward path, the flame which torments me stays at
full glow and continues to burn me, however many hours one
counts.

The flame I mean is the sweet name of Jesus. It consumes me to my
marrow and eats miraculously into my bones. O sweetness in pain!
O pain in sweetness! O stay in my heart still, stay there for ever.

Though my life fades away in pain and torment because the
arrows and darts of Jesus / pierce my mind and senses, Love, O my

Durchstreichen Mut und Sinn,
Doch nie so gar mich zehret
Die Liebe, Jesu mein,
Als gleich sie wieder nähret,
Und schenkt auch Freuden ein.

O Flämmlein süß ohn Maßen!
O bitter auch ohn Ziel!
Du machest mich verlassen
All ander Freud und Spiel;
Du zündest mein Gemüte,
Bringst mir groß Herzenleid,
Du kühlest mein Geblüte,
Bringst auch Ergetzlichkeit.

Ade zu tausend Jahren,
O Welt, zu guter Nacht:
Ade, laß mich nun fahren,
Ich längst hab dich veracht.
In Jesu Lieb ich lebe,
Sags rund von Herzengrund:
In lauter Lust ich schwebe,
Wie sehr ich bin verwundt.

Jesus, consumes me less than it refreshes me and pours out drink of
joy.
    O immeasurably sweet flame! O infinitely bitter too! You make
me neglect all other joy and recreation, you inflame my mind, you
bring me great sorrow, you cool my blood, and bring me comfort.
    Farewell for a thousand years, O World, good night! Farewell,
let me go now, I have despised you for a long time. I live in Jesus'
love, I say it openly and sincerely: however sorely I am wounded
I am in transports of delight.

Vom Ochs und Eselein bei der Krippen

Der Wind auf leeren Straßen
Streckt aus die Flügel sein,
Streicht hin gar scharf ohn Maßen
Zu Bethlems Krippen ein;
Er brummlet hin und wieder,
Der fliegend Winterbot,
Greift an die Gleich und Glieder
Dem frisch vermenschten Gott.

Ach, ach, laß ab von Brausen,
Laß ab, du schnöder Wind,
Laß ab von kaltem Sausen
Und schon dem schönen Kind!
Vielmehr du deine Schwingen
Zerschlag im wilden Meer,
Allda dich satt magst ringen,
Kehr nur nit wieder her.

Mit dir nun muß ich kosen,
Mit dir, o Joseph mein!
Das Futter misch mit Rosen
Dem Ochs und Eselein,

The Ox and the Ass at the Manger

The wind spreads its wings in the empty streets and blows fiercely into the manger at Bethlehem, it roars here and there, the flying messenger of winter, it chills the joints and limbs of the newly incarnated God.

But oh, stop blowing, stop, you wicked wind, stop this cold whistling and spare the lovely child! Go batter your wings in the wild sea, there you may wrestle as you like, but do not come back here!

Joseph, I have something to say to you, my Joseph! Mix roses with the fodder of the ox and the ass, / and make a fragrant mash for

Mach deinen frommen Tieren
So lieblichs Mischgemüs,
Bald, bald, ohn Zeit verlieren
Mach ihn den Atem süß.

Drauf blaset her, ihr beiden,
Mit süßem Rosenwind,
Ochs, Esel, wohl bescheiden,
Und wärmets nacket Kind.
Ach blaset her und hauchet:
Aha, aha, aha!
Fort, fort euch weidlich brauchet:
Aha, aha, aha!

MARTIN OPITZ

Lied

ACH Liebste, laß uns eilen,
Wir haben Zeit:
Es schadet das Verweilen
Uns beiderseit.

Der edlen Schönheit Gaben
Fliehn Fuß für Fuß,
Daß alles, was wir haben,
Verschwinden muß.

your pious beasts; quick, quick, make their breath sweet without delay!

Then ox and ass both of you, as you have been told, blow a sweet, rosy breeze and warm the naked child. Oh, blow and breathe away: Ah-ha, ah-ha! Go to it! Use your lungs! Ah-ha! Ah-ha!

Song

O BELOVED, let us hurry, for time is getting short; delay will harm both of us. The gifts of noble beauty flee step by step, and everything we have must pass away./The splendour of your cheeks

Der Wangen Zier verbleichet,
Das Haar wird greis,
Der Augen Feuer weichet,
Die Brunst wird Eis.

Das Mündlein von Korallen
Wird ungestalt,
Die Händ', als Schnee, verfallen,
Und du wirst alt.

Drum laß uns jetzt genießen
Der Jugend Frucht,
Eh' als wir folgen müssen
Der Jahre Flucht.

Wo du dich selber liebest,
So liebe mich.
Gib mir, daß, wann du gibest,
Verlier auch ich.

Lied

ITZUND kommt die Nacht herbei,
Vieh und Menschen werden frei,
Die gewünschte Ruh geht an,
Meine Sorge kommt heran.

will pale, your hair will be grey, the flash of your eyes will fade, the flame of your passion will turn to ice; your dear coral mouth will lose its shape, your hands will shrink like snow, and you will be old. So let us enjoy now the fruit of youth before we have to follow the flight of the years. If you love yourself, love me too; give me so that when you give I lose something too.

Song

Now night is coming on, cattle and people are released, desired rest begins, my sorrow approaches.

Schöne glänzt der Mondenschein,
Und die güldenen Sternelein,
Froh ist alles weit und breit,
Ich nur bin in Traurigkeit.

Zweene mangeln überall
An der schönen Sternen Zahl,
Die zween Sternen, so ich mein,
Sind der Liebsten Äugelein.

Nach dem Monden frag ich nicht,
Dunkel ist der Sternen Licht,
Weil sich von mir weggewend't,
Asteris, mein Firmament.

Wann sich aber naht zu mir
Dieser meiner Sonnen Zier,
Acht ich es das Beste sein,
Daß kein Stern noch Monde schein.

The moonlight and the little golden stars shine beautifully, everything all round is happy; only I am in sadness.

Two are lacking everywhere in the number of the beautiful stars; the two stars I mean are the dear eyes of my beloved.

The moon holds no charms for me, the light of the stars is dark since Asteris, my firmament, has turned away from me.

But when she, the beauty of my sun, approaches me again, I prefer neither star nor moon to shine.

FRIEDRICH VON LOGAU

Der Buchstabe tötet

Du tötest, Buchstabe;
Wem graut für dem Grabe,
Der lasse dich bleiben!
Drum hüten die Leute
So fleißig sich heute
Für lesen und schreiben.

Regiments-Verständige

Es ist ein Volk, das heißt Statisten,
Ist von Verstand und scharfen Listen;
Doch meinen viel, es sein nicht Christen.

Die Herzenskirche

Man kann zwar alle Kirchen schließen,
Doch nie die Kirchen im Gewissen.

The Letter Killeth

Letter, you kill; anyone who is afraid of the grave had better
leave you alone. That is why people nowadays are so careful to
avoid reading and writing.

Political Experts

There are folk called politicians, who have intelligence and crafty
ingenuity; but a good many people think they are not what you
would call honest.

The Church of the Heart

Authority can shut down all the churches, but never the church
in a man's conscience.

Herodes weiset und kümmt nicht

HERODES weist die Weisen
Wo sie zu Christus reisen,
Kümmt aber selbsten nicht
Und bringt ihm seine Pflicht;
Wer weiß was die wohl glauben,
Die uns zum Glauben schrauben?

Der Mai

DIESER Monat ist ein Kuß, den der Himmel gibt der
    Erde,
Daß sie jetzund seine Braut, künftig eine Mutter werde.

SIMON DACH

DER Mensch hat nichts so eigen
So wohl steht ihm nichts an,
Als daß er Treu erzeigen
Und Freundschaft halten kann;

Herod Shows the Way but Does not Go Himself

HEROD directs the Wise Men on their way to Christ, but does not
go himself to present his duty. Who knows what those believe who
are always driving us to belief?

May

THIS month is a kiss which the sky gives the earth to make her his
bride now and a mother in the future.

MAN has no more human trait, nothing befits him better, than
that he can show good faith and keep friendship,/when he is to

Wann er mit seinesgleichen
Soll treten in ein Band;
Verspricht sich nicht zu weichen
Mit Herzen, Mund und Hand.

Die Red ist uns gegeben,
Damit wir nicht allein
Vor uns nur sollen leben
Und fern von Leuten sein;
Wir sollen uns befragen
Und sehn auf guten Rat,
Das Leid einander klagen,
So uns betreten hat.

Was kann die Freude machen
Die Einsamkeit verhehlt?
Das gibt ein duppelt Lachen
Was Freunden wird erzählt;
Der kann sein Leid vergessen,
Der es von Herzen sagt;
Der muß sich selbst auffressen,
Der in geheim sich nagt.

Gott stehet mir vor allen,
Die meine Seele liebt;

enter into a bond with his fellows and with heart, mouth, and hand promises not to leave it.

Speech was not given to us for us only to live by ourselves and stay away from others. We ought to consult one another and look for good advice, and share with one another the sorrows that have befallen us.

What can joy do, concealed in solitude? What is told to friends gives double mirth. The man who speaks his sorrow from his heart can forget it; the man who worries in secret is likely to consume himself.

God is for me above all others whom my soul loves;/the man

Dann soll mir àuch gefallen,
Der mir sich herzlich gibt;
Mit diesen Bunds-Gesellen
Verlach ich Pein und Not,
Geh auf dem Grund der Hellen
Und breche durch den Tod.

Ich hab, ich habe Herzen
So treue, wie gebührt,
Die Heuchelei und Scherzen
Nie wissentlich berührt;
Ich bin auch ihnen wieder
Von Grund der Seelen hold,
Ich lieb euch mehr, ihr Brüder,
Als aller Erden Gold.

Brauttanz

Tanz, der du Gesetze
Unsern Füßen gibst,
Handdruck, Huldgeschwätze,
Scherz und Liebe liebst, [...]

who gives himself to me sincerely should delight me next. With
these allies I can laugh at sorrow and disaster, go to the bottom of
hell and break the bonds of death.

I have them, I have hearts as true as is meet, who have never
consciously had to do with hypocrisy and mockery: I am devoted
to them too from the bottom of my soul. I love you more, my
brothers, than all the gold on earth.

Bridal Dance

Dance, you who give laws to our feet and love the pressure of
hands, fond whispering, laughter and love,/it seems as though all

Sinnen, Augen, Ohren
Werden uns zu Hauf
Gleichsam wie beschworen
Zeucht dein Läger auf.

Wie die Bäum im Lenzen
Von der Blüte schwer,
Wie die Tauben glänzen,
Wie ein Kriegesheer:
So bist du zu schauen
Tanz, wenn du dich rührst,
Und an die Jungfrauen
Die Gesellen führst.

Auf, such zu begnügen
Dieses edle Paar,
Das sich jetzt will fügen
Um das neue Jahr,
Schaff, daß ihre Sachen
Wie im Tanze gehn,
Laß nur Lieb und Lachen
Allzeit um sie stehn. [...]

Hierauf stimm Schalmeien
Und Trompeten an,
Laß an deinen Reihen
Gehen was nur kann,

our senses, eyes, and ears together are enchanted when your train appears.

Like the trees in spring heavy with blossom, like gleaming doves, like an army in movement, so you seem, dance, when you set to and lead the men to the girls.

Up then, seek to please this noble pair who are to be joined together at the New Year; make it so that their affairs may go with a swing as in a dance, and that love and laughter may always be round them.

On this let the hautboys and trumpets blow; let all who can take part in your round;/live to give us pleasure, considering that

Leb uns zu gefallen,
Angesehn, daß Welt,
Zeit und Tod, samt allen,
Seinen Reihen hält.

Anno 1647 des Nachts, da ich vor Engbrüstigkeit nicht
schlafen können, auf dem Bette gemacht

WIE? Ist es denn nicht gnug, gern einmal sterben
   wollen?
Natur, Verhängnüs, Gott, was haltet ihr mich auf?
Kein Säumnüs ist bei mir, vollendet ist mein Lauf;
Soll ich die Durchfahrt euch denn tausendmal verzollen?
Was kränkt es, fertig sein und sich verweilen sollen!
Ist Sterben ein Gewinn? O mir ein teurer Kauf!
Mich töten so viel Jahr und Krankheiten zuhauf;
Ich lebe noch und bin wohl zehnmal tot erschollen.
Weib, Kinder, macht es ihr? Verlängert ihr mein Licht?
Seht meinen Jammer an! Ist dieses Liebespflicht,
Zu schlechtem Vorteil euch mein Vorteil mir nicht
   gönnen?

the World, Time, and Death, all things keep their places in the
dance.

Written in Bed in the Year 1647, at Night, when I could not
Sleep for Asthma

WHAT, is it not enough to be willing to die once? Nature, Fate,
God, why do you hold me back? There is no delay on my side,
my course is finished; must I pay you toll a thousand times for the
passage? How bitter it is to be ready and have to wait! Is death
gain? It is an expensive bargain indeed for me! So many years and
illnesses come together to kill me; I am still alive, and have been
given out for dead ten times at least. Wife, children, is it you that
are doing this? Are you prolonging my light? Look at my misery;
is this charity – grudging me my benefit for little benefit to your-
selves?/Oh, do not make things worse for me by your presence!

Ach kränket mich nicht mehr durch euer Angesicht!
Die allerletzte Pein ist, gläub ich, ärger nicht,
Als leben müssen, tot sein wollen und nicht können.

JOHANNES RIST

Betrachtung der zukünftigen unendlichen Ewigkeit

O EWIGKEIT, du Donnerwort,
O Schwert, das durch die Seele bohrt,
    o Anfang sonder Ende!
O Ewigkeit, Zeit ohne Zeit,
ich weiß vor großer Traurigkeit
    nicht, wo ich mich hinwende!
Mein ganz erschrocknes Herz erbebt,
daß mir die Zung am Gaumen klebt.

Kein Unglück ist in aller Welt,
das endlich mit der Zeit nicht fällt
    und ganz wird aufgehoben.

The last pain of all, I think, cannot be worse than having to stay alive, wanting to be dead, and not being able to die!

A Consideration of the Infinite Eternity to Come

O ETERNITY, you word of thunder, O word that pierces the soul, O beginning without end! O eternity, time without time, I do not know where to turn for great sadness! My terrified heart trembles so that my tongue cleaves to the roof of my mouth.

There is no misfortune in the world which does not come to an end with time itself and pass away. / But eternity has no end, it plays

Die Ewigkeit nur hat kein Ziel
sie treibet fort und fort ihr Spiel,
    läßt nimmer ab zu toben.
Ja, wie mein Heiland selber spricht:
aus ihr ist kein Erlösung nicht.

O Ewigkeit, du machst mir bang,
o ewig, ewig ist zu lang,
    hie gilt fürwahr kein Scherzen!
Drum, wenn ich diese lange Nacht
zusamt der großen Pein betracht,
    erschreck ich recht von Herzen.
Nichts ist zu finden weit und breit
so schrecklich als die Ewigkeit. [...]

O Ewigkeit, du Donnerwort,
O Schwert, das durch die Seele bohrt,
    O Anfang sonder Ende!
O Ewigkeit, Zeit ohne Zeit,
ich weiß vor großer Traurigkeit
    nicht, wo ich mich hinwende.
Herr Jesu, wenn es dir gefällt,
eil ich zu dir ins Himmelszelt.

its play for ever and ever and never ceases to rage. Yes, as my
Saviour Himself says, there is no release from it.
    O eternity you fill me with anxiety, O eternal, eternal is too
long, there is no jesting here! So when I consider that long night
together with the great pain, I am terrified from the bottom of my
heart. There is nothing that can be found anywhere so terrifying as
eternity.
    O eternity, you word of thunder, O sword that pierces the soul,
O beginning without end! O eternity, time without time, I do not
know where to turn for great sadness! Lord Jesus, if it be Thy will,
I will hasten to Thee into the tent of Heaven.

PAUL GERHARDT

Abendlied

Nun ruhen alle Wälder,
Vieh, Menschen, Städt und Felder,
Es schläft die ganze Welt:
Ihr aber, meine Sinnen,
Auf, auf, ihr sollt beginnen,
Was eurem Schöpfer wohlgefällt.

Wo bist du, Sonne, blieben?
Die Nacht hat dich vertrieben,
Die Nacht, des Tages Feind:
Fahr hin, ein andre Sonne,
Mein Jesus, meine Wonne,
Gar hell in meinem Herzen scheint.

Der Tag ist nun vergangen,
Die güldnen Sternlein prangen
Am blauen Himmelssaal:
So, so werd ich auch stehen,
Wenn mich wird heißen gehen
Mein Gott aus diesem Jammertal.

Evening Hymn: The Duteous Day now Closeth

Now all the woods are at rest, cattle, men, town, and country, the whole world is asleep. But you my senses, up, up, you must do what pleases your Creator.

Sun, where have you gone? The night has driven you away, night the enemy of day. No matter, another Sun, my Jesus, my joy, shines very brightly in my heart.

Now the day has gone the golden stars gleam in the blue hall of heaven; I, too, will be just like them when my God commands me to go from this vale of sorrow.

Der Leib, der eilt zur Ruhe,
Legt ab das Kleid und Schuhe,
Das Bild der Sterblichkeit:
Die zieh ich aus, dargegen
Wird Christus mir anlegen
Den Rock der Ehr und Herrlichkeit.

Das Häupt, die Füß und Hände
Sind froh, daß nun zum Ende
Die Arbeit kommen sei:
Herz, freu dich, du sollt werden
Vom Elend dieser Erden
Und von der Sünden Arbeit frei.

Nun geht, ihr matten Glieder
Geht, geht und legt euch nieder,
Der Betten ihr begehrt.
Es kommen Stund und Zeiten,
Da man euch wird bereiten
Zur Ruh ein Bettlein in der Erd.

Mein Augen stehn verdrossen,
Im Hui sind sie geschlossen;
Wo bleibt dann Leib und Seel?
Nimm sie zu deinen Gnaden,
Sei gut für allen Schaden,
Du Aug und Wächter Israel.

The body hastens to its rest, takes off clothes and shoes, the symbols of mortality. I take these off, but Christ in return will put the garment of glory and splendour on me.

Head, feet, and hands are glad that the toil is over now. Be joyful, heart, you will be released from the exile of this earth and from the tribulation of sin.

Now go, you weary limbs, go and lie down, you are longing for your bed. The hour and the time will come when a bed in the earth will be made ready for you to rest in.

My eyes are weary, in a moment they will be closed; where is body and soul then? Take them into thy grace, make good all damage, Thou the eye and watchman of Israel.

Breit aus die Flügel beide,
O Jesu, meine Freude,
Und nimm dein Küchlein ein.
Will Satan mich verschlingen,
So laß die Englein singen:
Dies Kind soll unverletzet sein.

Auch euch, ihr meine Lieben,
Soll heinte nicht betrüben
Kein Unfall noch Gefahr.
Gott laß euch ruhig schlafen,
Stell euch die güldnen Waffen
Ums Bett und seiner Helden Schar.

An das leidende Angesicht Jesu Christi

O HÄUPT voll Blut und Wunden,
Voll Schmerz und voller Hohn!
O Häupt, zu Spott gebunden
Mit einer Dornenkron!
O Häupt, sonst schön gezieret
Mit höchster Ehr und Zier,
Itzt aber hoch schimpfieret!
Gegrüßet seist du mir. [...]

Spread out both Thy wings, oh Jesus my joy, and receive Thy chick. If Satan seeks to devour me, let Thy angels sing: This child must go unharmed.

And may you too, dearly beloved, not be troubled this night by any accident or danger. May God let you sleep peacefully, and may He set His weapons of gold and the host of His champions about your beds.

The Suffering Countenance of Jesus Christ

O HEAD covered with blood and wounds, with pain and scorn! O head bound in mockery with a crown of thorns! O head, else splendidly decked with fairest honour and beauty, but now shamefully derided, I salute you!

Nun was du, Herr, erduldet,
Ist alles meine Last,
Ich hab es selbst verschuldet,
Was du getragen hast.
Schau her, hie steh ich Armer,
Der Zorn verdienet hat;
Gib mir, o mein Erbarmer,
Den Anblick deiner Gnad. [...]

Ich will hie bei dir stehen,
Verachte mich doch nicht;
Von dir will ich nicht gehen,
Wann dir dein Herze bricht;
Wann dein Herz wird erblassen
Im letzten Todesstoß,
Alsdann will ich dich fassen
In meinen Arm und Schoß. [...]

Wann ich einmal soll scheiden,
So scheide nicht von mir,
Wann ich den Tod soll leiden,
So tritt du dann herfür,
Wann mir am allerbängsten
Wird um das Herze sein,
So reiß mich aus den Ängsten
Kraft deiner Angst und Pein.

But what Thou, Lord, hast suffered is all my burden, I myself
have deserved what Thou hast borne. See, see here I stand, a poor
man who deserves Thy anger; give me, my merciful Lord, the
sight of Thy grace!

I will stand here with Thee, do not despise me; I will not leave
Thee when Thy heart breaks; when Thy heart pales in the last
agony of death I will hold Thee in my arms and in my lap.

When the time comes for me to depart, do not depart from me,
when the time comes for me to suffer death, then come forth; when
fear seizes most powerfully upon my heart, snatch me away from
anguish through Thy anguish and suffering.

Erscheine mir zum Schilde,
Zum Trost in meinem Tod,
Und laß mich sehn dein Bilde
In deiner Kreuzesnot,
Da will ich nach dir blicken,
Da will ich glaubensvoll
Dich fest an mein Herz drücken.
Wer so stirbt, der stirbt wohl.

PAUL FLEMING

Gedanken über der Zeit

IHR lebet in der Zeit und kennt doch keine Zeit;
So wißt ihr Menschen nicht, von und in was ihr seid.
Dies wißt ihr, daß ihr seid in einer Zeit geboren
Und daß ihr werdet auch in einer Zeit verloren.
Was aber war die Zeit, die euch in sich gebracht?
Und was wird diese sein, die euch zu nichts mehr macht?
Die Zeit ist was und nichts, der Mensch in gleichem Falle,
Doch was dasselbe Was-und-Nichts sei, zweifeln alle.

Manifest Thyself as my shield, as my consolation in death, and
let me see Thine image in Thine agony on the cross. Then I will
look towards Thee, and firm in faith will clasp Thee firmly to my
heart. Whoso dies thus dies well.

Thoughts on Time

YOU live in [finite] time and yet know no [infinite] time; thus you
men do not know whence you come and in what you are. This you
know, that you were born in a moment of time, and that you will
be lost in a moment of time. But what was that moment which
brought you into itself? And what will that one be, which will
make you into nothing? Time is something and nothing, man is in
the same state, yet all are in doubt about what this same 'something
and nothing' is./Time dies in itself, and renews itself out of itself.

Die Zeit, die stirbt in sich und zeugt sich auch aus sich.
Dies kömmt aus mir und dir, von dem du bist und ich.
Der Mensch ist in der Zeit; sie ist in ihm ingleichen,
Doch aber muß der Mensch, wenn sie noch bleibet,
    weichen.
Die Zeit ist, was ihr seid, und ihr seid, was die Zeit,
Nur daß ihr wen'ger noch, als was die Zeit ist, seid.
Ach daß doch jene Zeit, die ohne Zeit ist, käme
Und uns aus dieser Zeit in ihre Zeiten nähme,
Und aus uns selbsten uns, daß wir gleich könnten sein
Wie *der* itzt jener Zeit, die keine Zeit geht ein!

Andacht

ICH lebe; doch nicht ich. Derselbe lebt in mir,
Der mir durch seinen Tod das Leben bringt herfür.
Mein Leben war sein Tod, sein Tod war mir mein Leben,
Nur geb ich wieder ihm, was er mir hat gegeben.
Er lebt durch meinen Tod. Mir sterb ich täglich ab.

This, from which you and I derive, comes from you and me. Man
lives in [finite] time, it is equally in him, but man must go while
[finite] time remains. Time is what you are, and you are what time
is, except that you are even less than what time is. Oh, if only that
[infinite] time which is timeless would come and take us out of this
[finite] time into its eternities, and take us out of ourselves, that we
might be, as He now is, equal to that [infinite] time which at no
[moment of] time has a beginning [or ending]!

Meditation

I LIVE, yet not I; He lives in me who by His death brings forth life
in me. My life was His death, His death was life for me. I only give
back to Him what He has given to me. He lives through my death.
I die away to myself daily. / The body, my earthly portion, is the
grave of the soul; it only lives in seeming. He who does not wish to

Der Leib, mein irdnes Teil, der ist der Seelen Grab.
Er lebt nur auf den Schein. Wer ewig nicht will sterben,
Der muß hier in der Zeit verwesen und verderben,
Weil er noch sterben kann. Der Tod, der geistlich heißt,
Der ist alsdenn zu spat, wann uns sein Freund hinreißt,
Der unsern Leib bringt um. Herr, gib mir die Genade,
Daß dieses Leibes Brauch nicht meiner Seelen schade.
Mein Alles und mein Nichts, mein Leben, meinen Tod,
Das hab ich bei mir selbst. Hilfst du, so hats nicht Not.
Ich will, ich mag, ich soll, ich kann mir selbst nicht raten;
Dich will ichs lassen tun; du hast bei dir die Taten.
Die Wünsche tu ich nur. Ich lasse mich ganz dir.
Ich will nicht meine sein. Nimm mich, nur gib dich mir.

An die Nacht, als er bei ihr wachete

WIE aber eilst du so, du meiner Schmerzen Rast?
Deucht michs doch, daß ich kaum auf eine Viertel-
   stunde
Allhier gesessen bin bei diesem Rosenmunde,
Der meinen machet blaß! So merk' ich, daß du fast

die eternally must decompose and spoil here in finite time, while he
still can die. That death, who is called spiritual, comes too late when
his friend, who destroys our body, has snatched us away. Lord,
grant me grace that the custom of this body may not harm my soul.
My all and my nothing, my life, my death, all this I have in myself.
If Thou wilt help, then there is no danger. I will not, I cannot, I
ought not, I am not able to help myself; I will let Thee do it, the
deeds are with Thee. I can only make the wishes. I hand myself
over to Thee entirely. I do not wish to be mine. Take me, but give
me Thyself.

To the Night, when He was Awake with Her

HOW swiftly you go, you the repose of my pain! It seemed as
though I had only been sitting for a quarter of an hour here by the
rosy mouth which makes my mouth pale! But now I realize that
you have already

Dich an die Hälfte schon von uns entzogen hast.
Kehr' um und halte Fuß und gib uns Zeit zum Bunde,
Den wir hier richten auf von ganzem Herzengrunde.
Kehr' um und sei bei uns ein nicht so kurzer Gast.

Dein Sohn, der sanfte Schlaf, schleicht durch das stille
     Haus,
Und streut die leise Saat der Träume häufig aus,
Darmit du länger kannst bei unsrer Lust verweilen.

Verhüll' uns in ein Tuch, bis daß das dunkle Licht
Des halben Morgens dir durch deine Kleider bricht;
Denn ist es Zeit, daß wir mit dir von hinnen eilen.

Es ist umsonst, das Klagen

Es ist umsonst, das Klagen,
    Das du um mich,
    Und ich um dich,
Wir um einander tragen.
Sie ist umsonst, die harte Pein,
Mit der wir itzt umfangen sein.

half withdrawn yourself from us. Turn back and stop and give us time for the covenant which we are establishing here from the bottom of our hearts. Turn back and do not be such a fleeting guest with us!

Your son, soft sleep, steals through the silent house and scatters liberally the quiet seed of dreams so that you can stay longer with our pleasure.

Wrap us in a veil until the dim light of the half morning shines through your garments; then it will be time for us to hasten away with you.

It is all in vain, the lamenting that you make for me and I for you and we for each other. It is in vain, the hard sorrow with which we are now surrounded.

Laß das Verhängnüs walten.
    Was dich dort ziert
    Und mich hier führt,
Das wird uns doch erhalten.
Dies, was uns itzt so sehr betrübt,
Ists dennoch, das uns Freude gibt.

Sei unterdessen meine,
    Mein mehr als ich,
    Und schau' auf mich,
Daß ich bin ewig deine.
Vertraute Liebe weichet nicht,
Hält allzeit, was sie einmal spricht.

Auf alle meine Treue
    Sag ich dirs zu,
    Du bist es, du,
Der ich mich einig freue.
Mein Herze, das sich itzt so quält,
Hat dich und keine sonst erwählt.

Bleib, wie ich dich verlassen,
    Daß ich dich einst,
    Die du itzt weinst,
Mit Lachen mag umfassen.
Dies soll für diese kurze Pein
Uns ewig unsre Freude sein.

Let Fate take its course. What makes your beauty there and leads me here will surely keep us safe. What makes us so sad now is nonetheless what will give us joy.

Meanwhile stay mine, mine more than I am myself, and think of me, for I am always yours. Confident love does not give way and once it has made a promise always keeps it.

By all my fidelity I say to you: it is you, you only who give me delight. My heart, which is now in such distress, has chosen you and no other.

Stay as I left you, so that I may soon embrace you laughing, though you are weeping now. This shall be our everlasting joy in exchange for this short sorrow.

Eilt, lauft, ihr trüben Tage,
    Eilt, lauft vorbei,
    Eilt, macht mich frei
Von aller meiner Plage!
Eilt, kommt, ihr hellen Stunden ihr,
Die mich gewähren aller Zier!

An Sich

Sei dennoch unverzagt, gib dennoch unverloren,
Weich keinem Glücke nicht, steh' höher als der Neid,
Vergnüge dich an dir und acht' es für kein Leid,
Hat sich gleich wider dich Glück, Ort und Zeit ver-
    schworen.

Was dich betrübt und labt, halt alles für erkoren,
Nimm dein Verhängnüs an, laß alles unbereut,
Tu, was getan muß sein, und eh man dirs gebeut.
Was du noch hoffen kannst, das wird noch stets geboren.

Was klagt, was lobt man doch? Sein Unglück und sein
    Glücke
Ist ihm ein jeder selbst. Schau alle Sachen an.
Dies alles ist in dir, laß deinen eiteln Wahn,

    Hasten, run you dismal days, hasten, run by, hasten, make me
free from all my troubles! Hasten, come, you bright hours which
will grant me all beauty!

To Himself

Be undismayed in spite of everything; do not give up, despite
everything; give way to no twist of fortune; stand above envy; be
content with yourself and think it no disaster even if fortune, place,
and time have conspired against you.

    What saddens or refreshes you, think it chosen for you; accept
your fate, regret nothing, do what must be done and before you are
told to do it. What you can hope for may happen any day.

    What is it that we lament, or that we praise? Each man is his own
fortune and misfortune. Look round at everything – all this is
within you; leave your empty delusion,

Und eh du förder gehst, so geh' in dich zurücke.
Wer sein selbst Meister ist und sich beherrschen kann,
Dem ist die weite Welt und alles untertan.

LAß dich nur nichts nicht tauren
        Mit Trauren;
        Sei stille,
        Wie Gott es fügt,
        So sei vergnügt,
        Mein Wille.

Was willst du heute sorgen
        Auf morgen?
        Der Eine
        Steht allem für;
        Der gibt auch dir
        Das Deine.

Sei nur in allem Handel
        Ohn Wandel,
        Steh feste;
        Was Gott beschleußt,
        Das ist und heißt
        Das Beste.

and, before you go any farther, go back into yourself. The man
who is master of himself and can control himself has the wide
world and what is in it at his feet.

Do not let yourself be depressed by sadness; be calm, however
God may dispose, be content with it, my will.

Why worry today about tomorrow? There is One who controls
everything; He will give you your share too.

Be constant in everything you undertake, stand firm. What God
ordains is and is known to be best.

ANDREAS GRYPHIUS

Auf die Geburt des Herrn

DAS wesentliche Wort, das in den Ewigkeiten,
Eh eine Zeit entstund, Gott ist und Gott geschaut,
Das Wort, durch das Gott hat der Erden Haus gebaut,
Durch das der Himmel stund, das Licht, das uns wird
    leiten
(Das mehr denn lichte Licht), wenn Händ' und Füße
    gleiten,
Vor dem nichts finster ist, vor dem der Höllen graut
Und was mehr dunkel heißt, hat sich der Welt vertraut
Und nimmt an unser Fleisch und schwere Last der Zeiten.
Es ist vom Ehrenthron ins Tränental ankommen,
Und hat dies Leibes Zelt zur Wohnung angenommen,
Wiewol sein Eigentum sich stets ihm widersetzt.
Wer diesen Gast aufnimmt, wird augenblicks erkennen
Wie herrlich seine Gunst, er wird in Lieb' entbrennen,
In Liebe, die mit Lust und für und für ergetzt.

The Birth of the Lord

THAT essential Word which in the eternities before time was, is
God and saw God, the Word by which God built the house of
Earth; by which the heavens were fixed; the Light that will lead us
(the Light more bright than bright) when hands and feet slip; to
which nothing is dark, at which hell shudders and all other dark
things; it has entrusted itself to the world and takes upon itself our
flesh and our heavy burden of the ages. It has come from the throne
of honour into the vale of tears and has taken for its dwelling the
tent of this body, though its heritage has always been rebellious.
He who receives this guest will straightway realize how splendid
his favour is, he will burst into flames of love, of love which will
rejoice him with delight for ever.

Grabschrift Marianæ Gryphiæ, seines Brudern Pauli Töchterlein

GEBOREN in der Flucht, umringt mit Schwert und
    Brand,
Schier in dem Rauch erstickt, der Mutter herbes Pfand,
Des Vatern höchste Furcht, die an das Licht gedrungen,
Als die ergrimmte Glut mein Vaterland verschlungen:
Ich habe diese Welt beschaut und bald gesegnet,
Weil mir auf Einen Tag all' Angst der Welt begegnet;
Wo ihr die Tage zählt, so bin ich jung verschwunden,
Sehr alt, wofern ihr schätzt, was ich für Angst empfunden.

Auf den Sonntag des guten Sämanns

ICH höre nichts, wenn du mich heißest hören;
Dein werter Samen bringet wenig Frucht
In mir! Ach, Herr, der Höllenvogel sucht
Dein Wort in mir arglistig zu versehren.

Epitaph on Mariana Gryphius, his Brother Paul's little Daughter

BORN during the flight, surrounded with swords and conflagra-
tion, almost stifled in the smoke; my mother's bitter pledge, my
father's chief anxiety, I pressed forward to the light when the
furious fire had consumed my country; I looked upon this world
and soon said farewell to it, for in one day all the dread of the world
came upon me. If you count the days, I was young when I passed
away, but I was very old if you consider what dread I had experi-
enced.

The Sower: Sexagesima

I HEAR nothing when Thou commandest me to hear; Thy pre-
cious seed bears little fruit in me! O Lord, the bird of hell seeks
craftily to injure Thy word in me./When the flowering is about to

Wenn sich die Blüt' in meinem Geist will mehren,
Kränkt mich die Hitz', und (was ich oft verflucht)
Der Dornen Angst (ach, scharfe Dornenzucht)
Erstöckt in mir schier alle gute Lehren.
Schrecke die Vögel, Herr, die mich berauben,
Laß mich auch in der Versuchung dir glauben,
Und reiß die Disteln aus, die ganz mein Herz umgeben.
Laß mich durch Regen der Gnaden erquicken,
Schicke Geduld, wenn das Kreuze will drücken,
Daß an der Dornen Statt dein Wort mög' in mir leben!

Über die Erdkugel

DER Erden rundes Haus, das Vieh und Menschen trägt,
Ist noch nicht ganz beschaut, doch ist es ganz gemessen.
Was nie der Leib bezwang, hat doch der Geist besessen,
Der Land und Wellen Ziel hier, auch abwesend, legt.

multiply in my spirit the heat assails me and, what I have often
cursed, the fear of the thorns (O sharp breed of thorns) quite
chokes all good teachings in me. Lord scare the birds who rob me,
let me even in temptation believe in Thee, and tear out the thistles
which quite surround my heart. Let me be refreshed by the rain of
grace; send patience when the cross seems to chafe, so that instead
of the thorns Thy Word may live in me!

The Terrestrial Globe

THE round house of the earth which bears animals and men is not
yet completely surveyed, but it is completely measured out. What
the body never conquered has nonetheless been possessed by the
mind which, though absent, has set the bounds of land and sea.

Über die Himmelskugel

SCHAU hier des Himmels Bild, dies hat ein Mensch
erdacht,
Der doch auf Erden saß! O übergroße Sinnen,
Die mehr, denn jemand schaut, durch Forschen nur
gewinnen!
Soll dies nicht himmlisch sein, was selber Himmel
macht?

An Mariam

HIER ist kein Raum vor dich, das Haus ist voll Ge-
dränge:
Warum? Der, den du trägst, dem ist die Welt zu enge.

Betrachtung der Zeit

MEIN sind die Jahre nicht, die mir die Zeit genommen,
Mein sind die Jahre nicht, die etwa möchten kommen;
Der Augenblick ist mein, und nehm' ich den in Acht,
So ist der mein, der Jahr' und Ewigkeit gemacht.

The Celestial Globe

SEE here the image of heaven; a man, who sits on earth, has
thought this out! O superlative mental powers, which can by
searching achieve more than anyone can see! Must not that which
can make heaven, itself be heavenly?

No Room at the Inn

THERE is no room for you here, the house is crowded out. Why?
He whom you carry, the world itself is too narrow for Him.

Meditation on Time

THE years which time has taken from me are not mine; the years
which may still come are not mine either; the moment is mine, and
if I pay attention to that, then He is mine who made time and
eternity.

Über die Geburt Jesu

NACHT, mehr denn lichte Nacht! Nacht, lichter als der
　　Tag,
Nacht, heller als die Sonn', in der das Licht geboren,
Das Gott, der Licht, in Licht wohnhaftig, ihm erkoren:
O Nacht, die alle Nächt' und Tage trotzen mag!
O freudenreiche Nacht, in welcher Ach und Klag
Und Finsternis, und was sich auf die Welt verschworen,
Und Furcht und Höllenangst und Schrecken war
　　verloren!
Der Himmel bricht, doch fällt nunmehr kein Donner-
　　schlag.
Der Zeit und Nächte schuf, ist diese Nacht ankommen
Und hat das Recht der Zeit und Fleisch an sich genom-
　　men
Und unser Fleisch und Zeit der Ewigkeit vermacht.
Der Jammer trübe Nacht, die schwarze Nacht der
　　Sünden,
Des Grabes Dunkelheit muß durch die Nacht ver-
　　schwinden.
Nacht, lichter als der Tag! Nacht, mehr denn lichte
　　Nacht!

On the Birth of Christ

NIGHT, brighter-than-bright night! night brighter than the day;
night brighter than the sun, in which that light is born which God,
who is light, dwelling in light, has chosen for himself: O night,
which can defy all nights and days! O joyous night, in which wail-
ing and lamenting and darkness and everything that conspires with
the world, and dread and fear of hell and horror all were lost. The
sky breaks open, but no thunderbolt falls now. He who made time
and nights has come this night and taken upon himself the law of
time and flesh, and has given our flesh and time to eternity. The
dismal night of sorrow, the black night of sin, the darkness of the
grave must vanish through this night. Night, brighter than the day!
Night, brighter-than-bright night!

Tränen des Vaterlandes

WIR sind doch nunmehr ganz, ja mehr denn ganz
  verheeret!
Der frechen Völker Schar, die rasende Posaun,
Das vom Blut fette Schwert, die donnernde Kartaun
Hat aller Schweiß und Fleiß und Vorrat aufgezehret,
Die Türme stehn in Glut, die Kirch' ist umgekehret,
Das Rathaus liegt im Grauß, die Starken sind zerhaun,
Die Jungfern sind geschändt, und wo wir hin nur schaun,
Ist Feuer, Pest und Tod, der Herz und Geist durch-
  fähret.
Hier durch die Schanz und Stadt rinnt allzeit frisches
  Blut.
Dreimal sind schon sechs Jahr, als unser Ströme Flut,
Von Leichen fast verstopft, sich langsam fortgedrungen;
Doch schweig ich noch von dem, was ärger als der Tod,
Was grimmer denn die Pest und Glut und Hungersnot:
Daß auch der Seelen Schatz so vielen abgezwungen.

My Country's Tears

WE are now wholly – nay more than wholly – devastated! The
band of presumptuous nations, the blaring trumpet, the sword
greasy with blood, the thundering cannon have consumed every-
one's sweat and industry and provisions. The towers are on fire, the
church is cast down, the town hall lies in ruins, the strong are
maimed, the virgins raped, and wherever we look there is [nothing
but] fire, plague, and death that pierces heart and mind. Here
through the bulwarks and the town ever-fresh blood is running.
Three times six years ago the water of our rivers slowly found its
way past the corpses that almost blocked it; but I will say nothing
of what is worse than death itself, more dreadful than the plague
and fire and famine – that so many have been despoiled of the
treasure of the soul.

An die Sternen

Ihr Lichter, die ich nicht auf Erden satt kann schauen,
Ihr Fackeln, die ihr Nacht und schwarze Wolken trennt,
Als Diamante spielt und ohn' Aufhören brennt;
Ihr Blumen, die ihr schmückt des großen Himmels Auen,
Ihr Wächter, die, als Gott die Welt auf wollte bauen,
Sein Wort, die Weisheit selbst, mit rechten Namen nennt,
Die Gott allein recht mißt, die Gott allein recht kennt,
(Wir blinden Sterblichen, was wollen wir uns trauen!)
Ihr Bürgen meiner Lust, wie manche schöne Nacht
Hab' ich, indem ich euch betrachtete, gewacht?
Herolden dieser Zeit, wenn wird es doch geschehen,
Daß ich, der eurer nicht allhier vergessen kann,
Euch, derer Liebe mir steckt Herz und Geister an,
Von andern Sorgen frei werd' unter mir besehen?

To the Stars

You lights, of which I cannot see my fill here on earth, you torches
which pierce night and black clouds, glitter like diamonds and burn
unceasingly; you flowers which adorn the meadows of the wide
sky, you watchmen whom, when God set out to construct the
world, his word, wisdom itself, named by your right names; whom
only God measures aright, whom only God knows aright (we blind
mortals, how can we presume!); you sureties of my joy, how many
lovely nights have I stayed awake watching you! Heralds of that
time, when will it be that I, who cannot forget you here, shall see
you, love for whom inflames my heart and spirits, below me, when
I am freed from all other cares?

Abend

DER schnelle Tag ist hin, die Nacht schwingt ihre
    Fahn'
Und führt die Sternen auf. Der Menschen müde Scharen
Verlassen Feld und Werk; wo Tier' und Vögel waren,
Traurt itzt die Einsamkeit. Wie ist die Zeit vertan!
Der Port naht mehr und mehr sich zu der Glieder Kahn.
Gleich wie dies Licht verfiel, so wird in wenig Jahren
Ich, du, und was man hat, und was man sieht, hinfahren.
Dies Leben kömmt mir vor als eine Rennebahn:
Laß, höchster Gott, mich doch nicht auf dem Laufplatz
    gleiten,
Laß mich nicht Ach, nicht Pracht, nicht Lust, nicht Angst
    verleiten,
Dein ewig heller Glanz sei vor und neben mir,
Laß, wenn der müde Leib entschläft, die Seele wachen,
Und wenn der letzte Tag wird mit mir Abend machen,
So reiß mich aus dem Tal der Finsternis zu dir!

Evening

THE swift day is over, the night brandishes her banner and leads
on the stars. The weary companies of men leave field and work;
where animals and birds were, solitude now mourns. How time has
been wasted! The harbour approaches closer and closer to the boat
of the limbs. Just as this light vanished, so I and you and all that
people have and see, will pass away in a few years. This life seems to
resemble a race-course; O highest God, let me not slip on the
track, let neither lament nor splendour nor pleasure nor fear lead
me astray, let Thy eternally bright glory be always before me and
beside me. Let, when the weary body falls asleep, let the soul re-
main awake and, when the last day brings my evening on, then
snatch me out of the vale of darkness to Thee!

Auf seinen Geburtstag

DAß du den Bau gemacht, den Bau der schönen Welt,
Und so viel tausend Heer' unendlich heller Lichter
Und Körper, die die Kraft gleichfallender Gewichter
An dem gesetzten Ort durch deinen Schluß erhält,
Daß du die Körper selbst mit so viel Schmuck bestellt
Und auf der Erden Haus unzählig' Angesichter,
Die ungleich, dennoch gleich, als vorgesetzte Richter
Aussprechen, daß nur dir nichts gleich wird hier ver-
    meldt:
Dies rühm' ich; doch noch mehr, daß du mir wollen
    gönnen,
Daß, Herr, dein Wunderwerk ich habe rühmen können,
Daß du die Augen mir, zu schauen, aufgemacht:
Dies rühm' ich; doch noch mehr, daß du mir mehr willt
    zeigen,
Als diese Welt begreift, und mir versprichst zu eigen
Dein Haus, mehr, dich, den nichts satt schaut und satt
    betracht.

On His Birthday

THAT Thou hast made the fabric, the fabric of the beautiful world, and so many thousand hosts of infinitely bright lights and bodies, which the force of equally falling weights holds by Thy command in the place appointed; that Thou hast furnished these bodies themselves with such beauty and that on the house of earth countless faces which, unequal and yet equal, speak forth as pre-ordained judges, that to Thee only nothing can be called equal; all this I praise, but more that Thou hast deigned to allow me, Lord, to praise Thy wonderful works, that Thou hast opened my eyes that I might see; all this I praise, but yet more that Thou wilt show me more than this world contains, and promisest me as a possession Thy house, and even more Thyself, whom nothing can see and contemplate enough.

JOHANN KLAJ

Aus dem *Leidenden Christus*

Im lieblichen Frühling wird alles erneuet, · erfreuet, ·
gedeihet,
Und du, und du, Herr Christ,
Der du der Menschen Freude bist, · klagest,
Der du der Welt Gedeihen bist, · zagest.
Mußt du meine Sündenplagen, · geschlagen, · tragen?
Ach mir Armen! · Ist denn kein Erbarmen?
Ist kein Recht mehr in der Welt?
Unrecht Recht, Recht Unrecht fällt.

Wir holen Violen in blümichten Auen,
Narzissen entsprießen von perlenen Tauen,
Es grünet und grunet das fruchtige Land,
Es glänzet im Lenzen der wäßrige Strand.
Jesu, wie bist du gemutet!
Händ und Beine sind zerrissen,
Deine Schultern wundgeschmissen,
Und der ganze Leib sehr blutet!

Es lallen mit Schallen, von Bergen her fallen,
Sie rieseln in Kieseln die Silberkristallen,

From: *Christ's Passion*

In pleasant spring-time everything is renewed, delighted and pros-
pered, and Thou, and Thou, Lord Christ, who art the joy of
mankind, lamentest, Thou that art the prospering of the world,
faintest. Must Thou, scourged, bear the torments of my sins? Alas
for me, is there no mercy? Is there no longer any justice in the
world? Injustice administers justice and justice injustice!

We seek for violets in flowery meadows, daffodils spring among
pearly dewdrops, the fruitful land greens and smells of vegetation,
the watery shore gleams in the spring. Jesus, in what state art
Thou! Thy hands and legs are torn, Thy shoulders flayed by
scourging and Thy whole body bleeds exceedingly.

The silver crystal waters murmur and echo as they fall from the
mountains, they purl among the pebbles, / they gleam, they moisten
the gravid field, they flow and irrigate the pregnant world.

Sie leuchten, befeuchten das trächtige Feld,
Sie fließen, durchgießen die schwangere Welt.
    Jesu, deiner Seite Brunnen,
    Deine Wunden, deine Narben
    Kommen mit blutroten Farben
    Von dem Kreuze hergerunnen!

Die Nachtigall zwittert und kittert in Klüften,
Die Haubellerch tiretilieret in Lüften,
Die Stiegelitz zitschert und zwitschert im Wald,
Der Fröschefeind klappert, der Widerhall schallt.
    Jesu, was für Jammerklagen,
    Was für gallenbittre Schmerzen
    Pressen dir aus deinem Herzen
    Solches Zittern, solches Zagen!

Die Buchen und Eichen verbinden sich feste,
Sie strecken, bedecken die laubichten Äste,
Sie schatten die Matten, sie breiten sich aus,
Sie zieren, vollfuhren ein lebendes Haus.
    Jesu, du bist ausgespannet,
    Deine Glieder sind zerrecket,
    Deine Hände weitgestrecket,
    Ja, dein Leben ist verbannet!

Jesus, the fountains from Thy side, Thy wounds, Thy scars, stream from the cross in blood-red colours!

The nightingale twitters and titters in the dells, the crested lark trills soaring in the air, the goldfinch chirrups and chirps in the wood, the [stork] foe to frogs rattles his beak, the echo resounds. Jesus, oh what agonized laments, what pains bitter as gall, such trembling, such fainting press out of Thy heart!

The beeches and oaks anchor themselves firmly, they stretch out and cover their leafy branches, they shade the meadows, they spread themselves out, they adorn and complete a living house. Jesus, Thou art stretched out, Thy limbs are wrenched asunder, Thy hands spread far apart, oh, Thy life is exiled from Thee!

CHRISTIAN HOFMANN VON
HOFMANNSWALDAU

Arie

IHR hellen Mörderin', ihr Augen! schließt euch zu,
Jedoch die schönen Brüste,
Als Zunder meiner Lüste,
Genießen keine Ruh,
Ihr aufgeblähter Schnee rafft alle Kraft zusammen,
Und bläst in meine Flammen.

Es muß dein Atem ja wohl Glut und Hitze sein,
Denn was daraus erquillet,
Ist auch mit Brand erfüllet:
Der edlen Flammen Schein
Bezeuget als Rubin sich auf der Berge Spitzen,
Mich Armen zu erhitzen.

Du schläfst in sich'rer Ruh, ich aber wach' allhier,
Verirret in den Schranken
Voll schlüpfriger Gedanken,
Ich schaue dich in mir,
Und ich bemühe mich, den Unmut zu versüßen,
Im Geiste dich zu küssen.

Aria

EYES, you bright murderesses, you close, but the fair breasts, as
though tinder to my desires, enjoy no rest; their inflated snow sum-
mons all its power and blows upon my flames.

Your breath must be flame and heat indeed, for what flows forth
from it is filled with fire too: the glow of those noble flames shows
as rubies on the tops of the mountains, to increase my doleful heat.

You are sleeping in assured quiet, but I am awake here, lost in
the maze full of hazardous thoughts; I see you in my mind's eye,
and to sweeten my annoyance I try to kiss you in the spirit.

Ich fühle, wie mich hier des Ambers Lieblichkeit,
Den deine Zunge gibet,
Wenn sie am schärfsten liebet,
Mit Anmut überstreut,
Und wünsche, daß dein Geist auch in dem Schlafe spüre,
Was ich im Sinne führe.

Es muß ein süßer Traum von Liebes-Schelmerei
Dir durch die Adern dringen,
Und dich zu etwas zwingen,
So dir ganz fremde sei,
So dich zu früher Zeit, so bald du wirst erwachen,
Auch schamrot könne machen.

Der Liebes-Engel selbst, so neidisch ist wie du,
Der will sich itzt bemühen
Den Vorhang vorzuziehen,
Von wegen deiner Ruh;
Doch mußt du mit der Zeit mir ungescheut entdecken,
Wie dir die Träume schmecken.

I can feel how even here the deliciousness of musk, which your tongue imparts when it loves most intensely, casts desire upon me, and I wish your spirit would feel even in sleep what I have in mind.

A sweet dream of amorous roguery must find its way through your veins and force you to something which would be quite foreign to you, which might make you blush for shame in the morning as soon as you wake up.

The angel of love himself, who is as grudging as you, now tries to draw the curtain to protect your sleep; but some time you must explain frankly to me how you like these dreams.

Vergänglichkeit der Schönheit

Es wird der bleiche Tod mit seiner kalten Hand
Dir endlich mit der Zeit um deine Brüste streichen,
Der liebliche Korall der Lippen wird verbleichen;
Der Schultern warmer Schnee wird werden kalter Sand,

Der Augen süßer Blitz, die Kräfte deiner Hand,
Für welchen solches fällt, die werden zeitlich weichen.
Das Haar, das izund kann des Goldes Glanz erreichen,
Tilgt endlich Tag und Jahr als ein gemeines Band.

Der wohlgesetzte Fuß, die lieblichen Gebärden,
Die werden teils zu Staub, teils nichts und nichtig
    werden,
Denn opfert keiner mehr der Gottheit deiner Pracht.

Dies und noch mehr als dies muß endlich untergehen.
Dein Herze kann allein zu aller Zeit bestehen,
Dieweil es die Natur aus Diamant gemacht.

The Transitoriness of Beauty

In time, Death with his cold hand will at the last caress your breasts, the delicious coral of your lips will pale; the warm snow of your shoulders will turn to cold sand.

The sweet flash of your eyes, the powers of your hand will at last surrender to him, before whom all such things fall. Your hair, that now rivals the gleam of gold itself, the days and years will destroy like an ordinary ribbon.

Your neat foot, your delightful ways will turn to dust or to nothingness itself; then no one will pay homage any more to the divinity of your splendour.

This and much more than this must come to an end at last. Your heart alone can endure to all time, for Nature has fashioned it of diamond.

Verliebte Arie

Wo sind die Stunden
Der süßen Zeit,
Da ich zuerst empfunden,
Wie deine Lieblichkeit
Mich dir verbunden?
Sie sind verrauscht. Es bleibet doch dabei,
Daß alle Lust vergänglich sei.

Das reine Scherzen,
So mich ergetzt
Und in dem tiefen Herzen
Sein Merkmal eingesetzt,
Läßt mich in Schmerzen.
Du hast mir mehr als deutlich kund getan,
Daß Freundlichkeit nicht ankern kann.

Das Angedenken,
Der Zuckerlust
Will mich in Angst versenken.
Es will verdammte Kost
Uns zeitlich kränken.
Was man geschmeckt und nicht mehr schmecken soll,
Ist freudenleer und jammervoll.

Love Aria

Where are the hours of that sweet time when I first realized how
your loveliness had bound me to you? They have swept past. It
remains true what people say, that all pleasure is transitory.

That artless laughter which pleased me and left its mark in the
depths of my heart now leaves me in pain. You have made it more
than plain to me that friendliness is no anchor.

The memory of that sweet pleasure often bids fair to plunge me
into dread; this world's damned fare will always harm us. What one
has tasted once and may not taste any more is empty of joy and full
of misery.

Empfangene Küsse,
Ambrierter Saft,
Verbleibt nicht lange süße
Und kommt von aller Kraft;
Verrauschte Flüsse
Erquicken nicht. Was unsern Geist erfreut
Entspringt aus Gegènwärtigkeit.

Ich schwamm in Freude,
Der Liebe Hand
Spann mir ein Kleid von Seide;
Das Blatt hat sich gewandt,
Ich geh im Leide,
Ich wein itzund, daß Lieb und Sonnenschein
Stets voller Angst und Wolken sein.

Auf den Einfall der Kirchen zu St. Elisabeth

MIT starkem Krachen brach der Bau des Herren ein,
Die Pfeiler gaben nach, die Balken mußten biegen,
Die Ziegel wollten sich nicht mehr zusammenfügen:
Es trennte Kalk von Kalk und riß sich Stein von Stein.

Kisses received, musky liquor, do not stay sweet for long, and lose their savour. Dried-up rivers no longer quench. What delights our mind derives from the present.

I swam in joy, the hand of love spun me a robe of silk. Now the tables are turned, I walk in sorrow; now I weep that love and sunlight are always full of dread and clouds.

The Collapse of St. Elizabeth's Church [Breslau]

WITH a loud crash the Lord's house collapsed, the pillars gave way, the beams were forced to bend, the bricks no longer joined together, mortar parted from mortar and stone tore away from stone.

Der Mauern hohe Pracht, der süßen Orgeln Schein,
Die hieß ein Augenblick in einem Klumpen liegen:
Und was itzund aus Angst mein bleicher Mund ver-
    schwiegen,
Mußt abgetan, zersprengt und ganz vertilget sein.

O Mensch! Dies ist ein Fluch, der nach dem Himmel
    schmeckt,
Der dieses Haus gerührt und dein Gemüt erweckt.
Es spricht der Herren Herr: Du sollst mich besser ehren!

Die Sünde kommt von dir, das Scheitern kommt von
    Gott,
Und ist dein Herze Stein und dein Gemüte tot,
So müssen dich itzund die toten Steine lehren.

ANGELUS SILESIUS

Ein Christ ist Gottes Sohn

ICH auch bin Gottes Sohn, ich sitz' an seiner Hand:
Sein Geist, sein Fleisch und Blut ist ihm an mir bekannt.

The lofty splendour of the walls, the glow of the sweet organ, one moment made them all lie in a shapeless heap, and other things besides that my pale lips cannot utter now for fear, had to be pulled down, blasted away, and totally demolished.

O man, this is a curse that tastes of Heaven, which has struck this house and roused your spirit. The Lord of Lords speaks: You must worship me better!

The sin is yours, the wreck comes from God, and if your heart is stone and your spirit dead, the dead stones will have to teach you now.

A Christian is God's Son

I, TOO, am God's son. I sit at his side; His spirit, flesh, and blood are manifest to Him in me.

Die Zeit ist Ewigkeit

ZEIT ist wie Ewigkeit und Ewigkeit wie Zeit,
So du nur selber nicht machst einen Unterschied.

Ohne Warum

DIE Ros' ist ohn' Warum, sie blühet, weil sie blühet,
Sie acht't nicht ihrer selbst, fragt nicht, ob man sie siehet.

Zufall und Wesen

MENSCH, werde wesentlich! denn wann die Welt
vergeht,
So fällt der Zufall weg, das Wesen, das besteht.

Es mangelt nur an dir

ACH, könnte nur dein Herz zu einer Krippe werden,
Gott würde noch einmal ein Kind auf dieser Erden.

Time is Eternity

TIME is as Eternity is, and Eternity as Time only if you yourself
make no difference between them.

No Why

THERE is no 'why' about the rose, it blossoms because it blossoms,
pays no heed to itself and does not care whether it is seen.

Accident and Essence

MAN, make yourself partake of the Essence! for when the world
comes to an end accident drops away, but essence stands fast.

It Depends on You

OH, if only your heart could become a manger, God would once
again become a child on earth.

Dein Kerker bist du selbst

DIE Welt die hält dich nicht, du selber bist die Welt,
Die dich in dir mit dir so stark gefangen hält.

Die geheimste Gelassenheit

GELASSENHEIT fäht Gott; Gott aber selbst zu lassen,
Ist ein' Gelassenheit, die wenig Menschen fassen.

Die Nulle gilt vornean nichts

DAS Nichts, die Kreatur, wenn sich's Gott vorgesetzt,
Gilt nichts; steht's hinter ihm, dann wird es erst ge-
    schätzt.

Der Teufel der ist gut

DER Teufel ist so gut dem Wesen nach als du.
Was gehet ihm dann ab? Gestorb'ner Will' und Ruh'.

You Are Your Own Prison

IT is not the World that confines you, you yourself are the World,
which holds you so fast a prisoner with yourself in yourself.

Mystical Abandonment

ABANDONMENT ensnares God, but to abandon even God is an
abandonment which few men can comprehend.

A Nought before the Integer Has no Value

THE creature, which is nought, has no value if it comes before
God; it has significance only if it stands after Him.

The Devil Is Good

IN essence, the Devil is as good as you: what is it that he lacks?
Peace and extinguished will.

Wenn Gott am liebsten bei uns ist

GOTT, dessen Wollust ist, bei dir, o Mensch, zu sein,
Kehrt, wenn du nicht daheim, am liebsten bei dir ein.

Beschluß

FREUND, es ist auch genug. Im Fall du mehr willst
lesen,
So geh und werde selbst die Schrift und selbst das Wesen.

JESU, du mächtiger Liebesgott,
   Nah' dich zu mir,
Denn ich verschmachte fast bis in Tod
   Für Liebesgier;
Ergreif' die Waffen und in Eil'
Durchstich mein Herz mit deinem Pfeil,
   Verwunde mich!

When God most Delights to Be with Us

GOD, whose delight it is to be with you, O Man, prefers to come
into your house when you are not at home.

Conclusion

FRIEND, it is enough now: if you wish to read more go and your-
self become the Writing and its sense.

JESUS, Thou mighty God of love, come near to me for I am lan-
guishing almost to death in desire of love. Take up Thine arms and
swiftly pierce my heart with Thine arrow – oh, wound me!

Komm' meine Sonne, mein Lebenslicht,
  Mein Aufenthalt
Komm' und erwärme mich, daß ich nicht
  Bleib' ewig kalt;
Wirf deine Flammen in den Schrein
Mein's halbgefrornen Herzens ein,
  Entzünde mich!

O allersüßeste Seelenbrunst
  Durchglüh' mich ganz
Und überform' mich aus Gnad' und Gunst
  In deinen Glanz;
Blas' an das Feuer ohn' Verdruß
Daß dir mein Herz mit schnellem Fluß
  Vereinigt sei!

Dann will ich sagen, daß du mich hast
  Erlöst vom Tod
Und als ein lieblicher Seelengast
  Besucht in Not;
Dann will ich rühmen, daß du bist
Mein Bräut'gam, der mich liebt und küßt
  Und nicht verläßt.

Come my sun, the light of my life, my refuge, come and warm
me so that I do not stay cold for ever; throw Thy flames into the
casket of my half-frozen heart – oh, enflame me!

  O sweetest fire of the soul, glow all through me and transport
me by Thy grace and favour into Thy splendour; blow on the fire
untiringly, that my heart may quickly thaw and be united with
Thee!

  Then I will say that Thou hast saved me from death and hast
visited me in my distress as a kind guest of the soul. Then I will
boast that Thou art my Bridegroom, who loves me and kisses me
and will not forsake me.

Liebe, die du mich zum Bilde
Deiner Gottheit hast gemacht,
Liebe, die du mich so milde
Nach dem Fall hast wieder bracht:
Liebe, dir ergeb' ich mich
Dein zu bleiben ewiglich.

Liebe, die du mich erkoren
Eh' als ich geschaffen war,
Liebe, die du Mensch geboren
Und mir gleich wardst ganz und gar,
Liebe, dir ergeb' ich mich
Dein zu bleiben ewiglich.

Liebe, die für mich gelitten
Und gestorben in der Zeit,
Liebe, die mir hat erstritten
Ew'ge Lust und Seligkeit,
Liebe, dir ergeb' ich mich
Dein zu bleiben ewiglich. [...]

Liebe, die mich ewig liebet,
Die für meine Seele bitt't
Liebe, die das Lösgeld gibet
Und mich kräftiglich vertritt:
Liebe, dir ergeb' ich mich
Dein zu bleiben ewiglich.

Love, who createdst me to be the image of Thy Godhead; Love,
who in Thy mercy hast brought me back after the Fall: Love, I
give myself to Thee to remain Thine for ever.

Love, who hast chosen me before I was made, Love, who was
born as man and becamest like me in every way: Love, I give myself
to Thee to remain Thine for ever.

Love, who in this temporal world didst suffer and die for me,
Love, who hast won for me eternal joy and bliss, Love, I give my-
self to Thee to remain Thine for ever.

Love, who lovest me for ever, who intercedest for my soul,
Love, who givest the ransom and art my powerful advocate, Love,
I give myself to Thee to remain Thine for ever.

Liebe, die mich wird erwecken
Aus dem Grab der Sterblichkeit
Liebe, die mich wird umstecken
Mit dem Laub der Herrlichkeit:
Liebe, dir ergeb' ich mich
Dein zu bleiben ewiglich.

JOHANN JAKOB CHRISTOFFEL VON GRIMMELSHAUSEN

Komm Trost der Nacht

KOMM Trost der Nacht, o Nachtigall,
Laß deine Stimm mit Freudenschall
Aufs lieblichste erklingen;
Komm, komm und lob den Schöpfer dein,
Weil andre Vöglein schlafen sein
Und nicht mehr mögen singen!
Laß dein Stimmlein
Laut erschallen, dann vor allen
Kannst du loben
Gott im Himmel hoch dort oben.

Love, who wilt wake me out of the grave of mortality, Love, who wilt adorn me with the garland of glory, Love, I give myself to Thee to remain Thine for ever.

COME solace of the night, O nightingale, let your voice sound with joyous note as delightfully as may be; come, come and praise your creator, while other birds are asleep and cannot sing any more. Let your dear voice sound aloud, for you better than any can praise God in Heaven high above us.

Obschon ist hin der Sonnenschein
Und wir im Finstern müssen sein,
So können wir doch singen
Von Gottes Güt und seiner Macht,
Weil uns kann hindern keine Nacht,
Sein Lob zu vollenbringen.
Drum dein Stimmlein
Laß erschallen, dann vor allen
Kannst du loben
Gott im Himmel hoch dort oben.

Echo, der wilde Widerhall,
Will sein bei diesem Freudenschall
Und lässet sich auch hören.
Verweist uns alle Müdigkeit,
Der wir ergeben allezeit,
Lehrt uns den Schlaf betören.
Drum dein Stimmlein
Laß erschallen, dann vor allen
Kannst du loben
Gott im Himmel hoch dort oben.

Die Sterne, so am Himmel stehn,
Lassen sich zum Lob Gottes sehn,
Und tun ihm Ehr beweisen;

Though the sunlight has gone and we have to be in darkness,
we can sing nonetheless of God's goodness and His power, for no
night can prevent us from carrying out His praise. Therefore let
your dear voice sound, for you better than any can praise God in
Heaven high above us.

Echo, the wild resounder, likes to accompany this sound of joy
and lets her voice be heard too. She banishes all weariness, to
which we are at all times subject, and teaches us to outwit sleep.
Therefore let your dear voice sound, for you better than any can
praise God in Heaven high above us.

The stars in the sky show themselves to the glory of God and do
him homage; / even the owl that cannot sing shows by its screeching

Auch die Eul, die nicht singen kann,
Zeigt doch mit ihrem Heulen an,
Daß sie Gott auch tu preisen.
Drum dein Stimmlein
Laß erschallen, dann vor allen
Kannst du loben
Gott im Himmel hoch dort oben.

Nur her mein liebstes Vögelein,
Wir wollen nicht die fäulste sein
Und schlafend liegen bleiben,
Sondern bis daß die Morgenröt
Erfreuet diese Wälder öd,
Im Lob Gottes vertreiben.
Laß dein Stimmlein
Laut erschallen, dann vor allen
Kannst du loben
Gott im Himmel hoch dort oben.

ACH allerhöchstes Gut! du wohnest so im Finstern
Licht!
Daß man vor Klarheit groß den großen Glanz kann sehen
nicht.

that it, too, is praising God. Therefore let your dear voice sound,
for you better than any can praise God in Heaven high above us.

Come now, my dearest bird, we will not be among the idlest and
lie asleep, but pass the time in praise of God until the dawn rejoices
these wild woods. Let your dear voice sound aloud, for you better
than any can praise God in Heaven high above us.

O SUPREME Good! Thou hast Thy habitation in the Dark Light,
so that for very brightness we cannot see Thy glory.

KASPAR STIELER

Laß die Verstorbenen ruhen

Stirb, Filidor!
Warum willst du nicht willig sterben?
    Der Musen Chor
Verspricht dir deines Namens Erben,
    Ob Florilis schon meinet,
    Daß niemand um dich weinet.

    Zwar Florilis
Wird wegen deines Todes lachen;
    Sie wird gewiß
Sich lustig bei dem Sarge machen
    Und auf dem Grabe singen
    Mit Jauchzen und mit Springen.

    Wird jemand denn
Nach deinem Hinfall dein erwähnen
    Wie, wo und wenn,
So wird sie in der Gruft dich höhnen;
    Die abgefaulten Knochen
    Wird sie auch selbst bepochen.

Leave the Dead in Peace

Die, Filidor, why won't you die of your own free will? The choir
of the Muses promises you heirs to your name, even though Florilis
thinks that no one will mourn for you.

   Florilis, of course, will laugh at your death; she will certainly
crack jokes over your coffin and sing, whoop, and caper on your
grave.

   If anyone mentions your name after your decease, anyhow, any-
where, or at any time, she will mock you in your tomb; she will
even batter your rotting bones herself.

Doch denke nicht,
Daß ich es dir will, Stolze, schenken:
  Ein bleich Gesicht,
Das meinem gleichet, soll dich kränken;
    Mein Geist soll um dich stehen
    Und mit zu Bette gehen.

  Ein schwerer Traum
Soll dich oft aus dem Schlaf erwecken;
  Du glaubest kaum,
Wie ich alsdenn dich werd' erschrecken!
    Mit Werfen und mit Poltern
    Will ich dein Leben foltern!

  Wird man auf dir
Des Morgens blaue Flecken sehen,
  Sprich, daß von mir
Zur Rache dieses sei geschehen.
    Wirst du einmal denn kranken,
    Plag ich dich mit Gedanken.

  Drum besser dich,
Dieweil es Zeit ist, sich zu bessern.
  Verjagst du mich
Zu Acherontis Nebelwässern,
    So hilft alsdenn kein Klagen
    Wenn dich mein Geist wird plagen!

But do not imagine, proud girl, that I shall let you get away with it! A ghastly face, resembling mine, shall torment you; my ghost shall haunt you and go to bed with you.

An oppressive dream will often wake you out of sleep. You will hardly believe how I shall frighten you then: I shall make your life a misery with thumping and bumping.

If bruises are found on you in the morning, say that I have done it as my revenge. If you fall ill, I shall torment you in your thoughts.

So you had better reform while there is yet time to reform. If you banish me to the misty waters of Acheron, it will be no use complaining when my ghost torments you!

Nachtlast, Tageslust

Die Nacht,
Die sonst den Buhlern fügt und süße Hoffnung macht,
Die Ruh,
Die einem Liebenden sagt alle Wollust zu,
Bringt mir nur lauter Schmerzen
Und raubet mir das Licht,
Das meinem trüben Herzen,
Des Trostes Strahl verspricht.

Der Tag,
Dem sonst kein Paphoskind recht günstig werden mag,
Die Glut
Der goldnen Strahlen, die der Venus Schaden tut,
Erteilt mir lauter Freuden
Und gönnet mir das Glück,
Die Augen satt zu weiden
In meiner Liebsten Blick.

Wenn itzt
Apollens Feuergold der Berge Haupt erhitzt,
Und nu
Die aufgeweckte Welt entsaget ihrer Ruh:

Night's Burden, Day's Joy

NIGHT, which is usually kind to lovers and encourages them in their fond hopes; rest, which promises every joy to a lover, they bring me nothing but pain and rob me of the light which promises a ray of consolation to my sad heart.

Day, which is usually unfavourable to the children of Paphos; the glare of the golden rays which harm Venus, they give me nothing but joy and grant me the happiness of feasting my eyes on the sight of my beloved.

Now when Apollo's fiery gold heats the heads of the mountains and now the wakened world foregoes its rest,/Rosilla's cheek

Rührt mich Rosillens Wange
Mit einem feuchten Kuß
Und dieses währt so lange
Bis auf den Hesperus.

     Sobald
Der Sonne Kerze wird in Thetis' Schoße kalt,
     Laton'
In düstrer Wolkenluft führt auf den bleichen Mon,
So weicht mein Licht von hinnen,
Dann wird mir erst die Nacht,
Das Kind der Erebinnen,
Zur rechten Nacht gemacht.

     Drum geh',
Verhaßtes Sternenheer, gleich nimmer aus der See,
     Komm an,
Geliebter Lucifer, tritt auf Olympens Bahn.
Der Tag, der mich so liebet,
Soll meine Freude sein.
Die Nacht, die mich betrübet,
Weich' in die Höll hinein.

touches me with a moist kiss, and so it goes on until Hesperus appears.

As soon as the sun's candle cools in Thetis' lap and Latona leads up the pale moon in dim cloudy air, then night, the child of the daughters of Erebus, becomes night indeed for me.

May you, hateful army of stars, never rise out of the sea; come, beloved Lucifer, start on the path of Olympus. Day, which is so kind to me, shall be my joy; let Night, which makes me sad, flee into Hell!

Nacht-Glücke

WILLKOMMEN, Fürstin aller Nächte!
Prinz der Silberknechte,
Willkommen, Mon aus düstrer Bahn
Vom Ozean!
Dies ist die Nacht, die tausend Tagen
Trotz kann sagen:
Weil mein Schatz
Hier in Priapus' Platz
Erscheinen wird, zu stillen meine Pein.
Wer wird, wie ich, wohl so beglücket sein?

Beneidet, himmlische Laternen,
Weißgeflammte Sternen,
Mit einem scheelen Angesicht
Ach! mich nur nicht.
Kein Mensch, als ihr nur, möge wissen,
Wie wir küssen:
Alle Welt
Hat seine Ruh bestellt,
Wir beide nur, ich und mein Kind sind wach,
Und, Flammen, ihr an Bronteus' Wolkendach.

Night's Delight

WELCOME, princess of all nights! Prince of the silver servants,
moon, welcome on your dark path from the ocean! This is the
night, which can defy a thousand days, for my beloved will appear
here in Priapus' abode to calm my pain. Who can be made as happy
as I?

O heavenly lanterns, white-flamed stars, do not look with sour,
envious faces on me! No one but you must know how we kiss.
The whole world has gone to rest; only we two, my love and I, are
awake, and you, flames on Bronteus' cloudy roof.

Es säuselt Zephir aus dem Weste,
Durch Pomonen-Äste,
Es seufzet sein verliebter Wind
Nach meinem Kind.
Ich seh es gerne, da er spielet
Und sie kühlet,
Weil sie mir
Folgt durch die Gartentür,
Und doppelt den geschwinden Liebestritt.
Bring, West, sie bald und tausend Küsse mit!

Was werd ich, wenn sie kommt gegangen,
An- doch erstlichst -fangen,
Küß' ich die Hand, die Brust, den Mund
Zur selben Stund?
Ich werd (ich weiß) kein Wort nicht machen,
Soviel Sachen,
Die an Zier
Den Göttern gehen für
Und auf dies Schönchen sein gewendet an,
Erstaunen mich, daß ich nicht reden kann.

Komm, Flora, streue dein Vermügen
Dahin, wo wir liegen.

Zephyr rustles from the west through Pomona's branches, his lovesick wind sighs for my beloved. I am glad that he is at play and will cool her while she comes after me through the garden gate and quickens her swift lover's pace. West, bring her soon and a thousand kisses with her!

What shall I do first of all when she comes? Can I kiss her hand, her breast, her mouth all at once? I know I shall not waste time in talking, for so many things, which surpass the gods in beauty, and which have been lavished on this pretty piece, amaze me so that I cannot speak.

Come, Flora, spread your bounty where we shall lie; / a gay bed

Es soll ein bunter Rosenhauf
Uns nehmen auf,
Und Venus, du sollst in den Myrten
Uns bewirten,
Bis das Blut
Der Röt' herfür sich tut.
Was Schein ist das? Die Schatten werden klar.
Still! Lautenklang, mein Liebchen ist schon dar.

CHRISTIAN KNORR VON ROSENROTH

Morgenandacht

MORGENGLANZ der Ewigkeit,
Licht vom unerschöpften Lichte,
Schick uns diese Morgenzeit
Deine Strahlen zu Gesichte
Und vertreib durch deine Macht
Unsre Nacht.

Die bewölkte Finsternis
Müsse deinem Glanz entfliegen,
Die durch Adams Apfelbiß
Uns, die kleine Welt, bestiegen,
Daß wir, Herr, durch deinen Schein
Selig sein.

of roses shall receive us, and you, Venus, shall entertain us among the myrtles until the blood of dawn appears. What is that light? the shadows are brightening; hush, lute – my beloved is here!

Morning Prayer

MORNING splendour of eternity, light of inexhaustible light, send this morning thy rays to our eyes and with thy power drive away our night.

May the cloudy darkness which overpowered us, the microcosm, through Adam's bite of the apple flee before Thy glory, that we may be blessed through Thy light.

Deiner Güte Morgentau
Fall auf unser matt Gewissen:
Laß die dürre Lebensau
Lauter süßen Trost genießen
Und erquick uns, deine Schar,
Immerdar.

Gib, daß deiner Liebe Glut
Unsre kalten Werke töte
Und erweck uns Herz und Mut
Bei entstandner Morgenröte,
Daß wir, eh wir gar vergehn,
Recht aufstehn.

Laß uns ja das Sündenkleid
Durch des Bundes Blut vermeiden,
Daß uns die Gerechtigkeit
Mög als wie ein Rock bekleiden
Und wir so vor aller Pein
Sicher sein.

Ach, du Aufgang aus der Höh,
Gib, daß auch am Jüngsten Tage
Unser Leichnam aufersteh
Und, entfernt von aller Plage,
Sich auf jener Freudenbahn
Freuen kann.

May the morning dew of Thy blessing fall on our dull consciences; let the parched meadow of our life enjoy pure sweet comfort and revive us, Thy congregation, for ever.

Grant that the fire of Thy love may kill our dead works and awake our hearts and minds at the arrival of the dawn, so that we may truly arise before we depart for ever.

Let us put away this cloak of sin through the blood of the covenant, so that righteousness may clothe us as with a garment, and thus we may be preserved from all torment.

Oh, Thou dayspring from on high, grant that on the Judgement Day our bodies, too, may rise, and remote from all torment may rejoice in that place of joy.

Leucht uns selbst in jene Welt,
Du verklärte Gnadensonne;
Führ uns durch das Tränenfeld
In das Land der süßen Wonne,
Da die Lust, die uns erhöht,
Nie vergeht.

QUIRINUS KUHLMANN

Kühlpsalm 62 (II)

RECHT dunkelt mich das Dunkel,
Weil Wesenheit so heimlichst anbeginnt!
O seltner Glückskarfunkel!
Es strömt, was äußerlich verrinnt,
Und wird ein Meer, was kaum ein Bächlein gründt.

Je dunkler, je mehr lichter:
Je schwärzer alls, je weißer weißt sein Sam.
Ein himmlisch Aug ist Richter:
Kein Irdscher lebt, der was vernahm;
Es glänzt je mehr, je finster es ankam.

Light us the way Thyself into that world, Thou glorified Sun of
grace; lead us through the field of tears into the land of sweet joy,
where the joy which lifts us up will never pass away.

Kuhlmann's Cooling Psalm 62, Part II

IT is right that darkness darkens me, for it is thus that essentiality
most secretly begins. O rare carbuncle of fortune! What flows
away outwardly now streams [inwardly], and what hardly fills a
little brook becomes an ocean.

The darker the lighter; the blacker everything is, the whiter his
seed whitens. A heavenly eye is the judge: no mortal lives who per-
ceived anything of it. It gleams the more, the darker it approached.

Ach Nacht! Und Nacht, die taget!
O Tag, der Nacht vernünftiger Vernunft!
Ach Licht, das Kaine plaget
Und helle strahlt der Abelzunft!
Ich freue mich ob deiner finstern Kunft.

O längst erwart'tes Wunder,
Das durch den Kern des ganzen Baums auswächst!
Du fängst neu Edens Zunder,
Ei, Lieber, sieh, mein Herze lechzt!
Es ist genug! Hör, wie es innig ächzt!

O unaussprechlichst Blauen!
O lichtste Röt! O übergelbes Weiß!
Es bringt, was ewigst, schauen,
Beerdt die Erd als Paradeis;
Entflucht den Fluch, durchsegnet jeden Reis.

O Erdvier! Welches Strahlen!
Der Finsterst ist als vor die lichtste Sonn.
Kristallisiertes Prahlen!
Die Welt bewonnt die Himmelswonn:
Sie quillt zurück, als wäre sie der Bronn.

O night! And night that dawns! O day, the night of reasonable
reason! O light, that torments Cain and beams brightly to the tribe
of Abel! I rejoice at your dark approach.

O long expected miracle, which grows up through the core of
the whole tree! Thou takest Eden's tinder anew! O beloved, see,
my heart is parched! It is enough! Hear how it groans within me!

O most ineffable blueing! O gleamingest redness! O white
beyond all yellow! It brings to view what is most eternal, enearths
the earth as Paradise, it breaks the curse's curse, sends blessing
through each twig.

O square of earth! What radiance! The darkest part is as the
brightest sun was before. Crystallized splendour! The joy of
Heaven fills the world with joy, the world gives back streams, as
though it were itself the source.

Welch wesentliches Bildnis?
Erscheinst du so, geheimste Kraftfigur?
Wie richtigst, was doch Wildnis?
O was vor Zahl? Ach welche Spur?
Du bist, nicht ich! Dein ist Natur und Kur!

Die Kron ist ausgefüllet,
Die Tausend sind auch überall ersetzt:
Geschehen, was umhüllet;
Sehr hoher Röt, höchst ausgeätzt,
Daß alle Kunst an ihr sich ausgewetzt.

Die Lilien und Rosen
Sind durch sechs Tag gebrochen spat und früh:
Sie kränzen mit Liebkosen
Nun dich und mich aus deiner Müh.
Dein Will ist mein, mein Will ist dein, vollzieh.

Im jesuelschen Schimmer
Pfeiln wir zugleich zur jesuelschen Kron:
Der Stolz ist durch dich nimmer!
Er liegt zu Fuß im höchsten Hohn.
Ein ander ist mit dir der Erb und Sohn.

What is this essential symbol? Is it thus that Thou appearest,
most secret pattern of power? How canst Thou make straight what is
a wilderness? O what number? O what trace? Thou art, not I! Thine
is the Nature and thine the choice!

The crown is completed, the thousand are supplanted every-
where; what was concealed has come to pass; most lofty dawn,
supremely etched out, so that all art is blunt by comparison.

The lilies and roses have been picked morning and evening for
six days. They now crown Thee and me with loving caresses by
Thy pain. Thy will is mine, my will is Thine: fulfil it!

In Jesuelic glory we speed together like arrows to the Jesuelic
crown. Through Thee pride is no more! It lies on the ground in
utmost scorn. Another is heir and son with Thee.

JOHANN CHRISTIAN GÜNTHER

Abschied von seiner ungetreuen Liebsten

Wie gedacht,
Vor geliebt, itzt ausgelacht.
Gestern in die Schoß gerissen,
Heute von der Brust geschmissen,
Morgen in die Gruft gebracht.

Dieses ist
Aller Jungfern Hinterlist:
Viel versprechen, wenig halten,
Sie entzünden und erkalten
Öfters, eh ein Tag verfließt.

Dein Betrug,
Falsche Seele, macht mich klug.
Keine soll mich mehr umfassen,
Keine soll mich mehr verlassen;
Einmal ist fürwahr genug.

Denke nur,
Ungetreue Kreatur,
Denke, sag' ich, nur zurücke
Und betrachte deine Tücke
Und erwäge deinen Schwur.

On Parting from His Faithless Beloved

As I expected, once loved, now laughed to scorn; yesterday clasped to your bosom, today thrust from your breast, tomorrow carried to the tomb.

This is the deception every girl practises; they make many promises and keep few of them, they catch fire and cool down several times before one day is over.

Your deceit, false soul, makes me wise. No one shall embrace me any more, no one shall leave me any more. Once is quite enough.

Faithless creature, think, think back, I say, and consider your spite and weigh your solemn promise.

Hast du nicht
Ein Gewissen, das dich sticht,
Wenn die Treue meines Herzens,
Wenn die Größe meines Schmerzens
Deinem Wechsel widerspricht?

Bringt mein Kuß
Dir so eilends Überdruß,
Ei, so geh und küsse diesen,
Welcher dir sein Geld gewiesen,
Das dich wahrlich blenden muß.

Bin ich arm,
Dieses macht mir wenig Harm;
Tugend steckt nicht in dem Beutel,
Gold und Schmuck macht nur den Scheitel,
Aber nicht die Liebe warm.

Und wie bald,
Mißt die Schönheit die Gestalt!
Rühmst du gleich von deiner Farbe,
Daß sie ihresgleichen darbe,
Ach, die Rosen werden alt.

Have you no conscience which pricks you when my heart's
fidelity and the magnitude of my pain contrasts with your fickle-
ness?

If you tire so quickly of my kiss, well, then, go and kiss the other
who has shown you his money, which, of course, is bound to dazzle
you.

Though I am poor, it does not distress me; virtue does not live
in one's purse; gold and jewels warm the head but do not warm
love.

And how soon beauty can lose its looks! Though you boast that
your complexion has no equal, even roses wither.

Weg mit dir,
Falsches Herze, weg von mir!
Ich zerreiße deine Kette,
Denn die kluge Henriette
Stellet mir was bessers für.

Die unwiederbringliche Zeit

Ich weiß noch wohl die liebe Zeit,
In der ich mich genug gefreut;
Was waren das vor süße Tage!
Die Schläfe trugen Blum' und Glut
Und kannten weder Wunsch noch Plage,
Noch was den Greisen bange tut.

Mein Sorgen ging auf Lust und Scherz,
Mein Herz war Amaranthens Herz,
Wir zählten weder Kuß noch Stunden;
Tanz, Schauplatz, Gärte, Spiel und Wein
Und aller Vorteil der Gesunden
Nahm Blut und Geist mit Wollust ein.

Away with you, faithless heart, away from me! I will break your chain, for Harriet, who knows a thing or two, has something better in store for me.

Irretrievable Time

Well do I remember that dear time in which I had pleasure enough; what charming days they were! My temples were adorned with flowers and radiance and knew neither desire nor distress, nor what worries the aged.

My concern was with pleasure and laughter, my heart was Amaranthe's heart; we counted neither kisses nor hours; dancing, theatre, garden, gaming and wine, and all the advantages of good health our blood and mind absorbed with gusto.

Wie? Was erzähl' ich einen Traum?
Zum wenigsten gedenkt mich's kaum.
Mein Gott, wie ist die Zeit entronnen!
Was hast du, Herz, von aller Lust?
Dies, daß du Reu' und Leid gewonnen
Und wissen und entbehren mußt.

Ihr, die ihr die Natur versteht,
Und durch die Kunst oft höher geht,
Ihr könnt euch mir recht sehr verbinden:
Ach, sagt mir doch, ich fleh' euch an,
Wie soll ich die Maschine finden,
Die Zeit und Jugend hemmen kann?

CHRISTIAN FÜRCHTEGOTT GELLERT

Die Geschichte von dem Hute

Das erste Buch

DER erste, der mit kluger Hand
Der Männer Schmuck, den Hut, erfand,
Trug seinen Hut unaufgeschlagen;
Die Krempen hingen flach herab;

What? Why am I telling you a dream? I can hardly even remember it! Oh, God, how time has flowed past! What is left to you, heart, of all this pleasure? Only this, that you have gained remorse and sorrow and must know and renounce.

You people who understand how Nature works and who by your art can rise much higher, you can put me under a profound obligation: tell me, oh, I beg of you, how can I find a machine which will arrest time and youth?

The History of the Hat

Book I

THE first man who, with clever fingers, invented the hat, that ornament of man, wore his hat with the brim turned down: the brim

Und dennoch wußt' er ihn zu tragen,
Daß ihm der Hut ein Ansehn gab.

Er starb, und ließ bei seinem Sterben
Den runden Hut dem nächsten Erben.

Der Erbe weiß den runden Hut
Nicht recht gemächlich anzugreifen;
Er sinnt, und wagt es kurz und gut,
Er wagt's, zwo Krempen aufzusteifen.
Drauf läßt er sich dem Volke sehn;
Das Volk bleibt vor Verwundrung stehn
Und schreit: «Nun läßt der Hut erst schön!»

Er starb, und ließ bei seinem Sterben
Den aufgesteiften Hut dem Erben.

Der Erbe nimmt den Hut und schmält.
«Ich,» spricht er, «sehe wohl, was fehlt.»
Er setzt darauf mit weisem Mute
Die dritte Krempe zu dem Hute.
«O!» rief das Volk, «der hat Verstand!
Seht was ein Sterblicher erfand!
Er, er erhöht sein Vaterland!»

was floppy, / but all the same, he wore it with such an air that the hat
brought him respect.
He died, and at his death left the round hat to his next of kin.
The heir cannot do anything with the round hat; he thinks
things over and finally he takes a risk, he risks stiffening the brim
on two sides, and then he lets himself be seen. People stand still for
very admiration, and shout: 'Now the hat looks fine at last.'
He died and at his death left the stiffened hat to his heir.
The heir takes the hat and criticizes it. 'I,' he said, 'can see what
is the matter with it.' With crafty daring he takes up the brim on the
third side. 'Oh,' people cry, 'he is a clever man! See what it has
been given to a mortal man to invent! He reflects credit on his
country.'

Er starb, und ließ bei seinem Sterben
Den dreifach spitzen Hut dem Erben.

Der Hut war freilich nicht mehr rein;
Doch sagt, wie konnt' es anders sein?
Er ging schon durch die vierten Hände.
Der Erbe färbt ihn schwarz, damit er was erfände.
«Beglückter Einfall!» rief die Stadt,
«So weit sah keiner noch, als der gesehen hat.
Ein weißer Hut ließ lächerlich;
Schwarz, Brüder, schwarz! so schickt es sich.»

Er starb, und ließ bei seinem Sterben
Den schwarzen Hut dem nächsten Erben.

Der Erbe trägt ihn in sein Haus,
Und sieh, er ist sehr abgetragen;
Er sinnt, und sinnt das Kunststück aus,
Ihn über einen Stock zu schlagen
Durch heiße Bürsten wird er rein;
Er faßt ihn gar mit Schnüren ein.
Nun geht er aus, und alle schreien:
«Was sehn wir? Sind es Zaubereien?
Ein neuer Hut! O glücklich Land,

He died, and at his death left the three-cornered hat to his heir. The hat, of course, was no longer clean, but, I ask you, what can you expect? It was already fourth-hand. The heir has it dyed black, just to make a change. 'A happy thought!' the town cries. 'No one was so far-seeing as he. A white hat looked ridiculous. Black, brothers, black, that is the right thing.'
He died, and at his death left the black hat to his next of kin.
The heir takes it home and look, it is very worn. He thinks it over and comes on the idea of turning it inside out over a block. Hot brushes get it clean; he even binds it with braid. Then he goes out and everyone cries 'What is this? Is this magic? A new hat! O happy country,/where delusion and obscurantism vanish. No mortal can discover more than this great mind has discovered!'

Wo Wahn und Finsternis verschwinden!
Mehr kann kein Sterblicher erfinden,
Als dieser große Geist erfand.»

Er starb, und ließ bei seinem Sterben
Den umgewandten Hut dem Erben.

Erfindung macht die Künstler groß
Und bei der Nachwelt unvergessen;
Der Erbe reißt die Schnüre los,
Umzieht den Hut mit goldnen Tressen,
Verherrlicht ihn durch einen Knopf
Und drückt ihn seitwärts auf den Kopf.
Ihn sieht das Volk und taumelt vor Vergnügen.
Nun ist die Kunst erst hoch gestiegen!
«Ihm,» schrie es, «ihm allein ist Witz und Geist verliehn!
Nichts sind die andern gegen ihn!»

Er starb, und ließ bei seinem Sterben
Den eingefaßten Hut dem Erben.
Und jedesmal ward die erfundne Tracht
Im ganzen Lande nachgemacht.

Ende des ersten Buches.

. . . .

He died and at his death left the reversed hat to his heir.

Invention is what makes an artist great and remembered by
posterity; the heir tears off the braiding, surrounds the hat with
gold lace, adorns it with a button, and wears it on the side of his
head. People see him and are transported with delight: 'Now at
last,' they shout, 'art has reached its zenith! He, he alone, is en-
dowed with intelligence and wit; the others are nothing compared
with him!'

He died and at his death left the newly adorned hat to his heir.
And each time the newly created fashion was imitated throughout
the country.

End of Book I

Was mit dem Hute sich noch ferner zugetragen,
Will ich im zweiten Buche sagen.
Der Erbe ließ ihm nie die vorige Gestalt.
Das Außenwerk war neu; er selbst, der Hut, blieb alt.
Und, daß ich's kurz zusammenzieh',
Es ging dem Hute fast wie der Philosophie.

FRIEDRICH GOTTLIEB KLOPSTOCK

Das Rosenband

Im Frühlingsschatten fand ich sie;
Da band ich sie mit Rosenbändern.
Sie fühlt' es nicht und schlummerte.

Ich sah sie an; mein Leben hing
Mit diesem Blick an ihrem Leben!
Ich fühlt' es wohl und wußt' es nicht.

Doch lispelt' ich ihr sprachlos zu
Und rauschte mit den Rosenbändern:
Da wachte sie vom Schlummer auf.

The subsequent fortunes of the hat will be related in the second
book. The heirs never left it as they found it; the externals were
new, but the hat itself was and remained old. And, to cut a long
story short, the hat had much the same fate as philosophy.

The Chain of Roses

I found her in the spring shade and I bound her with chains of
roses; she did not feel it and went on slumbering.

I looked at her; by this glance my life hung from her life. I felt
this, but did not realize it.

But I whispered speechlessly to her and rustled the chains of
roses. Then she woke up from her sleep.

Sie sah mich an; ihr Leben hing
Mit diesem Blick an meinem Leben,
Und um uns ward's Elysium.

Die frühen Gräber

WILLKOMMEN, o silberner Mond,
Schöner, stiller Gefährt' der Nacht!
Du entfliehst? Eile nicht, bleib, Gedankenfreund!
Sehet, er bleibt, das Gewölk wallte nur hin.

Des Maies Erwachen ist nur
Schöner noch wie die Sommernacht,
Wenn ihm Tau, hell wie Licht, aus der Locke träuft,
Und zu dem Hügel herauf rötlich er kommt.

Ihr Edleren, ach, es bewächst
Eure Male schon ernstes Moos!
O wie war glücklich ich, als ich noch mit euch
Sahe sich röten den Tag, schimmern die Nacht.

She looked at me: by that glance her life hung from my life, and round us suddenly was Elysium.

The Graves of Friends who Died Young

WELCOME, O silver moon, lovely tranquil companion of the night! You withdraw? Do not hasten away, stay, you friend to thought! Look, she is staying, after all, it was only the clouds which passed over.

The only thing that is even more lovely than the summer night is the awakening of May, when dew, bright as light, drops from her hair and she comes up redly over the hill.

You noble ones, alas, mournful moss is already growing on your monuments! How happy I was, when in your company I saw the day redden and night shimmer!

Wißbegierde

AUCH Gott spricht. Von der Sprache des Ewigen
Erblickt das Auge mehr wie das Ohr von ihr
   Hört; und nur leis' ist seine Stimme,
     Wenn uns die Traub' und die Blume labet.

Dort in den Welten tun den Bewohnenden
Viel Geistesführer weiter die Schöpfung auf,
   Viel Sinne. Reicher, schöner Kenntnis
     Freuen sie droben sich, Gott vernehmend.

Es sank die Sonne, Dämmerung kam, der Mond
Ging auf, begeisternd funkelte Hesperus:
   O, welche inhaltsvolle Worte
     Gottes, der redete, sah mein Auge!

Das Licht schwand. Donner halleten, Sturm, des Meers
Getös war schön und schrecklich, erhob das Herz:
   O, welche inhaltsvolle Worte
     Gottes, der redete, hört' ich tönen!

Desire for Knowledge

EVEN God speaks! The eye sees more of the language of the
Eternal than the ear hears, and when grape and flower refresh us
His voice is only faint.

In the worlds above many guides of the spirit – many senses –
will make further revelations of the creation to those who dwell
there. There they enjoy richness and beauty of knowledge in
apprehending God.

The sun went down, twilight came; the moon rose, Hesperus
shone and inspired me. Oh, how pregnant with meaning were the
words of God – for it was He who was speaking – which my eye
saw!

The light faded. Thunderclaps rumbled, the storm and the roar-
ing of the sea were beautiful and awe-inspiring and exalted my heart.
Oh, how pregnant with meaning were the words of God – for it
was He who was speaking – which I heard sounding!

Gott herrschet, winkend, leitend, wie Wesen auch,
Die frei sind, handeln, herrscht für die Gegenwart
   Und für die Zukunft! Spricht durch Tat auch,
     Welche die Sterblichen tun, die Gottheit?

Wenn dieses ist, (wer glühet, der Unruh' voll,
Nicht hier vom Durst, zu wissen!): was tut sie kund
   Durch Siege derer, die des Menschen
     Rechte nicht nur, die sie selber leugnen?

Weil am Gestad' ich wandle des Ozeans,
Auf dem wir all' einst schweben, enthüll' ich's bald.
   Ich will die heiße Wißbegier denn
     Löschen! Sie bleibt; sie ist heilig Feuer!

Saat sä'n sie, deren Ernte Verwildrung ist!
Des Menschen Rechte leugnen sie, leugnen Gott!
   Schweigt jetzt, nicht leitend, Gott? und kannst du,
     Furchtbares Schweigen, nur du uns bessern?

God rules, beckoning, directing, as beings act who are free; He rules the present and the future. Does God speak, too, through the deeds mortals do?

If this is so (and who does not glow with restless thirst to know?) what does He reveal through the triumphs of those who deny not only human rights but even God Himself?

As I wander on the shores of the ocean, on which we shall all of us drift at last, I shall soon discover it. I want to quench my burning desire for knowledge. It remains, it is a holy fire!

They sow a seed, the harvest of which is desolation. They deny human rights and deny God. Does not God now keep silence, withholding His guidance? And can you alone, terrible silence, save us?

MATTHIAS CLAUDIUS

Abendlied

DER Mond ist aufgegangen,
die goldnen Sternlein prangen
am Himmel hell und klar;
der Wald steht schwarz und schweiget,
und aus den Wiesen steiget
der weiße Nebel wunderbar.

Wie ist die Welt so stille
und in der Dämmrung Hülle
so traulich und so hold!
Als eine stille Kammer,
wo ihr des Tages Jammer
verschlafen und vergessen sollt.

Seht ihr den Mond dort stehen? –
Er ist nur halb zu sehen,
und ist doch rund und schön!
So sind wohl manche Sachen,
die wir getrost belachen,
weil unsre Augen sie nicht sehn.

Evening Hymn

THE moon has risen, the little golden stars are shining out bright
and clear in the sky; the forest stands out black and silent, and the
white mist rises wondrously from the meadows.

How quiet the world is, how cosy and friendly in the mantle of
the dusk, like a quiet room where you may sleep away the sorrows
of the day and forget them.

Can you see the moon up there? Only half of it is visible, but it
is round and beautiful for all that. It is the same with many things
which we laugh at without thinking, because our eyes cannot see
them.

Wir stolze Menschenkinder
sind eitel arme Sünder,
und wissen gar nicht viel;
wir spinnen Luftgespinste
und suchen viele Künste
und kommen weiter von dem Ziel.

Gott, laß uns dein Heil schauen,
auf nichts Vergänglichs trauen,
nicht Eitelkeit uns freun!
Laß uns einfältig werden,
und vor dir hier auf Erden
wie Kinder fromm und fröhlich sein!

Wollst endlich sonder Grämen
aus dieser Welt uns nehmen
durch einen sanften Tod!
Und, wenn du uns genommen,
laß uns in Himmel kommen,
du unser Herr und unser Gott!

So legt euch denn, ihr Brüder,
in Gottes Namen nieder;
kalt ist der Abendhauch.
Verschon uns, Gott! mit Strafen,
und laß uns ruhig schlafen!
Und unsern kranken Nachbar auch!

We proud human beings are only poor sinners and have but
little knowledge. We spin fabrics out of air and run after many
tricks and only get farther away from the goal.

God, let us see Thy salvation, let us not trust to any transitory
thing nor take pleasure in vanity! Give us simplicity and let us be
happy and gentle as children before Thee here on earth.

We pray Thee at the last to take us from the world without regret
by an easy death, and when Thou hast taken us, let us go to Heaven,
Thou our Lord and our God!

Then brothers, lie down in God's name; the evening breeze is
chill. Punish us not O God, and let us sleep peacefully – and our
sick neighbour too.

Ein Wiegenlied, bei Mondenschein zu singen

So schlafe nun, du Kleine!
Was weinest du?
Sanft ist im Mondenscheine
und süß die Ruh'.

Auch kommt der Schlaf geschwinder,
und sonder Müh';
Der Mond freut sich der Kinder,
und liebet sie.

Er liebt zwar auch die Knaben,
doch Mädchen mehr,
gießt freundlich schöne Gaben
von oben her

auf sie aus, wenn sie saugen,
recht wunderbar;
schenkt ihnen blaue Augen
und blondes Haar.

Alt ist er wie ein Rabe,
sieht manches Land;
mein Vater hat als Knabe
ihn schon gekannt.

Lullaby by Moonlight

Now sleep little girl, why are you crying? Rest is soft and sweet
in the moonlight, and sleep comes quicker and easier. The moon
delights in children and loves them. He likes little boys, but he
likes little girls better, and in his friendly way he pours marvellous
gifts down upon them when they suck, gives them blue eyes and
fair hair. He is as old as a raven, and sees a lot of the world; when
my father was a boy he already knew him,/and soon after her

Und bald nach ihren Wochen
hat Mutter mal
mit ihm von mir gesprochen:
sie saß im Tal,

in einer Abendstunde,
den Busen bloß,
ich lag mit offnem Munde
in ihrem Schoß.

Sie sah mich an, für Freude
ein Tränchen lief,
der Mond beschien uns beide,
ich lag und schlief.

Da sprach sie: «Mond, o! scheine,
ich hab' sie lieb,
schein Glück für meine Kleine!»
Ihr Auge blieb

noch lang am Monde kleben
und flehte mehr.
Der Mond fing an zu beben,
als hörte er,

und denkt nun immer wieder
an diesen Blick,

churching my mother spoke to him about me. She was sitting in the
valley in the evening; her bosom was open, and I lay in her lap, my
mouth gaping. She looked at me, and a tear of joy ran down her
face; the moon shone on us both; I lay and slept. Then she said:
'O moon, shine down happiness on my little girl, I love her.' Her
eyes remained fixed on the moon for a long time and begged for
more things too. The moon began to quiver, as if he had heard,
and now he keeps thinking of that look / and shines down nothing

und scheint von hoch hernieder
mir lauter Glück.

Er schien mir unterm Kranze
ins Brautgesicht,
und bei dem Ehrentanze;
du warst noch nicht.

Motetto als der erste Zahn durch war

VIKTORIA! Viktoria!
Der kleine weiße Zahn ist da.
Du Mutter! komm, und Groß und Klein
im Hause! kommt, und kuckt hinein,
und seht den hellen weißen Schein.

Der Zahn soll Alexander heißen.
Du liebes Kind! Gott halt' ihn dir gesund,
und geb' dir Zähne mehr in deinen kleinen Mund,
und immer was dafür zu beißen!

but happiness upon me. He shone into my face under my bridal
garland, and at my wedding dance; you weren't there yet.

Motet, when the First Tooth Was Through

HURRAH hurrah, the little white tooth is there. Mother come, and
everyone in the house, grown-ups and children, look inside and see
the bright white gleam! The tooth shall be called William the Con-
queror! Dear child, God preserve it for you, and give you more
teeth in your little mouth, and always something for them to bite
on!

Der Tod und das Mädchen

Das Mädchen: VORÜBER! Ach, vorüber!
geh, wilder Knochenmann!
Ich bin noch jung, geh, Lieber!
und rühre mich nicht an.

Der Tod: Gib deine Hand, du schön und zart
Gebild!
Bin Freund und komme nicht zu strafen.
Sei gutes Muts! ich bin nicht wild,
sollst sanft in meinen Armen schlafen!

GOTTFRIED AUGUST BÜRGER

Lenore

LENORE fuhr um's Morgenrot
Empor aus schweren Träumen:
«Bist untreu, Wilhelm, oder tot?
Wie lange willst du säumen?» –
Er war mit König Friedrichs Macht
Gezogen in die Prager Schlacht
Und hatte nicht geschrieben,
Ob er gesund geblieben.

Death and the Girl

THE GIRL: Go past, oh, go past, go cruel man of bones! I am still young, please go, and do not touch me!

Death: Give me your hand, you fair and tender creature; I am a friend and do not come to punish. Do not be afraid, I am not cruel. You shall sleep softly in my arms.

Lenore

LENORE started up at dawn out of heavy dreams: 'William, are you faithless, or dead? How much longer will you delay?' He had gone with King Frederick's army into the Battle of Prague and had not written to say that he was safe.

Der König und die Kaiserin,
Des langen Haders müde,
Erweichten ihren harten Sinn
Und machten endlich Friede;
Und jedes Heer, mit Sing und Sang,
Mit Paukenschlag und Kling und Klang
Geschmückt mit grünen Reisern,
Zog heim zu seinen Häusern.

Und überall, all überall,
Auf Wegen und auf Stegen,
Zog Alt und Jung dem Jubelschall
Der Kommenden entgegen.
«Gottlob!» rief Kind und Gattin laut,
«Willkommen!» manche frohe Braut.
Ach! aber für Lenoren
War Gruß und Kuß verloren.

Sie frug den Zug wohl auf und ab
Und frug nach allen Namen;
Doch keiner war, der Kundschaft gab,
Von allen, so da kamen.

The King and the Empress, weary of long strife, had softened
their hard hearts and made peace at last. And both armies, with
singing and shouting, with drums beating and bands playing,
decked with green branches, were returning back to their homes.

And everywhere, all over the place, on high roads and by-roads,
old and young went out towards the joyous noise of the returning
soldiers. 'Thank God,' cried children and wives aloud. 'Welcome,'
cried many glad brides. But ah, no greeting and kiss was in store for
Lenore.

She went up and down the ranks asking, and asked the name of
each man; but there was no one, of all those who returned, who
gave her any information. / And when the army had passed through

Als nun das Heer vorüber war,
Zerraufte sie ihr Rabenhaar
Und warf sich hin zur Erde
Mit wütiger Gebärde.

Die Mutter lief wohl hin zu ihr:
«Ach, daß sich Gott erbarme!
Du trautes Kind, was ist mit dir?»
Und schloß sie in die Arme. –
«O Mutter, Mutter! hin ist hin!
Nun fahre Welt und alles hin!
Bei Gott ist kein Erbarmen.
O weh, o weh mir Armen!» –

«Hilf Gott, hilf! Sieh uns gnädig an!
Kind, bet' ein Vaterunser!
Was Gott tut, das ist wohlgetan.
Gott, Gott erbarmt sich unser!» –
«O Mutter, Mutter! eitler Wahn!
Gott hat an mir nicht wohlgetan!
Was half, was half mein Beten?
Nun ist's nicht mehr vonnöten.» –

she tore her raven hair and threw herself with crazed movements on the ground.

Her mother indeed ran to her: 'Oh, may God have mercy on us! Dear child, what is the matter with you?' and took her in her arms. 'Oh, mother, mother, what's gone is gone! Now the world and everything can go too! God has no mercy. Alas, alas for me!'

'Help us, O God, help us, look down in Thy mercy upon us! Child, say the Lord's prayer! What God does is well done indeed. God, God does have mercy on us!' 'Oh, mother, mother, that is foolish delusion, God has not done well by me! What was the use, what was the use of my prayers? Now there is no need for them.'

«Hilf Gott, hilf! Wer den Vater kennt,
Der weiß, er hilft den Kindern.
Das hochgelobte Sakrament
Wird deinen Jammer lindern.»
«O Mutter, Mutter, was mich brennt,
Das lindert mir kein Sakrament!
Kein Sakrament mag Leben
Den Toten wiedergeben.» –

«Hör', Kind! Wie, wenn der falsche Mann
Im fernen Ungarlande
Sich seines Glaubens abgetan
Zum neuen Ehebande?
Laß fahren, Kind, sein Herz dahin!
Er hat es nimmermehr Gewinn:
Wann Seel' und Leib sich trennen,
Wird ihn sein Meineid brennen.» –

«O Mutter, Mutter! hin ist hin!
Verloren ist verloren!
Der Tod, der Tod ist mein Gewinn!
O wär' ich nie geboren!
Lisch aus, mein Licht, auf ewig aus!
Stirb hin, stirb hin in Nacht und Graus!
Bei Gott ist kein Erbarmen;
O weh, o weh mir Armen!» –

'Help us, O God, help us! Who knows the Father knows that
He helps His children. The holy sacrament will ease your sorrow.'
'Oh, mother, mother, no sacrament will ease what is burning me!
No sacrament can give back life to the dead!'
'Listen, child, what if the false-hearted man has renounced his
faith in distant Hungary to enter a new marriage bond? Let his
heart go, my child, he will never profit from it! When soul and
body part his perjury will burn him!'
'Oh, mother, mother, what's gone is gone and what's lost is lost
for good! Death, death is what I shall gain, oh, I wish I had never
been born! Go out, my candle, out for ever, die, die in night and
horror! God has no mercy! Alas, alas for me!'

«Hilf Gott, hilf! Geh' nicht ins Gericht
Mit deinem armen Kinde!
Sie weiß nicht, was die Zunge spricht;
Behalt' ihr nicht die Sünde!
Ach, Kind, vergiß dein irdisch Leid
Und denk' an Gott und Seligkeit,
So wird doch deiner Seelen
Der Bräutigam nicht fehlen.»

«O Mutter! was ist Seligkeit?
O Mutter! was ist Hölle?
Bei ihm, bei ihm ist Seligkeit,
Und ohne Wilhelm Hölle! –
Lisch aus, mein Licht, auf ewig aus!
Stirb hin, stirb hin in Nacht und Graus!
Ohn' ihn mag ich auf Erden,
Mag dort nicht selig werden.»

So wütete Verzweifelung
Ihr in Gehirn und Adern.
Sie fuhr mit Gottes Vorsehung

'Help, God, help! Enter not into judgement with Thy poor child! She does not know what her tongue is saying, reckon it not to her as a sin! Oh, child, forget your earthly sorrow and think of God and salvation, if you do this your soul will have its bridegroom!'

'Oh, mother, what is salvation? Oh, mother, what is hell? Salvation is with him, and without William it is hell! Go out, my candle, out for ever, die, die in night and horror! Without him there is no salvation for me on earth or in heaven!'

Thus despair raged in her brain and veins; she went on presumptuously repining against God's providence,/beat her breast

Vermessen fort zu hadern,
Zerschlug den Busen und zerrang
Die Hand bis Sonnenuntergang,
Bis auf am Himmelsbogen
Die goldnen Sterne zogen.

Und außen, horch! ging's trapp trapp trapp,
Als wie von Rosseshufen,
Und klirrend stieg ein Reiter ab
An des Geländers Stufen.
Und horch! und horch! den Pfortenring
Ganz lose, leise, klinglingling!
Dann kamen durch die Pforte
Vernehmlich diese Worte:

«Holla, holla! Tu auf, mein Kind!
Schläfst, Liebchen, oder wachst du?
Wie bist noch gegen mich gesinnt?
Und weinest oder lachst du?» –
«Ach, Wilhelm, du? ... So spät bei Nacht? ...
Geweinet hab' ich und gewacht;
Ach, großes Leid erlitten!
Wo kommst du hergeritten?» –

and wrung her hands until sundown, until the golden stars came up
in the arch of heaven.
    And outside, hark, the sound of clop, clop, clop like horse's
hooves; and a rider got down jingling at the bottom of the steps.
And hark, and hark, the loose ring on the gate went tinglingling!
Then these words came audibly through the gate:
    'Hallo there! open the gate my child! Are you asleep, love, or
awake? How do you feel about me, and are you crying or laughing?'
    'Oh, William, it's you? So late at night? I have been lying awake
crying – Oh I have gone through great sorrow! Where have you
come from?'

«Wir satteln nur um Mitternacht.
Weit ritt ich her von Böhmen.
Ich habe spät mich aufgemacht
Und will dich mit mir nehmen.» –
«Ach, Wilhelm, erst herein geschwind!
Den Hagedorn durchsaust der Wind,
Herein, in meinen Armen,
Herzliebster, zu erwarmen!» –

«Laß sausen durch den Hagedorn.
Laß sausen, Kind, laß sausen!
Der Rappe scharrt; es klirrt der Sporn.
Ich darf allhier nicht hausen.
Komm, schürze, spring und schwinge dich
Auf meinen Rappen hinter mich!
Muß heut' noch hundert Meilen
Mit dir ins Brautbett eilen.» –

«Ach! Wolltest hundert Meilen noch
Mich heut' ins Brautbett tragen?
Und horch! es brummt die Glocke noch,
Die elf schon angeschlagen.» –

'We do not saddle till midnight. I have ridden all the way from Bohemia. I started late and I will take you with me.' 'Oh, William, quickly, come inside first! The wind is whistling through the thorn, come in, into my arms, to get warm!'

'Let it whistle through the thorn, let it whistle, child, let it whistle! My black horse is stamping, my spurs jingle, I cannot spend the night here. Come, tuck in your skirt, jump up and vault on to my black behind me. I still have hundred miles to go with you to our bridal bed!'

'What, would you want to take me a hundred miles today to our bridal bed? And listen, the bell is still booming, it has already begun to strike eleven!'/'That's neither here nor there, the moon is shining

«Sieh hin, sieh her! der Mond scheint hell.
Wir und die Toten reiten schnell.
Ich bringe dich, zur Wette,
Noch heut' ins Hochzeitbette.» –

«Sag' an, wo ist dein Kämmerlein?
Wo? wie dein Hochzeitbettchen?» –
«Weit, weit von hier! ... Still, kühl und klein! ...
Sechs Bretter und zwei Brettchen!» –
«Hat's Raum für mich?» – «Für dich und mich!
Komm, schürze, spring und schwinge dich
Die Hochzeitsgäste hoffen;
Die Kammer steht uns offen.»

Schön Liebchen schürzte, sprang und schwang
Sich auf das Roß behende;
Wohl um den trauten Reiter schlang
Sie ihre Lilienhände;
Und hurre hurre, hop hop hop!
Ging's fort in sausendem Galopp,
Daß Roß und Reiter schnoben
Und Kies und Funken stoben.

---

bright. We and the dead ride quickly. I'll bring you, I'll wager, to your marriage bed before tomorrow!'

'But tell me, where is your room, where is it? and what is your marriage bed like?' 'Far, far from here, quiet, cool, and small, six planks and two boards!' 'Is there room for me?' 'For you and me! Come, tuck in your skirt, jump and vault up! The wedding guests are waiting, the bride chamber is open for us!'

His sweetheart tucked in her skirt, jumped and vaulted up nimbly on to the horse; she twined her lily-white hands round the dear horseman; and hey, hey, hop, hop, hop away they went at a rousing gallop so that horse and rider snorted and sparks and stones flew.

Zur rechten und zur linken Hand,
Vorbei an ihren Blicken,
Wie flogen Anger, Heid' und Land!
Wie donnerten die Brücken! –
«Graut Liebchen auch? ... Der Mond scheint hell!
Hurrah! Die Toten reiten schnell!
Graut Liebchen auch vor Toten?» –
«Ach nein! ... Doch laß die Toten!» –

Was klang dort für Gesang und Klang?
Was flatterten die Raben? ...
Horch Glockenklang! Horch Totensang:
«Laßt uns den Leib begraben!»
Und näher zog ein Leichenzug
Der Sarg und Totenbahre trug.
Das Lied war zu vergleichen
Dem Unkenruf in Teichen.

«Nach Mitternacht begrabt den Leib
Mit Klang und Sang und Klage!
Jetzt führ' ich heim mein junges Weib;
Mit, mit zum Brautgelage! ...

How the country on the right hand and on the left, village green
and heather, flew past their gaze, how the bridges thundered! 'Are
you afraid, sweetheart! The moon is shining bright' Hurrah! the
dead ride quickly! Are you afraid of the dead, sweetheart?' 'Oh,
no – but let the dead be!'
   What was that sound of music and song? Why did the ravens
flutter? Listen, the sound of bells! Listen, a funeral chant: 'Let us
commit the body to the earth!' And there approached a funeral pro-
cession, carrying coffin and bier, the chant sounded like bullfrogs
croaking in ponds.
   'Wait until after midnight to bury the body with chant and
music and lament! Now I am bringing home my young bride, come
with me to the bridal feast!/Come here, sexton, come with the choir

Komm, Küster, hier! komm mit dem Chor
Und gurgle mir das Brautlied vor!
Komm, Pfaff', und sprich den Segen,
Eh' wir zu Bett uns legen!»

Still Klang und Sang ... Die Bahre schwand ...
Gehorsam seinem Rufen,
Kam's, hurre hurre! nachgerannt
Hart hinters Rappen Hufen.
Und immer weiter, hop hop hop!
Ging's fort in sausendem Galopp,
Daß Roß und Reiter schnoben
Und Kies und Funken stoben.

Wie flogen rechts, wie flogen links
Die Hügel, Bäum' und Hecken!
Wie flogen links und rechts und links
Die Dörfer, Städt' und Flecken! –
«Graut Liebchen auch? ... Der Mond scheint hell!
Hurrah! Die Toten reiten schnell!
Graut Liebchen auch vor Toten?» –
«Ach! Laß sie ruhn, die Toten.» –

and bawl the bridal song to me! Come, parson, and pronounce
the blessing before we go to bed!'
 Music and song fell silent, the bier disappeared; obedient to his
call, they all came hey, hey running after right behind the black
horse's hooves. And still onward, hop, hop, hop they went at a
rousing gallop so that horse and rider snorted and stones and
sparks flew.
 How they flew on the right, how they flew on the left, hills,
trees, and hedges! How they flew, left and right and left again, vil-
lages, towns, and hamlets! – 'Are you afraid, sweetheart? The
moon is shining brightly. Hurrah! the dead ride quickly! Are you
afraid of the dead, sweetheart?' 'Oh, let the dead rest in peace!'

Sieh da! sieh da! Am Hochgericht
Tantz' um des Rades Spindel,
Halb sichtbarlich bei Mondenlicht,
Ein luftiges Gesindel.
«Sa sa! Gesindel, hier! komm hier!
Gesindel, komm und folge mir!
Tanz' uns den Hochzeitsreigen,
Wann wir das Bett besteigen!» –

Und das Gesindel, husch husch husch!
Kam hinten nachgeprasselt,
Wie Wirbelwind am Haselbusch
Durch dürre Blätter rasselt.
Und weiter, weiter, hop hop hop!
Ging's fort in sausendem Galopp,
Daß Roß und Reiter schnoben
Und Kies und Funken stoben.

Wie flog, was rund der Mond beschien,
Wie flog es in die Ferne!
Wie flogen oben überhin
Der Himmel und die Sterne! –

Look there, look there, by the gibbet, half visible in the moon-
light an airy gang is dancing round the axle of the wheel. 'Hey
there, you gang, come here! All of you come and follow me! Dance
the bridal dance for us when we get into bed!'

And the company, quick, quick, quick came bustling after them
as eddying winds rustle through dry leaves on the hazel bush. And
on they go hop, hop, hop, away at a rousing gallop so that horse
and rider snorted and stones and sparks flew.

How it all flew by, the moonlit scene, how it flew into the dis-
tance! How the stars and the sky above flew by over their heads!

«Graut Liebchen auch? ... Der Mond scheint hell!
Hurrah! Die Toten reiten schnell! –
Graut Liebchen auch vor Toten?» –
«O weh! Laß ruhn die Toten!» –

«Rapp'! Rapp'! mich dünkt, der Hahn schon ruft...
Bald wird der Sand verrinnen ...
Rapp'! Rapp'! ich wittre Morgenluft ...
Rapp'! tummle dich von hinnen!
Vollbracht, vollbracht ist unser Lauf!
Das Hochzeitbette tut sich auf!
Die Toten reiten schnelle! –
Wir sind, wir sind zur Stelle.»

Rasch auf ein eisern Gittertor
Ging's mit verhängtem Zügel;
Mit schwanker Gert' ein Schlag davor
Zersprengte Schloß und Riegel.
Die Flügel flogen klirrend auf,
Und über Gräber ging der Lauf;
Es blinkten Leichensteine
Rundum im Mondenscheine.

'Are you afraid, sweetheart? The moon is shining brightly!
Hurrah! The dead ride quickly! Are you afraid of the dead, sweet-
heart?' 'Oh, let the dead rest in peace!'
    'Up, black! – I think the cock is already crowing – soon the
sands will run out – up, black! I sniff the morning air – up, black!
quick away from here! Our ride is over, over! the marriage bed
opens! The dead ride quickly! We are there, we are there at last!'
    With loose reins he rode straight for an iron-barred gate, a blow
from his pliant switch burst lock and bolt. The gates flew open
with a clatter, and on they rode over graves. All around grave-
stones glittered in the moonlight.

Ha sieh! Ha sieh! Im Augenblick,
Huhu! ein gräßlich Wunder!
Des Reiters Koller, Stück für Stück,
Fiel ab wie mürber Zunder.
Zum Schädel ohne Zopf und Schopf,
Zum nackten Schädel ward sein Kopf,
Sein Körper zum Gerippe
Mit Stundenglas und Hippe.

Hoch bäumte sich, wild schnob der Rapp'
Und sprühte Feuerfunken;
Und hui! war's unter ihr hinab
Verschwunden und versunken.
Geheul! Geheul aus hoher Luft,
Gewinsel kam aus tiefer Gruft
Lenorens Herz mit Beben
Rang zwischen Tod und Leben.

Nun tanzten wohl bei Mondenglanz
Rundum herum im Kreise
Die Geister einen Kettentanz
Und heulten diese Weise:
«Geduld! Geduld! Wenn's Herz auch bricht!
Mit Gott im Himmel hadre nicht!
Des Leibes bist du ledig;
Gott sei der Seele gnädig!»

Ah, look, ah, look! in that moment ugh! a gruesome miracle!
The horseman's uniform, piece by piece, dropped off like rotten
tinder. His head turned into a skull, a naked skull without scalp or
queue; his body became a skeleton with hour-glass and scythe.

The black horse reared high and snorted wildly and gave off
sparks of fire; and in a trice it had sunk away and disappeared under
her. Shrieking, shrieking came from high in the air, wailing came
from deep in the tombs. Lenore's quaking heart battled between
death and life.

Now the spirits danced indeed by the light of the moon, a round
dance, hand in hand, and wailed these words: 'Patience! Patience!
Even if your heart breaks! Do not quarrel with God in heaven!
Your body you have lost, may God have mercy on your soul!'

LUDWIG HEINRICH CHRISTOPH HÖLTY

Vermächtnis

IHR Freunde, hänget, wann ich gestorben bin,
Die kleine Harfe hinter dem Altar auf,
    Wo an der Wand die Totenkränze
        Manches verstorbenen Mädchens schimmern.

Der Küster zeigt dann freundlich dem Reisenden
Die kleine Harfe, rauscht mit dem roten Band,
    Das, an der Harfe festgeschlungen,
        Unter den goldenen Saiten flattert.

Oft, sagt er staunend, tönen im Abendrot
Von selbst die Saiten, leise wie Bienenton;
    Die Kinder, hergelockt vom Kirchhof,
        Hörten's, und sahn, wie die Kränze bebten.

Bequest

FRIENDS, when I am dead, hang up the little harp on the wall behind the altar, where the funeral wreaths of many dead maidens glimmer.

The friendly sexton will show the little harp to visitors and rustle the red ribbon that is tied to the harp and flutters beneath the golden strings.

'Often,' he will say, wondering, 'in the sunset the strings sound by themselves softly, like the hum of bees; the children, drawn here from the churchyard, have heard it and seen how the wreaths quivered.'

Auf den Tod einer Nachtigall

SIE ist dahin, die Maienlieder tönte,
    Die Sängerin,
Die durch ihr Lied den ganzen Hain verschönte,
    Sie ist dahin!
Sie, deren Ton mir in die Seele hallte,
    Wenn ich am Bach,
Der durch Gebüsch im Abendgolde wallte,
    Auf Blumen lag!

Sie gurgelte tief aus der vollen Kehle
    Den Silberschlag:
Der Widerhall in seiner Felsenhöhle
    Schlug leis ihn nach.
Die ländlichen Gesäng' und Feldschalmeien
    Erklangen drein;
Es tanzeten die Jungfraun ihre Reihen
    Im Abendschein.

Auf Moose horcht' ein Jüngling mit Entzücken
    Dem holden Laut,
Und schmachtend hing an ihres Lieblings Blicken
    Die junge Braut;

On the Death of a Nightingale

SHE is gone, the singer who sang May-time songs, who with her singing made the whole wood seem more beautiful, she is gone. She, whose note echoed in my soul when I lay among the flowers by the stream as it swirled through the bushes in the gold of the evening.

She trilled her silvery notes from the depths of her sonorous throat; the echo in its rocky cavern softly repeated them. Rustic songs and pipes mingled with them; the girls used to dance their rounds in the evening glow.

Lying on the moss, a young man listened transported to the delightful sound, and his young betrothed watched with emotion every glance of her beloved;/at every one of your fugues they

Sie drückten sich bei jeder deiner Fugen
   Die Hand einmal,
Und hörten nicht, wenn deine Schwestern schlugen,
   O Nachtigall!

Sie lauschten dir, bis dumpf die Abendglocke
   Des Dorfes klang
Und Hesperus, gleich einer goldnen Flocke,
   Aus Wolken drang;
Und gingen dann im Wehn der Maienkühle
   Der Hütte zu,
Mit einer Brust voll zärtlicher Gefühle,
   Voll süßer Ruh.

JOHANN WOLFGANG VON GOETHE

Mailied

W IE herrlich leuchtet
Mir die Natur!
Wie glänzt die Sonne!
Wie lacht die Flur!

Es dringen Blüten
Aus jedem Zweig
Und tausend Stimmen
Aus dem Gesträuch

pressed each other's hands and did not listen, O nightingale, when your sisters sang.

They listened to you until the faint sound of the village curfew was heard and Hesperus, like a flake of gold, came out of the clouds; and then, in the cool evening breeze of May they went down to the cottage, their breasts filled with tenderness, filled with sweet peace.

May Song

How splendidly nature glows for me! How the sun shines, how the fields laugh!

Blossoms burst out of every twig and a thousand voices out of the bushes

Und Freud' und Wonne
Aus jeder Brust.
O Erd', o Sonne!
O Glück, o Lust!

O Lieb', o Liebe!
So golden schön,
Wie Morgenwolken
Auf jenen Höhn!

Du segnest herrlich
Das frische Feld,
Im Blütendampfe
Die volle Welt.

O Mädchen, Mädchen,
Wie lieb' ich dich!
Wie blickt dein Auge!
Wie liebst du mich!

So liebt die Lerche
Gesang und Luft,
Und Morgenblumen
Den Himmelsduft,

And joy and pleasure from every breast. O earth, O sun, O
happiness, O delight!
O love, O love, so golden and beautiful like morning clouds on
the mountains up there.
You bless the fresh field with splendour, the plenteous world in
the haze of blossom.
O sweetheart, sweetheart, how I love you! How your eyes
gleam! How you love me!
The lark loves song and air, and morning flowers love the scent
of the sky in the same way

Wie ich dich liebe
Mit warmem Blut,
Die du mir Jugend
Und Freud und Mut

Zu neuen Liedern
Und Tänzen gibst.
Sei ewig glücklich,
Wie du mich liebst!

Heidenröslein

SAH ein Knab ein Röslein stehn,
Röslein auf der Heiden,
War so jung und morgenschön,
Lief er schnell, es nah zu sehn,
Sah's mit vielen Freuden.
Röslein, Röslein, Röslein rot,
Röslein auf der Heiden.

Knabe sprach: Ich breche dich,
Röslein auf der Heiden!

As I love you with warm blood, you who give me youth and joy
and courage
To make new songs and dance new dances. Be everlastingly
happy with this happiness in which you love me!

Rose on the Common

A BOY saw a rose growing, a rose on the common, it was so young,
and beautiful as the morning, he ran quickly to see it more closely
and looked at it with great pleasure. Rose, rose, red rose, rose on
the common.

The boy said: I am going to pick you, rose on the common.

Röslein sprach: Ich steche dich,
Daß du ewig denkst an mich,
Und ich will's nicht leiden.
Röslein, Röslein, Röslein rot,
Röslein auf der Heiden.

Und der wilde Knabe brach
's Röslein auf der Heiden;
Röslein wehrte sich und stach,
Half ihr doch kein Weh und Ach,
Mußt' es eben leiden.
Röslein, Röslein, Röslein rot,
Röslein auf der Heiden.

Willkommen und Abschied

Es schlug mein Herz, geschwind zu Pferde!
Es war getan fast eh gedacht.
Der Abend wiegte schon die Erde,
Und an den Bergen hing die Nacht;
Schon stand im Nebelkleid die Eiche,
Ein aufgetürmter Riese, da,
Wo Finsternis aus dem Gesträuche
Mit hundert schwarzen Augen sah.

The rose said: I shall prick you so badly that you will always re-member me, and I will not let you. Rose, rose, red rose, rose on the common.

And the rough boy picked the rose on the common. The rose defended herself and pricked him, no cries and complaints were any use, she had to put up with it. Rose, rose, red rose, rose on the common.

Welcome and Farewell

My heart beat: go quickly, on horseback! it was done almost be-fore the thought was over. The evening was already cradling the earth, and night hung on the mountains. The oak, a towering giant, already stood in its cloak of mist where darkness peered out of the bushes with a hundred black eyes.

Der Mond von einem Wolkenhügel
Sah kläglich aus dem Duft hervor,
Die Winde schwangen leise Flügel,
Umsausten schauerlich mein Ohr;
Die Nacht schuf tausend Ungeheuer,
Doch frisch und fröhlich war mein Mut:
In meinen Adern welches Feuer!
In meinem Herzen welche Glut!

Dich sah ich, und die milde Freude
Floß von dem süßen Blick auf mich;
Ganz war mein Herz an deiner Seite
Und jeder Atemzug für dich.
Ein rosenfarbnes Frühlingswetter
Umgab das liebliche Gesicht,
Und Zärtlichkeit für mich – ihr Götter!
Ich hofft' es, ich verdient' es nicht!

Doch ach, schon mit der Morgensonne
Verengt der Abschied mir das Herz:
In deinen Küssen welche Wonne!
In deinem Auge welcher Schmerz!
Ich ging, du standst und sahst zur Erden,

The moon from a hill of clouds looked out mournfully through
the haze; the winds moved quiet wings and brushed tremulously
past my ears. The night created a thousand monsters, but my cour-
age was joyous and determined. What fire in my veins, what a glow
in my heart!

I saw you, and the generous joy flowed upon me from your
sweet glance. My heart was wholly at your side, and every breath I
drew was for you. Rosy spring sunshine surrounded your delight-
ful face, and tenderness for me – ye Gods, I hoped for it, I did not
deserve it!

But alas, with the morning sun parting already constricted my
heart. What delight was in your kisses, what pain in your eyes. I
went, you stood looking at the ground,/and looked after me with

Und sahst mir nach mit nassem Blick:
Und doch, welch Glück, geliebt zu werden!
Und lieben, Götter, welch ein Glück!

Ganymed

WIE im Morgenglanze
Du rings mich anglühst,
Frühling, Geliebter!
Mit tausendfacher Liebeswonne
Sich an mein Herz drängt
Deiner ewigen Wärme
Heilig Gefühl,
Unendliche Schöne!

Daß ich dich fassen möcht'
In diesen Arm!

Ach, an deinem Busen
Lieg ich, schmachte,
Und deine Blumen, dein Gras
Drängen sich an mein Herz.
Du kühlst den brennenden
Durst meines Busens,

wet eyes. And yet, what bliss to be loved, and to love, ye gods what bliss!

Ganymede

BELOVED, Spring, how you glow at me in the morning light! With thousandfold joy of love the sanctified feeling of your everlasting warmth penetrates to my heart, infinite beauty!

Oh, that I could embrace you in my arms!

Alas, I lie at your breast, languishing, and your flowers, your grass nestle at my heart. You cool the burning thirst of my breast,

Lieblicher Morgenwind!
Ruft drein die Nachtigall
Liebend nach mir aus dem Nebeltal.

Ich komm, ich komme!
Wohin? Ach, wohin?

Hinauf! Hinauf strebt's.
Es schweben die Wolken
Abwärts, die Wolken
Neigen sich der sehnenden Liebe.
Mir! Mir!
In euerm Schoße
Aufwärts!
Umfangend umfangen!
Aufwärts an deinen Busen,
All liebender Vater!

Der König in Thule

Es war ein König in Thule
Gar treu bis an das Grab,
Dem sterbend seine Buhle
Einen goldnen Becher gab.

---

delightful morning breeze! The nightingale calls lovingly to me out of the mist-filled valley.

I am coming, I am coming! Where to, oh, where?

Up! Upwards I strive. The clouds descend gently, the clouds bow down to yearning love. To me! to me! In your lap, upwards! Embracing, embraced! Upwards to Thy bosom, all-loving Father.

The King in Thule

THERE was a King in Thule, faithful to the grave, to whom his consort on her deathbed gave a golden cup.

Es ging ihm nichts darüber,
Er leert' ihn jeden Schmaus;
Die Augen gingen ihm über,
So oft er trank daraus.

Und als er kam zu sterben,
Zählt' er seine Städt' im Reich,
Gönnt' alles seinen Erben,
Den Becher nicht zugleich.

Er saß beim Königsmahle,
Die Ritter um ihn her,
Auf hohem Vätersaale,
Dort auf dem Schloß am Meer.

Dort stand der alte Zecher,
Trank letzte Lebensglut,
Und warf den heiligen Becher
Hinunter in die Flut.

Er sah ihn stürzen, trinken
Und sinken tief ins Meer.
Die Augen täten ihm sinken;
Trank nie einen Tropfen mehr.

He valued nothing higher, he emptied it at every feast, the tears ran from his eyes every time he drank from it.

And when he came to die, he counted up the cities in his kingdom, left everything gladly to his heirs, but not his cup.

He sat at the royal feast table, the knights round him, in the lofty ancestral hall yonder in the castle by the sea.

There he stood, the aged toper, drank the last glow of life, and threw the sanctified cup down into the waves.

He saw it fall, fill, and sink deep down into the sea. His eyes closed, he never drank another drop.

Prometheus

BEDECKE deinen Himmel, Zeus,
Mit Wolkendunst
Und übe, dem Knaben gleich,
Der Disteln köpft,
An Eichen dich und Bergeshöhn;
Mußt mir meine Erde
Doch lassen stehn
Und meine Hütte, die du nicht gebaut,
Und meinen Herd,
Um dessen Glut
Du mich beneidest.

Ich kenne nichts Ärmeres
Unter der Sonn' als euch, Götter!
Ihr nähret kümmerlich
Von Opfersteuern
Und Gebetshauch
Eure Majestät
Und darbtet, wären
Nicht Kinder und Bettler
Hoffnungsvolle Toren.

Prometheus

COVER your heaven, Zeus, with cloudy vapour and try out your strength, like a boy beheading thistles, on oaks and mountain-tops; even so, you have to let my earth stand and my cottage, which you did not build, and my hearth, whose glow you envy me.

I do not know anything more miserable under the sun than you, gods. You feed your majesty scantily on sacrificed tribute and the breath of prayer, and you would starve if children and beggars were not hopeful fools.

Da ich ein Kind war,
Nicht wußte, wo aus noch ein,
Kehrt ich mein verirrtes Auge
Zur Sonne, als wenn drüber wär'
Ein Ohr, zu hören meine Klage,
Ein Herz wie meins,
Sich des Bedrängten zu erbarmen.

Wer half mir
Wider der Titanen Übermut?
Wer rettete vom Tode mich,
Von Sklaverei?
Hast du nicht alles selbst vollendet,
Heilig glühend Herz?
Und glühtest jung und gut,
Betrogen, Rettungsdank
Dem Schlafenden da droben?

Ich dich ehren? Wofür?
Hast du die Schmerzen gelindert
Je des Beladenen?
Hast du die Tränen gestillet

When I was a child and had come to my wit's end, I turned my confused eye towards the sun, as though there were an ear above it to hear my lament, a heart like mine to take pity on me in my straits. Who helped me against the arrogant Titans? Who saved me from death and slavery? Holy glowing heart, did you not achieve all this yourself? And did you not radiate, betrayed in your youth and innocence, thanks for your deliverance to the sleeper up above?

I honour you? What for? Have you ever soothed my pains when I was heavy laden? Have you ever dried my tears/when I was

Je des Geängsteten?
Hat nicht mich zum Manne geschmiedet
Die allmächtige Zeit
Und das ewige Schicksal,
Meine Herrn und deine?

Wähntest du etwa,
Ich sollte das Leben hassen,
In Wüsten fliehen,
Weil nicht alle
Blütenträume reiften?

Hier sitz ich, forme Menschen
Nach meinem Bilde,
Ein Geschlecht, das mir gleich sei,
Zu leiden, zu weinen,
Zu genießen und zu freuen sich,
Und dein nicht zu achten,
Wie ich!

Gretchen am Spinnrade

MEINE Ruh' ist hin,
Mein Herz ist schwer;
Ich finde sie nimmer
Und nimmermehr.

---

frightened? Was it not almighty time and eternal fate, my masters and yours, who forged me into a man?

Did you imagine that I would hate life, flee into the wilderness because all my flowery dreams did not mature?

I sit here, make men in my image, a race which shall be like me, to suffer, to weep, to enjoy and be glad, and to ignore you, as I do!

Gretchen at the Spinning-wheel

MY peace is gone, my heart is heavy; I shall never find peace again, never any more.

Wo ich ihn nicht hab',
Ist mir das Grab,
Die ganze Welt
Ist mir vergällt.

Mein armer Kopf
Ist mir verrückt,
Mein armer Sinn
Ist mir zerstückt.

Meine Ruh' ist hin,
Mein Herz ist schwer;
Ich finde sie nimmer
Und nimmermehr.

Nach ihm nur schau' ich
Zum Fenster hinaus,
Nach ihm nur geh' ich
Aus dem Haus.

Sein hoher Gang,
Sein' edle Gestalt,
Seines Mundes Lächeln,
Seiner Augen Gewalt,

Any place where I have not got him is the grave to me, the whole world is soured.

My poor head is turned, my poor mind is in pieces.

My peace is gone, my heart is heavy; I shall never find peace again, never any more.

When I look out of the window I am looking out for him, when I leave the house I am going to him.

His stately gait, his noble figure, the smile of his mouth, the power of his eyes

Und seiner Rede
Zauberfluß,
Sein Händedruck,
Und ach, sein Kuß!

Meine Ruh' ist hin,
Mein Herz ist schwer;
Ich finde sie nimmer
Und nimmermehr.

Mein Busen drängt
Sich nach ihm hin.
Ach dürft' ich fassen
Und halten ihn,

Und küssen ihn,
So wie ich wollt',
An seinen Küssen
Vergehen sollt'!

And the magic stream of his speech, the pressure of his hand and ah! his kiss!

My peace is gone, my heart is heavy; I shall never find peace again, never any more.

My bosom yearns towards him – oh, if only I could embrace him and hold him

And kiss him to my heart's desire, so that my senses would swoon under his kisses!

Auf dem See

UND frische Nahrung, neues Blut
Saug ich aus freier Welt;
Wie ist Natur so hold und gut,
Die mich am Busen hält!
Die Welle wieget unsern Kahn
Im Rudertakt hinauf,
Und Berge, wolkig himmelan,
Begegnen unserm Lauf.

Aug, mein Aug, was sinkst du nieder?
Goldne Träume, kommt ihr wieder?
Weg, du Traum! so gold du bist;
Hier auch Lieb und Leben ist.

Auf der Welle blinken
Tausend schwebende Sterne,
Weiche Nebel trinken
Rings die türmende Ferne;
Morgenwind umflügelt
Die beschattete Bucht,
Und im See bespiegelt
Sich die reifende Frucht.

On the Lake

AND I suck fresh nourishment, new blood out of untrammelled nature: how gracious and generous is Nature, who holds me to her bosom! The waves rock our boat to the rhythm of the oars, and mountains, cloudily reaching for heaven, meet our course.

Eye of mine, why do you droop? Golden dreams, are you coming back? Away, dreams, golden as you are; here, too, there is love and life.

On the waves a thousand hovering stars gleam, soft mists drink up the towering horizon round us; the morning breeze flutters round the shaded bay and the ripening fruit is reflected in the lake.

Herbstgefühl

FETTER grüne, du Laub,
Am Rebengeländer
Hier mein Fenster herauf!
Gedrängter quellet,
Zwillingsbeeren, und reifet
Schneller und glänzend voller!
Euch brütet der Mutter Sonne
Scheideblick, euch umsäuselt
Des holden Himmels
Fruchtende Fülle;
Euch kühlet des Mondes
Freundlicher Zauberhauch,
Und euch betauen, ach!
Aus diesen Augen
Der ewig belebenden Liebe
Vollschwellende Tränen.

Wanderers Nachtlied I

DER du von dem Himmel bist,
Alles Leid und Schmerzen stillest,
Den, der doppelt elend ist,
Doppelt mit Erquickung füllest,

Autumn

GREEN more lushly, you leaves on the vine trellis climbing up to
my window! Swell tighter, you pairs of berries and ripen faster and
gleamingly fuller! The farewell glance of mother sun is hatching
you out, the fruiting bounty of the generous sky is rustling round
you, the friendly magic breath of the moon is cooling you, and you
are bedewed, alas, by great welling tears of ever-vivifying love
from my eyes.

Wanderer's Song at Night I

YOU, who come from Heaven and calm all sorrow and pain, and
fill those who are doubly wretched with double consolation, / Oh,

Ach, ich bin des Treibens müde!
Was soll all der Schmerz und Lust?
Süßer Friede,
Komm, ach komm in meine Brust!

Wanderers Nachtlied II

ÜBER allen Gipfeln
Ist Ruh,
In allen Wipfeln
Spürest du
Kaum einen Hauch:
Die Vögelein schweigen im Walde.
Warte nur! Balde
Ruhest du auch.

An den Mond

FÜLLEST wieder Busch und Tal
Still mit Nebelglanz,
Lösest endlich auch einmal
Meine Seele ganz;

I am weary of it all, where is the sense in all this pain and joy?
Sweet peace, come, oh, come, into my breast.

Wanderer's Song at Night II

CALM is over all the hill-tops, in all the tree-tops you can hardly
feel a breath. The little birds are hushed in the wood. Wait, soon you
will be calm too.

To the Moon

AGAIN you quietly fill coppice and valley with misty splendour, and
at long last too, you set my spirit free.

Breitest über mein Gefild
Lindernd deinen Blick,
Wie des Freundes Auge mild
Über mein Geschick.

Jeden Nachklang fühlt mein Herz
Froh- und trüber Zeit,
Wandle zwischen Freud' und Schmerz
In der Einsamkeit.

Fließe, fließe, lieber Fluß!
Nimmer werd' ich froh!
So verrauschte Scherz und Kuß,
Und die Treue so.

Ich besaß es doch einmal,
Was so köstlich ist!
Daß man doch zu seiner Qual
Nimmer es vergißt!

Rausche, Fluß, das Tal entlang,
Ohne Rast und Ruh,
Rausche, flüstre meinem Sang
Melodien zu!

You spread your comforting glance over my landscape, like the gentle eye of a friend surveying my fate.

My heart feels every echo of pleasant and sad times; I walk between joy and pain, in solitude.

Flow, flow on, dear river! I shall never be happy. Laughter and kisses faded away like this, and faithfulness too.

Once, after all, I did possess what is so precious! and to think that to one's misery one can never forget it!

Roar, river, along the valley, restless and unquiet! Roar, whisper the music to my song,

Wenn du in der Winternacht
Wütend überschwillst,
Oder um die Frühlingspracht
Junger Knospen quillst.

Selig, wer sich vor der Welt
Ohne Haß verschließt,
Einen Freund am Busen hält
Und mit dem genießt,

Was, von Menschen nicht gewußt,
Oder nicht bedacht,
Durch das Labyrinth der Brust
Wandelt in der Nacht.

Gesang der Geister über den Wassern

D ES Menschen Seele
Gleicht dem Wasser:
Vom Himmel kommt es,
Zum Himmel steigt es,
Und wieder nieder
Zur Erde muß es,
Ewig wechselnd.

When in winter nights you rage and overflow or purl round the
spring glory of young buds.

Happy the man who can withdraw without resentment from the
world, keep a friend at his side, and enjoy with him

What, unknown or neglected by men, walks in the night through
the labyrinth of the heart.

Song of the Spirits over the Waters

THE soul of man is like water: it comes from heaven, it rises to
heaven and is bound to return back to the earth, alternating ever-
lastingly.

Strömt von der hohen
Steilen Felswand
Der reine Strahl,
Dann stäubt er lieblich
In Wolkenwellen
Zum glatten Fels,
Und leicht empfangen
Wallt er verschleiernd,
Leisrauschend
Zur Tiefe nieder.

Ragen Klippen
Dem Sturz entgegen,
Schäumt er unmutig
Stufenweise
Zum Abgrund.

Im flachen Bette
Schleicht er das Wiesental hin,
Und in dem glatten See
Weiden ihr Antlitz
Alle Gestirne.

Wind ist der Welle
Lieblicher Buhler;
Wind mischt vom Grund aus
Schäumende Wogen.

The pure jet streams from the high, steep cliff, then entrancingly
it turns to cloudy waves of vapour against the smooth rock, and,
gently received, it undulates, veiling everything and softly murmur-
ing, down to the valley.

If rocks stand out against its descent it foams angrily step by
step down into the abyss.

In the even bed it steals through the valley meadows, and in the
smooth lake all the constellations joyously mirror their faces.

The wind is the delightful lover of the wave, wind mixes foam-
ing combers from the ground swell.

Seele des Menschen,
Wie gleichst du dem Wasser!
Schicksal des Menschen,
Wie gleichst du dem Wind!

Grenzen der Menschheit

WENN der uralte,
Heilige Vater
Mit gelassener Hand
Aus rollenden Wolken
Segnende Blitze
Über die Erde sät,
Küß ich den letzten
Saum seines Kleides,
Kindliche Schauer
Treu in der Brust.

Denn mit Göttern
Soll sich nicht messen
Irgendein Mensch.
Hebt er sich aufwärts
Und berührt
Mit dem Scheitel die Sterne,

Soul of man, how like water you are! Fate of man, how like the wind!

Bounds of Humanity

WHEN the ancient holy Father with tranquil hand sows beneficent lightning flashes out of rolling clouds over the earth, I kiss the extreme hem of his garment, childlike tremors faithful in my breast.

For no man may measure himself against the gods. If he lifts himself upwards and touches the stars with his head,/then his un-

Nirgends haften dann
Die unsichern Sohlen,
Und mit ihm spielen
Wolken und Winde.

Steht er mit festen,
Markigen Knochen
Auf der wohlgegründeten
Dauernden Erde,
Reicht er nicht auf,
Nur mit der Eiche
Oder der Rebe
Sich zu vergleichen.

Was unterscheidet
Götter von Menschen?
Daß viele Wellen
Vor jenen wandeln,
Ein ewiger Strom:
Uns hebt die Welle,
Verschlingt die Welle,
Und wir versinken.

Ein kleiner Ring
Begrenzt unser Leben,
Und viele Geschlechter
Reihen sich dauernd
An ihres Daseins
Unendliche Kette.

certain feet find no hold anywhere and he becomes the plaything of clouds and winds.

If he stands with firm sturdy bones on the firmly founded lasting earth, he does not reach up far enough to bear comparison even with the oak or the vine.

What distinguishes gods from men? Before them many waves progress, an eternal river; we are lifted by the wave and swallowed up by the wave, and we sink down and away.

A narrow ring bounds our life, and many generations are continually linking on to the endless chain of their existence.

Erlkönig

WER reitet so spät durch Nacht und Wind?
Es ist der Vater mit seinem Kind;
Er hat den Knaben wohl in dem Arm,
Er faßt ihn sicher, er hält ihn warm.

«Mein Sohn, was birgst du so bang dein Gesicht?» –
Siehst, Vater, du den Erlkönig nicht?
Den Erlenkönig mit Kron' und Schweif? –
«Mein Sohn, es ist ein Nebelstreif.»

«Du liebes Kind, komm, geh mit mir!
Gar schöne Spiele spiel' ich mit dir;
Manch' bunte Blumen sind an dem Strand,
Meine Mutter hat manch gülden Gewand.»

Mein Vater, mein Vater, und hörest du nicht,
Was Erlenkönig mir leise verspricht? –
«Sei ruhig, bleibe ruhig, mein Kind;
In dürren Blättern säuselt der Wind.»

«Willst, feiner Knabe, du mit mir gehn?
Meine Töchter sollen dich warten schön;
Meine Töchter führen den nächtlichen Reihn,
Und wiegen und tanzen und singen dich ein.»

Erlking

WHO is that riding so late through the dark and the wind? It is the father with his child. He has the boy snug in his arms, he holds him safely, he keeps him warm.

'My son, why are you scared and hiding your face?' – 'Father, can't you see the Erlking, the Erlking with crown and robe?' – 'My son, it is a wisp of cloud.'

'You, darling child, come, go with me! I will play lovely games with you; there are heaps of bright flowers on the shore; my mother has lots of golden clothes.'

'Father, father, can't you hear what the Erlking whispers and promises me?' – 'Hush, don't fret, my son, it is the wind rustling in the dry leaves.'

Mein Vater, mein Vater, und siehst du nicht dort
Erlkönigs Töchter am düstern Ort? –
«Mein Sohn, mein Sohn, ich seh' es genau:
Es scheinen die alten Weiden so grau.»

«Ich liebe dich, mich reizt deine schöne Gestalt;
Und bist du nicht willig, so brauch' ich Gewalt.» –
Mein Vater, mein Vater, jetzt faßt er mich an!
Erlkönig hat mir ein Leids getan! –

Dem Vater grauset's, er reitet geschwind,
Er hält in Armen das ächzende Kind,
Erreicht den Hof mit Müh' und Not;
In seinen Armen das Kind war tot.

Harfenspieler

WER nie sein Brot mit Tränen aß,
Wer nie die kummervollen Nächte
Auf seinem Bette weinend saß,
Der kennt euch nicht, ihr himmlischen Mächte.

'Pretty boy, will you come with me? My daughters shall look after you nicely, every night they will dance the round and will rock and dance and sing you to sleep.'/
'Oh, father, oh, father, can't you see the Erlking's daughters over there at that dismal place?' – 'My son, my son, I can see it plain; it is the old willows that gleam all grey.'
'I love you, your beautiful shape excites me, and if you won't come willingly I will use force.' – 'Father, father, now he's taking hold of me! He has hurt me, the Erlking has!' –
The father is terrified, he rides fast, he holds the groaning child in his arms, it is all he can do to reach the farm; in his arms the child was dead.

The Harper's Song

WHO never ate his bread with tears, who never sat weeping the long miserable nights away on his bed, does not know you, you heavenly powers!

Ihr führt ins Leben uns hinein,
Ihr laßt den Armen schuldig werden,
Dann überlaßt ihr ihn der Pein:
Denn alle Schuld rächt sich auf Erden.

Mignon

KENNST du das Land, wo die Zitronen blühn,
Im dunkeln Laub die Gold-Orangen glühn,
Ein sanfter Wind vom blauen Himmel weht,
Die Myrte still und hoch der Lorbeer steht,
Kennst du es wohl? Dahin! Dahin
Möcht ich mit dir, o mein Geliebter, ziehn.

Kennst du das Haus? Auf Säulen ruht sein Dach,
Es glänzt der Saal, es schimmert das Gemach,
Und Marmorbilder stehn und sehn mich an:
Was hat man dir, du armes Kind, getan?
Kennst du es wohl? Dahin! Dahin
Möcht ich mit dir, o mein Beschützer, ziehn.

You lead us into life, you let the poor wretch incur guilt, then you leave him to his torment, for all guilt brings vengeance upon itself on earth.

Mignon

Do you know the country where the lemon-trees flower, and the golden oranges glow in the dark foliage, where a gentle wind blows from the blue sky, where the myrtle stands quiet and the bay-tree towers up? Do you know it? That is where, oh, that is where, I would like to go with you, O my beloved!
You know the house? Its roof rests on pillars, the hall gleams, the rooms glitter, and marble statues stand and look at me: 'Poor child, what have they done to you?' You know it? That is where, oh, that is where I would like to go with you, O my protector!

Kennst du den Berg und seinen Wolkensteg?
Das Maultier sucht im Nebel seinen Weg,
In Höhlen wohnt der Drachen alte Brut,
Es stürzt der Fels und über ihn die Flut;
Kennst du ihn wohl? Dahin! Dahin
Geht unser Weg! O Vater, laß uns ziehn!

Parzenlied

Es fürchte die Götter
Das Menschengeschlecht!
Sie halten die Herrschaft
In ewigen Händen
Und können sie brauchen,
Wie's ihnen gefällt.

Der fürchte sie doppelt,
Den je sie erheben!
Auf Klippen und Wolken
Sind Stühle bereitet
Um goldene Tische.

You know the mountain range and its cloudy path? The mule seeks its way there in the mist; the ancient brood of dragons dwells in caves; the cliff falls sheer and the stream over it. You know it? That is there, oh, that is where our way leads, oh, father, let us go!

Song of the Fates

THE children of men must fear the gods! They bear rule in their eternal hands and can use it as they please.

The man they lift up must fear them doubly! On precipices and clouds seats are prepared round golden tables.

Erhebet ein Zwist sich,
So stürzen die Gäste,
Geschmäht und geschändet,
In nächtliche Tiefen,
Und harren vergebens,
Im Finstern gebunden,
Gerechten Gerichtes.

Sie aber, sie bleiben
In ewigen Festen
An goldenen Tischen.
Sie schreiten vom Berge
Zu Bergen hinüber:
Aus Schlünden der Tiefe
Dampft ihnen der Atem
Erstickter Titanen,
Gleich Opfergerüchen,
Ein leichtes Gewölke.

Es wenden die Herrscher
Ihr segnendes Auge
Von ganzen Geschlechtern,
Und meiden, im Enkel
Die ehmals geliebten
Still redenden Züge
Des Ahnherrn zu sehn.

When a quarrel arises the guests fall, scorned and shamed, into depths of night and bound in darkness await a fair trial in vain.

But they, they stay in eternal feasting at golden tables. They stride across from mountain to mountain; the breath of stifled Titans steams up to them from crevasses in the depths, like savours of sacrifice, a faint vapour.

The rulers turn away their auspicious eye from whole families and avoid recognizing in the grandson the once loved, quietly eloquent features of his ancestor.

So sangen die Parzen;
Es horcht der Verbannte
In nächtlichen Höhlen,
Der Alte, die Lieder,
Denkt Kinder und Enkel
Und schüttelt das Haupt.

Römische Elegien V

Froh empfind ich mich nun auf klassischem Boden
    begeistert;
    Vor- und Mitwelt spricht lauter und reizender mir.
Hier befolg' ich den Rat, durchblättre die Werke der
    Alten
    Mit geschäftiger Hand, täglich mit neuem Genuß.
Aber die Nächte hindurch hält Amor mich anders
    beschäftigt;
    Werd' ich auch halb nur gelehrt, bin ich doch doppelt
    beglückt.

So sang the Fates; the exile, the aged one, listens in caves of
night to the songs, thinks of his children and grandchildren and
shakes his head.

Roman Elegies V

Here on classic ground I feel joyously inspired; the worlds of the
past and of the present speak to me more distinctly and enchant-
ingly. Here I do as [Horace] advised and with eager hand I turn the
pages of the classics every day with fresh enjoyment. But all
through the nights Amor keeps me busy in quite a different way;
even if I am only being half instructed, I am being made doubly
happy./And am I not gaining instruction when I see the shape of a

Und belehr' ich mich nicht, indem ich des lieblichen
    Busens
    Formen spähe, die Hand leite die Hüften hinab?
Dann versteh ich den Marmor erst recht; ich denk und
    vergleiche,
    Sehe mit fühlendem Aug, fühle mit sehender Hand.
Raubt die Liebste denn gleich mir einige Stunden des
    Tages,
    Gibt sie Stunden der Nacht mir zur Entschädigung
    hin.
Wird doch nicht immer geküßt, es wird vernünftig
    gesprochen;
    Überfällt sie der Schlaf, lieg' ich und denke mir viel.
Oftmals hab ich auch schon in ihren Armen gedichtet
    Und des Hexameters Maß leise mit fingernder Hand
Ihr auf den Rücken gezählt. Sie atmet in lieblichem
    Schlummer,
    Und es durchglühet ihr Hauch mir bis ins Tiefste die
    Brust.
Amor schüret die Lamp indes und denket der Zeiten,
    Da er den nämlichen Dienst seinen Triumvirn getan.

lovely bosom and let my hands glide down over the hips? Then at
last I understand the marbles, I think and compare, see with a sen-
tient eye and feel with a seeing hand. Even though my sweetheart
may rob me of a few hours of day, she gives me hours of the night
as a compensation. After all, we do not kiss all the time, we often
indulge in serious conversation. If sleep comes upon her I lie and
think hard. I have often even made poetry in her arms and softly
counted the measure of the hexameter on her back with my fingers.
She breathes in delightful sleep, and her breath glows through me
to the bottom of my heart. Amor trims the lamp and thinks back to
the times when he used to perform the same service for his trium-
virs [Catullus, Tibullus and Propertius].

Römische Elegien IX

HERBSTLICH leuchtet die Flamme vom ländlich
geselligen Herde,
Knistert und glänzet, wie rasch! sausend vom Reisig
empor.
Diesen Abend erfreut sie mich mehr; denn eh noch zur
Kohle
Sich das Bündel verzehrt, unter die Asche sich neigt,
Kommt mein liebliches Mädchen. Dann flammen Reisig
und Scheite,
Und die erwärmete Nacht wird uns ein glänzendes
Fest.
Morgen frühe geschäftig verläßt sie das Lager der Liebe,
Weckt aus der Asche behend Flammen aufs neue
hervor.
Denn vor andern verlieh der Schmeichlerin Amor die
Gabe,
Freude zu wecken, die kaum still wie zu Asche
versank.

Roman Elegies IX

THE flame shines autumnally from the rustic sociable hearth,
crackles and gleams – how quickly – and speeds up from the
kindling. This evening it will give me greater pleasure, for before
the faggot has burnt down to an ember and bends under the ash,
my lovely girl will be here. Then kindling and logs will flare up and
we shall make the warmed night into a glowing festivity. To-
morrow morning she will busily leave the couch of love and
nimbly rouse fresh flames out of the ashes. For, above all gifts,
Amor gave this engaging creature that of awakening joys which had
barely sunk, like ashes, into quietness.

Römische Elegien XIV

ZÜNDE mir Licht an, Knabe! – «Noch ist es hell. Ihr verzehret
  Öl und Docht nur umsonst. Schließet die Läden doch nicht!
Hinter die Häuser entwich, nicht hinter den Berg, uns die Sonne!
  Ein halb Stündchen noch währt's bis zum Geläute der Nacht.» –
Unglückseliger! Geh und gehorch! Mein Mädchen erwart' ich.
  Tröste mich, Lämpchen, indes, lieblicher Bote der Nacht!

Nähe des Geliebten

ICH denke dein, wenn mir der Sonne Schimmer
  Vom Meere strahlt;
Ich denke dein, wenn sich des Mondes Flimmer
  In Quellen malt.

Roman Elegies XIV

BOY, light the lamp! 'It is still bright, you will only use oil and wick all for nothing. Why, do not close the shutters! The sun has only gone behind the houses, not behind the mountains! It will be half an hour before the evening angelus.' Go, wretch, and do as you are told! I am expecting my sweetheart. Meanwhile, lamp, you must console me, you delightful messenger of night!

Presence of the Beloved

I THINK of you when the shimmer of the sun gleams from the sea;
I think of you when the glimmering light of the moon is reflected in the springs.

Ich sehe dich, wenn auf dem fernen Wege
Der Staub sich hebt,
In tiefer Nacht, wenn auf dem schmalen Stege
Der Wandrer bebt.

Ich höre dich, wenn dort mit dumpfem Rauschen
Die Welle steigt.
Im stillen Haine geh' ich oft zu lauschen,
Wenn alles schweigt.

Ich bin bei dir, du seist auch noch so ferne,
Du bist mir nah!
Die Sonne sinkt, bald leuchten mir die Sterne.
O wärst du da!

Dauer im Wechsel

HIELTE diesen frühen Segen,
Ach, nur Eine Stunde fest!
Aber vollen Blütenregen
Schüttelt schon der laue West.

I see you when the dust rises on the distant road; in deep night, when the traveller trembles on the narrow bridge.

I hear you, when the waves surge with a dull roar; I often go into the quiet copse to listen when all is still.

I am with you; however far away you may be, you are near me. The sun is setting, soon the stars will be shining down on me. If only you were here!

Permanence in Change

IF only even one hour could hold fast this early bounty! But the warm west wind already shakes down a full rain of blooms. / Shall I

Soll ich mich des Grünen freuen,
Dem ich Schatten erst verdankt?
Bald wird Sturm auch das zerstreuen,
Wenn es falb im Herbst geschwankt.

Willst du nach den Früchten greifen,
Eilig nimm dein Teil davon!
Diese fangen an zu reifen,
Und die andern keimen schon;
Gleich mit jedem Regengusse
Ändert sich dein holdes Tal,
Ach, und in demselben Flusse
Schwimmst du nicht zum zweitenmal.

Du nun selbst! Was felsenfeste
Sich vor dir hervorgetan,
Mauern siehst du, siehst Paläste
Stets mit andern Augen an.
Weggeschwunden ist die Lippe,
Die im Kusse sonst genas,
Jener Fuß, der an der Klippe
Sich mit Gemsenfreche maß.

take delight in the green which has just given me shade? When it has fluttered discoloured in the autumn some storm will soon disperse that too.

If you would reach for the fruit, take your share of it promptly! While these are beginning to ripen the others are already germinating. Your gracious vale changes with every shower of rain, and alas you will never swim a second time in the same river.

And you yourself! What stood out before you firm as a rock, you see them all, ramparts and palaces, all the time with changing eyes. The lip, which used to come to life in a kiss, the foot which used to try its strength on the mountains with chamois-like boldness, they have disappeared.

Jene Hand, die gern und milde
Sich bewegte, wohlzutun,
Das gegliederte Gebilde,
Alles ist ein andres nun.
Und was sich an jener Stelle
Nun mit deinem Namen nennt,
Kam herbei wie eine Welle,
Und so eilt's zum Element.

Laß den Anfang mit dem Ende
Sich in Eins zusammenzichn!
Schneller als die Gegenstände
Selber dich vorüberfliehn!
Danke, daß die Gunst der Musen
Unvergängliches verheißt,
Den Gehalt in deinem Busen
Und die Form in deinem Geist.

Gefunden

Ich ging im Walde
So für mich hin,
Und nichts zu suchen,
Das war mein Sinn.

That hand, which used to move with loving generosity to do good, the whole articulated formation, is all something different now. And what now in its place calls itself by your name came like a wave, and like a wave it hastens to its element.

Let the beginning and the end contract into one, let yourself fly by more swiftly than the objects. Give thanks that the favour of the muses promises what is imperishable – the import in your breast and the form in your spirit.

Found

I was walking in the woods all by myself without looking for anything in particular.

Im Schatten sah ich
Ein Blümchen stehn,
Wie Sterne leuchtend,
Wie Äuglein schön.

Ich wollt' es brechen,
Da sagt' es fein:
Soll ich zum Welken
Gebrochen sein?

Ich grub's mit allen
Den Würzlein aus,
Zum Garten trug' ich's
Am hübschen Haus.

Und pflanzt' es wieder
Am stillen Ort;
Nun zweigt es immer
Und blüht so fort.

In a shady place I saw a little flower, glowing like stars, beautiful
as a pair of little eyes.

I was just going to pick it when it said softly, 'Am I to be picked
only to wither?'

I dug it up with all its roots, and carried it to the garden by the
lovely house.

And planted it again in that quiet place; now it keeps putting out
shoots and goes on blossoming.

Selige Sehnsucht

SAGT es niemand, nur den Weisen,
Weil die Menge gleich verhöhnet:
Das Lebend'ge will ich preisen
Das nach Flammentod sich sehnet.

In der Liebesnächte Kühlung,
Die dich zeugte, wo du zeugtest,
Überfällt dich fremde Fühlung
Wenn die stille Kerze leuchtet.

Nicht mehr bleibest du umfangen
In der Finsternis Beschattung,
Und dich reißet neu Verlangen
Auf zu höherer Begattung.

Keine Ferne macht dich schwierig,
Kommst geflogen und gebannt,
Und zuletzt, des Lichts begierig,
Bist du Schmetterling verbrannt.

Und so lang du das nicht hast,
Dieses: Stirb und werde!
Bist du nur ein trüber Gast
Auf der dunklen Erde.

Trance and Transformation

Do not tell anyone but the wise, because the mob will mock immediately: stuff of life is what I praise, that longs to die in flames.

In the assuagement of those nights of love which begot you, in which you have begotten, strange presentiments come upon you when the quiet candle gleams.

You remain no longer held in the overshadowing darkness, and new desire sweeps you upward to more exalted mating.

No distance makes you hesitate, you come flying and enchanted and at last, a moth eager for the light, you are burnt.

And until you have grasped this – 'Die and be transformed!' – you will be nothing but a sorry guest on the sombre earth.

Lied und Gebilde

MAG der Grieche seinen Ton
Zu Gestalten drücken,
An der eignen Hände Sohn
Steigern sein Entzücken;

Aber uns ist wonnereich
In den Euphrat greifen
Und im flüss'gen Element
Hin und wider schweifen.

Löscht' ich so der Seele Brand,
Lied, es wird erschallen;
Schöpft des Dichters reine Hand,
Wasser wird sich ballen.

AN vollen Büschelzweigen,
Geliebte, sieh nur hin!
Laß dir die Früchte zeigen,
Umschalet stachlig grün.

Poetry and Plastic Form

LET the Greek mould his clay into shapes, let him increase his
delight by the fruit of his own hands;
   But our delight is to dip our hands into the Euphrates and to
roam here and there in the fluid element.
   When I have thus cooled the ardour of the soul, song will sound
by itself; when the poet takes it in his pure hand, water will take
shape.

ON the full clustered branches – beloved, look – let me show you
the fruits, husked, prickly-green.

Sie hängen längst geballet,
Still, unbekannt mit sich;
Ein Ast, der schaukelnd wallet,
Wiegt sie geduldiglich.

Doch immer reift von innen
Und schwillt der braune Kern,
Er möchte Luft gewinnen
Und säh' die Sonne gern.

Die Schale platzt, und nieder
Macht er sich freudig los;
So fallen meine Lieder
Gehäuft in deinen Schoß.

Urworte. Orphisch

ΔAIMΩN, *Dämon*

WIE an dem Tag, der dich der Welt verliehen,
Die Sonne stand zum Gruße der Planeten,
Bist alsobald und fort und fort gediehen
Nach dem Gesetz, wonach du angetreten.

They have been hanging there clenched for a long time, quietly,
unbeknown to themselves; a branch, rocking and swaying, has
cradled them patiently.

But all the time the brown heart has been ripening and swelling
from within; it wants to reach the air and would like to see the sun.

The husk splits and down it falls, joyfully freeing itself; just so
my songs fall heaped into your lap.

Words of Ancient Wisdom. Orphic

Fate

As the sun stood to receive the salute of the planets on the day
which gave you to the world, so you began to grow and have con-
tinued ever since, according to the law which governed your set-
ting out./Thus you must be, you cannot escape from yourself, so

So mußt du sein, dir kannst du nicht entfliehen,
So sagten schon Sibyllen, so Propheten;
Und keine Zeit und keine Macht zerstückelt
Geprägte Form, die lebend sich entwickelt.

ΤΥΧΗ, *das Zufällige*

Die strenge Grenze doch umgeht gefällig
Ein Wandelndes, das mit und um uns wandelt;
Nicht einsam bleibst du, bildest dich gesellig,
Und handelst wohl so, wie ein andrer handelt:
Im Leben ists bald hin-, bald widerfällig,
Es ist ein Tand und wird so durchgetandelt.
Schon hat sich still der Jahre Kreis geründet,
Die Lampe harrt der Flamme, die entzündet.

ΕΡΩΣ, *Liebe*

Die bleibt nicht aus! – Er stürzt vom Himmel nieder,
Wohin er sich aus alter Öde schwang,
Er schwebt heran auf luftigem Gefieder
Um Stirn und Brust den Frühlingstag entlang,

Sibyls spoke long ago and Prophets too; and no time and no power can shatter minted form which develops as it lives.

Chance

Yet an element of change which goes with us and about us circumvents the stern law to our delight. You do not stay lonely, you fit yourself into society and act much as others act. In life things are sometimes favourable and sometimes unfavourable, they are toys and we toy with them for what they are worth. Already the cycle of years has quietly completed itself; the lamp awaits the flame which shall set it alight.

Love

That is not withheld! He swoops from heaven, whither he had risen from ancient wastes, he flutters to us with airy wings and hovers all through the spring day round our heads and breasts,

Scheint jetzt zu fliehn, vom Fliehen kehrt er wieder:
Da wird ein Wohl im Weh, so süß und bang.
Gar manches Herz verschwebt im Allgemeinen,
Doch widmet sich das edelste dem Einen.

ΑΝΑΓΚΗ, *Nötigung*

Da ists denn wieder, wie die Sterne wollten:
Bedingung und Gesetz; und aller Wille
Ist nur ein Wollen, weil wir eben sollten,
Und vor dem Willen schweigt die Willkür stille;
Das Liebste wird vom Herzen weggescholten,
Dem harten Muß bequemt sich Will und Grille.
So sind wir scheinfrei denn, nach manchen Jahren,
Nur enger dran, als wir am Anfang waren.

ΕΛΠΙΣ, *Hoffnung*

Doch solcher Grenze, solcher ehrnen Mauer
Höchst widerwärtige Pforte wird entriegelt,
Sie stehe nur mit alter Felsendauer!
Ein Wesen regt sich leicht und ungezügelt:

sometimes he seems to retreat, but returns from his retreating; then
there comes joy in suffering, so sweet and tremulous. Many a heart
tends to diffusion, but it is the noblest that gives itself to the One.

Necessity

Then it is again as the stars decreed: limit and law, and all will is
only a willing because we simply had to, and free choice is silent in
the face of the will; what is most loved is driven with scolding from
the heart, and will and fancy submit to stern compulsion. Thus after
many years we, seemingly free, are only more hemmed in than we
were at the beginning.

Hope

But even this most hideous gate in the brazen boundary walls
can be unlocked, even though it stands with ancient rocklike per-
manence. A Being moves lightly and unconstrainedly, / lifts us up

Aus Wolkendecke, Nebel, Regenschauer
Erhebt sie uns, mit ihr, durch sie beflügelt,
Ihr kennt sie wohl, sie schwärmt durch alle Zonen –
Ein Flügelschlag – und hinter uns Äonen!

WEIß wie Lilien, reine Kerzen,
Sternen gleich, bescheidner Beugung,
Leuchtet aus dem Mittelherzen
Rot gesäumt die Glut der Neigung.

So frühzeitige Narzissen
Blühen reihenweis im Garten.
Mögen wohl die guten wissen,
Wen sie so spaliert erwarten.

DÄMMRUNG senkte sich von oben,
Schon ist alle Nähe fern;
Doch zuerst emporgehoben
Holden Lichts der Abendstern!
Alles schwankt ins Ungewisse,
Nebel schleichen in die Höh;
Schwarzvertiefte Finsternisse
Widerspiegelnd ruht der See.

with her out of cloud cover, fog, and showers of rain and gives us
wings: you know her well, she permeates all zones; one wing-beat
and aeons are behind us!

WHITE as lilies, pure candles, like stars, gently bowing, out of the
hearts in the centre, rimmed with red, the glow of love gleams.
   Thus early narcissi bloom in rows in the garden. Perhaps these
simple flowers know for whom they are on parade.

DUSK descended from above, near things are already far off, but
first comes lifted up the evening star with its gracious light! Every-
thing blurs into indistinctness, mists creep upward, the lake rests
and reflects deepened black darknesses.

Nun im östlichen Bereiche
Ahn ich Mondenglanz und -Glut,
Schlanker Weiden Haargezweige
Scherzen auf der nächsten Flut.
Durch bewegter Schatten Spiele
Zittert Lunas Zauberschein,
Und durchs Auge schleicht die Kühle
Sänftigend ins Herz hinein.

FRIEDRICH ('MALER') MÜLLER

Auf Amors Köcher

M IT furchtbaren Zügen
Des Schicksals leuchtet
Auf Amors gewaltigem
Köcher die Schrift:
Ich trage die süßesten
Pfeile der Wonne;
Ich fasse die bittersten
Pfeile der Schmerzen;
Olympos, Erebus
Ruhen in mir.

Now in the eastern region I sense the gleam and glow of the moon, the branchy hair of the slim willows plays on the near water, the magic light of Luna trembles through the play of moving shadows, and coolness steals through the eye calming into the heart.

Love's Quiver

ON Love's mighty quiver in terrible characters of fate the legend shines: 'I bear the sweetest arrows of joy; I contain the bitterest arrows of pain; Olympus and Erebus both rest in me.'

J. M. R. LENZ

Wo bist du itzt

Wo bist du itzt, mein unvergeßlich Mädchen,
Wo singst du itzt?
Wo lacht die Flur, wo triumphiert das Städtchen,
Das dich besitzt?

Seit du entfernt, will keine Sonne scheinen,
Und es vereint
Der Himmel sich, dir zärtlich nachzuweinen,
Mit deinem Freund.

All unsre Lust ist fort mit dir gezogen,
Still überall
Ist Wald und Feld. Dir nach ist sie geflogen,
Die Nachtigall.

O komm zurück! Schon rufen Hirt und Herden
Dich bang herbei.
Komm bald zurück! Sonst wird es Winter werden
Im Monat Mai.

Where are you now, my unforgettable maiden, where are you singing now? Where is the smiling countryside, where the town that can boast of possessing you?

Since you went the sun will refuse to shine and the sky joins with your admirer in weeping tenderly at your departure.

All our pleasure is gone with you. Silence reigns everywhere over field and woodland. The nightingale, too, has flown after you.

Oh, do come back! Already the shepherds and their flocks anxiously call for you. Come back soon, or it will be winter in the month of May!

C. A. TIEDGE

Elegie auf dem Schlachtfelde bei Kunersdorf

NACHT umfängt den Wald; von jenen Hügeln
Stieg der Tag ins Abendland hinab;
Blumen schlafen, und die Sterne spiegeln
In den Seen ihren Frieden ab.

Mich laßt hier in dieses Waldes Schauern,
Wo der Fichtenschatten mich verbirgt;
Hier soll einsam meine Seele trauern
Um die Menschheit, die der Wahn erwürgt.

Drängt euch um mich her, ihr Fichtenbäume!
Hüllt mich ein, wie eine tiefe Gruft!
Seufzend, wie das Atmen schwerer Träume,
Weh um mich die Stimme dieser Luft.

Hier an dieses Hügels dunkler Spitze
Schwebt, wie Geisterwandel, banges Graun;
Hier, hier will ich vom bemoosten Sitze
Jene Schädelstätten überschaun.

Dolche blinken dort im Mondenscheine,
Wo das Erntefeld des Todes war;
Durcheinander liegen die Gebeine
Der Erschlagnen um den Blutaltar.

Elegy on the Battlefield of Kunersdorf

NIGHT embraces the woods; from those hills the day has gone
down into the west; flowers sleep and the stars reflect their peace
into the lakes. Leave me here in the tremors of this forest where the
shadow of the firs cover me; here my soul shall mourn in solitude
over humanity butchered by delusion. Cluster round me, you pine-
trees, encompass me like a deep vault! Let the voice of this air
breathe round me sighing like the heavy breathing in dreams.
Here, over the dark crest of this hill, fearful horror hovers like the
haunting of spirits. Here, here, from the mossy seat I will look
over this Golgatha.

Daggers gleam over there in the moonlight where the harvest
field of death was. The bones of the slaughtered lie mingled round
the altar of blood./Here lies a head leaning on the enemy's breast,

Ruhig liegt, wie an der Brust des Freundes,
Hier ein Haupt, an Feindes Brust gelehnt,
Dort ein Arm vertraut am Arm des Feindes. –
Nur das Leben haßt, der Tod versöhnt.
O, sie können sich nicht mehr verdammen,
Die hier ruhn; sie ruhen Hand an Hand!
Ihre Seelen gingen ja zusammen,
Gingen über in ein Friedensland;
Haben gern einander dort erwidert,
Was die Liebe gibt und Lieb erhält.
Nur der Sinn der Menschen, noch entbrüdert,
Weist den Himmel weg aus dieser Welt.
Hin eilt dieses Leben, hin zum Ende,
Wo herüber die Zypresse hängt:
Darum reicht einander doch die Hände,
Eh die Gruft euch an einander drängt!

Aber hier, um diese Menschentrümmer,
Hier auf öder Wildnis ruht ein Fluch;
Durch das Feld hin streckt sich Mondenschimmer,
Wie ein weites, weißes Leichentuch.
Dort das Dörfchen unter Weidenbäumen;
Seine Väter sahn die grause Schlacht:

quiet as though on the breast of a friend, there an arm links the arm
of an enemy. – It is life that hates; death reconciles. Oh, they can-
not condemn one another any more, those who lie here; they rest
hand in hand. Their souls went together into a land of peace; there
they gladly return what love gives and what keeps love alive. It is
only the mind of men, still divided from their brothers, that shuts
heaven out of this world. This life hurries on to its close, where the
cypress hangs. Therefore give one another your hands before the
grave forces you together!
    But there is a curse here, round these human ruins, here in this
uncultivated wilderness. The moonlight spreads out over the fields
like a broad white shroud. There the hamlet under the willow-trees;
its fathers saw the dreadful battle./Oh, they rest in peace and in

O sie schlafen ruhig, und verträumen
In den Gräbern jene Flammennacht!
Vor den Hütten, die der Asch entstiegen,
Ragt der alte Kirchenturm empor,
Hält in seinen narbenvollen Zügen
Seine Welt noch *unsern* Tagen vor.
Lodernd fiel um ihn das Dorf zusammen;
Aber ruhig, wie der große Sinn
Seiner Stiftung, sah er auf die Flammen
Der umringenden Verwüstung hin.
Finster blickt er, von der Nacht umgrauet,
Und von Mondesanblick halb erhellt,
Über diesen Hügel, und beschauet,
Wie ein dunkler Geist, das Leichenfeld.

Mag, o Lenz, dein Angesicht hier lächeln?
Jeder Windstoß, der den Wald bewegt,
Ist ein großer Seufzer, der das Röcheln
Der Gefallnen durch die Wildnis trägt.
Diese Greisin, diese düstre Fichte
Zeigt die Narben, die auch *sie* empfing,
Weist dahin, wo blutig die Geschichte
Böser Zeiten ihr vorüberging. [...]

their graves dream away that night of flames. The old church tower stands out in front of the cottages that have risen from the ashes and in its scarred features still holds up its world as a reproach to our days. Round it the village crashed in flames; but tranquil, like the great significance of its foundation, it looked down upon the flames of circumambient destruction. Now it looks grimly out over the hill and, surrounded by grey night, half illumined by the glance of the moon, it gazes like a dark spirit over the field of corpses.

Spring, can your face smile here? Every gust of wind that moves the wood is a great sob, which carries the death-rattle of the fallen through the wilderness. This ancient, this sinister pine shows the scars that it, too, received and points to where the events of evil times passed by.

Hier der See, und dort des Stromes Fluten
Spiegelten zurück das Todesschwert;
Dieser Himmel sah das Opfer bluten;
Dieser Hügel war ein Opferherd;
Hier im Bach hat Menschenblut geflossen;
Wo der Halm im Monde zuckend nickt,
Hat vielleicht ein Auge, halb geschlossen,
Nach der Heimatgegend hingeblickt. [...]
Und der stille Wandrer, welcher traurig
Sich dem Graun der Gegend überläßt,
Fühlt ein dumpfes Ahnen, das so schaurig
Ihm den Atemzug zusammenpreßt.

War es Klang von einer fernen Quelle,
Was so dumpf zu meinem Herzen sprach?
Oder schwebt Geseufz um jede Stelle,
Wo ein Herz, ein Herz voll Liebe, brach?
Ist es Wandel einer düstern Trauer,
Was am Sumpf dem Hagebusch entrauscht,
Und nun schweigt, und, wie ein dunkelgrauer
Nebelstreif, im Nachtgeflüster lauscht? [...]

Sagt, was ist, was gilt ein Menschenleben,
Was die Menschheit vor dem Weltengeist,

The lake here and the waves of the river there reflected the sword
of death; this sky saw the victim bleed, this hill was a place of burnt
offering; here in the stream the blood of men has flowed; where the
grass nods and quivers in the moonlight perhaps an eye, half
closed, looked in the direction of home. And the silent visitor, who
sadly abandons himself to the horror of the scene, feels a dark
premonition which chokes his trembling breath.

Was it the sound of a distant spring which spoke so darkly to my
heart? Or does sobbing float around in every place where a heart,
a loving heart, has broken? Is it the haunting of a dismal grief
which rustles from the hawthorn by the marsh and now is silent and
listening like a dark grey streak of mist in the whispering of night?

Say, what is a human life? what value has it, has humanity in the
eyes of the spirit of the universe/when savage death thus tears the

Wenn der wilde Tod aus den Geweben
Ihres Daseins so die Faden reißt?
Welche Faden sind hier abgerissen!
Und was fällt, wenn nur *ein* Haupt zerfällt! –
Hier stehn wir, und hinter Finsternissen
Steht der hohe Genius der Welt!

Stürme fahren aus dem Schoß der Stille,
Und die Zeit, mit Trümmern wüst umringt,
Zählt am Uferrand der Lebensfülle
Jeden Tropfen, den der Sand verschlingt.
Schwankend irren wir im finstern Sturme;
Wechseltod beherrscht die Finsternis;
Er beraubt den Halm und gibt dem Wurme,
Gibt dem Halm, was er dem Wurm entriß.

Luftig spielt das Laub des Ulmenbaumes
An den frischen Ästen um den Stamm:
Regt darin sich noch ein Rest des Traumes,
Der einmal in Nervensäften schwamm? [...]
Dieser Staub am Wege hing um Seelen;
Wo ich trete, stäubt vielleicht ein Herz.
Gott! und hier aus diesen Augenhöhlen
Starrete zu dir hinauf der Schmerz.

threads from the tissue of its existence? And what threads have been
snapped here! And how much falls, when even one head falls! Here
we stand and behind veils of darkness stands the mighty Genius of
the World!

Storms flash out of the bosom of quiet, and time, surrounded by
a waste of ruins, on the verge of life's profusion counts every drop
which the sand swallows up. We totter aimlessly in the dark storm,
mutual death rules the darkness: he robs the grass to give to the
worm, and gives the grass what he wrested from the worm.

The leaves of the elm dance gracefully on the vigorous branches
round the trunk; is this movement a remnant of a dream which
once swam in corporeal lymph? This dust by the wayside has cur-
tained souls: where I walk perhaps a heart eddies up in dust. And
out of these sockets, O God, pain stared up to Thee.

Welch ein Anblick! – Hieher, Volksregierer,
Hier, bei dem verwitternden Gebein
Schwöre, deinem Volk ein sanfter Führer,
Deiner Welt ein Friedensgott zu sein.
Hier schau her, wenn dich nach Ruhme dürstet!
Zähle diese Schädel, Völkerhirt,
Vor dem Ernste, der dein Haupt, entfürstet,
In die Stille niederlegen wird!
Laß im Traum das Leben dich umwimmern,
Das hier unterging in starres Graun!
Ist es denn so herrlich, sich mit Trümmern
In die Weltgeschichte einzubaun?

Einen Lorbeerkranz verschmähn, ist edel!
Mehr als Heldenruhm ist Menschenglück!
Ein bekränztes Haupt wird auch zum Schädel,
Und der Lorbeerkranz zum Rasenstück!
Cäsar fiel an einem dunkeln Tage
Ab vom Leben, wie entstürmtes Laub;
Friedrich liegt im engen Sarkophage;
Alexander ist ein wenig Staub.

What a sight is this! Hither, ruler of the people, here over the weathered bones swear to be a gentle leader to your people and a god of peace to your world. See here, if you thirst for fame! Count these skulls, shepherd of the nations, in contemplation of the severity which will lay your head, unprinced, away into the stillness. Let the lives which were lost here in rigid horror wail around you in your dreams. Is it so splendid to build yourself a place in the history of the world with ruins?

It is noble to despise a laurel wreath! Human happiness is more than heroes' fame. Even a garlanded head turns to a skull and the laurel wreath to a sod of turf! One dark day Caesar fell from life like a leaf torn off by the gale; Frederic lies in his narrow coffin; Alexander is a little dust. / The great world-stormer is small now; it

Klein ist nun der große Weltbestürmer;
Es verhallte, lauten Donnern gleich;
Längst schon teilten sich in ihn die Würmer,
So wie die Satrapen in sein Reich.

Fließt das Leben auch aus einer Quelle,
Die durch hochbekränzte Tage rinnt;
Irgendwo erscheint die dunkle Stelle,
Wo das Leben stille steht und sinnt. [...]

Dort, dort unten, wo zur letzten Krümme,
Wie ein Strahl, der Lebensweg sich bricht,
Tönet eine feierliche Stimme,
Die dem Wandrer dumpf entgegen spricht:
«Was nicht rein ist, wird in Nacht verschwinden;
Des Verwüsters Hand ist ausgestreckt;
Und die Wahrheit wird den Menschen finden,
Ob ihn Dunkel oder Glanz versteckt!»

all died away, like loud thunderclaps; long ago the worms shared him out as the satraps shared out his empire.

Though life flows from one source which runs through gaily garlanded days, somewhere the dark place becomes apparent where life stands still and reflects.

There, down there where the path of life breaks off like a lightning flash at the last bend in the road, a solemn voice is heard which addresses the wanderer in hollow tones: 'What is not clean will disappear into night; the hand of the destroyer is outstretched; and truth will search man out, whether he hides in darkness or in splendour!'

FRIEDRICH VON SCHILLER

Nänie

Auch das Schöne muß sterben! Das Menschen und
  Götter bezwinget,
  Nicht die eherne Brust rührt es des stygischen Zeus.
Einmal nur erweichte die Liebe den Schattenbeherrscher,
  Und an der Schwelle noch, streng, rief er zurück sein
  Geschenk.
Nicht stillt Aphrodite dem schönen Knaben die Wunde,
  Die in den zierlichen Leib grausam der Eber geritzt.
Nicht errettet den göttlichen Held die unsterbliche
  Mutter,
  Wann er, am skäischen Tor fallend, sein Schicksal
  erfüllt.
Aber sie steigt aus dem Meer mit allen Töchtern des
  Nereus,
  Und die Klage hebt an um den verherrlichten Sohn.
Siehe! Da weinen die Götter, es weinen die Göttinnen
  alle,
  Daß das Schöne vergeht, daß das Vollkommene stirbt.
Auch ein Klaglied zu sein im Mund der Geliebten ist
  herrlich,
  Denn das Gemeine geht klanglos zum Orkus hinab.

Lament

Even beauty has to die; what overcomes men and gods does not
move the iron breast of the Zeus of the Styx. Only once did love
soften the ruler of the shades, and even then he sternly called back
his gift at the very threshold. Aphrodite cannot cure the lovely boy
of the wound the boar savagely ripped in his delicate flesh. When
the god-like hero falls at the Scaean gate and falling fulfils his
destiny, his immortal mother cannot save him; but she rises from
the sea with all the daughters of Nereus, and laments her glorified
son. Look, the gods are weeping and all the goddesses too, weeping
that beauty must pass, that perfect things must die. There is splen-
dour even in this – to be a lament in the mouths of those we loved,
for what has no distinction goes down to Orcus unsung.

Der Abend

Senke, strahlender Gott – die Fluren dürsten
Nach erquickendem Tau, der Mensch verschmachtet,
 Matter ziehen die Rosse –
  Senke den Wagen hinab!

Siehe, wer aus des Meers kristallner Woge
Lieblich lächelnd dir winkt! Erkennt dein Herz sie?
 Rascher fliegen die Rosse,
  Tethys, die göttliche, winkt.

Schnell vom Wagen herab in ihre Arme
Springt der Führer, den Zaum ergreift Cupido,
 Stille halten die Rosse,
  Trinken die kühlende Flut.

An dem Himmel herauf mit leisen Schritten
Kommt die duftende Nacht; ihr folgt die süße
 Liebe. Ruhet und liebet!
  Phöbus, der liebende, ruht.

Evening

Let it descend, radiant god – the fields are thirsty for refreshing dew, man's strength is failing, your horses are dragging, – let your chariot descend!

See who is beckoning to you with welcoming smile from the crystal waves of the sea! Does your heart know her? The horses fly more swiftly; Tethys, the divine, beckons to you.

Swiftly the driver leaps from the chariot into her arms, Cupid seizes the reins, the horses stand still and drink the cooling main.

With silent steps fragrant night ascends into the sky; after her comes sweet love. Rest, and love one another. Phoebus, the lover, is at rest.

Der Handschuh

VOR seinem Löwengarten,
Das Kampfspiel zu erwarten,
Saß König Franz,
Und um ihn die Großen der Krone,
Und rings auf hohem Balkone
Die Damen in schönem Kranz.

Und wie er winkt mit dem Finger,
Auftut sich der weite Zwinger,
Und hinein mit bedächtigem Schritt
Ein Löwe tritt
Und sieht sich stumm
Rings um,
Mit langem Gähnen,
Und schüttelt die Mähnen
Und streckt die Glieder
Und legt sich nieder.

Und der König winkt wieder,
Da öffnet sich behend
Ein zweites Tor,
Daraus rennt
Mit wildem Sprunge
Ein Tiger hervor.

The Glove

KING FRANCIS was sitting at his lion-pit waiting for the fight, round him the lords of the land, and all around, on a high balcony, a fair garland of ladies.

And as he gives a sign with his finger the wide arena opens and with measured tread a lion enters. And looks round without a sound, with a long yawn, and shakes his mane and stretches his legs and lies down.

And again the King gives a sign, and a second gate opens quickly and with a wild bound a tiger rushes out. / When he sees the lion he

Wie der den Löwen erschaut,
Brüllt er laut,
Schlägt mit dem Schweif
Einen furchtbaren Reif
Und recket die Zunge,
Und im Kreise scheu
Umgeht er den Leu
Grimmig schnurrend,
Drauf streckt er sich murrend
Zur Seite nieder.

Und der König winkt wieder,
Da speit das doppelt geöffnete Haus
Zwei Leoparden auf einmal aus,
Die stürzen mit mutiger Kampfbegier
Auf das Tigertier;
Das packt sie mit seinen grimmigen Tatzen,
Und der Leu mit Gebrüll
Richtet sich auf – da wird's still,
Und herum im Kreis,
Von Mordsucht heiß,
Lagern die greulichen Katzen.

Da fällt von des Altans Rand
Ein Handschuh von schöner Hand
Zwischen den Tiger und den Leun
Mitten hinein.

roars loudly, waves his tail in a fearsome ring, flicks his tongue, and cautiously circles the lion, fiercely snarling. Then he lies down at one side, growling.

And the King again gives a sign and the double-doored cage suddenly vomits forth two leopards. In eager lust for battle they fall upon the tiger. He seizes them with his fierce claws, and the lion rises to his feet with a roar – a hush falls, as the dreadful cats hot with lust for slaughter crouch round in a circle.

Then, over the edge of the balcony a glove drops from a fair hand, between the tiger and the lion, right in the middle of them.

Und zu Ritter Delorges spottender Weis'
Wendet sich Fräulein Kunigund:
«Herr Ritter, ist Eure Lieb so heiß,
Wie Ihr mir's schwört zu jeder Stund,
Ei, so hebt mir den Handschuh auf!»

Und der Ritter in schnellem Lauf
Steigt hinab in den furchtbarn Zwinger
Mit festem Schritte,
Und aus der Ungeheuer Mitte
Nimmt er den Handschuh mit keckem Finger.

Und mit Erstaunen und mit Grauen
Sehen's die Ritter und Edelfrauen,
Und gelassen bringt er den Handschuh zurück.
Da schallt ihm sein Lob aus jedem Munde,
Aber mit zärtlichem Liebesblick –
Er verheißt ihm sein nahes Glück –
Empfängt ihn Fräulein Kunigunde.
Und er wirft ihr den Handschuh ins Gesicht:
«Den Dank, Dame, begehr' ich nicht!»
Und verläßt sie zur selben Stunde.

And the Lady Kunigund turns mockingly to the knight de Lorges: 'Sir Knight, if your love is as hot as you constantly swear to me it is, why, pick up my glove for me!'

And the knight with a swift movement steps down into the dreadful pit with sure foot, and with nimble fingers he picks up the glove from between the monsters.

And the knights and the noble ladies watch with amazement and with horror, and nonchalantly he brings back the glove. Then his praise rises from every mouth to meet him, but Lady Kunigund receives him with a tender glance of love – which assures him his bliss is near. And he flings the glove into her face: 'I do not desire your thanks, Lady!' And he leaves her from that moment.

Die Kraniche des Ibykus

ZUM Kampf der Wagen und Gesänge,
Der auf Korinthus' Landesenge
Der Griechen Stämme froh vereint,
Zog Ibykus, der Götterfreund.
Ihm schenkte des Gesanges Gabe,
Der Lieder süßen Mund Apoll;
So wandert' er, an leichtem Stabe,
Aus Rhegium, des Gottes voll.

Schon winkt auf hohem Bergesrücken
Akrokorinth des Wandrers Blicken,
Und in Poscidons Fichtenhain
Tritt er mit frommem Schauder ein.
Nichts regt sich um ihn her, nur Schwärme
Von Kranichen begleiten ihn,
Die fernhin nach des Südens Wärme
In graulichtem Geschwader ziehn.

«Seid mir gegrüßt, befreundte Scharen,
Die mir zur See Begleiter waren!
Zum guten Zeichen nehm' ich euch,
Mein Los, es ist dem euren gleich:

Ibycus' Cranes

IBYCUS, the friend of the gods, was on his way to the contest of
chariots and of song which unites the peoples of Greece on the
isthmus of Corinth. Apollo had given him the gift of song, the
sweet voice of poetry. And so he was journeying from Rhegium,
travelling light, inspired by the god.

Already on its high ridge Acrocorinth beckons to the traveller's
eye, and with pious awe he enters Poseidon's pine grove. Nothing
stirs round him, his only companions are flocks of cranes, who in
their grey squadrons are flying to the warmth of the distant south.

'I greet you, friendly bands who were my companions at sea!
I take you to be a good omen. My fate is like yours. /We both come

Von fernher kommen wir gezogen
Und flehen um ein wirtlich Dach.
Sei uns der Gastliche gewogen,
Der von dem Fremdling wehrt die Schmach!»

Und munter fördert er die Schritte
Und sieht sich in des Waldes Mitte –
Da sperren, auf gedrangem Steg,
Zwei Mörder plötzlich seinen Weg.
Zum Kampfe muß er sich bereiten,
Doch bald ermattet sinkt die Hand,
Sie hat der Leier zarte Saiten,
Doch nie des Bogens Kraft gespannt.

Er ruft die Menschen an, die Götter,
Sein Flehen dringt zu keinem Retter;
Wie weit er auch die Stimme schickt,
Nichts Lebendes wird hier erblickt.
«So muß ich hier verlassen sterben,
Auf fremdem Boden, unbeweint,
Durch böser Buben Hand verderben,
Wo auch kein Rächer mir erscheint!»

from afar, and beg for a sheltering roof; may the hospitable power
that protects the stranger from ill-treatment be favourable to us!'

And he goes forward cheerfully until he finds himself in the
middle of the forest when, on a narrow path, two murderers sud-
denly bar his way. He has to make ready to fight, but soon his hand
sinks exhausted; it is used to stretching the gentle strings of the
lyre but never yet the strength of the bow.

He calls on men and on gods; his cry reaches no deliverer; how-
ever far he sends his voice, no living thing can be seen here. 'Then
I must die here forsaken, on foreign soil, unwept, and come to my
end at the hand of evil scoundrels in a place where I cannot even
find an avenger!'

Und schwer getroffen sinkt er nieder,
Da rauscht der Kraniche Gefieder,
Er hört, schon kann er nicht mehr sehn,
Die nahen Stimmen furchtbar krähn.
«Von euch, ihr Kraniche dort oben,
Wenn keine andre Stimme spricht,
Sei meines Mordes Klag' erhoben!»
Er ruft es, und sein Auge bricht.

Der nackte Leichnam wird gefunden,
Und bald, obgleich entstellt von Wunden,
Erkennt der Gastfreund in Korinth
Die Züge, die ihm teuer sind.
«Und muß ich so dich wiederfinden,
Und hoffte mit der Fichte Kranz
Des Sängers Schläfe zu umwinden,
Bestrahlt von seines Ruhmes Glanz!»

Und jammernd hören's alle Gäste,
Versammelt bei Poseidons Feste,
Ganz Griechenland ergreift der Schmerz,
Verloren hat ihn jedes Herz;

And as he falls, sorely wounded, the rushing of the cranes' wings comes over; he can no longer see, but he hears the dreadful honking of their call. 'If no other voice is raised, may you, cranes here above me, bring the indictment for my murder!' Thus he cries, and expires.

The naked body is found, and soon his host in Corinth recognizes the features he loved, though they are disfigured by wounds. 'And to think that I have to find you like this, when I had hoped to twine the wreath of pine round the singer's brow, irradiated by the splendour of his fame!'

And all the guests who had gathered for the festival of Poseidon hear the news with mourning, the whole of Greece is moved by sorrow, the loss is felt in every heart;/and the people crowd angrily

Und stürmend drängt sich zum Prytanen
Das Volk, es fordert seine Wut,
Zu rächen des Erschlag'nen Manen,
Zu sühnen mit des Mörders Blut.

Doch wo die Spur, die aus der Menge,
Der Völker flutendem Gedränge,
Gelocket von der Spiele Pracht,
Den schwarzen Täter kenntlich macht?
Sind's Räuber, die ihn feig erschlagen?
Tat's neidisch ein verborgner Feind?
Nur Helios vermag's zu sagen,
Der alles Irdische bescheint.

Er geht vielleicht mit frechem Schritte
Jetzt eben durch der Griechen Mitte,
Und während ihn die Rache sucht,
Genießt er seines Frevels Frucht;
Auf ihres eignen Tempels Schwelle
Trotzt er vielleicht den Göttern, mengt
Sich dreist in jene Menschenwelle,
Die dort sich zum Theater drängt.

to the Magistrate, their rage demands that the ghost of the murdered man be avenged and the crime washed out in the murderer's blood.

But where is the clue to distinguish the black culprit out of the crowd, out of the surging multitude of peoples attracted by the splendour of the games? Was it bandits who foully slew him? Was it the envious work of some hidden enemy? Only Helios, who shines on all earthly things, can say.

Perhaps even now he is walking with confident tread amid the Greeks and enjoys the fruits of his crime while vengeance is still looking for him; perhaps he is defying the gods on the threshold of their own temples, mingling brazenly with the surge of people pressing towards the theatre.

Denn Bank an Bank gedränget sitzen,
Es brechen fast der Bühne Stützen,
Herbeigeströmt von fern und nah,
Der Griechen Völker wartend da;
Dumpfbrausend wie des Meeres Wogen,
Von Menschen wimmelnd, wächst der Bau
In weiter stets geschweiftem Bogen
Hinauf bis in des Himmels Blau.

Wer zählt die Völker, nennt die Namen,
Die gastlich hier zusammenkamen?
Von Theseus' Stadt, von Aulis' Strand,
Von Phocis, vom Spartanerland,
Von Asiens entlegner Küste,
Von allen Inseln kamen sie
Und horchen von dem Schaugerüste
Des Chores grauser Melodie,

Der streng und ernst, nach alter Sitte,
Mit langsam abgemeßnem Schritte
Hervortritt aus dem Hintergrund,
Umwandelnd des Theaters Rund.

For there the peoples of Greece who have streamed in from far
and near are sitting waiting on crowded benches, the timbers of the
stand are strained to breaking point; filled with a hoarse mutter like
the sound of the sea, swarming with people, the edifice rises, one
curved tier above another, up to the blue of heaven.

Who can count the peoples, name the names of all those who
have come together as visitors in this place? From the city of
Theseus, from the shores of Aulis, from Phocis, from the country
of the Spartans, from the distant coast of Asia, from all the islands
they have come, and listen from the stand to the awesome chant of
the chorus,

as it comes from behind the scene and proceeds round the circle
of the theatre, austere and solemn, according to ancient rite, with

So schreiten keine ird'schen Weiber,
Die zeugete kein sterblich Haus!
Es steigt das Riesenmaß der Leiber
Hoch über menschliches hinaus.

Ein schwarzer Mantel schlägt die Lenden,
Sie schwingen in entfleischten Händen
Der Fackel düsterrote Glut,
In ihren Wangen fließt kein Blut;
Und wo die Haare lieblich flattern,
Um Menschenstirnen freundlich wehn,
Da sieht man Schlangen hier und Nattern
Die giftgeschwollnen Bäuche blähn.

Und schauerlich gedreht im Kreise
Beginnen sie des Hymnus Weise,
Der durch das Herz zerreißend dringt,
Die Bande um den Frevler schlingt.
Besinnungraubend, herzbetörend
Schallt der Erinnyen Gesang,
Er schallt, des Hörers Mark verzehrend,
Und duldet nicht der Leier Klang:

slow and measured step./No earthly women walk like this, no
mortal race engendered them! The gigantic proportions of their
bodies far surpass mere human measure.

Black garments sweep their loins, in their fleshless hands they
brandish the dull red glow of the torches, no blood flows in their
cheeks; and where round human brows friendly locks of hair wave
in sweet movement, here snakes and adders can be seen inflating
their poison-bloated bellies.

And formed into a gruesome circle they begin to sing the
piercing, heart-rending chant which casts toils round the evil-
doer. Trance-inducing, heart-numbing sounds and re-sounds the
spine-chilling song of the Erinnyes and drowns the accompaniment
of the lyre:

«Wohl dem, der frei von Schuld und Fehle
Bewahrt die kindlich reine Seele!
Ihm dürfen wir nicht rächend nahn,
Er wandelt frei des Lebens Bahn.
Doch wehe, wehe, wer verstohlen
Des Mordes schwere Tat vollbracht!
Wir heften uns an seine Sohlen,
Das furchtbare Geschlecht der Nacht.

Und glaubt er fliehend zu entspringen,
Geflügelt sind wir da, die Schlingen
Ihm werfend um den flücht'gen Fuß,
Daß er zu Boden fallen muß.
So jagen wir ihn, ohn' Ermatten,
Versöhnen kann uns keine Reu,
Ihn fort und fort bis zu den Schatten,
Und geben ihn auch dort nicht frei.»

So singend tanzen sie den Reigen,
Und Stille wie des Todes Schweigen
Liegt überm ganzen Hause schwer,
Als ob die Gottheit nahe wär.

'Blessed the man who, free from guilt and crime, has kept his
soul childlike and pure! We may not visit him with vengeance, he
walks in freedom on the path of life. But woe, woe to him who has
secretly done the fell deed of murder! We, the dreadful brood of
night, dog his footsteps.

'And if he hopes to escape by flight, on our wings we come upon
him, casting snares before his fleeing foot and bring him to the
ground. And thus we tirelessly pursue him, no remorse can appease
us, on and on down into the shades, nor do we release him even
there.'

And to this song they tread the round, and silence like the hush
of death lies heavy over the whole house, as though the deity was
near./And solemnly, according to ancient rite, they proceed round

Und feierlich, nach alter Sitte,
Umwandelnd des Theaters Rund,
Mit langsam abgemeßnem Schritte
Verschwinden sie im Hintergrund.

Und zwischen Trug und Wahrheit schwebet
Noch zweifelnd jede Brust und bebet'
Und huldiget der furchtbarn Macht,
Die richtend im Verborgnen wacht,
Die unerforschlich, unergründet
Des Schicksals dunkeln Knäuel flicht,
Dem tiefen Herzen sich verkündet,
Doch fliehet vor dem Sonnenlicht.

Da hört man auf den höchsten Stufen
Auf einmal eine Stimme rufen:
«Sieh da! Sieh da, Timotheus,
Die Kraniche des Ibykus!» –
Und finster plötzlich wird der Himmel,
Und über dem Theater hin
Sieht man, in schwärzlichtem Gewimmel,
Ein Kranichheer vorüberziehn.

the circle of the theatre and with slow, measured steps disappear
behind the scene.

And each man's breast trembles, poised between delusion and
truth, and worships the fearful power which watches and judges in
secret, which ties, inscrutable and unfathomed, the dark knot of
fate and manifests itself to the depths of the heart though it flees the
light of day.

Then suddenly a voice is heard on one of the topmost tiers cry-
ing: 'Look, look, Timotheus – Ibycus's cranes!' And the sky sud-
denly grows dark and a host of cranes is seen passing over the
theatre, black and thronging.

«Des Ibykus!» – Der teure Name
Rührt jede Brust mit neuem Grame,
Und wie im Meere Well' auf Well',
So läuft's von Mund zu Munde schnell:
«Des Ibykus, den wir beweinen,
Den eine Mörderhand erschlug!
Was ist's mit dem? Was kann er meinen?
Was ist's mit diesem Kranichzug?»

Und lauter immer wird die Frage,
Und ahnend fliegt's mit Blitzesschlage
Durch alle Herzen: «Gebet acht,
Das ist der Eumeniden Macht!
Der fromme Dichter wird gerochen,
Der Mörder bietet selbst sich dar!
Ergreift ihn, der das Wort gesprochen,
Und ihn, an den's gerichtet war!»

Doch dem war kaum das Wort entfahren,
Möcht' er's im Busen gern bewahren;
Umsonst! Der schreckenbleiche Mund
Macht schnell die Schuldbewußten kund.

'Ibycus!' The cherished name moves each breast with fresh sorrow, and the words pass swiftly from mouth to mouth, as wave follows wave in the sea: 'Ibycus? whom we mourn, whom the hand of a murderer slew? What about him? What does that man mean? What about this flight of cranes?'

And the questioning grows louder and with lightning swiftness the realization flashes through all hearts: 'Give heed, this is the power of the Eumenides! The pious poet is avenged, the murderer is giving himself away! Seize the man who spoke and the man he spoke to!'

But he, hardly had the words escaped him before he wished he could have held them back in his breast. In vain! Lips pale with terror quickly betray their consciousness of guilt./Men seize them

Man reißt und schleppt sie vor den Richter,
Die Szene wird zum Tribunal,
Und es gestehn die Bösewichter,
Getroffen von der Rache Strahl.

Das Glück

SELIG, welchen die Götter, die gnädigen, vor der
      Geburt schon
    Liebten, welchen als Kind Venus im Arme gewiegt,
Welchem Phöbus die Augen, die Lippen Hermes gelöset
    Und das Siegel der Macht Zeus auf die Stirne gedrückt.
Ein erhabenes Los, ein göttliches, ist ihm gefallen,
    Schon vor des Kampfes Beginn sind ihm die Schläfe
      bekränzt.
Ihm ist, eh' er es lebte, das volle Leben gerechnet,
    Eh' er die Mühe bestand, hat er die Charis erlangt.
Groß zwar nenn' ich den Mann, der, sein eigner Bildner
      und Schöpfer,
    Durch der Tugend Gewalt selber die Parze bezwingt;
Aber nicht erzwingt er das Glück, und was ihm die
      Charis

and drag them before the judge, the stage becomes a tribunal, and
the evildoers, struck by the bolt of vengeance, confess their deed.

Good Fortune

THE man whom the gracious gods loved even before he was born,
whom Venus dandled when he was still a child, whose eyes were
opened by Phoebus and whose lips by Hermes and on whose fore-
head Zeus pressed his seal – he is happy. A noble, divine lot is his,
his brows are already crowned before the contest begins. A full life
is awarded him before he has lived it and Charis is already his be-
fore he has endured the toil. True, man who is his own maker and
shaper and himself compels the fate by the force of his own virtues,
he may well be called great; but he cannot compel fortune, and
courageous striving will never attain what Charis / has jealously

Neidisch geweigert, erringt nimmer der strebende
    Mut.
Vor Unwürdigem kann dich der Wille, der ernste,
    bewahren,
    Alles Höchste, es kommt frei von den Göttern herab.
Wie die Geliebte dich liebt, so kommen die himmlischen
    Gaben,
    Oben in Jupiters Reich herrscht, wie in Amors, die
    Gunst.
Neigungen haben die Götter, sie lieben der grünenden
    Jugend
    Lockigte Scheitel, es zieht Freude die Fröhlichen an.
Nicht der Sehende wird von ihrer Erscheinung beseligt,
    Ihrer Herrlichkeit Glanz hat nur der Blinde geschaut;
Gern erwählen sie sich der Einfalt kindliche Seele,
    In das bescheidne Gefäß schließen sie Göttliches ein.
Ungehofft sind sie da und täuschen die stolze Erwartung,
    Keines Bannes Gewalt zwinget die Freien herab.
Wem er geneigt, dem sendet der Vater der Menschen und
    Götter
    Seinen Adler herab, trägt ihn zu himmlischen Höhn.

withheld from him. An effort of will may preserve you from meanness, but the noblest gifts come from the gods unsought. Gifts from heaven come in the same way as love from the lover, and in Jupiter's kingdom above, as in Amor's, favouring is the rule. The gods have their preferences, they love the curly heads of burgeoning youth, and the Joyous Ones are attracted by joy. It is not the seeing who are blessed by their visitation; it is only the blind who have seen the splendour of their glory. They love to choose the childlike soul of the simple, and they enclose divine gifts in this modest vessel. Suddenly they are there and disappoint proud expectations, for no incantation can force the unfettered gods. The father of men and gods sends his eagle down to those who please him, to carry them up to the heights of heaven. / He chooses as he

Unter die Menge greift er mit Eigenwillen, und welches
    Haupt ihm gefället, um das flicht er mit liebender
    Hand
Jetzt den Lorbeer und jetzt die herrschaftgebende Binde,
    Krönte doch selber den Gott nur das gewogene
    Glück.
Vor dem Glücklichen her tritt Phöbus, der pythische
    Sieger,
    Und der die Herzen bezwingt, Amor, der lächelnde
    Gott.
Vor ihm ebnet Poseidon das Meer, sanft gleitet des
    Schiffes
    Kiel, das den Cäsar führt und sein allmächtiges Glück.
Ihm zu Füßen legt sich der Leu, das brausende Delphin
    Steigt aus den Tiefen, und fromm beut es den Rücken
    ihm an.
Zürne dem Glücklichen nicht, daß den leichten Sieg ihm
    die Götter
    Schenken, daß aus der Schlacht Venus den Liebling
    entrückt;
Ihn, den die Lächelnde rettet, den Göttergeliebten
    beneid' ich,
    Jenen nicht, dem sie mit Nacht deckt den verdunkelten
    Blick.

pleases from the crowd and binds with loving hand now the laurel wreath and now the fillet of sovereignty round the heads which please him, for it was Fortune who, after all, of her favour crowned the god himself. And the fortunate are visited by Phoebus, the victor in the Pythian Games, and Amor the smiling god who tames men's hearts. Poseidon makes the sea smooth in front of them, the keel of the ship glides smoothly that carries Caesar and his all-powerful fortune. At their feet lions lie down, the dripping dolphins rise from the depths and dutifully offer their backs. Do not be angry with the fortunate because the gods give them easy victories or because Venus snatches her favourite out of the battle. The man I envy is the one the smiling goddess saves, the beloved of the gods, not the man whose darkened eye she covers with night. / Was

War er weniger herrlich, Achilles, weil ihm Hephästos
  Selbst geschmiedet den Schild und das verderbliche
    Schwert,
Weil um den sterblichen Mann der große Olymp sich
    beweget?
  Das verherrlichet ihn, daß ihn die Götter geliebt,
Daß sie sein Zürnen geehrt und, Ruhm dem Liebling zu
    geben,
  Hellas' bestes Geschlecht stürzten zum Orkus hinab.
Zürne der Schönheit nicht, daß sie schön ist, daß sie
    verdienstlos
  Wie der Lilie Kelch prangt durch der Venus Ge-
    schenk;
Laß sie die Glückliche sein – du schaust sie, du bist der
    Beglückte,
  Wie sie ohne Verdienst glänzt, so entzücket sie dich.
Freue dich, daß die Gabe des Lieds vom Himmel herab-
    kommt,
  Daß der Sänger dir singt, was ihn die Muse gelehrt!
Weil der Gott ihn beseelt, so wird er dem Hörer zum
    Gotte,
  Weil er der Glückliche ist, kannst du der Selige sein.

Achilles less glorious because Hephaestus himself wrought his
shield and his death-dealing sword and because even great Olym-
pus was disturbed for the sake of this mortal man? That the gods
loved him, that they respected his anger and, to give fame to their
favourite, sent the noblest clan of Hellas headlong down to Orcus:
all this is part of his glory. Do not be angry with beauty because it
is beautiful, because by the gift of Venus it exists in undeserved
splendour like the flower of the lily! Let it be fortunate; you see it,
you are made happy by it, it delights you as it is in its undeserved
glory. Be glad that the gift of song comes down from heaven, that
the poet sings what the muse has taught him! Because the god in-
spires him he becomes a god to the listener: because he is fortunate
you can be happy./Themis may wield the scales on the busy
market-place and wages be measured out strictly according to toil;

Auf dem geschäftigen Markt, da führe Themis die Wage,
 Und es messe der Lohn streng an der Mühe sich ab;
Aber die Freude ruft nur ein Gott auf sterbliche Wangen,
 Wo kein Wunder geschieht, ist kein Beglückter zu
 sehn.
Alles Menschliche muß erst werden und wachsen und
 reifen,
 Und von Gestalt zu Gestalt führt es die bildende Zeit;
Aber das Glückliche siehest du nicht, das Schöne nicht
 werden,
 Fertig von Ewigkeit her steht es vollendet vor dir.
Jede irdische Venus ersteht, wie die erste des Himmels,
 Eine dunkle Geburt aus dem unendlichen Meer;
Wie die erste Minerva, so tritt, mit der Ägis gerüstet,
 Aus des Donnerers Haupt jeder Gedanke des Lichts.

Das Lied von der Glocke

VIVOS VOCO MORTUOS PLANGO FULGURA FRANGO

FEST gemauert in der Erden
Steht die Form, aus Lehm gebrannt.
Heute muß die Glocke werden!
Frisch, Gesellen, seid zur Hand!

but only a god can call joy to mortal cheeks, and happy folk are not seen where no miracles occur. All human things have to develop, grow, and mature, and the shaping power of time brings them from one form to another; but fortune and beauty you cannot see develop, they stand perfect before you from all eternity. Every earthly Venus, like the first, the heavenly Venus, appears as the mysterious child of the infinite ocean, and every luminous thought steps like the first Minerva armed with her aegis from the Thunderer's head.

The Lay of the Bell

THE mould of baked clay stands firmly bedded in the ground. The bell must be cast today. Come, boys, lend a hand./The sweat

Von der Stirne heiß
Rinnen muß der Schweiß,
Soll das Werk den Meister loben;
Doch der Segen kommt von oben.

Zum Werke, das wir ernst bereiten,
Geziemt sich wohl ein ernstes Wort;
Wenn gute Reden sie begleiten,
Dann fließt die Arbeit munter fort.
So laßt uns jetzt mit Fleiß betrachten,
Was durch schwache Kraft entspringt:
Den schlechten Mann muß man verachten,
Der nie bedacht, was er vollbringt.
Das ist's ja, was den Menschen zieret,
Und dazu ward ihm der Verstand,
Daß er im innern Herzen spüret,
Was er erschafft mit seiner Hand.

Nehmet Holz vom Fichtenstamme,
Doch recht trocken laßt es sein,
Daß die eingepreßte Flamme
Schlage zu dem Schwalch hinein!
Kocht des Kupfers Brei,
Schnell das Zinn herbei!

will have to run from your hot faces if the job is to be a credit to the master, but the blessing on it comes from on high.

A solemn word is suited to the job we solemnly prepare; work goes ahead more smoothly when good counsel goes with it. And so let us earnestly consider what our poor strength can achieve. The incompetent man who never considers what he is doing deserves nothing but contempt. What makes a human being is just this, that he can feel in his inmost heart what he fashions with his hands, and that is what his wits were given him for.

Bring pine faggots, and see that they are good and dry, so that the flame they hold captive strikes through the roof of the furnace. When the copper is molten, add the tin quickly,/to make the tough metal flow in the proper way.

Daß die zähe Glockenspeise
Fließe nach der rechten Weise!

Was in des Dammes tiefer Grube
Die Hand mit Feuers Hilfe baut,
Hoch auf des Turmes Glockenstube,
Da wird es von uns zeugen laut.
Noch dauern wird's in späten Tagen
Und rühren vieler Menschen Ohr
Und wird mit dem Betrübten klagen
Und stimmen zu der Andacht Chor.
Was unten tief dem Erdensohne
Das wechselnde Verhängnis bringt,
Das schlägt an die metallne Krone,
Die es erbaulich weiter klingt.

    Weiße Blasen seh' ich springen;
    Wohl! die Massen sind im Fluß.
    Laßt's mit Aschensalz durchdringen,
    Das befördert schnell den Guß.
      Auch von Schaume rein
      Muß die Mischung sein,
    Daß vom reinlichen Metalle
    Rein und voll die Stimme schalle.

The bell our hand builds in the dam's deep pit with the aid of fire will bear witness to us aloud in the bell-chamber of the tower. It will still be there in after days and reach the ears of many; it will mourn with the bereaved and join in the choir of devotion. Whatever the changing fates bring the sons of earth far beneath strikes the metal bow which rings it out for all to learn.

I see white bubbles rising. Good, the mass is fluid. Mix the potash in it to bring the casting on quicker. The mixture must be free from slag if the voice of the bell is to sound pure and full out of the pure metal.

Denn mit der Freude Feierklange
Begrüßt sie das geliebte Kind
Auf seines Lebens erstem Gange,
Den es in Schlafes Arm beginnt;
Ihm ruhen noch im Zeitenschoße
Die schwarzen und die heitern Lose,
Der Mutterliebe zarte Sorgen
Bewachen seinen goldnen Morgen. –
Die Jahre fliehen pfeilgeschwind.
Vom Mädchen reißt sich stolz der Knabe,
Er stürmt ins Leben wild hinaus,
Durchmißt die Welt am Wanderstabe.
Fremd kehrt er heim ins Vaterhaus,
Und herrlich, in der Jugend Prangen,
Wie ein Gebild aus Himmels Höhn,
Mit züchtigen, verschämten Wangen
Sieht er die Jungfrau vor sich stehn.
Da faßt ein namenloses Sehnen
Des Jünglings Herz, er irrt allein,
Aus seinen Augen brechen Tränen,
Er flieht der Brüder wilden Reihn.
Errötend folgt er ihren Spuren
Und ist von ihrem Gruß beglückt,
Das Schönste sucht er auf den Fluren,

The bell greets with solemn and joyous note the darling child as,
still in the arms of sleep, it makes the first journey of its life. Its
dark or bright lots as yet lie hidden in the womb of time; the tender
cares of mother's love watch over its golden morning. The years
pass swift as arrows. The boy tears himself proudly from the girl,
he rushes roughly out into life, and paces the world stick in hand.
He comes home a stranger to his parents' house, and sees before
him the maiden, resplendent in the flower of her youth like a figure
from heaven, with modestly suffused cheeks. Then a nameless long-
ing seizes upon the young man's heart, he wanders about alone,
tears start unbidden from his eyes, he avoids the rough gangs of his
mates. He follows her with blushing face, rejoices in her salutation,
and searches the fields for the fairest flowers/to grace his love. O

Womit er seine Liebe schmückt.
O zarte Sehnsucht, süßes Hoffen,
Der ersten Liebe goldne Zeit!
Das Auge sieht den Himmel offen,
Es schwelgt das Herz in Seligkeit.
O daß sie ewig grünen bliebe,
Die schöne Zeit der jungen Liebe!

Wie sich schon die Pfeifen bräunen!
Dieses Stäbchen tauch' ich ein:
Sehn wir's überglast erscheinen,
Wird's zum Gusse zeitig sein.
Jetzt, Gesellen, frisch!
Prüft mir das Gemisch,
Ob das Spröde mit dem Weichen
Sich vereint zum guten Zeichen.

Denn wo das Strenge mit dem Zarten
Wo Starkes sich und Mildes paarten,
Da gibt es einen guten Klang.
Drum prüfe, wer sich ewig bindet,
Ob sich das Herz zum Herzen findet!
Der Wahn ist kurz, die Reu' ist lang. –

tender yearning, sweet hope, the golden times of first love; the eye
sees Heaven open, the heart is full of bliss. If only it could last for
ever green, the lovely time of young love!

Ah, the tubes are browning now! I will dip in this rod and if
we see it come out glazed the time will be ripe for casting. Now,
come on, lads! test the mixture to see whether the brittle and soft
are combining in the proper way.

For where austerity has combined with mildness, and strength
with gentleness, the result is a harmonious sound. And so the man
who is going to tie himself for life must consider whether it is really
the heart which inspires him and his bride. Illusion lasts only a little
time, regret lives long./The bridal wreath sits charmingly in the

Lieblich in der Bräute Locken
Spielt der jungfräuliche Kranz,
Wenn die hellen Kirchenglocken
Laden zu des Festes Glanz.
Ach! des Lebens schönste Feier
Endigt auch den Lebensmai,
Mit dem Gürtel, mit dem Schleier
Reißt der schöne Wahn entzwei.
Die Leidenschaft flieht,
Die Liebe muß bleiben;
Die Blume verblüht,
Die Frucht muß treiben.
Der Mann muß hinaus
Ins feindliche Leben,
Muß wirken und streben
Und pflanzen und schaffen,
Erlisten, erraffen,
Muß wetten und wagen,
Das Glück zu erjagen.
Da strömet herbei die unendliche Gabe,
Es füllt sich der Speicher mit köstlicher Habe,
Die Räume wachsen, es dehnt sich das Haus.
Und drinnen waltet
Die züchtige Hausfrau,
Die Mutter der Kinder,
Und herrschet weise
Im häuslichen Kreise,

hair of the bride when the gay church bells invite to the splendour
of the occasion. But alas, the finest festivity of life means the end of
life's springtime, and with the girdle and the veil the sweet illusion
itself is torn apart. Passion is spent but love must remain, the
flower is over and the fruit must set; the husband must go out into
the hostile world, he must work and toil and plant and labour, gain
by cunning and gain by grasping, must wager and risk to achieve
fortune. Then the endless gift streams in, the barn fills with valuable
goods, the rooms grow bigger, the house expands. And inside, the
decent housewife is in control, and rules wisely in the family circle,

Und lehret die Mädchen
Und wehret den Knaben,
Und reget ohn' Ende
Die fleißigen Hände,
Und mehrt den Gewinn
Mit ordnendem Sinn,
Und füllet mit Schätzen die duftenden Laden,
Und dreht um die schnurrende Spindel den Faden,
Und sammelt im reinlich geglätteten Schrein
Die schimmernde Wolle, den schneeigten Lein,
Und füget zum Guten den Glanz und den Schimmer,
Und ruhet nimmer.

Und der Vater mit frohem Blick
Von des Hauses weitschauendem Giebel
Überzählet sein blühend Glück,
Siehet der Pfosten ragende Bäume
Und der Scheunen gefüllte Räume
Und die Speicher, vom Segen gebogen,
Und des Kornes bewegte Wogen,
Rühmt sich mit stolzem Mund:
Fest, wie der Erde Grund,
Gegen des Unglücks Macht
Steht mir des Hauses Pracht!

she teaches the girls and restrains the boys and keeps her active hands always busy, she increases the gain with her sense of order, and fills the fragrant drawers with treasures and twists the thread round the whirring spindle and puts away the glossy wool and snowy linen in the neatly polished cupboards, she confers a glow and a shimmer on good things, and never rests.

And the father looks out delighted from the towering roof of the house and counts over his flourishing fortune; he sees the posts standing up like trees, the filled spaces of the hay-loft and the barns bursting with the yield, and the heaving waves of corn, and he proudly boasts: 'The splendour of my house stands as firm as the foundations of the earth against the power of misfortune.'/But no

Doch mit des Geschickes Mächten
Ist kein ew'ger Bund zu flechten,
Und das Unglück schreitet schnell.

Wohl! nun kann der Guß beginnen,
Schön gezacket ist der Bruch.
Doch, bevor wir's lassen rinnen,
Betet einen frommen Spruch.
Stoßt den Zapfen aus!
Gott bewahr' das Haus!
Rauchend in des Henkels Bogen
Schießt's mit feuerbraunen Wogen.

Wohltätig ist des Feuers Macht,
Wenn sie der Mensch bezähmt, bewacht,
Und was er bildet, was er schafft,
Das dankt er dieser Himmelskraft;
Doch furchtbar wird die Himmelskraft,
Wenn sie der Fessel sich entrafft,
Einhertritt auf der eignen Spur,
Die freie Tochter der Natur.
Wehe, wenn sie losgelassen,
Wachsend ohne Widerstand
Durch die volkbelebten Gassen
Wälzt den ungeheuren Brand!

permanent alliance can be made with the powers of destiny, and misfortune strides apace.

Good, now the casting can begin; the metal has a fine jagged fracture. But before we let it run out let us say a short prayer. Knock the tap out! God preserve us all! The fiery brown waves rush smoking into the curve of the ear.

As long as man tames it and guards it the power of fire is beneficial, and he owes to this divine force everything he makes and creates. But the divine force becomes a thing of terror when it escapes from its bonds and starts out on its own path as the free daughter of Nature that it is! There is disaster when it is let loose, growing resistlessly, the vast fire rolls through the populous streets!

Denn die Elemente hassen
Das Gebild der Menschenhand.
Aus der Wolke
Quillt der Segen,
Strömt der Regen;
Aus der Wolke, ohne Wahl,
Zuckt der Strahl.
Hört ihr's wimmern hoch vom Turm!
Das ist Sturm!
Rot wie Blut
Ist der Himmel,
Das ist nicht des Tages Glut!
Welch Getümmel
Straßen auf!
Dampf wallt auf!
Flackernd steigt die Feuersäule,
Durch der Straße lange Zeile
Wächst es fort mit Windeseile.
Kochend wie aus Ofens Rachen
Glühn die Lüfte, Balken krachen,
Pfosten stürzen, Fenster klirren,
Kinder jammern, Mütter irren,
Tiere wimmern
Unter Trümmern,
Alles rennet, rettet, flüchtet,
Taghell ist die Nacht gelichtet.

For the elements hate what the hand of man has formed. From the clouds blessings flow, the rain streams down; from the clouds, too, the random lightning flashes. Can you hear the jangling from the top of the tower? That is the tocsin. The sky is red as blood. That is no ordinary daylight! What a confusion up and down the streets! Smoke billows up. The pillar of fire rises and blazes, along the whole row of the street it grows with the speed of the wind; the draught sears like the breath of an oven, beams crack, posts collapse, windows shatter, children cry and mothers dither, animals whine beneath the ruins; everyone is running, saving, fleeing, the night is lit up like day. / The bucket flies fast as can be along the

Durch der Hände lange Kette
Um die Wette
Fliegt der Eimer, hoch im Bogen
Spritzen Quellen, Wasserwogen.
Heulend kommt der Sturm geflogen,
Der die Flamme brausend sucht.
Prasselnd in die dürre Frucht
Fällt sie, in des Speichers Räume,
In der Sparren dürre Bäume,
Und als wollte sie im Wehen
Mit sich fort der Erde Wucht
Reißen in gewalt'ger Flucht,
Wächst sie in des Himmels Höhen
Riesengroß!
Hoffnungslos
Weicht der Mensch der Götterstärke,
Müßig sieht er seine Werke
Und bewundernd untergehen.

Leergebrannt
Ist die Stätte,
Wilder Stürme rauhes Bette;
In den öden Fensterhöhlen
Wohnt das Grauen,
Und des Himmels Wolken schauen
Hoch hinein.

long chain of hands; the springs and waters shoot up in a steep curve. The stormwind comes howling, pursuing the flame. It rushes into the compartments of the barn, crackling in the dry corn and in the dry wood of the joists, and as though it wanted to tear the weight of earth itself up with it in one mighty bound, it towers huge into the heights of the sky. Man, without hope, gives way before such god-like strength. Resigned and amazed, he sees his work destroyed.

   The site is burnt out, a rough bed of wild winds. Horror lives in the empty window openings, and the clouds in the sky look down on it from far above.

Einen Blick
Nach dem Grabe
Seiner Habe
Sendet noch der Mensch zurück –
Greift fröhlich dann zum Wanderstabe.
Was des Feuers Wut ihm auch geraubt,
Ein süßer Trost ist ihm geblieben:
Er zählt die Häupter seiner Lieben,
Und sieh! ihm fehlt kein teures Haupt.

In die Erd' ist's aufgenommen,
Glücklich ist die Form gefüllt;
Wird's auch schön zu Tage kommen,
Daß es Fleiß und Kunst vergilt?
Wenn der Guß mißlang?
Wenn die Form zersprang?
Ach! vielleicht, indem wir hoffen,
Hat uns Unheil schon getroffen.

Dem dunkeln Schoß der heil'gen Erde
Vertrauen wir der Hände Tat,
Vertraut der Sämann seine Saat
Und hofft, daß sie entkeimen werde
Zum Segen, nach des Himmels Rat.

Man gives one last look at the grave of his possessions, then
gladly reaches for the wanderer's staff. Whatever the rage of the
fire has robbed, one sweet consolation is left: he counts the heads
of his family and finds that not a single dear one is missing.

Now the earth has received it; the mould is well and truly filled.
Will it come out in a state to reward our work and skill? What if the
casting were to fail, if the mould were to crack? But even now as
we stand in hope, perhaps disaster has already come upon us.

We entrust the work of our hands to the dark bosom of Mother
Earth, as the sower entrusts his seed and hopes that it will sprout
and grow bountifully according to Heaven's ordinance. / We sadly

Noch köstlicheren Samen bergen
Wir trauernd in der Erde Schoß
Und hoffen, daß er aus den Särgen
Erblühen soll zu schönerm Los.

Von dem Dome,
Schwer und bang,
Tönt die Glocke
Grabgesang.
Ernst begleiten ihre Trauerschläge
Einen Wandrer auf dem letzten Wege.

Ach! die Gattin ist's, die teure,
Ach! es ist die treue Mutter,
Die der schwarze Fürst der Schatten
Wegführt aus dem Arm des Gatten,
Aus der zarten Kinder Schar,
Die sie blühend ihm gebar,
Die sie an der treuen Brust
Wachsen sah mit Mutterlust –
Ach! des Hauses zarte Bande
Sind gelöst auf immerdar,
Denn sie wohnt im Schattenlande,

hide in the earth's bosom a more precious seed than this, and hope
that it will spring from the coffin to a more gracious lot.

The bell sounds from the cathedral, slow and fearful, funeral
music. Its solemn mourning strokes accompany a pilgrim on his
last journey.

Alas, it is the beloved, the faithful wife and mother, that the
black ruler of the shades leads away out of the arms of her husband,
out of the company of tender children whom she bore him in her
bloom, whom with a mother's pride and joy she watched growing
at her faithful breast – alas, now the gentle domestic bonds are
loosed for ever, for she who was the mother of the family now lives
in the land of shades;/her conscientious control is gone now, her

Die des Hauses Mutter war,
Denn es fehlt ihr treues Walten,
Ihre Sorge wacht nicht mehr,
An verwaister Stätte schalten
Wird die Fremde, liebeleer.

    Bis die Glocke sich verkühlet,
    Laßt die strenge Arbeit ruhn;
    Wie im Laub der Vogel spielet,
    Mag sich jeder gütlich tun.
        Winkt der Sterne Licht,
        Ledig aller Pflicht
    Hört der Bursch die Vesper schlagen,
    Meister muß sich immer plagen.

Munter fördert seine Schritte
Fern im wilden Forst der Wandrer
Nach der lieben Heimathütte.
Blökend ziehen heim die Schafe,
Und der Rinder
Breitgestirnte, glatte Scharen
Kommen brüllend,
Die gewohnten Ställe füllend.
Schwer herein
Schwankt der Wagen,
Kornbeladen;

care no longer watches over them; in her place a loveless stranger will rule the orphaned family.

Let us rest from our strenuous work while the bell is cooling off. Every man may enjoy himself just as birds play among the leaves. When the starlight beckons, the apprentice hears the vesper bell ring; he is free from all duties, but the master always has to worry.

The wanderer far away in the wild forest joyfully directs his steps towards his longed-for cottage home. The sheep bleat on the way in and the wide-browed sleek cattle come lowing to fill their accustomed stalls. The cart loaded with corn lurches heavily in;/the

Bunt von Farben
Auf den Garben
Liegt der Kranz,
Und das junge Volk der Schnitter
Fliegt zum Tanz.
Markt und Straße werden stiller,
Um des Lichts gesell'ge Flamme
Sammeln sich die Hausbewohner,
Und das Stadttor schließt sich knarrend.
Schwarz bedecket
Sich die Erde,
Doch den sichern Bürger schrecket
Nicht die Nacht,
Die den Bösen gräßlich wecket,
Denn das Auge des Gesetzes wacht.

Heil'ge Ordnung, segenreiche
Himmelstochter, die das Gleiche
Frei und leicht und freudig bindet,
Die der Städte Bau gegründet,
Die herein von den Gefilden
Rief den ungesell'gen Wilden,
Eintrat in der Menschen Hütten,
Sie gewöhnt zu sanften Sitten
Und das teuerste der Bande
Wob, den Trieb zum Vaterlande!

garland, gay with colours, lies on the sheaves, and the young
reapers are off to the dance. Street and market grow quiet, families
collect round the social candle flame and the town gate creaks shut.
The earth covers itself with blackness, but night, which rouses the
wicked man in dread, holds no terrors for the assured citizen be-
cause the eye of the law stays awake.

Divine Order, bountiful daughter of heaven, who joins equals
in a voluntary, easy and joyful association, who laid the founda-
tions of towns, who called the asocial savage in from the
waste, entered into the cottages of men, accustomed them to gentle
ways, and wove the dearest bond of all, love of country!

Tausend fleiß'ge Hände regen,
Helfen sich in munterm Bund,
Und in feurigem Bewegen
Werden alle Kräfte kund.
Meister rührt sich und Geselle
In der Freiheit heil'gem Schutz,
Jeder freut sich seiner Stelle,
Bietet dem Verächter Trutz.
Arbeit ist des Bürgers Zierde,
Segen ist der Mühe Preis;
Ehrt den König seine Würde,
Ehret uns der Hände Fleiß.

Holder Friede,
Süße Eintracht,
Weilet, weilet
Freundlich über dieser Stadt!
Möge nie der Tag erscheinen,
Wo des rauhen Krieges Horden
Dieses stille Tal durchtoben,
Wo der Himmel,
Den des Abends sanfte Röte
Lieblich malt,
Von der Dörfer, von der Städte
Wildem Brande schrecklich strahlt!

A thousand industrious hands are busy with mutual help in
happy community, and everyone's energies show what they can do
in eager activity. Master and man set to in the hallowed protection
of freedom; each takes pride in his position and opposes the scorner.
Work is the crown of the citizen, bounty the reward of labour; if
the king is honoured by his royalty, what confers honour on us is
the industry of our hands.

Blessed peace, sweet accord, rest, oh, rest upon this city and
bless it! May the day never come when the wild hordes of war riot
through this quiet valley, when the sky, which now is coloured by
the soft red of evening, reflects in terrible glow the fierce con-
flagration of villages and towns!

Nun zerbrecht mir das Gebäude,
Seine Absicht hat's erfüllt,
Daß sich Herz und Auge weide
An dem wohlgelungnen Bild.
   Schwingt den Hammer, schwingt,
   Bis der Mantel springt!
Wenn die Glock' soll auferstehen,
Muß die Form in Stücken gehen.

Der Meister kann die Form zerbrechen
Mit weiser Hand, zur rechten Zeit,
Doch wehe, wenn in Flammenbächen
Das glühnde Erz sich selbst befreit!
Blindwütend, mit des Donners Krachen,
Zersprengt es das geborstne Haus,
Und wie aus offnem Höllenrachen
Speit es Verderben zündend aus.
Wo rohe Kräfte sinnlos walten,
Da kann sich kein Gebild gestalten;
Wenn sich die Völker selbst befrein,
Da kann die Wohlfahrt nicht gedeihn.

Weh, wenn sich in dem Schoß der Städte
Der Feuerzunder still gehäuft,
Das Volk, zerreißend seine Kette,

Now break the cope up, it has done its job; let heart and eye rejoice at the successfully completed piece. Swing those hammers, swing them till the mantle breaks. If the bell is to rise, the mould must be smashed.

The master can break the mould with his experienced hand at the right moment, but disaster ensues when the fiery metal frees itself in flaming streams! Blindly raging, with thunderous crash it bursts the cracked mould and spits out incendiary death as though from the open mouth of hell. Where crude forces are in senseless control no created form can take shape; when peoples free themselves welfare cannot prosper.

Disaster, when the fiery tinder has piled up in the bosom of the towns and the people rends its chains/and turns with dreadful mien

Zur Eigenhilfe schrecklich greift!
Da zerret an der Glocke Strängen
Der Aufruhr, daß sie heulend schallt
Und, nur geweiht zu Friedensklängen,
Die Losung anstimmt zur Gewalt.

Freiheit und Gleichheit! hört man schallen,
Der ruh'ge Bürger greift zur Wehr,
Die Straßen füllen sich, die Hallen,
Und Würgerbanden ziehn umher.
Da werden Weiber zu Hyänen
Und treiben mit Entsetzen Scherz,
Noch zuckend, mit des Panthers Zähnen,
Zerreißen sie des Feindes Herz.
Nichts Heiliges ist mehr, es lösen
Sich alle Bande frommer Scheu,
Der Gute räumt den Platz dem Bösen,
Und alle Laster walten frei.
Gefährlich ist's, den Leu zu wecken,
Verderblich ist des Tigers Zahn,
Jedoch der schrecklichste der Schrecken,
Das ist der Mensch in seinem Wahn.
Weh denen, die dem Ewigblinden
Des Lichtes Himmelsfackel leihn!

to help itself! Then revolt tugs at the ropes of the bell and makes it
wail aloud, and though it was consecrated to the tones of peace it
now sounds the signal for brute force!

'Liberty and Equality!' is the cry. The quiet citizen reaches for
his weapon, the streets and halls fill up, and thugs go about in
gangs. Then women turn into hyaenas and jest of dreadful things;
with panther's teeth they tear the still-quivering heart of their
enemy. Nothing is sacred now, all the restrictions of pious awe are
loosed, the good give place to the evil and all the vices have their
way. It is dangerous enough to wake the lion, the tiger's tooth is
deadly too, but the most fearful horror of all horrors is man in his
purblind delusion. Woe to those who lend him the heavenly torch

Sie strahlt ihm nicht, sie kann nur zünden
Und äschert Städt' und Länder ein.

Freude hat mir Gott gegeben!
Sehet! wie ein goldner Stern
Aus der Hülse, blank und eben,
Schält sich der metallne Kern.
Von dem Helm zum Kranz
Spielt's wie Sonnenglanz,
Auch des Wappens nette Schilder
Loben den erfahrnen Bilder.

Herein! herein!
Gesellen alle, schließt den Reihen,
Daß wir die Glocke taufend weihen!
Concordia soll ihr Name sein.
Zur Eintracht, zu herzinnigem Vereine
Versammle sie die liebende Gemeine.

Und dies sei fortan ihr Beruf,
Wozu der Meister sie erschuf:
Hoch überm niedern Erdenleben
Soll sie im blauen Himmelszelt
Die Nachbarin des Donners schweben
Und grenzen an die Sternenwelt,

of light, for it does not give him illumination, it can only set fire
to things and it reduces cities and nations to ashes.

God has given me joy! Look, like a golden star the metal kernel
peels out of the husk, shining and smooth. From crown to bow it
glistens like the sun. The sharply outlined shields of the coats of
arms reflect credit on the experienced craftsman.

Come along in, all you men! Stand round close, let us christen
and consecrate the bell. Its name shall be Concordia; may it call
together the loving congregation to concord, to sincere unity.

Let this be its purpose, the purpose to which the master made it:
high above the humble life of earth it shall hang in the blue vault of
heaven, a neighbour to the thunder, and border on the world of the
stars;/it shall be a voice from on high, like the bright concourse of

Soll eine Stimme sein von oben,
Wie der Gestirne helle Schar,
Die ihren Schöpfer wandelnd loben
Und führen das bekränzte Jahr.
Nur ewigen und ernsten Dingen
Sei ihr metallner Mund geweiht,
Und stündlich mit den schnellen Schwingen
Berühr' im Fluge sie die Zeit;
Dem Schicksal leihe sie die Zunge,
Selbst herzlos, ohne Mitgefühl,
Begleite sie mit ihrem Schwunge
Des Lebens wechselvolles Spiel.
Und wie der Klang im Ohr vergehet,
Der mächtig tönend ihr entschallt,
So lehre sie, daß nichts bestehet,
Daß alles Irdische verhallt.

    Jetzo mit der Kraft des Stranges
    Wiegt die Glock' mir aus der Gruft,
    Daß sie in das Reich des Klanges
    Steige, in die Himmelsluft.
      Ziehet, ziehet, hebt!
      Sie bewegt sich, schwebt.
    Freude dieser Stadt bedeute,
    Friede sei ihr erst Geläute.

the stars who in their courses praise their creator and lead in the garlanded year. May its metal mouth be consecrated to eternal and solemn things alone, and may time in his flight touch it hourly with his swift wings; may it lend its tongue to fate; heartless itself and without compassion though it is, may its pulse accompany the shifting patterns of life. And as the sound, which leaves the bell in mighty reverberation, dies in the ear, so let it teach us that nothing endures and that all earthly things pass away.

Now, with the power of the rope heave the bell up out of the pit, to let it rise into the realm of sound, into the air of heaven! Pull, pull, heave! It moves, it hangs free. May its first peal mean joy to this town, may it mean peace!

JOHANN PETER HEBEL

Auf den Tod eines Zechers

Do hen si mer e Ma vergrabe,
's isch schad für sini bsundre Gabe.
Gang, wo de witt, such no so ein!
Sel isch verbei, de findsch mer kein.

Er isch e Himmelsglehrte gsi.
In alle Dörfere her und hi
se het er gluegt vo Hus zu Hus:
hangt nienen echt e *Sternen* us?

Er isch e freche Ritter gsi.
In alle Dörfere her und hi
se het er gfrogt enanderno:
«sin *Leuen* oder *Bäre* do?»

E guete Christ, sel isch er gsi.
In alle Dörfere her und hi
se het er unter Tags und z'Nacht
zum *Chrütz* si stille Bueßgang gmacht.

On the Death of a Drunkard

THEY have just buried a man I knew, it is a pity about his special gifts. Search as you will to find another like him, he is gone, you will never find one.

He was learned in astronomy. Up and down in every village he went from house to house to see whether any of them showed a sign of a *Star*.

He was a bold knight too. Up and down in every village he was always asking, 'Is there such a thing as a *Lion* or a *Bear* here?'

He was a good Christian, that he was. Up and down in every village, day and night he made his inconspicuous penitential pilgrimage to the *Cross*.

Si Namen isch in Stadt und Land
bi große Here wohl bikannt.
Si allerliebste Kumpanie
sin alliwil d'*drei Künig* gsi.

Jez schloft er und weiß nüt dervo,
es chunnt e Zit, gohts alle so.

*Die Vergänglichkeit. Gespräch auf der Straße von Basel
zwischen Steinen und Brombach, in der Nacht*

Der Bueb seit zum Aetti:
F AST allmol, Aetti, wenn mer 's Röttler Schloß
so vor den Auge stoht, se denki dra,
öbs üsem Hus echt au e mol so goht.
Stohts denn nit dört, so schudrig, wie der Tod
im Basler Todtetanz? Es gruset eim,
wie länger as me's bschaut. Und üser Hus,
es sitzt jo wie ne Chilchli uffem Berg,
und d'Fenster glitzeren, es isch e Staat.
Schwetz, Aetti, gohts em echterst au no so?
I mein emol, es chönn schier gar nit sy.

His name is well known to the quality in town and country. *The
Duke of Wellington* and *The Marquess of Granby* were always his
favourite companions.

Now he is at rest and knows no more. The time will come when
we shall all be the same.

*Sic Transit: a Conversation on the Basel Road between Steinen
and Brombach, at Night*

THE boy says to his father: Father, nearly always when I see
Rötteln Castle stand out like that, I wonder whether our house will
go that way too. It stands up there, doesn't it, as gruesome as
Death in the Dance of Death at Basel. The longer you look at it
the more uncomfortable you feel. And our house sits up on the hill
like a church, and the windows glitter, it looks fine. Tell me, Father,
will it really go that way too? I think sometimes that it simply
couldn't!

Der Aetti seit:
Du guete Burst, 's cha frili sy, was meinsch?
'S chunnt alles jung und neu, und alles schliicht
si'm Alter zu, und alles nimmt en End,
und nüt stoht still. Hörsch nit, wie's Wasser ruuscht,
und siehsch am Himmel obe Stern an Stern?
Me meint, vo alle rühr si kein, und doch
ruckt alles witers, alles chunnt und goht.

Je, 's isch nit anderst, lueg mi a, wie d'witt.
De bisch no jung; närsch, i bi au so gsi;
jez würd's mer anderst, 's Alter, 's Alter chunnt;
und woni gang, go Gresgen oder Wies,
in Feld und Wald, go Basel oder heim,
's isch einerlei, i gang im Chilchhof zue, –
briegg, alder nit! – und bis de bisch wien ich,
e gstandene Ma, se bini nümme do,
und d'Schof und Geiße weiden uf mi'm Grab.
Jo wegerli, und 's Hus wird alt und wüest;
der Rege wäscht der's wüester alli Nacht,
und d'Sunne bleicht der's schwärzer alli Tag,

The father says: Bless you, of course it can, what do you think?
Everything starts young and new and everything goes on gently
towards old age, and everything has an end and nothing stands still.
Do you hear the water rushing? And do you see up there one star
beside the other in the sky? You'd think none of them budged, but
everything's on the move, everything comes and goes.

Yes, that's how it is, it's no use looking at me like that. You're
young still. Never mind, I was young too, I have changed now, and
age, old age is coming on, and everywhere I go, to Gresgen or
Wies, to the fields or the woods, to Basel or home, it's all the same,
I am on the way to the churchyard willy-nilly and by the time
you are as old as I am, a grown man, I shan't be there any more, and
the sheep and the goats will be grazing on my grave. Yes it's true,
and the house is growing old and dirty too; the rain washes it dirtier
every night and the sun bleaches it blacker every day / and the

und im Vertäfer popperet der Wurm.
Es regnet no dur d'Bühne ab, es pfift
der Wind dur d'Chlimse. Drüber thuesch du au
no d'Auge zu; es chömme Chindeschind
und pletze dra. Z'letzt fuults im Fundement,
und 's hilft nüt meh. Und wemme nootno gar
zweitusig zählt, isch alles z'semme g'keit.
Und 's Dörfli sinkt no selber in si Grab.
Wo d'Chilche stoht, wo 's Vogts und 's Here Hus,
goht mit der Zit der Pflueg. –

       Der Bueb seit:

                    Nei, was de seisch!

       Der Aetti seit:

Je, 's isch nit anderst, lueg mi a, wie d'witt!
Isch Basel nit e schöni tolli Stadt?
'S sin Hüser drinn, 's isch mengi Chilche nit
so groß, und Chilche, 's sin in mengem Dorf
nit so viel Hüser. 'S isch e Volchspiel, 's wohnt
e Riichthum drinn, und menge brave Her,
und menge, woni gchennt ha, lit scho lang
im Chrützgang hinterm Münsterplatz und schloft.

beetles tick in the wainscots. The rain will come through the loft,
the wind will whistle through the cracks. Meantime you will have
closed your eyes too and your children's children will come and
patch it up. At long last it will get the rot in the foundations and then
there'll be no help for it. And by the year two thousand everything
will have tumbled down, and the whole village will have sunk into
its grave. In time the plough will go where the church stands,
where the mayor's house is, and the rectory.

The boy says: Why, fancy that!

His father says: Yes, that's how it is; it's no use looking at me
like that. Basel is a fine town, a grand town, isn't it? There are
houses there, some churches aren't as big, and so many churches,
why some villages haven't as many houses. It is a crowd of people,
there is lots of money there and lots of fine gentlemen, and a lot of
people I have known lie in the cloisters behind the Minster Square
and sleep./There's nothing for it, son, the hour will strike when

'S isch eithue, Chind, es schlacht emol e Stund,
goht Basel au ins Grab, und streckt no do
und dört e Glied zum Boden us, e Joch,
en alte Thurn, e Giebelwand; es wachst
do Holder druf, do Büechli, Tanne dört,
und Moos und Farn, und Reiger niste drinn –
's isch schad derfür! – und sin bis dörthi d'Lüt
so närsch wie jez, se göhn au Gspenster um,
d'Frau Faste, 's isch mer jez, sie fang scho a,
me seits emol, – der Lippi Läppeli,
und was weiß ich, wer meh. Was stoßisch mi?

Der Bueb seit:
Schwätz lisli, Aetti, bis mer über d'Bruck
do sin, und do an Berg und Wald verbei!
Dört obe jagt e wilde Jäger, weisch?
Und lueg, do niden in de Hürste seig
gwiß 's Eiermeidli g'lege, halber fuul,
's isch Johr und Tag. Hörsch, wie der Laubi schnuuft?

Der Aetti seit:
Er het der Pfnüsel! Seig doch nit so närsch!
Hüst, Laubi, Merz! – und loß die Todte go,

even Basel will go down to the grave too, and just poke up a limb here and there out of the ground, a beam, an old tower, a gable; the elder will grow on it, beeches here, firs there, and moss and fern, and herons will nest in it – such a pity! and, if people then are as foolish as they are now, ghosts will walk there, Frau Faste (I have an idea she has already started, at least that's what they say) and Lippi-Läppeli and heaven knows what besides! What are you nudging me for?

The boy says: Not so loud, Father, until we are across the bridge and past the hill and the wood over there! There is a wild huntsman hunts up there, didn't you know? And look, it must have been down in the bushes there that girl who sold eggs was found, half decayed, a year ago. Listen, how Laubi [one of the pair of oxen drawing the cart] snorts.

His father says: He's got a cold. Don't be so silly! Gee up, Laubi, Merz! and let the dead be,/they can't do anything to you. What was

sie thüen der nüt meh! – Je, was hani gseit?
Vo Basel, aß es au emol verfallt. –
Und goht in langer Zit e Wandersma
ne halbi Stund, e Stund wit dra verbei,
se luegt er dure, lit ke Nebel druf,
und seit sim Cammerad, wo mittem goht:
«Lueg, dört isch Basel gstande! Selle Thurn
seig d'Peterschilche gsi, 's isch schad derfür!»

Der Bueb seit:
Nei, Aetti, ischs der Ernst? es cha nit sy!

Der Aetti seit:
Je, 's isch nit anderst, lueg mi a, wie d'witt,
und mit der Zit verbrennt die ganzi Welt.
Es goht e Wächter us um Mitternacht,
e fremde Ma, me weiß nit, wer er isch,
er funklet wie ne Stern, und rüeft: «Wacht auf!
Wacht auf, es kommt der Tag!» – Drob röthet si
Der Himmel, und es dundert überal,
z'erst heimlig, alsg'mach lut, wie sellemol,
wo Anno Sechsenünzgi der Franzos
so uding gschosse het. Der Bode schwankt,

I saying? About Basel, that it will fall down too one day. – And if
long after a traveller goes by, an hour or even half an hour away, he
will be able to look across, if there is no mist, and will say to his
mate who is with him: 'Look, that is where Basel stood. That
tower they say was St Peter's Church. A pity it's all gone.'

The boy says: No, Father, are you serious? I can't believe it.

His father says: Yes, that's how it is, it's no use looking at me
like that, and in time the whole world will burn up. A watchman
will go out at midnight, a foreign chap nobody knows, he'll glitter
like a star and cry, 'Awake! Behold, the day is come!' and the sky
will turn red and there'll be thunder everywhere, first soft, then
loud like that time in ninety-six when the French bombarded so
fiercely. The ground will shake/so that the church towers will rock,

aß d'Chilchthürn guge, d'Glocke schlagen a,
und lüte selber Betzit wit und breit,
und Alles betet. Drüber chunt der Tag;
o, b'hüetis Gott, me bruucht ke Sunn derzu,
der Himmel stoht im Blitz, und d'Welt im Glast.
Druf gschieht no viel, i ha jez nit der Zit;
und endli zündets a, und brennt und brennt,
wo Boden isch, und niemes löscht. Es glumst
wohl selber ab. Wie meinsch, siehts us derno?

Der Bueb seit:

O Aetti, sag mer nüt me! Zwor wie gohts
de Lüte denn, wenn alles brennt und brennt?

Der Aetti seit:

He, d'Lüt sind nümme do, wenns brennt, sie sin –
wo sin sie? Seig du frumm, un halt die wohl,
geb, wo de bisch, und bhalt di Gwisse rein!
Siesch nit, wie d'Luft mit schöne Sterne prangt!
'S isch jede Stern verglichlige ne Dorf,
und witer obe seig e schöni Stadt,

the bells will sound and ring out for the service by themselves to
all and sundry, and everyone will pray. Then the day will come;
O God preserve us, there will be no need of any sun, the sky will be
nothing but lightning and the world will be all afire. And a lot more
will happen that I've no time for now, and at last it will catch fire
and blaze and blaze, wherever there is any land, and no one to put
it out. I suppose it will burn out by itself. And what do you think
it will look like then?

The boy says: Oh, Father, don't tell me any more. But – what'll
happen to the people when everything blazes and blazes?

The father says: Why, the people won't be there when the fire
comes, they – well, where'll they be? You be good and live decent,
wherever you are and keep a clear conscience. Do you see how the
sky is splendid with bright stars? Each star is as it might be a vil-
lage, and farther up perhaps there is a fine town, / you can't see it

me sieht sie nit vo do, und haltsch di guet,
se chunnsch in so ne Stern, und 's isch der wohl,
und findsch der Aetti dört, wenn's Gottswill isch,
und 's Chüngi selig, d'Muetter. Oebbe fahrsch
au d'Milchstroß uf in die verborgni Stadt,
und wenn de sitwärts abe luegsch, was siehsch?
e Röttler Schloß! Der Belche stoht verchohlt,
der Blauen au, als wie zwee alti Thürn,
und zwische drinn isch alles use brennt,
bis tief in Boden abe. D'Wiese het
ke Wasser meh, 's isch alles öd und schwarz,
und todtestill, so wit me luegt – das siehsch,
und seisch di'm Cammerad, wo mitder goht:
«Lueg, dört isch d'Erde g'si, und selle Berg
het Belche gheiße! Nit gar wit dervo
isch Wisleth gsi, dört hani au scho glebt,
und Stiere g'wettet, Holz go Basel g'führt,
und broochet, Matte g'raust, und Liechtspöh g'macht,
und g'vätterlet, bis an mi selig End,
und möcht jez nümme hi.» – Hüst Laubi, Merz!

from here, and if you live decent you will go to one of those stars
and you'll be happy there, and you'll find your father there, if it is
God's will, and poor Bessie, your mother. Perhaps you'll drive up
the Milky Way into that hidden town, and if you look down to one
side, what'll you see – Rötteln Castle! The Belchen will be charred
and the Blauen too, like two old towers, and between the two every-
thing will be burnt out, right into the ground. There won't be any
water in the Wiese, everything will be bare and black and deathly
quiet, as far as you can see; you'll see that and say to your mate
that's with you: 'Look, that's where the earth was, and that moun-
tain was called the Belchen. And not far away was Wieslet; I used
to live there and harness my oxen, cart wood to Basel, and plough,
and drain meadows and make splints for torches, and potter about
until my death, and I wouldn't like to go back now!' Gee up,
Laubi, Merz!

JOHANN PETER HEBEL

An Herrn Pfarrer Jäck

[...] 'S ISCH wohr, Her Jäck, i ha kei eigene Baum,
i ha kei Huus, i ha kei Schof im Stal,
kei Pflueg im Feld, kei Immestand im Hof,
kei Chatz, kei Hüenli, mengmol au kei Geld.
'S macht nüt. 'S isch doch im ganze Dorf kei Buur
so rich as ich. Der wüsset wie me's macht.
Me meint, me heigs. So meini au, i heigs
im süesse Wahn, und wo ne Bäumli blüeiht,
's isch mi, und wo ne Feld voll Ähri schwankt,
's isch au mi; wo ne Säuli Eichle frißt,
es frißt sie us mim Wald.

So bin i rich. Doch richer bin i no
im Heuet, in der Erndt, im frohe Herbst.
I sag: Jez chömmet Lüt, wer will und mag,
und heuet, schnidet, hauet Trübli ab!
I ha mi Freud an allem gha, mi Herz
an alle Düften, aller Schöni g'labt.
Was übrig isch, isch euer. Tragets heim [...]

Letter to the Reverend Mr Jäck

IT's true, sir, I have no tree of my own, I've got no house, I've got
no sheep in the fold, no plough in the field, no beehive in my yard,
no cat, no hen, and very often no money either. It makes no odds;
even so, there's not a farmer in the village as rich as I am. You
know how it's done; you make believe you've got it. And so I
make believe I have it in sweet delusion, and wherever a tree is in
bloom it's mine, and wherever a field waves full of corn it's mine
too; and wherever a pig eats acorns it eats them in my woods.

And so, this way, I'm rich. But I'm even richer in the hay harvest,
at reaping time, in glad autumn. I say: 'Come along now every-
body, anyone who likes, and mow and reap and cut the grapes! I
have had my pleasure of all this, refreshed my heart with all the
scents, with all the beauty. The rest is yours. Take it home with
you.'

FRIEDRICH HÖLDERLIN

Abendphantasie

Vor seiner Hütte ruhig im Schatten sitzt
Der Pflüger, dem Genügsamen raucht sein Herd.
    Gastfreundlich tönt dem Wanderer im
       Friedlichen Dorfe die Abendglocke.

Wohl kehren jetzt die Schiffer zum Hafen auch,
In fernen Städten fröhlich verrauscht des Markts
    Geschäft'ger Lärm; in stiller Laube
       Glänzt das gesellige Mahl den Freunden.

Wohin denn ich? Es leben die Sterblichen
Von Lohn und Arbeit; wechselnd in Müh' und Ruh'
    Ist alles freudig; warum schläft denn
       Nimmer nur mir in der Brust der Stachel?

Am Abendhimmel blühet ein Frühling auf;
Unzählig blühn die Rosen, und ruhig scheint
    Die goldne Welt; o dorthin nehmt mich,
       Purpurne Wolken! und möge droben

Evening Fantasy

The ploughman is sitting quietly in front of his cottage in the shade, the smoke goes up from the frugal man's hearth. In the peaceful village the evening bell is sounding a welcoming note to the traveller.

Now I suppose the boatmen are returning to harbour too, and in distant cities the busy hum of the market is dying away; in some quiet bower a hospitable meal is shining on a table friends sit round.

But where am I to go? Mortals live by wages and work; in alternate toil and rest everyone finds satisfaction: why is it always in my breast that the goad is never still?

A springtime is blossoming in the evening sky, the roses bloom unnumbered, and the golden world seems to be at rest; oh, take me there with you, purple clouds, and may

In Licht und Luft zerrinnen mir Lieb und Leid! –
Doch, wie verscheucht von törichter Bitte, flieht
   Der Zauber; dunkel wird's, und einsam
     Unter dem Himmel, wie immer, bin ich. –

Komm du nun, sanfter Schlummer! zu viel begehrt
Das Herz; doch endlich, Jugend, verglühst du ja,
   Du ruhelose, träumerische!
     Friedlich und heiter ist dann das Alter.

Hyperions Schicksalslied

IHR wandelt droben im Licht
   Auf weichem Boden, selige Genien!
    Glänzende Götterlüfte
     Rühren euch leicht,
       Wie die Finger der Künstlerin
       Heilige Saiten.

Schicksallos, wie der schlafende
   Säugling, atmen die Himmlischen;

my love and sorrow dissolve there in the light and the air! But as though my foolish prayer has disturbed it, the magic is disappearing; darkness is falling and I stand here lonely under the sky, as always.

Come now, gentle sleep! the heart desires too much; but in the end, restless and dreamy years of youth, your glow will die away; then old age will be peaceful and serene.

Hyperion's Song of Fate

YOU walk up there in the light on soft ground, blessed genii! Glistening divine breezes touch you gently, as the harpist's fingers touch sacred strings.

The heavenly ones breathe fatelessly, like a sleeping infant;/their

Keusch bewahrt
In bescheidener Knospe
Blühet ewig
Ihnen der Geist,
Und die seligen Augen
Blicken in stiller
Ewiger Klarheit.

Doch uns ist gegeben
Auf keiner Stätte zu ruhn,
Es schwinden, es fallen
Die leidenden Menschen
Blindlings von einer
Stunde zur andern,
Wie Wasser von Klippe
Zu Klippe geworfen,
Jahrlang ins Ungewisse hinab.

An die Parzen

NUR einen Sommer gönnt, ihr Gewaltigen!
Und einen Herbst, zu reifem Gesange mir,
Daß williger mein Herz, vom süßen
Spiele gesättiget, dann mir sterbe.

spirit blooms eternally, chastely preserved in modest bud and their blissful eyes see with tranquil eternal clarity.

But on us it has been laid never to rest in any place; suffering human beings dwindle and fall headlong from one hour to the next, hurled like water from precipice to precipice down through the years into uncertainty.

To the Fates

GRANT me just one summer, you mighty ones, and one autumn to ripen my song, so that my heart, sated with sweet playing, may die more willingly.

Die Seele, der im Leben ihr göttlich Recht
Nicht ward, sie ruht auch drunten im Orkus nicht;
    Doch ist mir einst das Heil'ge, das am
      Herzen mir liegt, das Gedicht, gelungen:

Willkommen dann, o Stille der Schattenwelt!
Zufrieden bin ich, wenn auch mein Saitenspiel
    Mich nicht hinabgeleitet; einmal
      Lebt' ich, wie Götter, und mehr bedarf's nicht.

Erntezeit

REIF sind, in Feuer getaucht, gekochet
Die Früchte und auf der Erde geprüfet und ein Gesetz ist
Daß alles hineingeht, Schlangen gleich,
Prophetisch, träumend auf
Den Hügeln des Himmels. Und vieles
Wie auf den Schultern eine
Last von Scheitern ist
Zu behalten. Aber bös sind
Die Pfade. Nämlich unrecht,

The soul who has not received its divinely appointed rights in
life does not rest even in Orcus below; but if I ever achieve that
sacred thing which is my heart's desire, my poetry,
    Then welcome, tranquillity of the world of shades! I shall be
content, even if the music of my strings does not escort me down:
once I shall have lived as the gods live, and there is no need of
more.

Harvest-time

THE fruits are ripe, dipped in fire and cooked, and tested on the
earth, and it is a law that everything shall go into it, like snakes,
prophetic, dreaming on the hills of heaven. And much, like a load
of logs on the shoulders, has to be remembered. But the paths are
bad./For the captive elements and the ancient laws of the earth go

Wie Rosse, gehn die gefangenen
Element' und alten
Gesetze der Erd. Und immer
Ins Ungebundene gehet eine Sehnsucht. Vieles aber ist
Zu behalten. Und Not die Treue.
Vorwärts aber und rückwärts wollen wir
Nicht sehn. Uns wiegen lassen, wie
Auf schwankem Kahne der See.

Sonnenuntergang

Wo bist du? trunken dämmert die Seele mir
Von aller deiner Wonne; denn eben ist's,
    Daß ich gelauscht, wie, goldner Töne
        Voll, der entzückende Sonnenjüngling

Sein Abendlied auf himmlischer Leier spielt';
Es tönten rings die Wälder und Hügel nach,
    Doch fern ist er zu frommen Völkern,
        Die ihn noch ehren, hinweggegangen.

out of step, like horses. And always a longing reaches for the in-
finite. But much has to be remembered. And faithfulness is a need.
But we will not look forwards or backwards. Let ourselves be
cradled as in a swaying boat the lake cradles us.

Sunset

WHERE are you? My soul looms drunken with all your joy, for it
is just this moment that I was listening to the entrancing youthful
sun-god
    Playing his evening chant on a heavenly lyre; the woods and
hills re-echoed it. But he has gone, far away to pious peoples who
still revere him.

Brot und Wein

I

Ringsum ruhet die Stadt; still wird die erleuchtete
    Gasse,
Und, mit Fackeln geschmückt, rauschen die Wagen
    hinweg.
Satt gehn heim von Freuden des Tags zu ruhen die
    Menschen,
Und Gewinn und Verlust wäget ein sinniges Haupt
Wohlzufrieden zu Haus; leer steht von Trauben und
    Blumen
Und von Werken der Hand ruht der geschäftige Markt.
Aber das Saitenspiel tönt fern aus Gärten; vielleicht, daß
Dort ein Liebendes spielt oder ein einsamer Mann
Ferner Freunde gedenkt und der Jugendzeit; und die
    Brunnen
Immerquillend und frisch rauschen an duftendem Beet.
Still in dämmriger Luft ertönen geläutete Glocken,
Und der Stunden gedenk rufet ein Wächter die Zahl.
Jetzt auch kommet ein Wehn und regt die Gipfel des
    Hains auf,
Sieh! und das Schattenbild unserer Erde, der Mond,

Bread and Wine

I

ALL round us the city is at rest, the lighted street is growing quiet,
and the carriages, decked with torches, rattle off. People are coming
home sated from the pleasures of the day-time to rest, and crafty
heads are weighing up profit and loss contentedly at home; the busy
market-place is empty now of grapes and flowers and is resting from
the work of men's hands. But from distant gardens comes a sound
of strings; perhaps some lover is playing there or a lonely man is
thinking of distant friends and of his youth; and the fountains, ever
welling and fresh, are purling by the scented flower-beds. Pealed
bells are sounding quietly in the twilight air and a watchman mind-
ful of the hours is calling out their number. Now there is a breath
which moves the tree-tops in the wood, and look, now the shadow
image of our earth, the moon,/is on her way in secret too; night,

Kommet geheim nun auch; die Schwärmerische, die
   Nacht kommt,
Voll mit Sternen und wohl wenig bekümmert um uns,
Glänzt die Erstaunende dort, die Fremdlingin unter den
   Menschen
Über Gebirgeshöhn traurig und prächtig herauf.

II

Wunderbar ist die Gunst der Hocherhabnen und niemand
Weiß von wannen und was einem geschiehet von ihr.
So bewegt sie die Welt und die hoffende Seele der
   Menschen,
Selbst kein Weiser versteht, was sie bereitet, denn so
Will es der oberste Gott, der sehr dich liebet, und darum
Ist noch lieber, wie sie, dir der besonnene Tag.
Aber zuweilen liebt auch klares Auge den Schatten
Und versuchet zu Lust, eh' es die Not ist, den Schlaf,
Oder es blickt auch gern ein treuer Mann in die Nacht hin,
Ja, es ziemet sich ihr Kränze zu weihn und Gesang,
Weil den Irrenden sie geheiliget ist und den Toten,

the dream-laden, is coming; full of stars and, it seems, little con-
cerned with us, the astonishing one, the stranger among humans, is
gleaming forth sadly and splendidly up over the mountain tops.

II

The favour of lofty exalted night is miraculous and no one knows
whence her gifts come and what she brings about in our lives. Thus
she moves the world and the hoping soul of men, there is not even
a sage who understands what she has in store; for thus the supreme
God wills it, who loves you greatly, and that is why thoughtful day
is even dearer to you than she. But at times even clear eyes love the
shadow and seek to sleep for pleasure before it is time; or a faithful
man likes to gaze into the night; yes, it is fitting to dedicate gar-
lands to her and song, because she is consecrated to the bewildered
and the dead,/though she herself subsists eternally, utterly free in

294

Selber aber besteht, ewig, in freiestem Geist.
Aber sie muß uns auch, daß in der zaudernden Weile,
Daß im Finstern für uns einiges Haltbare sei,
Uns die Vergessenheit und das Heiligtrunkene gönnen,
Gönnen das strömende Wort, das, wie die Liebenden, sei
Schlummerlos, und vollern Pokal und kühneres Leben,
Heilig Gedächtnis auch, wachend zu bleiben bei Nacht.

III

Auch verbergen umsonst das Herz im Busen, umsonst
    nur
Halten den Mut noch wir, Meister und Knaben, denn wer
Möcht' es hindern und wer möcht' uns die Freude
    verbieten?
Göttliches Feuer auch treibet, bei Tag und bei Nacht,
Aufzubrechen. So komm! daß wir das Offene schauen,
Daß ein Eigenes wir suchen, so weit es auch ist.
Fest bleibt Eins; es sei um Mittag oder es gehe
Bis in die Mitternacht, immer bestehet ein Maß,
Allen gemein, doch jeglichem auch ist eignes beschieden,
Dahin gehet und kommt jeder, wohin er es kann.

spirit. But she must also grant us oblivion and holy intoxication so
that in the hesitating duration of time and in the darkness there
should be something for us to take hold of, she must grant us the
flowing word which, like lovers, shall be without sleep, and a fuller
cup and bolder life, holy remembrance, too, to stay awake at night.

III

Moreover, it is in vain that we, masters and apprentices, hide our
hearts in our breasts, in vain that we hold ourselves back, for who
would prevent it and who would forbid us this joy? For it is divine
fire which urges us by day and night to set out. Come then, let us
look at open spaces, let us seek something that is ours, however far
it may be. One thing is certain, whether at noon or towards mid-
night, there is always a measure common to all, but to each one a
measure of his own is allotted, every man must go and come where
he can. / So be it! and jubilant madness when it seizes upon the singer

Drum! und spotten des Spotts mag gern frohlockender
    Wahnsinn,
Wenn er in heiliger Nacht plötzlich die Sänger ergreift,
Drum an den Isthmos komm! dorthin, wo das offene
    Meer rauscht
Am Parnaß und der Schnee delphische Felsen umglänzt,
Dort ins Land des Olymps, dort auf die Höhe Cithärons,
Unter die Fichten dort, unter die Trauben, von wo
Thebe drunten und Ismenos rauscht im Lande des
    Kadmos,
Dorther kommt und zurück deutet der kommende Gott.

IV

Seliges Griechenland! du Haus der Himmlischen alle,
Also ist wahr, was einst wir in der Jugend gehört?
Festlicher Saal! der Boden ist Meer! und Tische die Berge,
Wahrlich zu einzigem Brauche vor alters gebaut!
Aber die Thronen, wo? die Tempel, und wo die Gefäße,
Wo mit Nektar gefüllt, Göttern zu Lust der Gesang?
Wo, wo leuchten sie denn, die fernhintreffenden Sprüche?
Delphi schlummert und wo tönet das große Geschick?

in holy night, loves to mock at mockery; therefore come to the
Isthmus! come where the open sea roars by Parnassus and the snow
gleams on Delphian cliffs, into the land of Olympus, there up to the
heights of Cithaeron, up there under the pines, under the clusters
of grapes, from where Thebe and Ismenus roar far below in the land
of Cadmus – that is where the coming god comes from, and it is
there that he points back to.

IV

Blessed Greece! You mansion of all the heavenly ones, so what we
heard in our youth is true, after all? Festive hall! Ocean the floor!
and mountains the tables, truly built before the ages for one use and
one use only! But where are the thrones, the temples, and where
the vessels, where the nectar-filled songs for the pleasure of the
gods? Where, oh, where do they shine now, those utterances which
used to strike home at a distance? Delphi sleeps, and where does the
great fate sound?/Where is swift fate? Where is the thunderous im-

Wo ist das schnelle? wo brichts, allgegenwärtigen Glücks
    voll
Donnernd aus heiterer Luft über die Augen herein?
Vater Äther! so riefs und flog von Zunge zu Zunge,
Tausendfach, es ertrug keiner das Leben allein;
Ausgeteilet erfreut solch Gut und getauschet, mit
    Fremden
Wirds ein Jubel, es wächst schlafend des Wortes Gewalt:
Vater! heiter! und hallt, so weit es gehet, das uralt
Zeichen, von Eltern geerbt, treffend und schaffend hinab.
Denn so kehren die Himmlischen ein, tiefschütternd
    gelangt so
Aus den Schatten herab unter die Menschen ihr Tag.

v

Unempfunden kommen sie erst, es streben entgegen
Ihnen die Kinder, zu hell kommet, zu blendend das Glück,
Und es scheut sie der Mensch, kaum weiß zu sagen ein
    Halbgott
Wer mit Namen sie sind, die mit den Gaben ihm nahn.
Aber der Mut von ihnen ist groß, es füllen das Herz ihm

pact upon the eye out of a clear sky, full of ubiquitous fortune?
'Father Æther!' thus they used to cry, and it flew from tongue to
tongue a thousandfold, no one could bear to live alone; such
treasure gives delight when shared, and when exchanged with
strangers it becomes jubilation, in sleep the power of the word
grows: 'Father! Serene!' and the ancient symbol inherited from
ancestors echoes down as far as it can, striking home and creating as
it goes. For this is how the heavenly ones enter in, in this way their
day-time descends, deeply convulsing, out of the shadows, to men.

v

At first they come unrecognized, the children press forward to
them, fortune comes too bright, too dazzling, and man avoids
them, even a demigod can hardly say who they are by name who
approach him with gifts. But they are magnanimous,/their joys fill

Ihre Freuden und kaum weiß er zu brauchen das Gut,
Schafft, verschwendet und fast ward ihm Unheiliges
     heilig,
Das er mit segnender Hand töricht und gütig berührt.
Möglichst dulden die Himmlischen dies; dann aber in
     Wahrheit
Kommen sie selbst, und gewohnt werden die Menschen
     des Glücks
Und des Tags und zu schaun die Offenbaren, das Antlitz
Derer, welche, schon längst Eines und Alles genannt,
Tief die verschwiegene Brust mit freier Genüge gefüllet,
Und zuerst und allein alles Verlangen beglückt;
So ist der Mensch; wenn da ist das Gut, und es sorget mit
     Gaben
Selber ein Gott für ihn, kennet und sieht er es nicht,
Tragen muß er zuvor; nun aber nennt er sein Liebstes,
Nun, nun müssen dafür Worte, wie Blumen entstehn.

VI

Und nun denkt er zu ehren in Ernst die seligen Götter,
Wirklich und wahrhaft muß alles verkünden ihr Lob.

his heart and he scarcely knows how to use this wealth; he works,
wastes, and is tempted to consider holy the profane things which
he touches foolishly, well-meaningly with beneficent hand. The
heavenly ones suffer this as long as they can; then they come them-
selves in truth, and men grow accustomed to joy and to the bright-
ness of day and to seeing the revealed ones, the faces of those who
long ago were called the One and the All, filled the silent breast with
liberal sufficiency and first and alone gratified all desire; man is like
that; when bounty is there and a god himself provides gifts for him,
he does not realize and see it. Beforehand he has to bear a load, but
now he names his most cherished, now – now words for it must
spring up like flowers.

VI

And now he means to worship the blessed gods in earnest, and
everything must show forth their praise truly and truthfully./Noth-

Nichts darf schauen das Licht, was nicht den Hohen
     gefället,
Vor den Äther gebührt Müßigversuchendes nicht.
Drum in der Gegenwart des Himmlischen würdig zu
     stehen,
Richten in herrlichen Ordnungen Völker sich auf
Untereinander und baun die schönen Tempel und Städte
Fest und edel, sie gehn über Gestaden empor –
Aber wo sind sie? wo blühn die Bekannten, die Kronen
     des Festes?
Thebe welkt und Athen; rauschen die Waffen nicht mehr
In Olympia, nicht die goldnen Wagen des Kampfspiels,
Und bekränzen sich denn nimmer die Schiffe Korinths?
Warum schweigen auch sie, die alten heil'gen Theater?
Warum freuet sich denn nicht der geweihete Tanz?
Warum zeichnet, wie sonst, die Stirne des Mannes ein
     Gott nicht,
Drückt den Stempel, wie sonst, nicht dem Getroffenen
     auf?
Oder er kam auch selbst und nahm des Menschen Gestalt
     an
Und vollendet' und schloß tröstend das himmlische Fest.

ing may see the light which does not please the high ones, in the
face of the Æther idle experiments are not fitting. And so, in order
to stand worthily in the presence of the heavenly ones, nations arise
in splendid hierarchies among themselves and build beautiful
temples and cities, strong and noble, they rise up on the shores – but
where are they now? where are the famous, the crowns of the
feast? Thebes is wilted and Athens too; do the arms no longer
rattle in Olympia, the golden cars of the chariot race, and are the
ships of Corinth no longer garlanded? Why are they silent now,
the ancient holy theatres? Why does the sacred dance no longer re-
joice? Why does it no longer happen that a god marks a man's fore-
head, no longer prints the stamp on the stricken? Or he even came
himself and took on human shape and perfected it and brought,
comforting, the heavenly feast to a close.

VII

Aber Freund! wir kommen zu spät. Zwar leben die
     Götter,
Aber über dem Haupt droben in anderer Welt.
Endlos wirken sie da und scheinens wenig zu achten,
Ob wir leben, so sehr schonen die Himmlischen uns.
Denn nicht immer vermag ein schwaches Gefäß sie zu
     fassen,
Nur zu Zeiten erträgt göttliche Fülle der Mensch.
Traum von ihnen ist drauf das Leben. Aber das Irrsal
Hilft, wie Schlummer, und stark machet die Not und die
     Nacht,
Bis daß Helden genug in der ehernen Wiege gewachsen,
Herzen an Kraft, wie sonst, ähnlich den Himmlischen
     sind.
Donnernd kommen sie drauf. Indessen dünket mir
     öfters
Besser zu schlafen, wie so ohne Genossen zu sein,
So zu harren und was zu tun indes und zu sagen,
Weiß ich nicht und wozu Dichter in dürftiger Zeit?

VII

But we have come too late, my friend. It is true that the gods are
still alive, but up there above our heads in another world. There
they are endlessly active and seem to care little whether we are
alive, so much do the heavenly ones spare us. For a weak vessel
cannot always contain them, man can only support divine plenty
from time to time. Life henceforward is a dream of them. But be-
wilderment helps, like slumber, and night and distress make us
strong, until enough heroes have grown in the brazen cradle,
enough hearts exist, as of old, like those of the heavenly ones. Then
they will come thundering. Meanwhile it often seems to me better
to sleep than to be without companions like this. I cannot wait like
this and I do not know what to do or say in the meantime, and what
is the use of poets in a poverty-stricken age?/But they are, you say,

Aber sie sind, sagst du, wie des Weingotts heilige
  Priester,
Welche von Lande zu Land zogen in heiliger Nacht.

VIII

Nämlich, als vor einiger Zeit, uns dünket sie lange,
Aufwärts stiegen sie all, welche das Leben beglückt,
Als der Vater gewandt sein Angesicht von den Menschen,
Und das Trauern mit Recht über der Erde begann,
Als erschienen zuletzt ein stiller Genius, himmlisch
Tröstend, welcher des Tags Ende verkündet' und
  schwand,
Ließ zum Zeichen, daß einst er da gewesen und wieder
Käme, der himmlische Chor einige Gaben zurück,
Derer menschlich, wie sonst, wir uns zu freuen ver-
  möchten,
Denn zur Freude, mit Geist, wurde das Größre zu groß
Unter den Menschen und noch, noch fehlen die Starken
  zu höchsten
Freuden, aber es lebt stille noch einiger Dank.
Brot ist der Erde Frucht, doch ists vom Lichte gesegnet,
Und vom donnernden Gott kommet die Freude des
  Weins.

like the holy priests of the wine god, who used to go from country
to country in holy night.

VIII

For, some time ago – it seems long to us – they went up, all of
them who had made life joyful, when the Father turned his face
away from mankind, and for good reason mourning began all over
the earth; when at last a quiet Genius appeared giving heavenly
comfort, who announced the end of the day and vanished, the
heavenly choir left, as a sign that he had been here once and would
come again, a few gifts behind at which we might be able to rejoice
humanly as of old, for what was greater became too great among
men for spiritual joy and now, even now, those who are strong
enough for the highest joys are lacking, though some thankfulness
still lives on quietly. Though bread is the fruit of the earth, it is
blessed by light, and the joy of wine derives from the thundering god.

Darum denken wir auch dabei der Himmlischen, die
  sonst
Da gewesen und die kehren in richtiger Zeit,
Darum singen sie auch mit Ernst, die Sänger, den
  Weingott
Und nicht eitel erdacht tönet dem Alten das Lob.

IX

Ja! sie sagen mit Recht, er söhne den Tag mit der Nacht
  aus,
Führe des Himmels Gestirn ewig hinunter, hinauf,
Allzeit froh, wie das Laub der immergrünenden Fichte,
Das er liebt, und der Kranz, den er von Efeu gewählt,
Weil er bleibet und selbst die Spur der entflohenen
  Götter
Götterlosen hinab unter das Finstere bringt.
Was der Alten Gesang von Kindern Gottes geweissagt,
Siehe! wir sind es, wir; Frucht von Hesperien ists!
Wunderbar und genau ists als an Menschen erfüllet,
Glaube, wer es geprüft! aber so vieles geschieht,
Keines wirket, denn wir sind herzlos, Schatten, bis unser
Vater Äther erkannt jeden und allen gehört.

So when we think of them we think of the heavenly ones who were
here of old and who will return when the time is right, and so they
sing with solemnity, the poets, to the wine god and their praise does
not sound as mere vain imaginings in the Ancient's ears.

IX

Yes, they are right when they say that he reconciles day with
night, leads the constellations everlastingly down and up the sky,
ever joyful like the foliage of the evergreen pine that he loves, and
the garland that he chose to be of ivy, because it lasts and even
brings the trace of the fugitive gods down to the godless into the
dark. What the song of the ancients prophesied about the children
of God – look, it is us, us! It is the fruit of Hesperia! It is miracu-
lously and exactly fulfilled as in men; let him who has tried it,
believe! But so much happens, nothing takes effect, for we are
heartless, shadows, until our Father Æther is recognized and

FRIEDRICH HÖLDERLIN

Aber indessen kommt als Fackelschwinger des Höchsten
Sohn, der Syrier, unter die Schatten herab.
Selige Weise sehns; ein Lächeln aus der gefangnen
Seele leuchtet, dem Licht tauet ihr Auge noch auf.
Sanfter träumet und schläft in Armen der Erde der Titan,
Selbst der neidische, selbst Cerberus trinket und schläft.

Hälfte des Lebens

MIT gelben Birnen hänget
Und voll mit wilden Rosen
Das Land in den See,
Ihr holden Schwäne,
Und trunken von Küssen
Tunkt ihr das Haupt
Ins heilignüchterne Wasser.

Weh mir, wo nehm' ich, wenn
Es Winter ist, die Blumen, und wo
Den Sonnenschein
Und Schatten der Erde?
Die Mauern stehn
Sprachlos und kalt, im Winde
Klirren die Fahnen.

belongs to each and to all./But meanwhile the son of the Highest
comes, the Syrian, sweeping the torch down to the shades. Blissful
sages can see it; a smile lights up from the captive soul, their eyes
yet thaw towards the light. The Titan dreams more softly and
sleeps in the arms of the earth, even the envious one, even Cerberus
drinks and sleeps.

The Middle of Life

THE land with yellow pears and full of wild roses hangs down into
the lake, you gracious swans, and drunk with kisses you dip your
heads into the sacredly sober water.

Alas for me, where shall I get the flowers when it is winter and
where the sunshine and shadow of earth? The walls stand speech-
less and cold, the weathervanes rattle in the wind.

NOVALIS

Aus: *Hymnen an die Nacht*

HINÜBER wall ich,
Und jede Pein
Wird einst ein Stachel
Der Wollust sein.
Noch wenig Zeiten
So bin ich los,
Und liege trunken
Der Lieb' im Schoß.
Unendliches Leben
Wogt mächtig in mir,
Ich schaue von oben
Herunter nach dir.
An jenem Hügel
Verlischt dein Glanz –
Ein Schatten bringet
Den kühlenden Kranz.
O! sauge, Geliebter,
Gewaltig mich an,
Daß ich entschlummern
Und lieben kann –
Ich fühle des Todes
Verjüngende Flut,

From: *Hymns to the Night*

I SHALL pass over, and then every torment will be a goad of
pleasure. Only a little time and I shall be free and lie in ecstasy in
the lap of love. Endless life will surge strongly in me, I shall look
down on you from above. Your glow will die away on that hill, a
shadow will bring a cooling garland. Oh, draw me, Beloved,
powerfully on, so that I can fall into slumber and can love. I feel
the rejuvenating stream of death,/I feel my blood turned into balm

Zu Balsam und Äther
Verwandelt mein Blut —
Ich lebe bei Tage
Voll Glauben und Mut
Und sterbe die Nächte
In heiliger Glut.

DER Jüngling bist du, der seit langer Zeit,
Auf unsern Gräbern steht in tiefem Sinnen;
Ein tröstlich Zeichen in der Dunkelheit —
Der höheren Menschheit freudiges Beginnen.
Was uns gesenkt in tiefe Traurigkeit,
Zieht uns mit süßer Sehnsucht nun von hinnen.
Im Tode ward das ewge Leben kund,
Du bist der Tod und machst uns erst gesund.

CLEMENS BRENTANO

Abendständchen

HÖR', es klagt die Flöte wieder
Und die kühlen Brunnen rauschen,
Golden weh'n die Töne nieder;
Stille, stille, lass' uns lauschen!

and aether — by day I live full of faith and courage, and each night
I die in sacred fire.

YOU are the youth who for long has stood on our graves in deep
contemplation; a comforting sign in the darkness — the joyous be-
ginning of higher humanity. What once plunged us into deep sad-
ness now draws us hence with sweet longing. Eternal life has been
revealed in death; you are death and it is only by you that we are
made whole.

Evening Serenade

LISTEN, the flute laments again and the cool fountains rustle,
Golden the notes waft down. Quiet, quiet, let us listen!

Holdes Bitten, mild Verlangen,
Wie es süß zum Herzen spricht!
Durch die Nacht, die mich umfangen,
Blickt zu mir der Töne Licht.

Nachklänge Beethovenscher Musik (2)

GOTT! Dein Himmel faßt mich in den Haaren,
Deine Erde reißt mich in die Hölle!
Herr, wo soll ich doch mein Herz bewahren,
Daß ich deine Schwelle sicher stelle?
Also fleh ich durch die Nacht, da fließen
Meine Klagen hin wie Feuerbronnen,
Die mit glühnden Meeren mich umschließen,
Doch inmitten hab ich Grund gewonnen,
Rage hoch gleich rätselvollen Riesen,
Memnons Bild, des Morgens erste Sonnen,
Fragend ihren Strahl zur Stirn mir schießen,
Und den Traum, den Mitternacht gesponnen,
Üb ich tönend, um den Tag zu grüßen.

Gracious asking, gentle yearning, how sweetly it speaks to the
heart! Through the night which holds me embraced, the light of the
notes flashes towards me.

Echoes of Beethoven's Music (2)

GOD, Thy heaven has me by the hair, Thy earth drags me into hell;
Lord, where shall I keep my heart so that I can keep safe Thy
threshold? Thus I implore Thee through the night, in which my
laments stream like fountains of fire which surround me with
flaming seas; but in the midst of it I have found foothold, I stand
forth like mysterious giants, Memnon's statue, the first suns of
morning shoot their questioning rays at my forehead, and the
dream which midnight spun I now rehearse to greet the day.

Was reif in diesen Zeilen steht,
Was lächelnd winkt und sinnend fleht,
Das soll kein Kind betrüben;
Die Einfalt hat es ausgesät,
Die Schwermut hat hindurch geweht,
Die Sehnsucht hat's getrieben.

Und ist das Feld einst abgemäht,
Die Armut durch die Stoppeln geht,
Sucht Ähren, die geblieben;
Sucht Lieb', die für sie untergeht,
Sucht Lieb', die mit ihr aufersteht,
Sucht Lieb', die sie kann lieben.

Und hat sie einsam und verschmäht,
Die Nacht durch, dankend in Gebet,
Die Körner ausgerieben,
Liest sie, als früh der Hahn gekräht,
Was Lieb' erhielt, was Leid verweht,
Ans Feldkreuz angeschrieben:
«O, Stern und Blume, Geist und Kleid,
Lieb', Leid und Zeit und Ewigkeit!»

What is ripe in these lines, what smilingly beckons and thought-fully implores, that will not hurt a child; simplicity has sown it, sorrow has blown across it, yearning has made it grow. And when the field is harvested, poverty goes through the stubble and looks for ears that are left; looks for love, which will go down to the grave with her, looks for love that will rise again with her, looks for love that she can love. And when she in her loneliness and neglect has ground the grain all through the night, giving thanks in prayer, she will read, when the cock has crowed in the morning, what has preserved love and dispersed sorrow, written on the crucifix in the field: 'O star and flower, spirit and garment, love, sorrow, and time and eternity.'

LUDWIG UHLAND

Der Schmied

Ich hör' meinen Schatz,
Den Hammer er schwinget,
Das rauschet, das klinget,
Das dringt in die Weite
Wie Glockengeläute
Durch Gassen und Platz.

Am schwarzen Kamin,
Da sitzet mein Lieber,
Doch geh' ich vorüber,
Die Bälge dann sausen,
Die Flammen aufbrausen
Und lodern um ihn.

Das Glück von Edenhall

Von Edenhall der junge Lord
Läßt schmettern Festtrommetenschall;
Er hebt sich an des Tisches Bord
Und ruft in trunkner Gäste Schwall:
«Nun her mit dem Glücke von Edenhall!»

The Smith

I can hear my sweetheart, he is swinging his hammer, it whistles and clangs, you can hear it a long way off like a peal of bells across the streets and the market-place.

My love sits at the black furnace, but when I go by the bellows groan, the flames roar up and blaze all round him.

The Luck of Edenhall

The young master of Edenhall has the festal trumpets sounded; he stands up at the table's edge and shouts into the crowd of drunken guests: 'Bring in the Luck of Edenhall!'

Der Schenk vernimmt ungern den Spruch,
Des Hauses ältester Vasall,
Nimmt zögernd aus dem seidnen Tuch
Das hohe Trinkglas von Kristall;
Sie nennens das Glück von Edenhall.

Darauf der Lord: «Dem Glas zum Preis
Schenk Roten ein aus Portugal!»
Mit Händezittern gießt der Greis:
Und purpurn Licht wird überall;
Es strahlt aus dem Glücke von Edenhall.

Da spricht der Lord und schwingts dabei:
«Dies Glas von leuchtendem Kristall
Gab meinem Ahn am Quell die Fei;
Drein schrieb sie: ‹Kommt dies Glas zu Fall,
Fahr wohl dann, o Glück von Edenhall!›

Ein Kelchglas ward zum Los mit Fug
Dem freud'gen Stamm von Edenhall:
Wir schlürfen gern in vollem Zug,
Wir läuten gern mit lautem Schall.
Stoßt an mit dem Glücke von Edenhall!»

The steward, the oldest vassal of the house, is concerned at this
order; hesitatingly he takes the tall drinking-glass of crystal out of
its silk cloth; they call it the 'Luck of Edenhall'.

At this his master says: 'In honour of the glass, fill it with red
wine from Portugal!' With trembling hands the old man pours,
and purple light gleams everywhere, it shines from the Luck of
Edenhall.

The master says, as he brandishes the glass: 'This glass of gleam-
ing crystal was given to my ancestor at the spring by the fairy. She
wrote on it: "If this glass do fall, Farewell the luck of Edenhall."

'It was appropriate that the fate of the joyous breed of Edenhall
should be bound up with a drinking-glass! We love to drink full
draughts, we love to clink glasses with a full note. Clink now with
the Luck of Edenhall!'

Erst klingt es milde, tief und voll,
Gleich dem Gesang der Nachtigall,
Dann wie des Waldstroms laut Geroll;
Zuletzt erdröhnt wie Donnerhall
Das herrliche Glück von Edenhall.

«Zum Horte nimmt ein kühn Geschlecht
Sich den zerbrechlichen Kristall;
Er dauert länger schon, als recht:
Stoßt an! Mit diesem kräftgen Prall
Versuch' ich das Glück von Edenhall.»

Und als das Trinkglas gellend springt,
Springt das Gewölb mit jähem Knall
Und aus dem Riß die Flamme dringt;
Die Gäste sind zerstoben all
Mit dem brechenden Glücke von Edenhall.

Einstürmt der Feind mit Brand und Mord,
Der in der Nacht erstieg den Wall:
Vom Schwerte fällt der junge Lord,
Hält in der Hand noch den Kristall,
Das zersprungene Glück von Edenhall.

At first it sounds soft, deep, and full like the song of the night-ingale, then like the loud roar of the mountain torrent, and finally it rolls like the rumble of thunder, the splendid Luck of Edenhall.
'Our bold family has taken fragile crystal as its talisman; it has lasted too long already. Clink with me! With this forceful thrust I'll test the luck of Edenhall!'
And as the goblet jars and splinters, the vaulting splits with a sudden crash, and through the crack the flame leaps; all the guests have scattered with the shattering of the Luck of Edenhall.
The enemy, who had climbed the wall during the night, rushes in to burn and murder. The young master falls by the sword, still holding in his hand the crystal glass, the splintered Luck of Edenhall.

Am Morgen irrt der Schenk allein,
Der Greis, in der zerstörten Hall':
Er sucht des Herrn verbrannt Gebein,
Er sucht im grausen Trümmerfall
Die Scherben des Glücks von Edenhall.

«Die Steinwand,» spricht er, «springt zu Stück,
Die hohe Säule muß zu Fall;
Glas ist der Erde Stolz und Glück:
In Splitter fällt der Erdenball
Einst, gleich dem Glücke von Edenhall.»

JOSEPH VON EICHENDORFF

Abschied

O Täler weit, o Höhen,
O schöner, grüner Wald,
Du meiner Lust und Wehen
Andächt'ger Aufenthalt!
Da draußen, stets betrogen,
Saust die geschäft'ge Welt,
Schlag noch einmal die Bogen
Um mich, du grünes Zelt!

In the morning the steward, the old man, wanders alone in the ruined hall; he seeks the burned bones of his lord, he seeks in the dreadful rubble the shards of the Luck of Edenhall.

'Walls of stone,' he says, 'burst in pieces, lofty pillars have to collapse in the end, earthly pride and happiness are nothing but glass; one day the globe of earth itself will disintegrate into splinters, like the Luck of Edenhall.'

Farewell

O broad valleys, O hills, O beautiful green forest, you pensive refuge of my joys and sorrows! Outside there, ever deluded, the busy world rushes; raise your arches round me once more, you green tent!

Wenn es beginnt zu tagen,
Die Erde dampft und blinkt,
Die Vögel lustig schlagen,
Daß dir dein Herz erklingt:
Da mag vergehn, verwehen
Das trübe Erdenleid,
Da sollst du auferstehen
In junger Herrlichkeit!

Da steht im Wald geschrieben
Ein stilles, ernstes Wort
Von rechtem Tun und Lieben,
Und was des Menschen Hort.
Ich habe treu gelesen
Die Worte, schlicht und wahr,
Und durch mein ganzes Wesen
Ward's unausprechlich klar.

Bald werd' ich dich verlassen,
Fremd in der Fremde gehn,
Auf buntbewegten Gassen
Des Lebens Schauspiel sehn;
Und mitten in dem Leben
Wird deines Ernsts Gewalt
Mich Einsamen erheben,
So wird mein Herz nicht alt.

When the day begins to break, the earth steams and gleams, the birds sing so merrily that your heart sings in answer. Then let dismal earthly sorrows vanish and blow away, you shall rise again in youthful splendour!

A quiet impressive statement is written in the forest of how to live and love aright, and what man's treasure is. I have read these simple and true words carefully and what they say became ineffably clear to me throughout my whole being.

Soon I shall have to leave you and go a stranger in strange places, and watch the pageant of life on gay and populous streets. And in the middle of that life the power of your authority will exalt me in my solitude, and so my heart will not grow old.

Auf meines Kindes Tod (8)

Von fern die Uhren schlagen,
Es ist schon tiefe Nacht,
Die Lampe brennt so düster,
Dein Bettlein ist gemacht.

Die Winde nur noch gehen
Wehklagend um das Haus,
Wir sitzen einsam drinne
Und lauschen oft hinaus.

Es ist, als müßtest leise
Du klopfen an die Tür,
Du hättst dich nur verirret,
Und kämst nun müd zurück.

Wir armen, armen Toren!
Wir irren ja im Graus
Des Dunkels noch verloren –
Du fandst dich längst nach Haus.

On the Death of my Child (8)

THE clocks strike far away, it is already deep in the night, the lamp burns dimly, your cot is made.

Only the winds still go keening round the house, we sit lonely inside and often listen out.

It is as though you were going to tap gently at the door, as if you had only lost your way and were coming back tired.

We poor foolish people! It is we who are still wandering, lost in the horror of darkness – you have long ago found your way home.

Der Einsiedler

Komm, Trost der Welt, du stille Nacht!
Wie steigst du von den Bergen sacht,
Die Lüfte alle schlafen,
Ein Schiffer nur noch, wandermüd,
Singt übers Meer sein Abendlied
Zu Gottes Lob im Hafen.

Die Jahre wie die Wolken gehn
Und lassen mich hier einsam stehn,
Die Welt hat mich vergessen,
Da tratst du wunderbar zu mir,
Wenn ich beim Waldesrauschen hier
Gedankenvoll gesessen.

O Trost der Welt, du stille Nacht!
Der Tag hat mich so müd gemacht,
Das weite Meer schon dunkelt,
Laß ausruhn mich von Lust und Not,
Bis daß das ew'ge Morgenrot
Den stillen Wald durchfunkelt.

The Hermit

Come, you solace of the world, quiet night! How softly you come down from the hills. The breezes are all sleeping; just one seaman, tired of journeying, sings his evening song to the glory of God in port across the sea.

The years go by like the clouds and pass me by in solitude here, the world has forgotten me, then you came miraculously to me as I was sitting here in thought among the murmuring of the woods.

O you solace of the world, quiet night! The day has made me so weary, the wide ocean is already darkening, let me rest from pleasure and distress until the eternal dawn glimmers through the quiet wood.

Das zerbrochene Ringlein

In einem kühlen Grunde
Da geht ein Mühlenrad,
Mein' Liebste ist verschwunden,
Die dort gewohnet hat.

Sie hat mir Treu' versprochen,
Gab mir ein'n Ring dabei,
Sie hat die Treu' gebrochen,
Mein Ringlein sprang entzwei.

Ich möcht' als Spielmann reisen
Weit in die Welt hinaus,
Und singen meine Weisen,
Und gehn von Haus zu Haus.

Ich möcht' als Reiter fliegen
Wohl in die blut'ge Schlacht,
Um stille Feuer liegen
Im Feld bei dunkler Nacht.

Hör' ich das Mühlrad gehen:
Ich weiß nicht, was ich will —
Ich möcht' am liebsten sterben,
Da wär's auf einmal still.

The Broken Ring

There is a cool valley where a mill-wheel turns. My sweetheart who used to live there has gone away.

She promised to be true and gave me a ring as a token. She broke her faith, my ring snapped in two.

I would like to go far out into the world as a travelling musician and go from house to house singing my tunes.

I would like to be a cavalryman and charge into the bloody battle, and lie round quiet fires in the dark night in the field.

When I hear the mill-wheel working I don't know what I want. Most of all, I would like to die — then all of a sudden it would be quiet.

Der Abend

SCHWEIGT der Menschen laute Lust:
Rauscht die Erde wie in Träumen
Wunderbar mit allen Bäumen,
Was dem Herzen kaum bewußt,
Alte Zeiten, linde Trauer,
Und es schweifen leise Schauer
Wetterleuchtend durch die Brust.

Mondnacht

Es war, als hätt' der Himmel
Die Erde still geküßt,
Daß sie im Blütenschimmer
Von ihm nun träumen müßt'.

Die Luft ging durch die Felder,
Die Ähren wogten sacht,
Es rauschten leis die Wälder,
So sternklar war die Nacht.

Evening

WHEN the loud merriment of men is silenced, the earth rustles
miraculously with all her trees as in a dream, what the heart is
hardly conscious of, old times, gentle sadness; and quiet tremors
sweep like summer lightning through my breast.

Moonlit Night

IT was as though the sky had quietly kissed the earth, so that she in
the glory of blossom now had to dream of him.

The breeze went across the fields, the ears of corn waved gently,
the woods rustled softly, the night was so starry-clear.

Und meine Seele spannte
Weit ihre Flügel aus,
Flog durch die stillen Lande,
Als flöge sie nach Haus.

Der Umkehrende (4)

Es wandelt, was wir schauen,
Tag sinkt ins Abendrot,
Die Lust hat eignes Grauen,
Und alles hat den Tod.

Ins Leben schleicht das Leiden
Sich heimlich wie ein Dieb,
Wir alle müssen scheiden
Von allem, was uns lieb.

Was gäb es doch auf Erden,
Wer hielt' den Jammer aus,
Wer möcht geboren werden,
Hieltst Du nicht droben Haus!

Du bists, der, was wir bauen,
Mild über uns zerbricht,
Daß wir den Himmel schauen –
Darum so klag ich nicht.

And my soul stretched its wings wide and flew through the tranquil counties as though it was flying home.

The Return (4)

WHAT we see is changing all the time, day sinks into the red of evening, pleasure has a horror of its own, and everything has its death.

Suffering steals into life stealthily like a thief; we must all of us leave what we love.

What would be left on earth, who could bear the misery, who could bear to be born if Thou didst not keep house above?

It is Thou that in thy mercy gently breakest above our heads everything we build, that we may see the sky; and so I do not complain.

Sehnsucht

Es schienen so golden die Sterne,
Am Fenster ich einsam stand
Und hörte aus weiter Ferne
Ein Posthorn im stillen Land.
Das Herz mir im Leib entbrennte,
Da hab' ich mir heimlich gedacht:
Ach, wer da mitreisen könnte
In der prächtigen Sommernacht!

Zwei junge Gesellen gingen
Vorüber am Bergeshang,
Ich hörte im Wandern sie singen
Die stille Gegend entlang:
Von schwindelnden Felsenschlüften,
Wo die Wälder rauschen so sacht,
Von Quellen, die von den Klüften
Sich stürzen in die Waldesnacht.

Sie sangen von Marmorbildern,
Von Gärten, die überm Gestein
In dämmernden Lauben verwildern,
Palästen im Mondenschein,

Longing

THE stars were shining so golden, I was standing by myself at the window and heard a posthorn from far away over the quiet countryside. My heart caught fire within me, and I thought secretly to myself: Oh, how wonderful to go along too, in the radiant summer night!

Two young apprentices passed by on the mountain slope, as they walked through the quiet scene I heard them singing: of dizzy rocky gorges where the woods rustle so softly, of streams which plunge from precipices into the night of the forest.

They sang of marble statues, of gardens which run to seed in twilit bowers above the naked rock, palaces in moonlight / where

Wo die Mädchen am Fenster lauschen,
Wann der Lauten Klang erwacht,
Und die Brunnen verschlafen rauschen
In der prächtigen Sommernacht.

FRIEDRICH RÜCKERT

Kehr' ein bei mir

Du bist die Ruh'
    Der Friede mild,
    Die Sehnsucht du
    Und was sie stillt.

Ich weihe dir
    Voll Lust und Schmerz
    Zur Wohnung hier
    Mein Aug' und Herz.

Kehr' ein bei mir
    Und schließe du
    Still hinter dir
    Die Pforten zu.

girls listen at the windows when the sound of the lute awakes, and the fountains purl sleepily in the radiant summer night.

Come In

You are tranquillity and gentle peace, you are desire and what satisfies desire.

I dedicate to you my eye and heart full of joy and pain for your dwelling here.

Come in and close the gates quietly behind you.

Treib andern Schmerz
　Aus dieser Brust!
　Voll sei dies Herz
　Von deiner Lust.

Dies Augenzelt
　Von deinem Glanz
　Allein erhellt,
　O füll' es ganz.

AUGUST VON PLATEN

Wer wußte je das Leben recht zu fassen,
Wer hat die Hälfte nicht davon verloren
Im Traum, im Fieber, im Gespräch mit Toren,
In Liebesqual, im leeren Zeitverprassen?

Ja, der sogar, der, ruhig und gelassen,
Mit dem Bewußtsein, was er soll, geboren,
Frühzeitig einen Lebensgang erkoren,
Muß vor des Lebens Widerspruch erblassen.

Drive out all other pain from my breast! Let my heart be full of
your joy.
　The tent of my eyes is lit by your glow alone. Oh, fill it quite!

Who has ever been able to seize life aright? Who has not had to
waste half of it in dreams, in feverish activity, in conversation with
fools, in pains of love, in empty squandering of time?
　Yes, even the man who is calm and composed, born with the
awareness of what he has to do, who early planned his life, even he
must pale before life's contradictoriness.

Denn jeder hofft doch, daß das Glück ihm lache,
Allein das Glück, wenn's wirklich kommt, ertragen,
Ist keines Menschen, wäre Gottes Sache.

Auch kommt es nie, wir wünschen bloß und wagen:
Dem Schläfer fällt es nimmermehr vom Dache,
Und auch der Läufer wird es nicht erjagen.

Es liegt an eines Menschen Schmerz, an eines Menschen
    Wunde nichts,
Es kehrt an das, was Kranke quält, sich ewig der Gesunde
    nichts;
Und wäre nicht das Leben kurz, das stets der Mensch vom
    Menschen erbt,
So gäb's Beklagenswerteres auf diesem weiten Runde
    nichts!
Einförmig stellt Natur sich her, doch tausendförmig ist
    ihr Tod,
Es fragt die Welt nach meinem Ziel, nach deiner letzten
    Stunde nichts;
Und wer sich willig nicht ergibt dem ehrnen Lose, das
    ihm dräut,

    For, after all, every man hopes that fortune will smile upon him,
but how to bear fortune when it really comes is no task for man, but
rather for God.
    But even so, it never comes, we simply indulge in wishes and
risks; it will not fall into the sleeper's lap, and even the runner will
never catch up with it.

ONE man's pain, one man's wounds are of no importance, the
healthy pays no heed to what torments the sick, and if this life, that
man keeps on inheriting from man, were not short, there would be
nothing more lamentable in the whole wide world. Nature repro-
duces herself uniformly, but her death may take a thousand shapes,
the world does not inquire about my goal or your last hour; and
the man who does not willingly submit to this iron fate, which
threatens him,/only worries himself into his grave in helpless anger,

Der zürnt ins Grab sich rettungslos und fühlt in dessen
    Schlunde nichts;
Dies wissen alle, doch vergißt es jeder gerne jeden Tag,
So komme denn, in diesem Sinn, hinfort aus meinem
    Munde nichts!
Vergeßt, daß euch die Welt betrügt und daß ihr Wunsch
    nur Wünsche zeugt,
Laßt eurer Liebe nichts entgehn, entschlüpfen eurer
    Kunde nichts!
Es hoffe jeder, daß die Zeit ihm gebe, was sie keinem gab,
Denn jeder sucht ein All zu sein, und jeder ist im Grunde
    nichts.

Der Pilgrim vor St. Just

NACHT ist's und Stürme sausen für und für,
Hispanische Mönche, schließt mir auf die Tür!

Laßt hier mich ruhn, bis Glockenton mich weckt,
Der zum Gebet Euch in die Kirche schreckt!

Bereitet mir, was Euer Haus vermag,
Ein Ordenskleid und einen Sarkophag!

---

and in fate's maw he feels nothing; everyone knows this, but each
man likes to forget it every day, so let me say nothing more of it.
Forget that the world deceives you and that the desire for it only
engenders more desire, let nothing elude your love or escape your
knowledge. Let each man hope that time will give him what it has
never given anyone, for each man tries to be a universal whole, and
every man is at bottom nothing at all.

The Pilgrim [the Emperor Charles V] at the Gates of S. Yuste

IT is night, and storm winds roar unceasingly. Spanish monks, un-
lock the gate for me! Let me rest here until the sound of the bell
wakes me that drives you into the church to prayer. Make ready for
me what your house can provide: a habit of your order and a
coffin!/Grant me a narrow cell, receive me into your order! More

Gönnt mir die kleine Zelle, weiht mich ein.
Mehr als die Hälfte dieser Welt war mein.

Das Haupt, das nun der Schere sich bequemt,
Mit mancher Krone ward's bediademt.

Die Schulter, die der Kutte nun sich bückt,
Hat kaiserlicher Hermelin geschmückt.

Nun bin ich vor dem Tod den Toten gleich,
Und fall' in Trümmer, wie das alte Reich.

ANNETTE VON DROSTE-HÜLSHOFF

Im Grase

Süsse Ruh, süßer Taumel im Gras,
von des Krautes Arom umhaucht,
tiefe Flut, tief tief trunkne Flut,
wenn die Wolk' am Azure verraucht,
wenn aufs müde, schwimmende Haupt
süßes Lachen gaukelt herab,
liebe Stimme säuselt und träuft
wie die Lindenblüt auf ein Grab.

than half of this world was mine. The head which now submits to the scissors was once diademed with many crowns. The shoulder which now bends to receive the cowl was once adorned with imperial ermine. Now before my death I am as the dead, and fall in ruins like the ancient Empire.

In the Long Grass

Sweet repose, sweet bemusement in the long grass, with the breath of the scent of herbs around you, a deep stream, deep, deep ecstatic stream, when the cloud evaporates into the azure, when sweet laughter dances down on to your weary swimming head, a dear voice murmurs and drifts like lime-blossom on to a grave;

Wenn im Busen die Toten dann,
jede Leiche sich streckt und regt,
leise, leise den Odem zieht,
die geschloßne Wimper bewegt,
tote Lieb', tote Lust, tote Zeit,
all die Schätze, im Schutt verwühlt,
sich berühren mit schüchternem Klang
gleich den Glöckchen, vom Winde umspielt.

Stunden, flüchtger ihr als der Kuß
eines Strahls auf den trauernden See,
als des ziehenden Vogels Lied,
das mir niederperlt aus der Höh',
als des schillernden Käfers Blitz,
wenn den Sonnenpfad er durcheilt,
als der heiße Druck einer Hand,
die zum letzten Male verweilt.

Dennoch, Himmel, immer mir nur
Dieses eine: nur für das Lied
jedes freien Vogels im Blau
eine Seele, die mit ihm zieht,

Then when the dead in your breast, every corpse stretches and stirs gently, gently draws breath, flutters its closed eyelashes – dead love, dead pleasure, dead time, all these treasures buried deep in rubble, touch one another with a hesitant note like little bells in the playful wind.

Hours, more fleeting you are than the kiss of a sunbeam on the mourning lake; than the migrating bird's call which comes down to me like pearls from the sky; than the flash of the brilliant beetle when he hurries across the sunlit path; than the warm pressure of a hand which lingers for the last time.

Even so, Heaven, grant me always just this one thing for myself: for the song of every free bird in the blue a soul to travel with it;

nur für jeden kärglichen Strahl
meinen farbigschillernden Saum,
jeder warmen Hand meinen Druck,
und für jedes Glück einen Traum.

Am letzten Tage des Jahres (Silvester)

Das Jahr geht um,
der Faden rollt sich sausend ab.
Ein Stündchen noch, das letzte heut,
und stäubend rieselt in sein Grab
was einstens war lebend'ge Zeit.
Ich harre stumm.

's ist tiefe Nacht!
Ob wohl ein Auge offen noch?
In diesen Mauern rüttelt dein
Verrinnen, Zeit! Mir schaudert, doch
Es will die letzte Stunde sein
einsam durchwacht,

Gesehen all,
was ich begangen und gedacht,
was mir aus Haupt und Herzen stieg:

only for every meagre ray my hem of iridescent colour; for every warm hand the pressure of my hand, and for every happiness a dream.

The Last Day of the Year (New Year's Eve)

The year is at the turn, whirring the thread unrolls. One hour more, the last of today, and what once was living time will flow dustily into its grave. I wait, in silence. It is deep night! Is there still an eye open? Your flowing passage, time, shakes at these walls! A shudder runs over me; but the last hour must be watched through in solitude, and everything must be seen that I have committed in deed and thought. What rose out of my head and heart/ now stands grim

Das steht nun eine ernste Wacht,
am Himmelstor. O halber Sieg!
O schwerer Fall!

Wie reißt der Wind
am Fensterkreuze! Ja, es will
auf Sturmesfittichen das Jahr
zerstäuben, nicht ein Schatten still
verhauchen unterm Sternenklar.
Du Sündenkind,

war nicht ein hohl
und heimlich Sausen jeden Tag
in deiner wüsten Brust Verließ,
wo langsam Stein an Stein zerbrach,
wenn es den kalten Odem stieß
vom starren Pol?

Mein Lämpchen will
verlöschen, und begierig saugt
der Docht den letzten Tropfen Öl.
Ist so mein Leben auch verraucht?
Eröffnet sich des Grabes Höhl'
mir schwarz und still?

guard at Heaven's gate. O half victory! O heavy fall! How the
wind tears at the transom! Yes, the year is going to scatter into dust
on the wings of the storm, not breathe its last as a quiet shadow
under the clearness of the stars. You child of sin, has there not been
a hollow secret rustling every day in the cell of your wild breast,
where slowly stone broke against stone as the cold breath thrust
from the frozen pole? My lamp is about to go out, and the wick
greedily sucks the last drop of oil. Has my life gone away in smoke
like that? Will the cave of the tomb open before me black and quiet/
within the circle which this year's course surrounds? My life is

Wohl in dem Kreis,
den dieses Jahres Lauf umzieht,
mein Leben bricht. Ich wußt’ es lang!
und dennoch hat dies Herz geglüht
in eitler Leidenschaften Drang!
Mir brüht der Schweiß

der tiefsten Angst
auf Stirn und Hand. – Wie? dämmert feucht
ein Stern dort durch die Wolken nicht?
Wär’ es der Liebe Stern vielleicht,
dir zürnend mit dem trüben Licht,
daß du so bangst?

Horch, welch Gesumm?
Und wieder? Sterbemelodie!
Die Glocke regt den ehrnen Mund.
O Herr, ich falle auf das Knie:
Sei gnädig meiner letzten Stund’!
Das Jahr ist um!

HEINRICH HEINE

Du bist wie eine Blume,
So hold und schön und rein;
Ich schau’ dich an, und Wehmut
Schleicht mir ins Herz hinein.

breaking, I have known it for a long time! And yet my heart has glowed in the pressure of idle passions! The sweat of deepest fear distils on forehead and hand. – Why, isn’t there a star there damply gleaming through the clouds? Could it be the star of love, chiding us with its faint light for being so afraid? Listen, what is that booming note? And again! The peal for the dying! The bell is moving its brazen mouth. O Lord, I fall on my knee: be merciful to my last hour! The year is over!

You are like a flower, so gracious and beautiful and pure. When I look at you, melancholy steals into my heart.

Mir ist, als ob ich die Hände
Aufs Haupt dir legen sollt',
Betend, daß Gott dich erhalte
So rein und schön und hold.

EIN Fichtenbaum steht einsam
Im Norden auf kahler Höh'.
Ihn schläfert; mit weißer Decke
Umhüllen ihn Eis und Schnee.

Er träumt von einer Palme,
Die fern im Morgenland
Einsam und schweigend trauert
Auf brennender Felsenwand.

Die Lorelei

ICH weiß nicht, was soll es bedeuten,
Daß ich so traurig bin;
Ein Märchen aus alten Zeiten,
Das kommt mir nicht aus dem Sinn.

I feel as though I ought to lay my hands on your head and pray
God to keep you so, pure and beautiful and gracious.

IN the north a lonely fir-tree stands on a bare height; he is sleepy; ice
and snow wrap him in a white covering.
    He dreams of a palm-tree who, far in the orient, mourns silent
and lonely on her cliff of scorching rock.

The Lorelei

I DO not know why it should be, but I am so sad: there is an old-
time fairy-tale which I can't put out of my mind.

Die Luft ist kühl und es dunkelt,
Und ruhig fließt der Rhein;
Der Gipfel des Berges funkelt
Im Abendsonnenschein.

Die schönste Jungfrau sitzet
Dort oben wunderbar,
Ihr goldnes Geschmeide blitzet,
Sie kämmt ihr goldnes Haar.

Sie kämmt es mit goldenem Kamme,
Und singt ein Lied dabei;
Das hat eine wundersame,
Gewaltige Melodei.

Den Schiffer im kleinen Schiffe
Ergreift es mit wildem Weh;
Er schaut nicht die Felsenriffe,
Er schaut nur hinauf in die Höh'.

Ich glaube, die Wellen verschlingen
Am Ende Schiffer und Kahn;
Und das hat mit ihrem Singen
Die Lorelei getan.

The air is cool and the twilight is falling and the Rhine is flowing calmly by; the top of the mountain is glittering in the evening sun.

Up there the most gorgeously beautiful maiden is sitting; her golden jewellery sparkles and she is combing her golden hair.

She is combing it with a golden comb and singing a song as she does so; it has a wonderful compelling melody.

It makes a wild nostalgia possess the boatman in his boat; he pays no attention to the submerged rocks, he can only look up and up.

In the end, if I remember rightly, the waves swallow up the boatman and his boat. And that is what she has done, the Lorelei and her singing.

Das Glück ist eine leichte Dirne
Und weilt nicht gern am selben Ort;
Sie streicht das Haar dir von der Stirne
Und küßt dich rasch und flattert fort.

Frau Unglück hat im Gegenteile
Dich liebefest ans Herz gedrückt;
Sie sagt, sie habe keine Eile,
Setzt sich zu dir ans Bett und strickt.

In der Fremde

Ich hatte einst ein schönes Vaterland.
Der Eichenbaum
Wuchs dort so hoch, die Veilchen nickten sanft.
Es war ein Traum.

Das küßte mich auf deutsch und sprach auf deutsch
(Man glaubt es kaum,
Wie gut es klang) das Wort: «Ich liebe dich!»
Es war ein Traum.

Fortune is a wanton creature and does not like to stay long in one place. She smooths your hair back from your forehead, gives you a quick kiss, and flits away.

Mrs Misfortune, on the other hand, soon takes you to her heart with firm affection. She says she is in no hurry, and sits and does her knitting by your bed.

In Exile

Once upon a time I had a fine country of my own where I was at home. The oaks grew tall there, the violets beckoned gently. It was a dream.

It kissed me in German and said in German – it's hard to believe how good it sounded – the words 'I love you'. It was only a dream.

Der Asra

TÄGLICH ging die wunderschöne
Sultanstochter auf und nieder
Um die Abendzeit am Springbrunn,
Wo die weißen Wasser plätschern.

Täglich stand der junge Sklave
Um die Abendzeit am Springbrunn,
Wo die weißen Wasser plätschern;
Täglich ward er bleich und bleicher.

Eines Abends trat die Fürstin
Auf ihn zu mit raschen Worten:
«Deinen Namen will ich wissen,
Deine Heimat, deine Sippschaft!»

Und der Sklave sprach: «Ich heiße
Mohamet, ich bin aus Yemmen,
Und mein Stamm sind jene Asra,
Welche sterben, wenn sie lieben.»

The Youth of the Tribe of Asra

EVERY day the beauteous daughter of the Sultan walked up and
down in the evening by the fountain where the white waters splash.
    Every day the young slave stood by the fountain in the evening
where the white waters splash; every day he grew paler and paler.
    One evening the princess went up to him and said suddenly: 'I
wish to know your name, your country, and your kindred!'
    And the slave said: 'My name is Mohamet, I am from Yemen,
and my tribe is those Asra who die when they love.'

Morphine

GROSS ist die Ähnlichkeit der beiden schönen
Jünglingsgestalten, ob der eine gleich
Viel blässer als der andre, auch viel strenger,
Fast möcht' ich sagen viel vornehmer aussieht
Als jener andre, welcher mich vertraulich
In seine Arme schloß — wie lieblich sanft
War dann sein Lächeln, und sein Blick wie selig!
Dann mocht' es wohl geschehn, daß seines Hauptes
Mohnblumenkranz auch meine Stirn berührte
Und seltsam duftend allen Schmerz verscheuchte
Aus meiner Seel' — doch solche Linderung,
Sie dauert kurze Zeit; genesen gänzlich
Kann ich nur dann, wenn seine Fackel senkt
Der andre Bruder, der so ernst und bleich. —
Gut ist der Schlaf, der Tod ist besser — freilich
Das beste wäre, nie geboren sein.

ICH war, o Lamm, als Hirt bestellt,
Zu hüten dich auf dieser Welt;
Hab' dich mit meinem Brot geätzt,
Mit Wasser aus dem Born geletzt.

Morphine

GREAT is the resemblance between the two beautiful youths,
though one looks much paler than the other, more austere too, I
might almost say more distinguished than that other one who used
to take me confidingly into his arms — how soft and loving his
smile was then, how happy his glance! Then sometimes the garland
of poppies on his head would touch my forehead too and drive all
pain from my mind with its strange scent — but such relief only lasts
a short time; I cannot recover completely until the other brother,
the serious, pale one, lowers his torch. Sleep is good, death is
better; but of course the best thing would be never to have been
born at all.

MY lamb, I was appointed as a shepherd to look after you in this
world. I have fed you with my bread and quenched your thirst

Wenn kalt der Wintersturm gelärmt,
Hab' ich dich an der Brust erwärmt.
Hier hielt ich fest dich angeschlossen;
Wenn Regengüsse sich ergossen,
Und Wolf und Waldbach um die Wette
Geheult im dunkeln Felsenbette,
Du bangtest nicht, hast nicht gezittert.
Selbst wenn den höchsten Tann zersplittert
Der Wetterstrahl – in meinem Schoß
Du schliefest still und sorgenlos.
    Mein Arm wird schwach, es schleicht herbei
Der blasse Tod! Die Schäferei,
Das Hirtenspiel, es hat ein Ende.
O Gott, ich leg' in deine Hände
Zurück den Stab. – Behüte du
Mein armes Lamm, wenn ich zur Ruh'
Bestattet bin – und dulde nicht,
Daß irgendwo ein Dorn sie sticht –
O schütz' ihr Vlies vor Dornenhecken
Und auch vor Sümpfen, die beflecken;
Laß überall zu ihren Füßen
Das allerliebste Futter sprießen;
Und laß sie schlafen, sorgenlos,
Wie einst sie schlief in meinem Schoß.

out of my well. / When the winter storms roared at you I warmed you in my bosom. I held you tightly clasped there when cloudbursts poured down and wolves and mountain torrents in their rocky beds howled round you as hard as they could. You were not afraid, you never trembled even when the lightning shattered the tallest pine – you slept softly and free from fear in my lap.

My arm is getting weak now, pale death is slinking up to me. Our Arcadia, our pastoral, is over. Oh, God, I return the shepherd's crook into Thy hands. Look after my poor lamb when I have been laid to rest, and do not suffer a thorn to prick her anywhere; oh, keep her fleece from the thorny hedges, and from the defiling morasses; let the nicest possible pasture spring up at her feet wherever she goes, and let her sleep as free from anxiety as she used once to sleep in my lap.

Der Scheidende

ERSTORBEN ist in meiner Brust
Jedwede weltlich eitle Lust,
Schier ist mir auch erstorben drin
Der Haß des Schlechten, sogar der Sinn
Für eigne und für fremde Not –
Und in mir lebt nur noch der Tod!
   Der Vorhang fällt, das Stück ist aus,
Und gähnend wandelt jetzt nach Haus
Mein liebes deutsches Publikum,
Die guten Leutchen sind nicht dumm;
Das speist jetzt ganz vergnügt zu Nacht
Und trinkt sein Schöppchen, singt und lacht –
Er hatte recht, der edle Heros,
Der weiland sprach im Buch Homeros':
Der kleinste lebendige Philister
Zu Stukkert am Neckar, viel glücklicher ist er
Als ich, der Pelide, der tote Held.
Der Schattenfürst in der Unterwelt.

On Departing

EVERY vain desire has died in my breast, even hatred of evil
things, even the feeling for my own and other people's distress, and
the only thing that still lives in me is death.

The curtain falls, the play is over, and my dear German audience
walks home, yawning. They are no fools, these good people, they're
having their suppers quite happily and drinking their pints and
singing and laughing. The noble hero was quite right who said
long ago in Homer's book that the meanest Philistine alive in
Stuttgart on the Neckar is much happier than I, the son of Peleus,
the dead champion, the prince of shades in the underworld.

Wo?

Wo wird einst des Wandermüden
Letzte Ruhestätte sein?
Unter Palmen in dem Süden?
Unter Linden an dem Rhein?

Werd' ich wo in einer Wüste
Eingescharrt von fremder Hand?
Oder ruh' ich an der Küste
Eines Meeres in dem Sand?

Immerhin! Mich wird umgeben
Gotteshimmel, dort wie hier,
Und als Totenlampen schweben
Nachts die Sterne über mir.

Es träumte mir von einer Sommernacht,
Wo bleich, verwittert, in des Mondes Glanze
Bauwerke lagen, Reste alter Pracht,
Ruinen aus der Zeit der Renaissance.

Where?

Where, when I am tired from my wanderings, will my last resting-place be? Under palms in the south? Under lime-trees on the Rhine?

Will some stranger bury me somewhere in a desert? Or shall I rest in the sand beside an ocean coast?

What does it matter? God's sky will be round me one way or the other, and above me the stars will hang down for funeral lamps at night.

I had a dream about a summer night, and in it, pale and weathered in the light of the moon, masonry lay about, remains of ancient glory, ruins of the Renaissance period.

Nur hie und da, mit dorisch ernstem Knauf,
Hebt aus dem Schutt sich einzeln eine Säule,
Und schaut ins hohe Firmament hinauf,
Als ob sie spotte seiner Donnerkeile.

Gebrochen auf dem Boden liegen rings
Portale, Giebeldächer und Skulpturen,
Wo Mensch und Tier vermischt, Centaur und Sphinx,
Satyr, Chimäre – Fabelzeitfiguren.

Es steht ein offner Marmorsarkophag
Ganz unverstümmelt unter den Ruinen,
Und gleichfalls unversehrt im Sarge lag
Ein toter Mann mit leidend sanften Mienen.

Karyatiden mit gerecktem Hals,
Sie scheinen mühsam ihn emporzuhalten.
An beiden Seiten sieht man ebenfalls
Viel basrelief gemeißelte Gestalten.

Hier sieht man des Olympos Herrlichkeit
Mit seinen liederlichen Heidengöttern,
Adam und Eva stehn dabei, sind beid'
Versehn mit keuschem Schurz von Feigenblättern.

Here and there a single pillar, with an austere doric capital, rises from the rubble and looks up into the sky as though in mockery of its thunderbolts.

All around there lie, shattered on the ground, portals and pediments and statues, in which men and beasts appear conjoined, centaur and sphinx, satyr and chimera – figures of a mythical age.

Among the ruins there stands, quite intact, an open marble sarcophagus and, also quite intact, a dead man was lying in the coffin with a suffering and gentle expression.

Caryatids with craning necks seem to have difficulty in supporting him. There are also to be seen on either side many figures chiselled in bas-relief.

The splendour of Olympus is here displayed with its wanton pagan gods; Adam and Eve stand there too, both equipped with a chaste apron of fig-leaves.

Hier sieht man Trojas Untergang und Brand,
Paris und Helena, auch Hektor sah man;
Moses und Aaron gleich daneben stand,
Auch Esther, Judith, Holofern und Haman.

Desgleichen war zu sehn der Gott Amur,
Phöbus Apoll, Vulkanus und Frau Venus,
Pluto und Proserpine und Merkur,
Gott Bacchus und Priapus und Silenus.

Daneben stand der Esel Balaams
– Der Esel war zum Sprechen gut getroffen –
Dort sah man auch die Prüfung Abrahams
Und Lot, der mit den Töchtern sich besoffen.

Hier war zu schaun der Tanz Herodias',
Das Haupt des Täufers trägt man auf der Schüssel,
Die Hölle sah man hier, und Satanas,
Und Petrus mit dem großen Himmelsschlüssel.

Abwechselnd wieder sah man hier skulpiert
Des geilen Jovis Brunst und Freveltaten,
Wie er als Schwan die Leda hat verführt,
Die Danaë als Regen von Dukaten.

Here can be seen the destruction and the fire of Troy, Paris and
Helen, and Hector too; Moses and Aaron stood close by, and Esther
as well, Judith, Holofernes, and Haman.

Also the god Amour was there, Phoebus Apollo, Vulcan and
Dame Venus, Pluto and Proserpine and Mercury, Bacchus the god,
Priapus and Silenus.

Beside them stood Balaam's ass – the ass was a speaking like-
ness; there you could see too the temptation of Abraham, and
Lot, who got drunk with his daughters.

Here was displayed the dance of Herodias; the Baptist's head is
borne upon a charger; Hell could be seen and Satan, and Peter with
the great key of heaven.

By contrast there were shown in sculpture the lust and crimes of
lecherous Jove, how he seduced Leda as a swan and Danae as a rain
of ducats.

Hier war zu sehn Dianas wilde Jagd,
Ihr folgen hochgeschürzte Nymphen, Doggen,
Hier sah man Herkules in Frauentracht,
Die Spindel drehend hält sein Arm den Rocken.

Daneben ist der Sinai zu sehn,
Am Berg steht Israel mit seinen Ochsen,
Man schaut den Herrn als Kind im Tempel stehn
Und disputieren mit den Orthodoxen.

Die Gegensätze sind hier grell gepaart,
Des Griechen Lustsinn und der Gottgedanke
Judäas! Und in Arabeskenart
Um beide schlingt der Epheu seine Ranke.

Doch, wunderbar! derweilen solcherlei
Bildwerke träumend ich bretrachtet habe,
Wird plötzlich mir zu Sinn, ich selber sei
Der tote Mann im schönen Marmorgrabe.

Zu Häupten aber meiner Ruhestätt'
Stand eine Blume, rätselhaft gestaltet,
Die Blätter schwefelgelb und violett,
Doch wilder Liebreiz in der Blume waltet.

Here was displayed Diana's wild hunt, with high kirtled nymphs
and mastiffs in her train, here, too, was Hercules dressed as a
woman, his arm holds the distaff as he turns the spindle.

Beside them Mount Sinai is shown, on the mountain stand the
children of Israel with their oxen, and you can see our Lord as a
child standing in the Temple and disputing with the orthodox.

The contrasts are glaringly paired off: the Greek sense of enjoy-
ment with Judea's theology! and like an arabesque the ivy winds
its trails around them both.

But, strange to say, while dreamingly gazing at these sculptured
things, I suddenly realize that the dead man in the splendid marble
grave must be me.

At the head of my resting-place, however, there was a flower,
mysteriously fashioned, the petals sulphur yellow and violet; but
the flower is filled with an untamed enchantment of love.

Das Volk nennt sie die Blum' der Passion
Und sagt, sie sei dem Schädelberg entsprossen,
Als man gekreuzigt hat den Gottessohn,
Und dort sein welterlösend Blut geflossen.

Blutzeugnis, heißt es, gebe diese Blum',
Und alle Marterinstrumente, welche
Dem Henker dienten bei dem Märtyrtum,
Sie trüge sie abkonterfeit im Kelche.

Ja, alle Requisiten der Passion
Sähe man hier, die ganze Folterkammer,
Zum Beispiel: Geißel, Stricke, Dornenkron',
Das Kreuz, den Kelch, die Nägel und den Hammer.

Solch eine Blum' an meinem Grabe stand,
Und über meinen Leichnam niederbeugend,
Wie Frauentrauer, küßt sie mir die Hand,
Küßt Stirne mir und Augen, trostlos schweigend.

Doch, Zauberei des Traumes! Seltsamlich,
Die Blum' der Passion, die schwefelgelbe,
Verwandelt in ein Frauenbildnis sich,
Und das ist sie – die Liebste, ja, dieselbe!

The common folk call it the flower of the passion, and say that it sprang from Golgatha when the Son of God was crucified and his world-redeeming blood flowed there.

They say this flower gives testimony of blood, and bears the image of all the instruments of torture which were used by the executioner at the martyrdom, all of them, in its calyx.

Yes, all the requisites of the Passion are here, they say, the whole torture chamber, the whips, ropes, crown of thorns, the cross, the cup, the nails, and the hammer.

That was the sort of flower that was growing at my graveside, and bending down over my corpse like a mourning woman, it kisses my hand, kisses forehead and eyes, inconsolably silent.

But, O magic of dreams, wondrously the sulphur-yellow flower of the passion is transformed into the portrait of a woman, and it is she herself, the beloved, yes it is she!

Du warst die Blume, du geliebtes Kind,
An deinen Küssen mußt' ich dich erkennen.
So zärtlich keine Blumenlippen sind,
So feurig keine Blumentränen brennen!

Geschlossen war mein Aug', doch angeblickt
Hat meine Seel' beständig dein Gesichte,
Du sahst mich an, beseligt und verzückt,
Und geisterhaft beglänzt vom Mondenlichte.

Wir sprachen nicht, jedoch mein Herz vernahm,
Was du verschwiegen dachtest im Gemüte –
Das ausgesprochene Wort ist ohne Scham,
Das Schweigen ist der Liebe keusche Blüte.

Lautloses Zwiegespräch! man glaubt es kaum,
Wie bei dem stummen, zärtlichen Geplauder
So schnell die Zeit verstreicht im schönen Traum
Der Sommernacht, gewebt aus Lust und Schauder.

Was wir gesprochen, frag' es niemals, ach!
Den Glühwurm frag', was er dem Grase glimmert,
Die Welle frage, was sie rauscht im Bach,
Den Westwind frage, was er weht und wimmert.

You were the flower, my beloved, I knew you by your kisses. No flower has lips as soft as this, no flower weeps tears that burn so fiery-hot.

My eyes were closed, but my soul continuously gazed at your face, and, irradiated by the ghostly light of the moon, you were looking at me in rapture and ecstasy.

We did not speak, but yet my heart perceived what you were secretly thinking in your soul – it is the spoken word that has no shame, the chaste flowering of love is silence.

A soundless dialogue! it is almost beyond belief how swiftly time passes with wordless tender conversation in the lovely dream of the summer night, woven of joy and horror.

What we said – ah, never ask! Ask the glow-worm what it glimmers to the grass, ask the wave what it murmurs in the brook, ask the west wind what it blows and whispers.

Frag', was er strahlet, den Karfunkelstein,
Frag', was sie duften, Nachtviol' und Rosen –
Doch frage nie, wovon im Mondenschein
Die Marterblume und ihr Toter kosen!

Ich weiß es nicht, wie lange ich genoß
In meiner schlummerkühlen Marmortruhe
Den schönen Freudentraum. Ach, es zerfloß
Die Wonne meiner ungestörten Ruhe!

O Tod! mit deiner Grabesstille, du,
Nur du kannst uns die beste Wollust geben;
Den Kampf der Leidenschaft, Lust ohne Ruh'
Gibt uns für Glück das albern rohe Leben!

Doch wehe mir! es schwand die Seligkeit,
Als draußen plötzlich sich ein Lärm erhoben;
Es war ein scheltend, stampfend wüster Streit,
Ach, meine Blum' verscheuchte dieses Toben!

Ja, draußen sich erhob mit wildem Grimm
Ein Zanken, ein Gekeife, ein Gekläffe,
Ich glaubte zu erkennen manche Stimm' –
Es waren meines Grabmals Basrelieffe.

Ask the carbuncle what it glows forth, ask the night violets and roses what they breathe out in perfume – but never ask what the flower of torture and its dead lover talk of in the moonlight.

I do not know how long I enjoyed the lovely dream of joy in my slumber-cool marble casket. Alas, the ecstasy of my undisturbed rest flowed away.

O death, you with your sepulchral quiet, you alone can give us the highest bliss; the convulsions of passion, pleasure without rest, that is all that foolish coarse life can give us instead of happiness.

But alas, the bliss disappeared, for suddenly a noise arose outside; it was a yelling, stamping bloody row, and oh, this racket drove away my flower!

Yes, outside a savage quarrelling, scolding, yelping started up with a vengeance; I thought I recognized several of the voices – it was the bas-reliefs on my monument.

Spukt in dem Stein der alte Glaubenswahn?
Und disputieren diese Marmorschemen?
Der Schreckensruf des wilden Waldgotts Pan,
Wetteifernd wild mit Mosis Anathemen!

O, dieser Streit wird enden nimmermehr,
Stets wird die Wahrheit hadern mit dem Schönen,
Stets wird geschieden sein der Menschheit Heer
In zwei Partei'n: Barbaren und Hellenen.

Das fluchte, schimpfte! gar kein Ende nahm's
Mit dieser Kontroverse, der langweil'gen,
Da war zumal der Esel Balaams,
Der überschrie die Götter und die Heil'gen!

Mit diesem I – A, I-A, dem Gewieh'r,
Dem schluchzend ekelhaften Mißlaut, brachte
Mich zur Verzweiflung schier das dumme Tier,
Ich selbst zuletzt schrie auf – und ich erwachte.

Does the old religious delusion still haunt the stone? and are these marble wraiths disputing among themselves? The dreadful cry of the wild wood-god Pan desperately trying to shout down the anathemas of Moses!

Oh, this conflict will never, never end, truth will always quarrel with beauty, the army of mankind will always be divided into two parties: barbarians and Hellenes.

They cursed and swore, and this dull controversy never seemed to finish; and moreover there was Balaam's ass too; he shouted down the gods and the saints.

The stupid beast nearly drove me mad with his braying Hee-haw Hee-haw, that sobbing nauseous discord, and at last I myself cried out – and I woke up.

NIKOLAUS LENAU

Bitte

WEIL' auf mir, du dunkles Auge,
Übe deine ganze Macht,
Ernste, milde, träumerische,
Unergründlich süße Nacht!

Nimm mit deinem Zauberdunkel
Diese Welt von hinnen mir,
Daß du über meinem Leben
Einsam schwebest für und für.

Der Postillion

LIEBLICH war die Maiennacht,
Silberwölklein flogen,
Ob der holden Frühlingspracht
Freudig hingezogen.

Schlummernd lagen Wies' und Hain,
Jeder Pfad verlassen;
Niemand als der Mondenschein
Wachte auf der Straßen.

Entreaty

REST upon me, you dark eye, exert all your power, solemn, gentle,
dreamy, unfathomably sweet night.

Take this world away from me with your magic darkness, so
that you alone brood over my life for ever and ever.

The Postilion

THE May night was delicious, silver clouds were flying joyfully on
their way above the gracious splendour of spring.

Meadow and copse were sleeping and every path was lonely; no
one but the moonlight was awake on the road.

Leise nur das Lüftchen sprach,
Und es zog gelinder
Durch das stille Schlafgemach
All der Frühlingskinder.

Heimlich nur das Bächlein schlich,
Denn der Blüten Träume
Dufteten gar wonniglich
Durch die stillen Räume.

Rauher war mein Postillion,
Ließ die Geißel knallen,
Über Berg und Tal davon
Frisch sein Horn erschallen.

Und von flinken Rossen vier
Scholl der Hufe Schlagen,
Die durchs blühende Revier
Trabten mit Behagen.

Wald und Flur im schnellen Zug
Kaum gegrüßt – gemieden;
Und vorbei, wie Traumesflug,
Schwand der Dörfer Frieden.

The breeze was only speaking softly, and it moved more gently
through the quiet bedchamber of all the children of spring.
The stream moved secretly and stealthily, for the dreams of the
blossoms spread a gorgeous scent through the quiet air.
My postilion was of rougher kind, cracked his whip and blew his
horn gaily across hill and valley.
And the hoof-beats of four nimble horses sounded as they
trotted easily through the countryside in bloom.
Past forest and common at rapid pace – hardly hullo before
good-bye – and the peace of the villages whisked by us like the
flight of dreams.

Mitten in dem Maienglück
Lag ein Kirchhof innen,
Der den raschen Wanderblick
Hielt zu ernstem Sinnen.

Hingelehnt an Bergesrand
War die bleiche Mauer,
Und das Kreuzbild Gottes stand
Hoch, in stummer Trauer.

Schwager ritt auf seiner Bahn
Stiller jetzt und trüber;
Und die Rosse hielt er an,
Sah zum Kreuz hinüber:

«Halten muß hier Roß und Rad,
Mag's Euch nicht gefährden;
Drüben liegt mein Kamerad
In der kühlen Erden!

Ein gar herzlieber Gesell!
Herr, 's ist ewig schade!
Keiner blies das Horn so hell,
Wie mein Kamerade!

In the middle of this Maytime happiness there lay a churchyard, which made the traveller's rapid glance pause for serious reflection.

The pale wall leaned against the slope of the hill and the figure of the crucified God stood out high in silent mourning.

The postilion was driving along more quietly and sadly now; he stopped the horses and looked over towards the cross.

'Horses and wheels must halt here, if you don't mind, sir. My mate lies buried over there in the cold ground.

'He *was* a good companion, it is a dreadful pity he died, sir; no one blew the horn so well as my mate.

Hier ich immer halten muß,
Dem dort unterm Rasen
Zum getreuen Brudergruß
Sein Leiblied zu blasen!»

Und dem Kirchhof sandt' er zu
Frohe Wandersänge,
Daß es in die Grabesruh'
Seinem Bruder dränge.

Und des Hornes heller Ton
Klang vom Berge wieder,
Ob der tote Postillion
Stimmt' in seine Lieder. –

Weiter ging's durch Feld und Hag
Mit verhängtem Zügel;
Lang mir noch im Ohre lag
Jener Klang vom Hügel.

A. W. FLORENTIN VON ZUCCALMAGLIO

Es fiel ein Reif in der Frühlingsnacht
er fiel auf die schönen Blaublümelein,
sie sind verwelket, verdorret.

'I always have to halt here to play his favourite tune as a fraternal
greeting to him where he lies under the turf.'

And he played joyous coaching tunes in the direction of the
churchyard, to force their way into the quiet of his mate's grave.

And the clear note of the horn echoed from the hill, as though
the dead postilion were joining in his tunes. –

Off we went again with loose reins through field and hedge; but
that echo from the hill stayed in my head for a long time.

A HOAR frost came in the spring night, it fell on the lovely blue
flowers, they are withered and dead.

Ein Knabe hatte ein Mägdlein lieb,
sie liefen heimlich von Hause fort,
es wußten's nicht Vater noch Mutter.

Sie liefen weit ins fremde Land,
sie hatten weder Glück noch Stern,
sie sind verdorben, gestorben.

EDUARD MÖRIKE

Gebet

HERR, schicke was du willt,
Ein Liebes oder Leides!
Ich bin vergnügt, daß beides
Aus deinen Händen quillt.

Wollest mit Freuden
Und wollest mit Leiden
Mich nicht überschütten!
Doch in der Mitten
Liegt holdes Bescheiden.

A young man loved a girl, they ran away from home secretly,
neither father nor mother knew of it.

They travelled far into a foreign country, they had no luck, they
are perished and dead.

Prayer

LORD, send what Thou wilt – pleasant things or unpleasant, I am
content that both flow from Thy hands.

Do not overwhelm me with joys or with sorrows! Gracious
sufficiency lies in the middle.

Verborgenheit

Lass, o Welt, o laß mich sein!
Locket nicht mit Liebesgaben!
Laßt dies Herz alleine haben
Seine Wonne, seine Pein!

Was ich traure, weiß ich nicht:
Es ist unbekanntes Wehe;
Immerdar durch Tränen sehe
Ich der Sonne liebes Licht.

Oft bin ich mir kaum bewußt,
Und die helle Freude zücket
Durch die Schwere, die mich drücket,
Wonniglich in meiner Brust.

Laß, o Welt, o laß mich sein!
Locket nicht mit Liebesgaben!
Laßt dies Herz alleine haben
Seine Wonne, seine Pein!

Withdrawal

World, let me, let me be! Do not entice me with gifts of love, let my heart keep its joy and its pain to itself.

I do not know what it is I mourn for, it is unknown sorrow; it is only through my tears that I can see the friendly light of the sun.

Often I barely realize it, and in my breast bright joy flashes rapturously through the melancholy which oppresses me.

World, let me, let me be! Do not entice me with gifts of love, let my heart keep its joy and its pain to itself.

Neue Liebe

KANN auch ein Mensch des andern auf der Erde
Ganz, wie er möchte, sein? –
In langer Nacht bedacht' ich mir's und mußte sagen:
  Nein!

So kann ich niemands heißen auf der Erde,
Und niemand wäre mein? –
Aus Finsternissen hell in mir aufzückt ein Freuden-
  schein:

Sollt' ich mit Gott nicht können sein,
So wie ich möchte, mein und dein?
Was hielte mich, daß ich's nicht heute werde?

Ein süßes Schrecken geht durch mein Gebein:
Mich wundert, daß es mir ein Wunder wollte sein,
Gott selbst zu eigen haben auf der Erde!

New Love

CAN one belong to any one on earth as one would wish to?
Through a long night I pondered on it and had to answer: No.

So I cannot be said to belong to anybody on earth, and no one to
belong to me? Out of the darknesses within me a bright gleam of
joy flashes out:

Couldn't I be mine and thine, as I would wish, with God? What
could prevent me from being so today?

A sweet tremor goes through me to the bone. I am amazed that
it could seem a miracle to me to possess God Himself on earth.

Frage und Antwort

Fragst du mich, woher die bange
Liebe mir zum Herzen kam,
Und warum ich ihr nicht lange
Schon den bittern Stachel nahm?

Sprich, warum mit Geisterschnelle
Wohl der Wind die Flügel rührt,
Und woher die süße Quelle
Die verborgnen Wasser führt!

Banne du auf seiner Fährte
Mir den Wind in vollem Lauf!
Halte mit der Zaubergerte
Du die süßen Quellen auf!

Gesang Weylas

Du bist Orplid, mein Land,
Das ferne leuchtet!
Vom Meere dampfet dein besonnter Strand
Den Nebel, so der Götter Wange feuchtet.

Question and Answer

Can you ask me where this miserable love came into my heart from, and why I have not long ago drawn its bitter sting?
Tell me why the wind beats its wings with ghostly swiftness and where the sweet spring gets its hidden waters from!
Just you try to hold up the wind in its path in full career! Just you try to stop the sweet springs with a magic wand!

Weyla's Song

You are Orphid, my country that glows afar. Your sunlit shore gives off the mist from the sea, the mist which moistens the cheeks of the gods.

Uralte Wasser steigen
Verjüngt um deine Hüften, Kind!
Vor deiner Gottheit beugen
Sich Könige, die deine Wärter sind.

Septembermorgen

Im Nebel ruhet noch die Welt,
Noch träumen Wald und Wiesen:
Bald siehst du, wenn der Schleier fällt,
Den blauen Himmel unverstellt,
Herbstkräftig die gedämpfte Welt
In warmem Golde fließen.

Pastoralerfahrung

Meine guten Bauern freuen mich sehr;
Eine «scharfe Predigt» ist ihr Begehr.
Und wenn man mir es nicht verdenkt,
Sag ich, wie das zusammenhängt.
Sonnabend, wohl nach elfe spat,
Im Garten stehlen sie mir den Salat;

Round your hips, child, ancient waters rise, their youth renewed! Kings who are your guardians, bow down before your godhead.

September Morning

The world is still at rest in the mist, woods and meadows are still dreaming. Soon, when the veil falls, you will see the blue sky unconcealed, the quietened world in its autumnal vigour, awash in warm gold.

A Clerical Experience

My good country folk lead me a fine dance; a 'powerful sermon' is what they ask for, and if they won't take it amiss I will explain how it comes about. On Saturday, some time after eleven at night, they steal the lettuce out of my garden;/at matins, at their ease, they

In der Morgenkirch' mit guter Ruh'
Erwarten sie den Essig dazu;
Der Predigt Schluß fein linde sei!
Sie wollen gern auch Öl dabei.

Zitronenfalter im April

GRAUSAME Frühlingssonne,
Du weckst mich vor der Zeit,
Dem nur in Maienwonne
Die zarte Kost gedeiht!
Ist nicht ein liebes Mädchen hier,
Das auf der Rosenlippe mir
Ein Tröpfchen Honig beut,
So muß ich jämmerlich vergehn
Und wird der Mai mich nimmer sehn
In meinem gelben Kleid.

Denk' es, o Seele

EIN Tännlein grünet wo,
Wer weiß, im Walde,
Ein Rosenstrauch, wer sagt,
In welchem Garten?

---

expect the vinegar to it. The end of the sermon has to be suitably
mild: they like to get the oil into the bargain!

Brimstone Butterfly in April

CRUEL spring sun, you have woken me too soon, for it is only in
the rapture of May that my delicate food can grow. If there is no
kind girl here to offer me a drop of honey on her rosy lips I must
perish miserably, and May will never see me in my yellow garment.

Oh, Soul, Remember This

A PINE sapling is growing somewhere, who knows where, in the
forest, a rose-bush in who can tell what garden./They are already

Sie sind erlesen schon –
Denk' es, o Seele! –
Auf deinem Grab zu wurzeln
Und zu wachsen.

Zwei schwarze Rößlein weiden
Auf der Wiese,
Sie kehren heim zur Stadt
In muntern Sprüngen.
Sie werden schrittweis gehn
Mit deiner Leiche,
Vielleicht, vielleicht noch eh'
An ihren Hufen
Das Eisen los wird,
Das ich blitzen sehe.

Im Frühling

HIER lieg' ich auf dem Frühlingshügel:
Die Wolke wird mein Flügel,
Ein Vogel fliegt mir voraus.
Ach, sag mir, alleinzige Liebe,
Wo du bleibst, daß ich bei dir bliebe!
Doch du und die Lüfte, ihr habt kein Haus.

---

pre-ordained – Oh, soul, remember this – to strike root and grow
on your grave.

Two black colts are grazing in the meadow, they come home
into the village with happy curvetings. They will go at foot-pace
with your corpse; perhaps, perhaps even before the horse-shoes,
which I can see gleaming, loosen on their hooves.

In the Spring

I LIE here on the spring-touched hill: the clouds become my wings,
a bird flies on ahead of me. Tell me, O one and only love, where
you are, so that I can be with you! But you have no house, you and
the breezes.

Der Sonnenblume gleich steht mein Gemüte offen,
Sehnend,
Sich dehnend
In Lieben und Hoffen.
Frühling, was bist du gewillt?
Wann werd' ich gestillt?

Die Wolke seh' ich wandeln und den Fluß,
Es dringt der Sonne goldner Kuß
Mir tief bis ins Geblüt hinein;
Die Augen wunderbar berauschet,
Tun, als schliefen sie ein,
Nur noch das Ohr dem Ton der Biene lauschet.

Ich denke dies und denke das,
Ich sehne mich und weiß nicht recht, nach was:
Halb ist es Lust, halb ist es Klage;
Mein Herz, o sage,
Was webst du für Erinnerung
In golden grüner Zweige Dämmerung! –
Alte unnennbare Tage!

My mind lies open like the sunflower, longing, stretching upward in love and hope. Spring, what do you want with me? When shall I be satisfied?

I can see the clouds moving and the river too, the golden kiss of the sun pierces deep into my blood. My eyes, strangely stuporladen, seem about to drop off to sleep, only my ear still takes in the sound of the bee.

I think about this and that, I wish longingly for something, I am not quite sure what; it is half pleasure, half mourning; oh, tell me, my heart, what memories are you weaving in the twilight of the golden green branches? Old times I dare not talk about.

Das verlassene Mägdlein

Früh, wann die Hähne krähn,
Eh' die Sternlein verschwinden,
Muß ich am Herde stehn,
Muß Feuer zünden.

Schön ist der Flammen Schein,
Es springen die Funken;
Ich schaue so drein,
In Leid versunken.

Plötzlich da kommt es mir,
Treuloser Knabe,
Daß ich die Nacht von dir
Geträumet habe.

Träne auf Träne dann
Stürzet hernieder:
So kommt der Tag heran –
O ging' er wieder!

The Jilted Servant Girl

Early when the cocks crow, before the little stars disappear, I have to stand at the range and light the fire.

The gleam of the flames is lovely, the sparks fly up; I just look vacantly, sunk in sorrow.

Suddenly it comes back to me, you faithless boy, that I dreamt about you last night.

Then one tear after another bursts from my eyes; and so the day comes up; – if it would only go away again!

Um Mitternacht

GELASSEN stieg die Nacht ans Land,
Lehnt träumend an der Berge Wand;
Ihr Auge sieht die goldne Wage nun
Der Zeit in gleichen Schalen stille ruhn.
   Und kecker rauschen die Quellen hervor,
    Sie singen der Mutter, der Nacht, ins Ohr
      Vom Tage,
Vom heute gewesenen Tage.

Das uralt alte Schlummerlied –
Sie achtet's nicht, sie ist es müd';
Ihr klingt des Himmels Bläue süßer noch,
Der flücht'gen Stunden gleichgeschwung'nes Joch.
   Doch immer behalten die Quellen das Wort,
    Es singen die Wasser im Schlafe noch fort
      Vom Tage
Vom heute gewesenen Tage.

At Midnight

CALMLY night has disembarked. She leans dreaming against the wall of hills, her eye sees the golden scales of time at rest in even balance, and the streams come forth more boldly with their purling, they sing into the ear of their mother night, about the day, the day that is over today.

The ancient venerable lullaby, she does not heed it, she is tired of it: the blue of the sky sounds sweeter to her, the evenly curved yoke of the fleeting hours. But the streams are still talking, they go on singing in their sleep about the day, the day that is over today.

Nachts

HORCH! auf der Erde feuchtem Grund gelegen,
Arbeitet schwer die Nacht der Dämmerung entgegen,
Indessen dort, in blauer Luft gezogen,
Die Fäden leicht, unhörbar fließen,
Und hin und wieder mit gestähltem Bogen
Die lust'gen Sterne goldne Pfeile schießen.

Im Erdenschoß, im Hain und auf der Flur,
Wie wühlt es jetzo rings in der Natur
Von nimmersatter Kräfte Gärung!
Und welche Ruhe doch und welch ein Wohlbedacht!
Mir aber in geheimer Brust erwacht
Ein peinlich Widerspiel von Fülle und Entbehrung
Vor diesem Bild, so schweigend und so groß.
Mein Herz, wie gerne machtest du dich los!
Du schwankendes, dem jeder Halt gebricht,
Willst, kaum entflohn, zurück zu deinesgleichen.
Trägst du der Schönheit Götterstille nicht,
So beuge dich! denn hier ist kein Entweichen.

At Night

LISTEN! Spread on the moist foundation of the earth, night
labours heavily towards the dawn, while up there the threads drawn
in the blue air flow inaudible, and now and then with flexed bow the
merry stars shoot golden arrows. In the lap of the earth, in the
copse and on the common, how the ferment of insatiable forces in
nature goes on churning now! And yet what peace! and what pur-
pose! But in my secret heart an embarrassing conflict of plenty and
austerity is awakened by this spectacle, so silent and so vast. My
heart, how gladly you would disengage yourself! You floundering
heart, with no firm hold of any kind, you have hardly escaped but
you want to return to your fellows. If you cannot support the
divine quiet of beauty, then bow, for here there is no escape.

Auf einem Kirchturm

EIN Glockentonmeer wallet
Zu Füßen uns und hallet
Weit über Stadt und Land.
So laut die Wellen schlagen,
Wir fühlen mit Behagen
Uns hoch zu Schiff getragen
Und blicken schwindelnd von dem Rand.

THEODOR STORM

Zur Nacht

VORBEI der Tag! Nun laß mich unverstellt
Genießen dieser Stunde vollen Frieden!
Nun sind wir unser; von der frechen Welt
Hat endlich uns die heil'ge Nacht geschieden.

Laß einmal noch, ehe sich dein Auge schließt,
Der Liebe Strahl sich rückhaltlos entzünden;
Noch einmal, eh im Traum sie sich vergißt,
Mich deiner Stimme lieben Laut empfinden!

On a Church Tower

AN ocean of bell notes surges at our feet and sounds far over town
and country. Loud as the waves beat we have the comfortable feel-
ing of being borne high up in a ship, and dizzily we look over the
edge.

At Night

THE day is over. Now let me without restraint enjoy the full peace
of this hour! Now we belong to one another; holy night has
separated us from the thrusting world.

Before your eyes close let the gleam of love light up once more
without reserve; let me feel once more the dear sound of your voice
before it loses itself in dreams!

Was gibt es mehr! Der stille Knabe winkt
Zu seinem Strande lockender und lieber;
Und wie die Brust dir atmend schwellt und sinkt,
Trägt uns des Schlummers Welle sanft hinüber.

Trost

So komme, was da kommen mag!
So lang du lebest, ist es Tag.

Und geht es in die Welt hinaus,
Wo du mir bist, bin ich zu Haus.

Ich seh dein liebes Angesicht,
Ich sehe die Schatten der Zukunft nicht.

Schliesse mir die Augen beide
Mit den lieben Händen zu!
Geht doch alles, was ich leide,
Unter deiner Hand zur Ruh.

What more can there be? The quiet boy beckons us ever more
friendlily and enticingly to his shore, and as your breast rises and
falls with your breathing, the wave of slumber gently carries us
across.

Consolation

Let come what will, as long as you are alive it is day.

And if I have to go out into the world, wherever you are is
home.

I see your dear face, and not the shadows of the future.

Close both my eyes with your dear hands, for all my suffering
goes to rest under your hand./And as the pain, wave after wave,

Und wie leise sich der Schmerz
Well' um Welle schlafen leget,
Wie der letzte Schlag sich regèt,
Füllest du mein ganzes Herz.

Februar

Im Winde wehn die Lindenzweige,
Von roten Knospen übersäumt;
Die Wiegen sind's, worin der Frühling
Die schlimme Winterzeit verträumt.

März

Und aus der Erde schauet nur
Alleine noch Schneeglöckchen;
So kalt, so kalt ist noch die Flur,
Es friert im weißen Röckchen.

calms down to sleep, and as the last ripple quivers, you fill my whole heart.

February

THE twigs of the limes wave in the wind, edged with red buds. They are the cradles in which the spring dreams away the hard winter.

March

And the only thing that looks out of the ground so far is the snowdrop. The ground is so cold, so cold, it shivers in its white skirt.

April

Das ist die Drossel, die da schlägt,
Der Frühling, der mein Herz bewegt;
Ich fühle, die sich hold bezeigen,
Die Geister aus der Erde steigen.
Das Leben fließet wie ein Traum –
Mir ist wie Blume, Blatt und Baum.

Mai

Die Kinder schreien «Vivat hoch!»
In die blaue Luft hinein;
Den Frühling setzen sie auf den Thron,
Der soll ihr König sein.

Die Kinder haben die Veilchen gepflückt,
All, all, die da blühten am Mühlengraben.
Der Lenz ist da; sie wollen ihn fest
In ihren kleinen Fäusten haben.

April

That is the thrush singing – spring-time which sets my heart beating; I feel the spirits rise out of the ground and show themselves well disposed. Life flows like a dream: I feel as flower, leaf, and tree must feel.

May

The children shout, 'Hurray, hurray!' into the blue sky. They set the spring upon a throne, he is to be their king.

The children have been picking all the violets that were out along the mill ditch, every one. Spring is here; they want to have him and hold him fast in their little fists.

Juli

Klingt im Wind ein Wiegenlied,
Sonne warm herniedersieht,
Seine Ähren senkt das Korn,
Rote Beere schwillt am Dorn,
Schwer von Segen ist die Flur –
Junge Frau, was sinnst du nur?

August

(*Inserat*)

Die verehrlichen Jungen, welche heuer
Meine Äpfel und Birnen zu stehlen gedenken,
Ersuche ich höflichst, bei diesem Vergnügen
Womöglich insoweit sich zu beschränken,
Daß sie daneben auf den Beeten
Mir die Wurzeln und Erbsen nicht zertreten.

July

A lullaby sounds on the breeze, the sun looks down warmly, the
corn bows its ears, the red berry swells on the thornbush, the land
is heavy with bounty – young wife, what are you pondering on?

August

(*Agony column*)

I beg to request the esteemed young gentlemen who intend to steal
my apples and pears this year to restrict themselves as far as pos-
sible to this form of enjoyment, and not to trample down the car-
rots and peas in my vegetable beds.

Am Aktentisch

Da hab ich den ganzen Tag dekretiert;
Und es hätte mich fast wie so manchen verführt:
Ich spürte das kleine dumme Vergnügen,
Was abzumachen, was fertigzukriegen.

An Klaus Groth

Wenn't Abend ward,
Und still de Welt un still dat Hart;
Wenn möd up't Knee di liggt de Hand,
Un ut din Husklock an de Wand
Du hörst den Parpendikelslag,
De nich to Woort keem över Dag;
Wenn't Schummern in de Ecken liggt,
Und buten all de Nachtswulk flüggt;
Wenn denn noch eenmal kiekt de Sünn
Mit golden Schiin to't Finster rin,

At the Office Desk

All day I have been issuing orders and the urge which leads so
many people astray nearly did so to me; I felt the small stupid
pleasure of 'finishing things off' and 'getting things done'.

To Klaus Groth

When evening comes and the world grows quiet and the heart too,
when your hand lies weary on your knee and you can hear the tick
of the pendulum from the clock on the wall which has not been able
to make itself heard all day; when dusk lies in the corners and the
nightjar flies round outside; when the sun looks in through the
window at you just once more with golden gleam, / when everything

Un, ehr de Slap kümmt un de Nacht,
Noch eenmal allens lävt un lacht, –
Dat is so wat vör't Minschenhart,
    Wenn't Abend ward.

KLAUS GROTH

De Fischer

Schön Anna stunn vær Stratendær,
Vær Stratendær,
De Fischer gung værbi:
Schön Anna knüttst du blaue Strümp,
De blauen Strümp,
De knüttst du wul vær mi?

«De Strümp de kriggt min Broder an,
Min Broder an,
Wul op de blaue See;
Du makst je sülm din Nett so grot,
Din Nett so grot,
Un Strümp bet anne Knee.»

is alive and laughing just once more before sleep and night come
upon you – that is something to make glad the heart of man, when
evening comes.

The Fisherman

Pretty Anna was standing at the door, at the street door; the
fisherman went by. 'Pretty Anna, so you're knitting blue socks;
I expect you're knitting those blue socks for me?'
    'My brother's going to wear these socks, my brother is, out on
the blue sea; you make your big net yourself, your big net, and
socks right up to the knee.'

Min Nett dat mak ik grot un wit,
So grot un wit
Man vær de dumme Stær:
Du knüttst din Strümp so fin un dicht,
So fin un dicht,
Dar geit keen Seel hindær.

Schön Anna, knüttst du fine Strümp
Son fine Strümp,
Un knüttst du se so blau:
Dar fangst du all de Fischers mit,
De Fischers mit,
Un weern se noch so slau.

Aflohnt

DE Sæn de harr er banni leef, se weer so week un fee.
De Ole schull int Hus herum: wat se sik inbilln de!

Se neem er Bündel ünnern Arm, vun Tran'n de Ogen
blank,
Se sä de Ole sacht adüs, se sä de Sæn: heff Dank!

'I only make my net so big and wide, so big and wide, to catch
the silly sturgeon; you knit your sock so close and thick, so close
and thick, that not a soul can get through.

'Pretty Anna if you knit close socks, as close as that, and if you
knit them so blue, you will catch all the fishermen in them, all the
fishermen, however clever they are.'

Paid Off

THE son was very fond of her, she was so soft and gentle. The old
man went round the house grumbling, saying, 'Who does she
think she is!'

She took her bundle under her arm, her eyes were bright with
tears; she gently said good-bye to the old man and she said, 'Thank
you' to his son.

Se gung bet um de Eck an Tun, un sett sik op den
    Steen.
De Ole schull int Hus herum, de Sæn de stunn un ween.

En Vergißmeinnicht

DE Dag de graut int Osten,
Dag ward dat æwerall;
Mi blifft dat grau un düster
Wo ik hin wandern schall,
    Dat blifft mi düster.

De Blöm un muntern Vageln
De sünd mi wulbekannt,
De Dau liggt op de Wischen
As in min Vaderland,
    Op gröne Wischen.

Ik plück mi vun de Heiloh
En Blom Vergißmeinnicht,
De Drapens an de Blæder
De köhlt mi dat Gesicht,
    De hellen Drapens.

She went round the corner of the fence and sat down on the
stone. The old man went round the house grumbling, his son stood
there in tears.

A Forget-me-not

THE dawn is greying in the east, soon it will be day everywhere.
But it stays grey and dark for me where I have to go, it stays dark.
    The flowers and the happy birds, I know them all, the dew lies
on the meadows just as it does at home, on the green meadows.
    I'll pick a forget-me-not flower in the moorland; the dewdrops
on the leaves will cool my face, the bright dewdrops.

Keen Graff is so breet un keen Müer so hoch,
Wenn Twee sik man gut sünd, so drapt se sik doch.

Keen Wedder so gruli, so düster keen Nacht,
Wenn Twee sik man sehn wüllt, so seht se sik sacht.

Dat gift wul en Maanschin, dar schint wul en Steern,
Dat gift noch en Licht oder Lücht un Lantern.

Dar finnt sik en Ledder, en Stegelsch un Steg:
Wenn Twee sik man leef hebbt – keen Sorg vær den Weg.

GOTTFRIED KELLER

Abendlied

Augen, meine lieben Fensterlein,
Gebt mir schon so lange holden Schein,
Lasset freundlich Bild um Bild herein:
Einmal werdet ihr verdunkelt sein!

Love Will Find Out a Way

There's no ditch so broad and no wall so high but if two are in love they will come together in spite of them.

There's no storm so wild and no night so dark but if two want to see each other they easily will.

There is somehow moonlight, or starlight shining, there is somehow a candle, or a light and a lantern.

There is somehow a ladder, a stile or a plank: if two are in love, there is always a way.

Song at Nightfall

Eyes, my beloved little windows, for such a long time you have given me delight and light and kindly let through picture after picture, the time will come when you will be darkened.

Fallen einst die müden Lider zu,
Löscht ihr aus, dann hat die Seele Ruh';
Tastend streift sie ab die Wanderschuh',
Legt sich auch in ihre finstre Truh'.

Noch zwei Fünklein sieht sie glimmend stehn
Wie zwei Sternlein, innerlich zu sehn,
Bis sie schwanken und dann auch vergehn,
Wie von eines Falters Flügelwehn.

Doch noch wandl' ich auf dem Abendfeld,
Nur dem sinkenden Gestirn gesellt;
Trinkt, o Augen, was die Wimper hält,
Von dem goldnen Überfluß der Welt!

Winternacht

NICHT ein Flügelschlag ging durch die Welt,
Still und blendend lag der weiße Schnee.
Nicht ein Wölklein hing am Sternenzelt,
Keine Welle schlug im starren See.

Then, when the tired lids drop and you extinguish, the soul will
be at rest; gropingly it slips off its walking-boots, and lies down too
in its dark chest.

It still sees two tiny sparks gleaming like two little stars inwardly
visible, until they flicker and go out as if quenched by the flutter of
a moth's wing.

Yet I am still walking in the field at sundown with only the set-
ting sun for a companion: eyes, drink as much as your lashes will
hold of the golden profusion of the world.

Winter Night

NOT even a wing beat went across the world, the white snow lay
quiet and glistening, not a cloud hung in the tent of the sky, not a
wave beat on the torpid lake.

Aus der Tiefe stieg der Seebaum auf,
Bis sein Wipfel in dem Eis gefror;
An den Ästen klomm die Nix' herauf,
Schaute durch das grüne Eis empor.

Auf dem dünnen Glase stand ich da,
Das die schwarze Tiefe von mir schied;
Dicht ich unter meinen Füßen sah
Ihre weiße Schönheit, Glied um Glied.

Mit ersticktem Jammer tastet' sie
An der harten Decke her und hin,
Ich vergess' das dunkle Antlitz nie,
Immer, immer liegt es mir im Sinn.

CONRAD FERDINAND MEYER

Eingelegte Ruder

MEINE eingelegten Ruder triefen,
Tropfen fallen langsam in die Tiefen.

Nichts, das mich verdroß! Nichts, das mich freute!
Niederrinnt ein schmerzenloses Heute!

Up from the depths rose the sunken tree, till its top froze fast in the ice; the water sprite climbed up its branches, peered upwards through the green ice.

I stood there on the thin glass which separated the black depths from me: close under my feet I saw her white beauty, limb by limb.

With stifled despair she groped back and forth against the hard ceiling. I shall never forget that dark face, it has always haunted me ever since.

Shipped Oars

My shipped oars are dripping, drops are falling into deep water.

Nothing that distressed me! Nothing that gave me pleasure! It is today, a painless day, that is trickling down.

Unter mir – ach, aus dem Licht verschwunden –
Träumen schon die schönern meiner Stunden.

Aus der blauen Tiefe ruft das Gestern:
Sind im Licht noch manche meiner Schwestern?

Schwarzschattende Kastanie

SCHWARZSCHATTENDE Kastanie,
Mein windgeregtes Sommerzelt,
Du senkst zur Flut dein weit Geäst,
Dein Laub, es durstet und es trinkt,
Schwarzschattende Kastanie!
Im Porte badet junge Brut
Mit Hader oder Lustgeschrei
Und Kinder schwimmen leuchtend weiß
Im Gitter deines Blätterwerks,
Schwarzschattende Kastanie!
Und dämmern See und Ufer ein
Und rauscht vorbei das Abendboot,
So zuckt aus roter Schiffslatern

Below me – ah, gone out of the light – my more pleasant hours already dream.

Yesterday calls up from the blue depths: are there more of my sisters up there in the light?

CHESTNUT-TREE with black shadows, my summer tent in which the breeze plays, you dip your broad branches down into the water, your leaves are thirsty and they drink, black-shadowing chestnut! In the harbour young people are bathing with quarrelsome or joyful shouts and children come swimming gleaming white in the trellis of your foliage, black-shadowing chestnut! And when lake and shore sink into dusk and the evening steamer goes rustling by,

Ein Blitz und wandert auf dem Schwung
Der Flut, gebrochnen Lettern gleich,
Bis unter deinem Laub erlischt,
Die rätselhafte Flammenschrift,
Schwarzschattende Kastanie!

Nachtgeräusche

MELDE mir die Nachtgeräusche, Muse,
Die ans Ohr des Schlummerlosen fluten!
Erst das traute Wachtgebell der Hunde
Dann der abgezählte Schlag der Stunde,
Dann ein Fischer-Zwiegespräch am Ufer,
Dann? Nichts weiter als der ungewisse
Geisterlaut der ungebrochnen Stille,
Wie das Atmen eines jungen Busens,
Wie das Murmeln eines tiefen Brunnens,
Wie das Schlagen eines dumpfen Ruders,
Dann der ungehörte Tritt des Schlummers.

a flash shoots from its red lantern and wanders on the swell of the
water, like broken lettering, until the mysterious flaming writing
fades out under your foliage, black-shadowing chestnut-tree!

Noises of the Night

TELL me, Muse, of the noises of the night which flood up to the
ear of those who cannot sleep! – First the familiar watchful barking
of the dogs, then the counted striking of the hour, then two fisher-
men talking on the shore, and then? Nothing, except the indis-
tinct ghostly sound of unbroken stillness, like the breathing of a
youthful breast, like the murmuring of a deep spring, like the beat
of a muffled oar, – then the unheard step of sleep.

Der römische Brunnen

Aufsteigt der Strahl und fallend gießt
Er voll der Marmorschale Rund,
Die, sich verschleiernd, überfließt
In einer zweiten Schale Grund;
Die zweite gibt, sie wird zu reich,
Der dritten wallend ihre Flut,
Und jede nimmt und gibt zugleich
                Und strömt und ruht.

Lethe

Jüngst im Traume sah ich auf den Fluten
Einen Nachen ohne Ruder ziehn.
Strom und Himmel stand in matten Gluten
Wie bei Tages Nahen oder Fliehn.

Saßen Knaben drin mit Lotoskränzen,
Mädchen beugten über Bord sich schlank,
Kreisend durch die Reihe sah ich glänzen
Eine Schale, draus ein jedes trank.

The Fountain in Rome

Up soars the jet and, falling, fills the circle of the marble bowl, which veils itself and overflows into the bottom of a second bowl;

The second becomes too affluent, welling up it gives its tide to the third, and each one takes and gives together, and streams and rests.

Lethe

Not long ago I dreamt I saw an oarless boat moving over the stream. River and sky had a dull glow, as at the approach or departure of the day.

In the boat were sitting youths with garlands of lotus, slim girls were leaning over the side; I saw a goblet gleaming as it went the round, and each one drank from it.

Jetzt erscholl ein Lied voll süßer Wehmut,
Das die Schar der Kranzgenossen sang –
Ich erkannte deines Nackens Demut,
Deine Stimme, die den Chor durchdrang.

In die Welle taucht' ich. Bis zum Marke
Schaudert' ich, wie seltsam kühl sie war.
Ich erreicht' die leise zieh'nde Barke,
Drängte mich in die geweihte Schar.

Und die Reihe war an dir zu trinken,
Und die volle Schale hobest du,
Sprachst zu mir mit trautem Augenwinken:
«Herz, ich trinke dir Vergessen zu!»

Dir entriß in trotz'gem Liebesdrange
Ich die Schale, warf sie in die Flut,
Sie versank, und siehe, deine Wange
Färbte sich mit einem Schein von Blut.

Now a song filled with sweet melancholy sounded, which the
band of garlanded companions was singing – I recognized the
humility of your neck, and your voice rising above the choir.

I plunged into the water. I shivered to the marrow, so strangely
chill it was. I reached the gently moving boat and thrust myself
among the sacred band.

And it was your turn to drink, and you lifted the full goblet and
said to me with a friendly glance: 'Dear heart, I drink to your for-
getting.'

In a rebellious surge of love I wrenched the goblet from you,
threw it into the stream, it sank, and see! your cheek coloured with
a glow of blood.

Flehend küßt' ich dich in wildem Harme,
Die den bleichen Mund mir willig bot,
Da zerrannst du lächelnd mir im Arme
Und ich wußt' es wieder – du bist tot.

FRIEDRICH NIETZSCHE

Ecce Homo

JA! Ich weiß, woher ich stamme!
Ungesättigt gleich der Flamme
Glühe und verzehr' ich mich.
Licht wird alles, was ich fasse,
Kohle alles, was ich lasse.
Flamme bin ich sicherlich!

Imploring I kissed you in wild grief as you willingly offered me
your pale mouth, then you smilingly dissolved in my arms and I
remembered – you are dead.

Ecce Homo

YES, I know where I spring from! Unsated like the flame I glow
and consume myself. Everything I grasp turns to light, everything
I leave to cinder, flame is certainly what I am!

Der Wanderer und sein Schatten

NICHT mehr zurück? Und nicht hinan?
Auch für die Gemse keine Bahn?

So wart' ich hier und fasse fest,
Was Aug' und Hand mich fassen läßt!

Fünf Fuß breit Erde, Morgenrot,
Und *unter* mir – Welt, Mensch und Tod!

Das trunkene Lied

O MENSCH! Gib acht!
Was spricht die tiefe Mitternacht?
«Ich schlief, ich schlief –
Aus tiefem Traum bin ich erwacht:–
Die Welt ist tief,
Und tiefer als der Tag gedacht.
Tief ist ihr Weh –,
Lust – tiefer noch als Herzeleid!
Weh spricht: Vergeh!
Doch alle Lust will Ewigkeit –,
Will tiefe, tiefe Ewigkeit.»

The Wanderer and his Shadow

I CANNOT go back? Cannot go on? No path even for a chamois?
Then I shall wait here and take a firm grip on what my eye and hand
let me hold. Five foot broad of earth, dawn, and below me – world,
man, and death!

The Song of Ecstasy

O MAN take heed! What does the depth of midnight say? 'I was
asleep, asleep – I have woken up out of deep dreaming: the world
is deep and deeper than day ever conceived. Its pain is deep – joy
deeper even than the heart's grief! Pain says: Pass away; but all joy
seeks eternity – seeks deep, deep eternity!'

ARNO HOLZ

Barocke Marine

See,
See, sonnigste See,
soweit
du ... siehst!

Über die rollenden Wasser hin,
lärmend, jauchzjohlend, wonnejubelnd, lustlachend, schwärmend,
sich grunzwölternd, sich wälzwerfend, sich
rückenschleudernd,
sich
wärmend,
sich hohlhandzurufend, sich hohlhandzuschreiend, sich
hohlhandzugröhlend,
tanggrünhaarig, schuppenglitzleiberig, störschwanzflossig,
schwimmtauchblinkend, schwimmfauchflinkend,
schwimmpustpfasend
wie
rasend, Drommetenschneckenhörner blasend,
tausend ... Tritonen!

Auf
blanken
Delphinrückenfinnen,
muschelempor,
hoch
ein Weib!

Baroque Sea Scape

SEA, sea, sunniest sea, as far as you can see!

Over the rolling waters, noisemaking, joybawling, pleasurecarolling, joylaughing, emotion-pouring, grunt-wallowing, hurlrolling, backdiving, warming themselves, shouting to each other, bawling to each other, yelling to each other through the megaphones of their hands, seaweedgreenhairy, scaleslipperybodied, sturgeontailflippered, swimdiveglittering, swimhissgleaming, swimpuffspluttering like mad, blowing gasteropodous conchtrumpets, a thousand tritons!

On bright dolphin dorsalfins aloft in a seashell, high, a woman!

Ihre herrliche, strahlende, ihre blendende, prahlende, ihre
leuchtende, prangende,
göttliche
Nacktheit ... in die
Sonne!

Unter ihr, schwaddelnd, unter ihr, paddelnd, unter ihr,
triefend,
die
steilen, die flinkernden, die buntschillerigen Perlmutterglattwände,
immer wieder von Neuem
hinan,
dick, feist, verliebt,
wie Kröten,
sieben alte, sieben
glamserige,
sieben
seehundsglotzäugige, seebärenschnurrborstige,
seeelefantenrüsselnäsige, seelöwenstrubbelklatschmähnige,
walroßwulstplumptonnenhalsige
Meertaper!

Die
Gesichter!!
Das ... Gestöhn!! Das ... Geklöhn!!
Das ... Gehuste!! ... Und ... das ... Gepruste!!

Da,
plötzlich,
wütend, mit ... Ruck
hinter meinem schäumenden, wiehernd sich bäumenden,
schnaubenden, gleißen, schnaufenden, weißen,

Her splendid radiant, her dazzling eyecatching, her glowing gor-
geous divine nakedness in the sun!

Beneath her swashing, beneath her sploshing, beneath her drip-
ping, constantly approaching the steep, the gleaming, the many-
colouredglistening slippery mother-of-pearl walls, stout, fat,
amorous, like toads, seven old, seven slimy, seven sealpopeyed,
seabearbristlebearded, seaelephantproboscisnosed, sealionshock-
headeddrippingmaned, walrusrollfatbarrelnecked sea-tapirs!

The faces! The groans! The backchat! The coughing! And the
spluttering!

Then, all at once, furious, with a sudden jolt, behind my foam-
ing, neighing, and rearing, snorting, shining, blowing, white,

schaufelpratzenruderigen Zwölfgespann,
ich,
mitten aus der Tiefe!
Mein ... Bart
blitzt!
«Neptun!!»
«Sauve qui peut!!»
«Halunken!! ... Ich ... werde euch!!»
Und
plitschplatsch,
klitschklatsch, ritschratsch
mein ... Dreizack
den
faden, maladen,
insolenten, impotenten, insolventen
Schlappschwänzen
um die Ohren, um die Backentaschen, um die Glatzen!

Die
krietschen!!

Die ... heulen!! Die ... brüllen!!

Dann, schnell,
hier noch ein paar Tatschen, da noch ein paar Patschen
dort
noch ein
Prallbackengesäß, noch ein Kranzfransengefräß,
noch
ein Froschbauch:
weg
sind sie!

shovelpawruddered twelve-in-hand, I, out of the depths into the
middle of them! My beard flashes! 'Neptune!' 'Sauve qui peut!'
'Scoundrels! I'll teach you!' And plitch-platch, clitch-clatch,
ritch-ratch my trident round their ears, their pendulous cheeks,
their bald pates, the dismal, sick-and-sorry, insolent, impotent, in-
solvent drooptails.
  They shriek!
  They yell! They bawl!
  Then, quick, a few smacks here, a few slaps there, another fat-
cherub bum, another garlandfringed gob, another frogpaunch:
they're gone.

Die
Schöne … lächelt.

«Monsieur?» … «Madame?»
Und
nach einer scharmanten, weltmännischst gewandten,
sie
in meine galante, sie in meine brillante,
sie
in meine
amüsante, extravagante,
durchbrochen
bernsteinblitzige, korallenglitzige, doppelsitzige
Donnerkalesche
allerrespektvollst leger einladenden Handbewegung, respektive Verbeugung,
sans façon
sause ich mit ihr
in
meine komfortabelste, brause ich mit ihr in meine admirabelste,
entblickschwinde ich mit ihr
in meine ämabelste, in meine agreabelste,
in
meine
irreproschabelste, inkomparabelste,
wunderdämmerigste, zauberschummerigste,
rubintraumlichtkarfunkelndste
Purpurgrotte!

The lady smiles.
'Monsieur?' 'Madame?' And after a charming, most man-of-
the-world-accomplished gesture or, if you prefer it, bow, frivol-
ously inviting her with the greatest respect into my gallant, into
my brilliant, into my amusing, extravagant, window-pierced, amber-
flashing, coralgleaming, stupendous two-seater calèche, *sans façon*
I sweep off with her into my most comfortable, I roar off with her
into my most admirable, I disappear from view with her into my
most delicious, most agreeable, into my most irreproachable, most
incomparable, most marveltwilit, most magicalhalflit, most ruby-
dreamlightcarbunclesparkling purple grotto!

—

This poem has been set in a smaller size of type from the rest of
the book, in order to preserve the poet's 'Mittelachsenpoesie'
arrangement without breaking lines. See biographical note, p. xxi.

RICHARD DEHMEL

Gleichnis

Es ist ein Brunnen, der heißt Leid;
Draus fließt die lautre Seligkeit.
Doch wer nur in den Brunnen schaut,
Den graut.

Er sieht im tiefen Wasserschacht
Sein lichtes Bild umrahmt von Nacht.
O trinke! da zerrinnt dein Bild:
Licht quillt.

STEFAN GEORGE

Fenster wo ich einst mit dir
Abends in die landschaft sah
Sind nun hell mit fremdem licht.

Pfad noch läuft vom tor wo du
Standest ohne umzuschaun
Dann ins tal hinunterbogst.

Parable

There is a well that is called sorrow; pure happiness runs out of
it. But horror seizes anyone who just looks into the well.

In the deep watery shaft he sees his own picture bright but
framed by night. Oh, but drink! then your picture dissolves; light
wells in.

Windows, from which I once looked out over the countryside in
the evening with you, are now bright with alien light.

The path still goes from the gate where you stood without look-
ing round and then turned down hill into the valley.

Bei der kehr warf nochmals auf
Mond dein bleiches angesicht ...
Doch es war zu spät zum ruf.

Dunkel – schweigen – starre luft
Sinkt wie damals um das haus.
Alle freude nahmst du mit.

D ᴇʀ hügel wo wir wandeln liegt im schatten ·
Indes der drüben noch im lichte webt
Der mond auf seinen zarten grünen matten
Nur erst als kleine weisse wolke schwebt.

Die strassen weithin-deutend werden blasser ·
Den wandrern bietet ein gelispel halt ·
Ist es vom berg ein unsichtbares wasser
Ist es ein vogel der sein schlaflied lallt?

Der dunkelfalter zwei die sich verfrühten
Verfolgen sich von halm zu halm im scherz ...
Der rain bereitet aus gesträuch und blüten
Den duft des abends für gedämpften schmerz.

At the curve the moon caught your pale face once more ... but
it was too late for me to call to you.
Darkness – silence – rigid air sinks round the house as it did
then. You took all joy away with you.

Tʜᴇ hill where we are walking lies in shadow, while the hill across
there is still enmeshed in light; the moon in her tender green mea-
dows is as yet only a drifting little cloud.
The roads that point far into the distance grow paler, a whisper-
ing makes the wanderers stay – is it an unseen stream from the
mountain, or is it a bird that is crooning its lullaby?
Two dark moths, come out before their time, chase one another
playfully from grass stem to grass stem. ... The hedgerow distils
out of bush and flower the scent of evening for muted grief.

K OMM in den totgesagten park und schau:
Der schimmer ferner lächelnder gestade ·
Der reinen wolken unverhofftes blau
Erhellt die weiher und die bunten pfade.

Dort nimm das tiefe gelb, das weiche grau
Von birken und von buchs · der wind ist lau ·
Die späten rosen welkten noch nicht ganz ·
Erlese küsse sie und flicht den kranz ·

Vergiss auch diese letzten astern nicht ·
Den purpur um die ranken wilder reben
Und auch was übrig blieb von grünem leben
Verwinde leicht im herbstlichen gesicht.

W IR schreiten auf und ab im reichen flitter
Des buchenganges beinah bis zum tore
Und sehen aussen in dem feld vom gitter
Den mandelbaum zum zweitenmal im flore.

C OME into the park they say is dead and look: the gleam of distant
smiling shores, the unhoped-for blue of the pure clouds shed a
light on the ponds and the variegated paths.
 Gather the deep yellow, the soft grey of birches and of box – the
breeze is mild – the late roses have not yet quite withered; choose
them, kiss them, and wind the garland,
 And do not forget these last asters either; twine in with gentle
hands the purple round the tendrils of the wild vine and, with the
autumn scene before you, whatever there is left of the green life.

U P and down we walk in the speckled richness of the beech avenue
nearly up to the gate, and from the fence we can see outside in the
field the almond-tree in bloom for the second time.

Wir suchen nach den schattenfreien bänken
Dort wo uns niemals fremde stimmen scheuchten ·
In träumen unsre arme sich verschränken ·
Wir laben uns am langen milden leuchten

Wir fühlen dankbar wie zu leisem brausen
Von wipfeln strahlenspuren auf uns tropfen
Und blicken nur und horchen wenn in pausen
Die reifen früchte an den boden klopfen.

MEIN kind kam heim.
Ihm weht der seewind noch im haar ·
Noch wiegt sein tritt
Bestandne furcht und junge lust der fahrt.

Vom salzigen sprühn
Entflammt noch seiner wange brauner schmelz:
Frucht schnell gereift
In fremder sonnen wildem duft und brand.

Sein blick ist schwer
Schon vom geheimnis das ich niemals weiss
Und leicht umflort
Da er vom lenz in unsern winter traf.

We look for the seats out of the shade, where alien voices never intruded on us, our arms link in dreams, and we take comfort from the long mellow glow.

We feel with thankfulness how fragments of sunbeams fall like drops upon us from the tree-tops as they softly rustle, and we only look up and listen when at intervals the ripe fruits thud upon the ground.

MY son came home. The sea breeze is still in his hair. Fear overcome swings in his gait and youthful joy in travel.

The brown glow of his cheek still burns with the salt spray. Fruit, ripened rapidly in the wild scents and heat of foreign suns.

His glance is already heavy with a secret I shall never know, and slightly clouded as he came from springtime into our winter.

So offen quoll
Die knospe auf dass ich fast scheu sie sah
Und mir verbot
Den mund der einen mund zum kuss schon kor.

Mein arm umschliesst
Was unbewegt von mir zu andrer welt
Erblüht und wuchs –
Mein eigentum und mir unendlich fern.

«Streut diesen sand und zweimal könnt ihr keltern
Und dreschen und das vieh ist doppelt melk.
Nun schwelgt und spottet eurer kargen eltern …»
Doch übers jahr bleibt alles brach und welk.

Grelltönende saite ziehn sie auf ihre leiern:
«Gott aber tier» «ein aber kein» «grad und doch krumm.»
Welten und zeiten durchrauscht nun! ein staunen! ein
feiern!
Doch wer die grundnote hört der lacht und bleibt stumm.

The bud has burst so wide open that I looked on it almost with
awe and held myself back from the mouth which had already chosen
another mouth to kiss.

My arm enfolds something that has grown unmoved towards
another world away from me – something that is mine, and in-
finitely remote from me.

'Scatter this sand and you will press the grapes and thresh twice
in a year, and the cattle will yield twice the milk. Live on the fat of
the land and laugh at your sparing parents.' But when the year is
over everything will be fallow and withered as it was before.

They stretch a harsh-sounding string on to their lyres: 'God,
but Animal', 'One, but None', 'Straight, but Crooked'. Through
worlds and epochs they sweep – what amazement! What celebra-
tions! But he who can hear the fundamental laughs and says
nothing.

Der Gehenkte

Der Frager:

DEN ich vom galgen schnitt · wirst du mir reden?

Der Gehenkte:

Als unter der verwünschung und dem schrei
Der ganzen stadt man mich zum tore schleppte
Sah ich in jedem der mit steinen warf
Der voll verachtung breit die arme stemmte
Der seinen finger reckte auf der achsel
Des vordermanns das aug weit aufgerissen ·
Dass in ihm einer meiner frevel stak
Nur schmäler oder eingezäumt durch furcht.
Als ich zum richtplatz kam und strenger miene
Die Herrn vom Rat mir beides: ekel zeigten
Und mitleid mußt ich lachen: «ahnt ihr nicht
Wie sehr des armen sünders ihr bedürft?»
Tugend – die ich verbrach – auf ihrem antlitz
Und sittiger frau und maid · sei sie auch wahr ·
So strahlen kann sie nur wenn ich so fehle!
Als man den hals mir in die schlinge steckte

The Hanged Man

THE Questioner: You whom I cut down from the gallows, will you speak to me?

The Hanged Man: When amid the curses and the shouts of the whole town I was dragged to the gates, I saw – in each man who threw a stone at me, who set his arms akimbo full of contempt, who with staring eyes pointed his finger at me across the shoulder of the man in front – I saw that one of my crimes was latent in each, only narrower or hemmed in by fear. When I came to the place of execution and the aldermen showed both disgust and pity for me in their stern faces, I was moved to laughter: 'Do you not realize how greatly you need the poor sinner?' Virtue – against which I had offended – on their faces, and on the faces of decent wives and girls, however real it may be, can only glow as it does if I sin as I do! When they put my neck into the noose/my malice showed me

Sah schadenfroh ich den triumf voraus:
Als sieger dring ich einst in euer hirn
Ich der verscharrte ... und in eurem samen
Wirk ich als held auf den man lieder singt
Als gott ... und eh ihrs euch versahet · biege
Ich diesen starren balken um zum rad.

CHRISTIAN MORGENSTERN

Das Nasobēm

Auf seinen Nasen schreitet
einher das Nasobēm,
von seinem Kind begleitet.
Es steht noch nicht im Brehm.

Es steht noch nicht im Meyer.
Und auch im Brockhaus nicht.
Es trat aus meiner Leyer
zum ersten Mal ans Licht.

Auf seinen Nasen schreitet
(wie schon gesagt) seitdem,
von seinem Kind begleitet,
einher das Nasobēm.

---

my future triumph: I the buried man will enter as a conqueror into your brains ... and I will be active in your seed as a hero about whom songs are sung, as a god ... and before you have had time to realize it I shall bend this stiff bar round into a wheel.

The Nosibeme

The stately nosibeme stalks along on its noses, accompanied by its young. It has not yet got into the Britannica, or even yet into Chambers' or into Everyman's; it was out of my lyre that it first stepped into the light of day. Upon its noses stalks (as I have already said), accompanied by its young, the stately nosibeme.

Der Lattenzaun

Es war einmal ein Lattenzaun,
mit Zwischenraum, hindurchzuschaun.

Ein Architekt, der dieses sah,
stand eines Abends plötzlich da –

und nahm den Zwischenraum heraus
und baute draus ein großes Haus.

Der Zaun indessen stand ganz dumm,
mit Latten ohne was herum,

ein Anblick gräßlich und gemein.
Drum zog ihn der Senat auch ein.

Der Architekt jedoch entfloh
nach Afri – od – Ameriko.

The Fence

Once upon a time there was a fence of palings with space between
them so you could see through them.

An architect, who noticed this, suddenly turned up one evening
and took away the space between and built a large house with it.

The fence meantime felt rather foolish in its palings without any-
thing round them, an unseemly and disgraceful sight; and so the
borough council had it taken away.

The architect, however, made off meanwhile to Africa or
America.

Die Behörde

KORF erhält vom Polizeibüro
ein geharnischt Formular,
wer er sei und wie und wo.

Welchen Orts er bis anheute war,
welchen Stands und überhaupt,
wo geboren, Tag und Jahr.

Ob ihm überhaupt erlaubt,
hier zu leben und zu welchem Zweck,
wieviel Geld er hat und was er glaubt.

Umgekehrten Falls man ihn vom Fleck
in Arrest verführen würde, und
drunter steht: Borowsky, Heck.

Korf erwidert darauf kurz und rund:
«Einer hohen Direktion
stellt sich, laut persönlichem Befund,

The Official Form

KORF receives from the police a strongly worded printed form,
demanding who he is, and how, and where;
in what place he was domiciled hitherto; whether married, single,
or divorced, and if not why not; place, day, and year of birth;
whether he has a permit to live here at all, and if so for what
purpose; what his means are and what his creed is;
in the contrary case he will be conveyed into custody; and at the
bottom are the signatures Borowsky, Heck.
Korf replies with extreme brevity: 'To the Chief Commissioner:
the undermanufactured certifies himself per personal inspection / and

untig angefertigte Person
als nichtexistent im Eigen-Sinn
bürgerlicher Konvention

vor und aus und zeichnet, wennschonhin
mitbedauernd nebigen Betreff,
Korf. (An die Bezirksbehörde in ....).»

Staunend liest's der anbetroffne Chef.

Die Mausefalle

I

PALMSTRÖM hat nicht Speck im Haus
dahingegen eine Maus.

Korf, bewegt von seinem Jammer,
baut ihm eine Gitterkammer.

Und mit einer Geige fein
setzt er seinen Freund hinein.

Nacht ist's, und die Sterne funkeln.
Palmström musiziert im Dunkeln.

has the honour to present himself as non-existent within the mean-
ing of the Act and remains, associating himself with you in deeply
regretting the circumstances hereinbefore set out, Yours etc: Korf.
(To the Blankshire County Police).'
The Competent Authority reads this in deep perplexment.

The Mouse-trap

I

PALMSTRÖM, though he has no bacon, has a mouse in the house.
Korf, touched by his distress, builds him a room out of trellis work,
and he puts his friend, with an exquisite violin, inside. It is night,
and the stars are sparkling; Palmström makes music in the dark.

Und derweil er konzertiert,
kommt die Maus hereinspaziert.

Hinter ihr, geheimer Weise,
fällt die Pforte leicht und leise.

Vor ihr sinkt in Schlaf alsbald
Palmströms schweigende Gestalt.

II

Morgens kommt von Korf und lädt
das so nützliche Gerät

in den nächsten, sozusagen
mittelgroßen Möbelwagen,

den ein starkes Roß beschwingt
nach der fernen Waldung bringt,

wo in tiefer Einsamkeit
er das seltne Paar befreit.

Erst spaziert die Maus heraus,
und dann Palmström, nach der Maus.

And, while he is performing, the mouse comes walking in. The trapdoor closes gently and noiselessly, in secret fashion, behind it. In front of it, in due course, Palmström's silent figure sinks into sleep.

II

In the morning von Korf comes and loads this useful device on to the nearest pantechnicon of – as it were – medium size, which a powerful horse nimbly takes to the distant forest, and here, in profound solitude, he liberates the unusual pair. First the mouse comes walking out, and then Palmström, after the mouse. / The creature,

Froh genießt das Tier der neuen
Heimat, ohne sich zu scheuen.

Während Palmström, glückverklärt,
mit von Korf nach Hause fährt.

KORF erfindet eine Art von Witzen,
die erst viele Stunden später wirken.
Jeder hört sie an mit langer Weile.

Doch als hätt' ein Zunder still geglommen,
wird man nachts im Bette plötzlich munter,
selig lächelnd wie ein satter Säugling.

Die Geruchsorgel

PALMSTRÖM baut sich eine Geruchs-Orgel
und spielt drauf von Korfs Nießwurz-Sonate.

Diese beginnt mit Alpenkräuter-Triolen
und erfreut durch eine Akazien-Arie.

without taking fright, eagerly enjoys its new home; Palmström,
meanwhile, drives home with von Korf, transfigured with delight.

Delayed-action Jokes

KORF invents a special sort of joke which does not take effect for
hours. People listen, bored.

But, as though a fuse had been quietly glowing, in bed at night
they suddenly cheer up, smiling blissfully like a well-fed baby.

The Olfactory Organ

PALMSTROM constructs an olfactory organ and plays von Korf's
sneezewort [hellebore] sonata on it.

It begins with triplets of alpine herbs and produces an enchanting
effect with an acacia-blossom aria.

Doch im Scherzo, plötzlich und unerwartet,
zwischen Tuberosen und Eukalyptus,

folgen die drei berühmten Nießwurz-Stellen,
welche der Sonate den Namen geben.

Palmström fällt bei diesen Ha-Cis-Synkopen
jedesmal beinahe vom Sessel, während

Korf daheim, am sichern Schreibtisch sitzend,
Opus hinter Opus aufs Papier wirft ...

AUGUST STRAMM

Schwermut

SCHREITEN Streben
Leben sehnt
Schauern Stehen
Blicke suchen
Sterben wächst
Das Kommen
Schreit!
Tief
Stummen
Wir.

But in the scherzo, sudden and unexpected, between tuberoses
and eucalyptus, there ensue the three famous sneezewort passages,
from which the sonata takes its name.
    At each of these [B–C♯] atishoo syncopations Palmström nearly
falls off his chair, while
    Korf at home, sitting safely at his desk, hurls opus after opus on
to the paper ...

Melancholy

STRIDING striving. Life yearns. Shuddering standing. Looks seek.
Dying grows. Coming screams. Deep down we [are] dumb.

Verzweifelt

DROBEN schmettert ein greller Stein
Nacht grant Glas
Die Zeiten stehn
Ich
Steine.
Weit
Glast
Du!

Patrouille

DIE Steine feinden
Fenster grinst Verrat
Äste würgen
Berge Sträucher blättern raschlig
Gellen
Tod

Desperate

UP there a harsh stone smashes. Night powders glass. The times
stand still. I stone: You glass afar!

Patro

THE stones are hostile. Window grins treachery. Branches strangle.
Mountainous bushes rustling scale off shrieking death.

HUGO VON HOFMANNSTHAL

Die Beiden

SIE trug den Becher in der Hand,
– Ihr Kinn und Mund glich seinem Rand –,
So leicht und sicher war ihr Gang,
Kein Tropfen aus dem Becher sprang.

So leicht und fest war seine Hand:
Er ritt auf einem jungen Pferde,
Und mit nachlässiger Gebärde
Erzwang er, daß es zitternd stand.

Jedoch, wenn er aus ihrer Hand
Den leichten Becher nehmen sollte,
So war es beiden allzuschwer:
Denn beide bebten sie so sehr,
Daß keine Hand die andre fand
Und dunkler Wein am Boden rollte.

Terzinen über Vergänglichkeit

NOCH spür ich ihren Atem auf den Wangen:
Wie kann das sein, daß diese nahen Tage
Fort sind, für immer fort, und ganz vergangen?

The Two

SHE carried the cup in her hand – her chin and mouth were like its rim – her gait was so light and assured, not a drop spilled out of the cup.

His hand was equally light and firm; he rode on a young horse, and with a careless movement he made it stand still, quivering.

But when he was to take the light cup from her hand, it was too heavy for both of them: for both trembled so much that no hand found the other hand, and dark wine flowed on the ground.

On Transitoriness, in Terza Rima

I CAN still feel their breath on my cheeks; how can it be that these recent days are gone, gone for ever and utterly disappeared?

Dies ist ein Ding, das keiner voll aussinnt,
Und viel zu grauenvoll, als daß man klage:
Daß alles gleitet und vorüberrinnt

Und daß mein eignes Ich, durch nichts gehemmt,
Herüberglitt aus einem kleinen Kind
Mir wie ein Hund unheimlich stumm und fremd.

Dann: daß ich auch vor hundert Jahren war
Und meine Ahnen, die im Totenhemd,
Mit mir verwandt sind wie mein eignes Haar,

So eins mit mir als wie mein eignes Haar.

Eigene Sprache

WUCHS dir die Sprache im Mund, so wuchs in die Hand
  dir die Kette:
Zieh nun das Weltall zu dir! Ziehe! Sonst wirst du
  geschleift!

This is a thing that no one ever fully grasps, and much too
dreadful to lament about: that everything is gliding and flowing
by us,
  and that my own self, unhindered, glided across to me out of a
small child as dumb and strange to me as a dog.
  And then – that I was there a hundred years ago and my for-
bears, who are in their shrouds, are as related to me as my own hair
is, are as much part of me as my own hair.

Individual Language

LANGUAGE has grown in your mouth, and in the same way a
chain has grown into your hand: pull the universe towards you!
Pull! Or else you will be dragged.

Manche freilich ...

MANCHE freilich müssen drunten sterben,
Wo die schweren Ruder der Schiffe streifen,
Andre wohnen bei dem Steuer droben,
Kennen Vogelflug und die Länder der Sterne.

Manche liegen immer mit schweren Gliedern
Bei den Wurzeln des verworrenen Lebens,
Andern sind die Stühle gerichtet
Bei den Sibyllen, den Königinnen,
Und da sitzen sie wie zu Hause,
Leichten Hauptes und leichter Hände.

Doch ein Schatten fällt von jenen Leben
In die anderen Leben hinüber,
Und die leichten sind an die schweren
Wie an Luft und Erde gebunden:

Ganz vergessener Völker Müdigkeiten
Kann ich nicht abtun von meinen Lidern,
Noch weghalten von der erschrockenen Seele
Stummes Niederfallen ferner Sterne.

WHILE some, it is true, have to die down there where the heavy oars
of the galleys scour, others live aloft by the helm, know the flight of
birds and the countries of the stars.

Some will always lie with heavy limbs close to the roots of
tangled life, while for others seats are set with the sibyls, the queens,
and they sit there as though they were at home, graceful of head
and graceful handed.

But a shadow falls from those lives across into the other lives,
and the light ones are bound to the heavy ones as much as to air and
earth:

I cannot put off from my eyelids the weariness of totally for-
gotten peoples, nor can I ward off from my terrified soul the silent
fall-out of distant stars.

Viele Geschicke weben neben dem meinen,
Durcheinander spielt sie alle das Dasein,
Und mein Teil ist mehr als dieses Lebens
Schlanke Flamme oder schmale Leier.

Lebenslied

DEN Erben laß verschwenden
An Adler, Lamm und Pfau
Das Salböl aus den Händen
Der toten alten Frau!
Die Toten, die entgleiten,
Die Wipfel in dem Weiten –
Ihm sind sie wie das Schreiten
Der Tänzerinnen wert!

Er geht wie den kein Walten
Vom Rücken her bedroht.
Er lächelt, wenn die Falten
Des Lebens flüstern: Tod!
Ihm bietet jede Stelle
Geheimnisvoll die Schwelle;
Es gibt sich jeder Welle
Der Heimatlose hin.

The fates of many weave alongside mine, existence shuffles them
all, and my part is more than the flame or the narrow lyre of this life
alone.

Song of Life

LET the heir squander on eagle, lamb, and peacock the anointing
oil out of the hands of the dead old woman! The dead who slip
away, the tree-tops in the distance, he values them as he does the
steps of ballet dancers!

He walks as one whom no authority threatens from behind. He
smiles when the wrinkles of life whisper: 'Death'. Every place
mysteriously offers him the threshold; the homeless man surrenders
himself to every wave.

Der Schwarm von wilden Bienen
Nimmt seine Seele mit;
Das Singen von Delphinen
Beflügelt seinen Schritt:
Ihn tragen alle Erden
Mit mächtigen Gebärden.
Der Flüsse Dunkelwerden
Begrenzt den Hirtentag!

Das Salböl aus den Händen
Der toten alten Frau
Laß lächelnd ihn verschwenden
An Adler, Lamm und Pfau:
Er lächelt der Gefährten.—
Die schwebend unbeschwerten
Abgründe und die Gärten
Des Lebens tragen ihn.

RAINER MARIA RILKE

Liebes-Lied

WIE soll ich meine Seele halten, daß
sie nicht an deine rührt? Wie soll ich sie
hinheben über dich zu andern Dingen?

The swarm of wild bees bears his soul along; the singing of
dolphins gives wings to his pace. All earths carry him with power-
ful gesture. The darkening of rivers sets bounds to the shepherd's
day.

The anointing oil out of the hands of the dead old woman, let
him squander it smilingly on eagle, lamb, and peacock; he smiles at
these companions. — The buoyant weightless abysses and the
gardens of life bear him up.

Song of Love

HOW shall I hold my soul so that it does not touch yours? How
shall I lift it across you to other things?/How gladly I would stow

Ach gerne möcht ich sie bei irgendwas
Verlorenem im Dunkel unterbringen
an einer fremden stillen Stelle, die
nicht weiterschwingt, wenn deine Tiefen schwingen.
Doch alles, was uns anrührt, dich und mich,
nimmt uns zusammen wie ein Bogenstrich,
der aus zwei Saiten *eine* Stimme zieht.
Auf welches Instrument sind wir gespannt?
Und welcher Geiger hat uns in der Hand?
O süßes Lied.

O SAGE, Dichter, was du tust? – Ich rühme.
Aber das Tödliche und Ungetüme,
wie hältst du's aus, wie nimmst du's hin? – Ich rühme.
Aber das Namenlose, Anonyme,
wie rufst du's, Dichter, dennoch an? – Ich rühme.
Woher dein Recht, in jeglichem Kostüme,
in jeder Maske wahr zu sein? – Ich rühme.
Und daß das Stille und das Ungestüme
wie Stern und Sturm dich kennen? : – Weil ich rühme.

it away with some lost thing in the dark in a strange quiet place
which does not vibrate when your depths vibrate! But everything
that touches us, you and me, takes us together like one stroke of the
bow which draws one voice out of two strings. On what instru-
ment are we stretched? And what fiddler has us in his hands? O
sweet melody!

TELL us, poet, what it is you do. – I praise. – But the deadly and
monstrous things, how can you bear them, how can you accept
them? – I praise. – But even what is nameless, what is anonymous,
how can you call upon it? – I praise. – What right have you to be
true in every disguise, beneath every mask? – I praise. – And how
is it that both calm and violent things, like star and storm, know you
for their own? – Because I praise.

Handinneres

INNERES der Hand. Sohle, die nicht mehr geht
als auf Gefühl. Die sich nach oben hält
und im Spiegel,
himmlische Straßen empfängt, die selber
Wandelnden.
Die gelernt hat, auf Wasser zu gehn,
wenn sie schöpft,
die auf den Brunnen geht,
aller Wege Verwandlerin.
Die auftritt in anderen Händen,
die ihresgleichen
zur Landschaft macht:
wandert und ankommt in ihnen,
sie anfüllt mit Ankunft.

Duineser Elegien, 6

FEIGENBAUM, seit wie lange schon ists mir bedeutend,
wie du die Blüte beinah ganz überschlägst
und hinein in die zeitig entschlossene Frucht,
ungerühmt, drängst dein reines Geheimnis.

Palm of the Hand

PALM of the hand. Sole that no longer walks, except on feeling.
Which is turned upwards and in its mirror reflects heavenly high-
ways which themselves are walking. It has learnt to walk on water
when it takes it from the well, it walks on fountains and transforms
all paths. It enters in other hands, it turns its own kind into land-
scape: journeys and ends its journey in them, fills them with
arrival.

Duino Elegies, 6

FIG-TREE, for a long time now I have found meaning in the way
you almost entirely overleap the stage of blossom and thrust your
pure mystery, unsung, into the early set fruit!/Like the pipe of a

Wie der Fontäne Rohr treibt dein gebognes Gezweig
abwärts den Saft und hinan: und er springt aus dem
    Schlaf,
fast nicht erwachend, ins Glück seiner süßesten Leistung.
Sieh: wie der Gott in den Schwan.
                     .... Wir aber verweilen,
ach, uns rühmt es zu blühn, und ins verspätete Innre
unserer endlichen Frucht gehn wir verraten hinein.
Wenigen steigt so stark der Andrang des Handelns,
daß sie schon anstehn und glühn in der Fülle des Herzens,
wenn die Verführung zum Blühn wie gelinderte Nacht-
    luft
ihnen die Jugend des Munds, ihnen die Lider berührt:
Helden vielleicht und den frühe Hinüberbestimmten,
denen der gärtnernde Tod anders die Adern verbiegt.
Diese stürzen dahin: dem eigenen Lächeln
sind sie voran, wie das Rossegespann in den milden
muldigen Bildern von Karnak dem siegenden König.

Wunderlich nah ist der Held doch den jugendlich Toten.
    Dauern

fountain your bent branches carry the sap downwards and up
again: and it leaps out of sleep, hardly awake yet, into the bliss of
its sweetest achievement. Look, like Jupiter into the swan. ... We,
alas, take our time, for it is praiseworthy for us to bloom and we
enter into the belated core of our finite fruit and find ourselves be-
trayed. Few feel the urge of action surging so strongly in them that,
as soon as the temptation to blossom touches their lids and the
youthfulness of their mouths as though with a mild night breeze,
they already stand waiting and glowing in the fullness of their
hearts: heroes perhaps, and those marked out for early departure
whose veins Death the gardener bends in a different way. These
rush onward: they forerun their own smile, as the team of horses in
the gentle low-relief carvings of Karnak precede the victorious
king.
    The hero is strangely akin to those who die young. Duration

ficht ihn nicht an. Sein Aufgang ist Dasein; beständig
nimmt er sich fort und tritt ins veränderte Sternbild
seiner steten Gefahr. Dort fänden ihn wenige. Aber,
das uns finster verschweigt, das plötzlich begeisterte
    Schicksal
singt ihn hinein in den Sturm seiner aufrauschenden Welt.
Hör ich doch keinen wie ihn. Auf einmal durchgeht mich
mit der strömenden Luft sein verdunkelter Ton.

Dann, wie verbärg ich mich gern vor der Sehnsucht: O
    wär ich,
wär ich ein Knabe und dürft es noch werden und säße
in die künftigen Arme gestützt und läse von Simson,
wie seine Mutter erst nichts und dann alles gebar.

War er nicht Held schon in dir, o Mutter, begann nicht
dort schon, in dir, seine herrische Auswahl?
Tausende brauten im Schooß und wollten *er* sein,
aber sieh: er ergriff und ließ aus, wählte und konnte.
Und wenn er Säulen zerstieß, so wars, da er ausbrach

does not touch him. His morning is existence; all the time he is
taking himself away and stepping into the changed constellation of
his continual danger. Few are likely to find him there. But Fate,
who surrounds us with sinister silence, suddenly enraptured calls
him with song into the tempest of his upward rushing world. But I
hear no one so clearly as him. Suddenly amid the blast of air his
darkened voice pierces me.

    Then, how gladly I would hide from longing for it: oh, if only
I were a small boy and could become a hero, and were sitting
propped upon my growing arms, and were reading about Samson
and how his mother at first bore nothing and then everything.

    Oh, mother, was he not already a hero inside you, did not his
imperious selection already begin there, in you? Thousands were
brewing in the womb and wanted to be him, but see, he seized and
let go, chose and achieved. And if he broke pillars asunder, it was
when he broke/out of the world of your womb into the narrower

aus der Welt deines Leibs in die engere Welt, wo er
    weiter
wählte und konnte. O Mütter der Helden,
o Ursprung reißender Ströme! Ihr Schluchten, in die sich
hoch von dem Herzrand, klagend,
schon die Mädchen gestürzt, künftig die Opfer dem
    Sohn.
Denn hinstürmte der Held durch Aufenthalte der Liebe,
jeder hob ihn hinaus, jeder ihn meinende Herzschlag,
abgewendet schon, stand er am Ende der Lächeln, anders.

Die Sonette an Orpheus

I. 9

Nur wer die Leier schon hob
auch unter Schatten,
darf das unendliche Lob
ahnend erstatten.

Nur wer mit Toten vom Mohn
aß, von dem ihren,
wird nicht den leisesten Ton
wieder verlieren.

world where he further chose and achieved. O mothers of heroes,
O source of ravaging streams! You gorges, into which girls have
hurled themselves from the high edge of the heart, lamenting,
future victims of the son. For when the hero rushed through the
bowers of love, each one, each heartbeat which loved him could
only lift him beyond it; but already withdrawn he stood at the end
of the smiles, different.

Sonnets to Orpheus

Only he who has raised the lyre even among the shades may sense
and dispense the infinite praise.

Only he who ate of their poppy with the dead will never lose
even the softest note.

Mag auch die Spieglung im Teich
oft uns verschwimmen:
Wisse das Bild.

Erst in dem Doppelbereich
werden die Stimmen
ewig und mild.

II. 10

ALLES Erworbne bedroht die Maschine, solange
sie sich erdreistet, im Geist, statt im Gehorchen, zu sein.
Daß nicht der herrlichen Hand schöneres Zögern mehr
        prange,
zu dem entschlossenern Bau schneidet sie steifer den
        Stein.

Nirgends bleibt sie zurück, daß wir ihr *ein* Mal entrönnen
und sie in stiller Fabrik ölend sich selber gehört.
Sie ist das Leben, – sie meint es am besten zu können,
die mit dem gleichen Entschluß ordnet und schafft und
        zerstört.

Though the reflection in the pond may often dissolve before us –
know the symbol!
    Only in the double realm will the voices be lasting and gentle.

THE machine will always menace everything we have achieved as
long as it presumes to exist in the sphere of mind instead of in that
of obedience. It cuts the stone to a more rigid line for some more
determined building, so that the lovelier hesitation of the masterly
hand need no longer show its beauty.
    It cannot be left behind anywhere, so that we might escape from
it just for once and let it belong to itself, lubricating in the quiet fac-
tory. It *is* life, it thinks it knows best as it orders, produces, and
destroys with equal resolve.

Aber noch ist uns das Dasein verzaubert; an hundert
Stellen ist es noch Ursprung. Ein Spielen von reinen
Kräften, die keiner berührt, der nicht kniet und bewun-
 dert.

Worte gehen noch zart am Unsäglichen aus ...
Und die Musik, immer neu, aus den bebendsten Steinen,
baut im unbrauchbaren Raum ihr vergöttlichtes Haus.

II. 12

WOLLE die Wandlung. O sei für die Flamme begeistert,
drin sich ein Ding dir entzieht, das mit Verwandlungen
 prunkt;
jener entwerfende Geist, welcher das Irdische meistert,
liebt in dem Schwung der Figur nichts wie den wenden-
 den Punkt.

Was sich ins Bleiben verschließt, schon *ists* das Erstarrte;
wähnt es sich sicher im Schutz des unscheinbaren Grau's?
Warte, ein Härtestes warnt aus der Ferne das Harte,
Wehe –: abwesender Hammer holt aus!

But existence is still enchanted for us; in hundreds of places it is
still pristine. A play of pure forces, which no one can touch without
kneeling and adoring.
 Words still peter out into what cannot be expressed. ... And
music, ever new, builds out of the most tremulous stones her
divinely consecrated house in unexploitable space.

ASPIRE to be changed! Oh, rejoice at the flame in which a thing
splendid in its changes escapes from you! That drafting spirit
which overcomes what is earthly, of all the sweep of the design
loves nothing so much as the turning-point.
 What shuts itself away into permanence is already petrified; does
it feel safe in the shelter of inconspicuous grey? Wait, what is hard
is warned from afar by something that is hardest. Ah! an absent
hammer is drawing back for the blow!

Wer sich als Quelle ergießt, den erkennt die Erkennung;
und sie führt ihn entzückt durch das heiter Geschaffne,
das mit Anfang oft schließt und mit Ende beginnt.

Jeder glückliche Raum ist Kind oder Enkel von Tren-
    nung,
den sie staunend durchgehn. Und die verwandelte
    Daphne
will, seit sie lorbeern fühlt, daß du dich wandelst in Wind.

II. 15

O BRUNNEN-MUND, du gebender, du Mund,
der unerschöpflich Eines, Reines, spricht, –
du, vor des Wassers fließendem Gesicht,
marmorne Maske. Und im Hintergrund

der Aquädukte Herkunft. Weither an
Gräbern vorbei, vom Hang des Apennins
tragen sie dir dein Sagen zu, das dann
am schwarzen Altern deines Kinns

Whoever pours himself out like a spring, Knowing knows him
and leads him delighted through the tranquil creation that often
ends at beginning and begins at ending.

Every glad space is child or grandchild of parting, which they
pass through amazed. And Daphne metamorphosed, since she has
felt as laurels feel, desires you to change into a breeze.

O FOUNTAIN mouth, you always giving, you mouth which in-
exhaustibly utters one thing, one pure thing – you, a marble mask
before the flowing face of water. And at the back of you
    aqueducts and their origin. From far away, past graves, from the
slopes of the Apennines, they bring you your utterance, that then
past the black agedness of your chin

vorüberfällt in das Gefäß davor.
Dies ist das schlafend hingelegte Ohr,
das Marmor-Ohr, in das du immer sprichst.

Ein Ohr der Erde. Nur mit sich allein
redet sie also. Schiebt ein Krug sich ein,
so scheint es ihr, daß du sie unterbrichst.

AUSGESETZT auf den Bergen des Herzens. Siehe, wie
    klein dort,
siehe: die letzte Ortschaft der Worte, und höher
aber wie klein auch, noch ein letztes
Gehöft von Gefühl. Erkennst du's? –
Ausgesetzt auf den Bergen des Herzens. Steingrund
unter den Händen. Hier blüht wohl
einiges auf; aus stummem Absturz
blüht ein unwissendes Kraut singend hervor.
Aber der Wissende? Ach, der zu wissen begann
und schweigt nun, ausgesetzt auf den Bergen des
    Herzens.
Da geht wohl, heilen Bewußtseins,
manches umher, manches gesicherte Bergtier,

falls down into the vessel in front. This is the sleeping recumbent ear, the marble ear, into which you are ever speaking.

An ear of the earth's. It is only with herself that she speaks like this. If a pitcher is interposed, it seems to her as though you are interrupting her.

EXPOSED on the mountains of the heart. Look, how tiny there, look – the last village of words, and higher up – but look how small it is – one last croft of feeling. Can you see it? Exposed on the mountains of the heart. Stony ground under your hands. There is some vegetation here; out of the dumb cliff an unsuspecting plant grows, singing. But the perceptive man? Oh, he who began to perceive and is silent now – exposed on the mountains of the heart. Many creatures walk here, in unimpaired consciousness, many surefooted mountain animals,/changing their pastures and staying for a

wechselt und weilt. Und der große geborgene Vogel
kreist um der Gipfel reine Verweigerung. – Aber
ungeborgen, hier auf den Bergen des Herzens ...

HANS CAROSSA

Der alte Brunnen

Lösch aus dein Licht und schlaf! Das immer wache
Geplätscher nur vom alten Brunnen tönt.
Wer aber Gast war unter meinem Dache,
Hat sich stets bald an diesen Ton gewöhnt.

Zwar kann es einmal sein, wenn du schon mitten
Im Traume bist, daß Unruh geht ums Haus,
Der Kies beim Brunnen knirscht von harten Tritten,
Das helle Plätschern setzt auf einmal aus,

Und du erwachst, – dann mußt du nicht erschrecken!
Die Sterne stehn vollzählig überm Land,
Und nur ein Wandrer trat ans Marmorbecken,
Der schöpft vom Brunnen mit der hohlen Hand.

while. And the great protected bird circles round the pure refusal
of the peaks. – But, unprotected, exposed, here on the mountains
of the heart. ...

The Old Fountain

Put out your light and go to sleep! The only sound is the ever-
wakeful purling of the old fountain. But everyone who has been a
guest under my roof has always soon got accustomed to this sound.
    It may be, though, that when you are already in the middle of
your dream a restlessness will go round the house, the gravel by the
fountain grates under heavy steps, the light purling suddenly stops,
    and you wake up – you must not be startled! The stars are still
standing above the earth, all of them, and it is only a wanderer who
has walked up to the marble basin and is taking up water in his
cupped hand.

Er geht gleich weiter, und es rauscht wie immer.
O freue dich, du bleibst nicht einsam hier.
Viel Wandrer gehen fern im Sternenschimmer,
Und mancher noch ist auf dem Weg zu dir.

Abendländische Elegie

(1943)

WIRD Abend über uns, o Abendland?
Was wir erdulden, haben Deine Seher
Vorausgelitten, vorausgesagt.
Sie schaun das Kommende, doch nur von fern.
Sie wissen auch, wodurch wir uns verfehlen;
Doch wenden sie nichts, und wenn Verhängnis eintrifft,
Erkennen sie's nicht mehr, nennen es Rettung.

Kein Seher bin ich, wäre gern dein Freund.
Du aber hast so viele Angesichte,
Und keines weiß von andern.
Inmitten deiner Wälder ward ich alt.
Ich lernte, was man lehrt in deinen Schulen.

Soon he'll go off again and the rushing noise will go on as it always does. You should be pleased, you are not alone here. Many wanderers are walking afar in the starlight, and many more of them are on their way to you.

Occidental Elegy

O WESTERN World, is evening coming upon us? Your seers have already suffered and already told what we now endure. They see what is to come, but they only see it from a long way off. They know too, what it is that makes us sin; but they cannot alter anything, and when fated disaster comes they no longer recognize it, they talk of 'saving'.

I am no seer, I would like to be your friend. But you have so many faces, and none of them knows about the others. Among your woods I grew old. I learnt what your schools teach./But today,

Heut aber, schaltend mit Erinnerungen,
Ahn ich nur wieder, was die Pflanze weiß,
Die Sonnenblume dort vor meinem Fenster,
daß es ein Stern doch ist, auf dem wir wohnen –
Wer ließ uns dies vergessen?
Was frommt es, für Jahrtausende zu planen,
Wenn die Sekunde nicht mehr klingt?

Im Gnadenlosen suchten wir die Leuchte,
Die uns den Weiterweg erhellen soll,
Und wundern uns, daß es noch tiefer finstert.
Selbst riefen wir die grauen Furienchöre,
Die nun durch unsern Heimathimmel jagen,
Entsetzen streuend: Stadt um Stadt erliegt.
Nur wie durch Feindes Huld steht noch der Dom,
Wo immer in den Frühlingen die Kinder,
Den leichten geistigen Wangenschlag empfangen,
Der sie gemahnt ans unsichtbare Sein.
Die starken Türme freun sich ihrer Dauer
Und ihrer Höhe dicht am Zug der Wolken,
Doch ist vielleicht ein Drache schon im Anflug,
Der sie aus ihren Gleichgewichten hebt.

marshalling my memories, I can only sense again what the plant, the sunflower there in front of my window, knows: that it is after all a star we live on – who allowed us to forget it? What is the use of planning for decades of centuries when the seconds no longer sound?

We have sought the light to lighten our way through the forest in the merciless, the grace-less, and then we wonder why it goes on getting darker ... it was ourselves who called the grey choirs of Furies who now hunt across the sky of our land scattering terror: town by town goes down. It is only as if by favour of the enemy that the cathedral still stands, in which children always, in the spring, receive the gentle spiritual blow on the cheek which reminds them of the invisible world. ... The strong towers are glad of their duration and of their height close to the procession of the clouds, yet perhaps a dragon is already flying which will lift them out of their equilibrium. / Then the bells will ring for the last time in

Zum letzten Male schlagen dann die Glocken
Im Riesensturz, der Wiege und Gruft verschüttet,
Und Altarbilder werden Todeszieren.

Zu viel Vernichtung haben wir gesehn.
Wie leuchtete das Haus am Park so gastlich,
Wo still im Lesesaal die Denker sannen,
Beraten von den Schriftwerken der Völker,
Und jeder suchte Wahrheit, Wahrheit, Wahrheit –
Was find ich dort? Ruinenschutt und Kohle.
Grau kriecht noch Rauch aus dem zerborstnen Globus,
Bücher vergehn, vom Feuer aufgeblättert,
Doch seitwärts welkt ein schwerer dunkler Grabkranz,
Und aus der Trümmertiefe schleicht Verwesung.

Benommen stehn die Menschen um das Irrsal.
Wer will sie trösten? Wer darf sagen,
Daß nicht mehr Fortgehn hilft, nicht Haßgelöbnis?
Den Armen wurde Grauen zu Gewöhnung.
Bald, bald verlöschen ihre Liebeskerzen,
Ein jeder hört den andern irre reden,
Und wer noch Strahlen in sich hegt, verbirgt sie.

the huge collapse which will bury cradle and grave, and altar-pieces
will become grave-monuments.

We have seen too much destruction. How hospitable the gleam
of the house by the park where the thinkers meditated in the read-
ing-room, counselled by the writings of the nations, and each man
sought for truth, truth, truth – what can I find there? Rubble and
charred wood ... Greyly the smoke creeps out of the shattered
globe, books pass away, their pages riffled open by fire, but on one
side a heavy dark funeral-wreath withers and corruption slinks up
from the depths of the ruins.

People stand sick at heart round the confusion. Who will con-
sole them, guide them? Who can say that it is no use any more to
go away or swear undying hatred? Horror has become familiar to
the unfortunate. Soon, soon their candles of love will go out, each
man hears the others talking wildly, and anyone who still bears
radiance within himself hides it.

Drum trag ich ab die Schichten meines Lebens,
Bis die vergessene Frühe wieder freiliegt,
Wo ich noch wachse, leicht, mir selbst unkenntlich:
Der Ölwald steht auf ockerbraunem Hang,
Zitronenblüte haucht aus dunklem Garten,
Und längs den Reihn der kleinen Goldschmiedbuden,
Die sich auf der uralten Brücke drängen,
Kehr ich zurück in deine schönste Stadt.
Rauh schmeichelt Wind um graue Trutzgebäude,
Die Treppe steigt an wappenbunter Wand,
Aus rauschenden Brunnen singt ein seliges Wissen –
Gehn hier noch Freunde? Keinem wohl begegn' ich,
Doch zieht mich leis in ihren kühlen Tempel
Die große nackte Schlummernde, die Nacht,
Zeitlose Mutter aller unsrer Tage,
An ihr gehn die Jahrhunderte vorüber.

Der Meister fand sie einst im weißen Stein,
Dem schimmernden, in dem sich Leichenblässe
Mit Glanz des Lebens feierlich vereint.
Heimweh nach ihr ist unser holdes Erbteil,
Und jede Liebe sucht in ihr den Himmel.

And so I will excavate the strata of my life until I expose the for-
gotten early layer in which I am still growing, gently and un-
recognizably even to myself: the olive-grove stands on an ochre-
brown slope, lemon blossom breathes out of a dark garden, and
along the rows of little goldsmiths' booths which cluster on the
ancient bridge, I come back into your loveliest city. ... Roughly the
wind caresses grey defensive works, the staircase rises against a
wall gay with coats of arms, blessed knowledge sings from rushing
fountains – do friends still walk here? I shall not meet anyone, I
expect, but the great naked sleeping figure Night draws me gently
into her temple, the timeless mother of all our days, she whom the
centuries pass by.

The master found her long ago in the white, the shimmering
stone, in which deathly pallor and splendour of life had solemnly
united. Longing for her is our fair heritage and every love seeks
heaven in her. / Look how softly she rests on the youth's coffin, head

Sieh, wie sie sanft ruht auf dem Sarg des Jünglings,
Das Haupt geneigt, und Mond und Stern im Haar,
Im fast geschlossenen Aug ein Tränenlicht!
Mohn reift bei ihr, der Zaubervogel wacht,
Und auch der Traumgott mahnt mit Wahnsinnsmaske,
Sehr still zu sein
Und nichts in diesen Schlaf hineinzusprechen
Als was er in Musik verwandeln kann.

Was würden wir ihr melden, was ihr preisen,
Von was für neuen Wundern ihr erzählen,
Um einen vollen Liebesklang zu wecken?
Vielleicht von glatten fernesüchtigen Straßen?
Tragenden Schiffen? Stolz erdachten Brücken?
Flugbooten, die das Dasein überqueren?
Geräten, grausam feinen, der Vernichtung?
Von Leitungen der Töne durch den Äther
Für wahres wie für trügerisches Wort?
O still, dies alles, alles bist nicht du,
Dies alles überholen andere bald,
Und was wir sonst ersinnen und erbilden,
Gilt es denn schon? Harrt es nicht noch der Weisung
von innen, die es adelt und bestätigt?

bent and moon and star in hair, in her all but closed eyes a gleam of
tears. Poppy ripens with her, the magic bird keeps watch, and the
god of dreams too with the mask of madness warns us to be very
quiet and not to disturb this sleep with any speech but what he can
transform into music.

What would we relate to her, what would we praise to her, of
what new wonders would we tell her, in order to awaken a full
note of love? Perhaps about smooth roads eager for distance?
Ships that can carry? Proudly designed bridges? Flying boats
which traverse existence? Instruments – cruelly delicate – of des-
truction? Of transmissions of sounds through the ether for true
words as for false? O hush, all this, you are not all this, all this will
be superseded soon by others, and everything else we think out and
construct, has it any value yet? Or is it not still waiting for the
command from within which shall ennoble and confirm it?/We

Wir kränken dich, indem wir es bereden.
Die Nacht, sie schweigt, voll Schönheit und voll Schmerz –
Wir wollen lieber von ihr trauern lernen,
Das trostentwöhnte, das geduldige Trauern,
Wo die Gedanken seltner irre gehn,
Und ihr ein schlichtes Zeichen hinterlassen,
Das älter ist als alle Menschenmühsal.

Dem Volk der Griechen galt als Weihegabe
Das Öl von den Oliven der Athena,
Als höchster Siegeslohn der frische Palmzweig –
Komm, legen wir der Schläferin die Blume,
Die große Sonnenblume, in den Arm!
Die war ein Pflänzchen einst, ein fast gestorbnes,
Von Fremden übern Zaun hereingeworfen,
Mit matten Wurzeln, abgefreßnen Blättern,
Und eilig wollten wirs zum Kehricht fegen;
Der alte Gärtner aber nahm es auf
Und grub es ein bei seinen hohen Lilien.
Welk bog der Stengel sich, ein grüner Wurm,
Wir lächelten zum Fleiß zittriger Hände,
Die dem verlornen Siechling Wasser brachten
Und seine Schwäche an ein Stäbchen knüpften,

affront you by talking about it. But Night, she is silent, full of beauty and full of pain. We will rather learn from her how to mourn, patient mourning divorced from consolation, mourning in which thoughts wander less often, and we will leave her a simple symbol which is older than all the toil of men. ...

Among the Greeks oil from Athene's olives was a sacred offering, the fresh palm branch the highest reward for the victor – come, we will lay the flower, the great sunflower, in the arms of the sleeping woman. It was a little plant once, nearly dead, thrown over the fence by strangers, with tired roots and gnawed leaves, and we in our hurry were about to put it with the rubbish; but the old gardener picked it up and planted it by his tall lilies. Its withered stalk coiled like a green worm, and we smiled at the labour of the trembling hands which brought water to the hopeless invalid and tied its weakness to a cane,/but one morning we did not recognize it.

Doch eines Morgens kannten wirs nicht mehr.
Dem Licht entgegen trug sich frei der Schaft,
Beim toten Laubrest sproß ein frisches Blättchen,
Ein zweites folgte. Lange noch verbarg sich
Die fest geschloßne grüne Kelchrosette,
Getreulich Wachstum hütend, und nun sieh
Die Neugeburt aus zögernder Genesung!
Das Feuergloriennrad ist aufgetan,
Im runden Keimkorb weben Blütenkreise
So dicht wie Stimmen gehn im Chorgesang
Und hauchen goldnes Mehl aufs eigne Laub.

Dies Zeichen, diese kleine Gegensonne,
Wird keinen Traum der Schläferin verstören;
Die Blüte stirbt, jedoch ihr Sinn ist ewig.
Durch sie grüßt uns geheim das Morgenland,
Wo Tiger glühn, von Heiligen gemildert,
Und königliche Pilger dich ersehnen.
O Abendland, so reich in der Verarmung,
Blick auf! Laß das Vergängliche vergehn!
Du weißt es doch, daß in der obern Sphäre
Nicht alles mitstürzt, was im Irdischen fällt.
Wer alles retten möchte, rettet nichts.

The stem stood up firmly towards the light, by the dead remnant of leaf a new shoot was sprouting, a second followed. The tightly closed green rosette of the calyx stayed hidden for a long time, faithfully guarding its growth, and now look at the rebirth from hesitant recovery! The wheel of fiery glory is revealed, in the round seed-basket circles of bloom weave as close as voices go in unison, and breathe golden flour on the plant's own leaves.

This sign, this little counter-sun, will not disturb the dreams of the sleeping woman; the blossom dies, but its sense is eternal. Through it a secret greeting comes to us from the orient where tigers glow, tamed by saints, and royal pilgrims long for you. O Occident, so rich in your poverty, look upward! Let what must pass pass! You know that what falls in the earthly realm does not carry with it the things in the sphere above. If one tries to save everything one saves nothing.

Noch gehen Schicksalsschwestern durch die Lande,
Zu diesen will ich sagen: «Ihr Erlauchten,
Gedenket unser! Küret uns ein Kind
Und hüllet es im Augenblick der Zeugung
Ins geisterliche feiende Gespinste,
Damit es wachse heil in kranker Welt,
Unnahbar der dämonischen Schlupfwespe,
Die gierig edle Keime sucht und ansticht,
Um ihnen die Vergängnis einzusenken,
Bevor die Schwingenkraft in ihnen aufwacht!»

Dann hoffe wieder, fieberndes Abendland,
Und schöpfe Mut, wenn die bewahrte Seele
Ein blind Zerstörtes in sich selbst neu stiftet!
Sie wird uns allen liebe Arbeit geben,
Aus Trümmern steigt einmal ein Segentag,
Wo wir das Licht nicht mehr verhehlen müssen
Und wieder frei mit Urgewalten spielen.
Ja wärs kein Tag, wärs eine Stunde nur,
Wo wir in einem reinen Anfang stehn,
Mitwebend an dem Sternenplan der Erde,
Wir trügen froh die Jahre der Verdunklung.

Sisters of destiny still go through the world and I will say to
them 'Illustrious ones, think of us! Choose for us a child and in the
moment of conception wrap it in charmed ghostly tissues so that it
may grow, healthy in a sick world, inaccessible to the daemonic
ichneumon fly which greedily seeks out noble germs and stings
them to inject them with mortality before the strength of their
wings wakes in them!'

Then, hectic occident, you may hope again and take courage
when the preserved soul re-founds in itself something once blindly
destroyed! It will give welcome work to all of us. Out of the ruins
a day of blessings will rise, when we shall not have to hide the
light any more, and shall be able to play freely with ancient
forces. ... Even if it were not a day, if it were only to be an hour,
in which we shall stand at the blameless inception of a thing, help-
ing to weave the star-pattern of the earth, then gladly would we
bear the years of darkened night.

RUDOLF ALEXANDER SCHRÖDER

OB dir ein Leib beschieden ward
    Von Fleisch und Bein,
Und ob die Prüfung noch so hart,
    Dein Herz soll härter sein.

Mag dir ein Herz gegeben sein,
    Das wünscht und trauert:
Die Zeit verlangt es, werde Stein.
    Stein trägt und überdauert.

ICH such den Splitter nicht
        In eurem Aug,
Weil ich nicht im Gericht
        Zum Richter taug.

Auch leist ich gern Verzicht
        Aufs Mein und Dein.
Mich lockt der Bettel nicht
        Im fremden Schrein.

Ach, Wandrer, weile nicht
        Bei solchem Graun,
Daß dir das Herz nicht bricht
        Es anzuschaun.

THOUGH you were given a body of flesh and bone, and though the test be never so hard, your heart must be harder.

Even if a heart was given you that desires and grieves, the times demand: turn to stone. Stone supports and lasts.

I DO not seek the mote in your eye, because I am not fit to judge in that court.

I gladly renounce what is mine and thine. The rubbish in another's treasure-box does not tempt me.

Oh, wanderer, do not pause at horror such as this, lest your heart should break from looking at it.

Kehr um und folge nicht
  Der Narrenspur,
Draus aller Jammer spricht
  Der Kreatur!

Doch leider darf ich's nicht. –
  Ich schau, gebannt,
Im fremden Schandgesicht
  Die eigne Schand.

WILHELM LEHMANN

Ahnung im Januar

MÜNCHHAUSENS Horn ist aufgetaut,
Zerbrochene Gefangenschaft!
Erstarrter Ton wird leise laut,
In Holz und Stengel treibt der Saft.

Dem Anruf als ein Widerhall,
Aus Lehmesklumpen, eisig, kahl,
Steigt Ammernleib, ein Federball,
Schon viele Male, erstes Mal!

Turn back, do not follow the tracks of fools, out of which the whole agony of creation speaks!
But alas, I cannot. – What, fascinated, I see in the stranger's face of shame, is my own shame.

Presentiment in January

MUNCHAUSEN's horn has thawed out – smashed imprisonment! Numbed sound becomes gently audible, sap rises in wood and stalk.
Like an echo to my call the bunting's body, a feather ball, rises out of clods of clay – icy, bare – for the thousandth time – for the first time!

Ob Juniflut den Stier umblaut,
Den Winterstall ein Wald durchlaubt?
Ist es Europa, die ihn kraut?
Leicht richtet er das schwere Haupt.

So warmen Fußes, Sommergeist,
Daß unter dir das Eis zerreißt –
Verheißung, und schon brenne ich,
Erfüllung, wie ertrag ich dich?

ERNST STADLER

Kleine Stadt

DIE vielen kleinen Gassen, die die langgestreckte
    Hauptstraße überqueren
Laufen alle ins Grüne.
    Überall fängt Land an.
Überall strömt Himmel ein und Geruch von Bäumen
    und der starke Duft der Äcker.
Überall erlischt die Stadt
    in einer feuchten Herrlichkeit von Wiesen,

Is it June haze that blues around the bull? Is it forest leafage that grows out through the winter stable? Is it Europa who is stroking him? Lightly he trains his heavy head.

Spirit of summer, with such warm feet that the ice splits under you – only an earnest, and I am already afire! Fulfilment, how shall I be able to bear you?

Small Town

ALL of the many little narrow streets which cross the long-drawn-out high street run into the country-side. Everywhere the country begins. On all sides the sky streams in and the smell of trees and the strong scent of the fields. On all sides the town peters out in a moist splendour of meadows, / and through the grey openings between low

Und durch den grauen Ausschnitt
   niedrer Dächer schwankt
Gebirge, über das die Reben klettern,
   die mit hellen Stützen in die Sonne leuchten.
Darüber aber schließt sich Kiefernwald: der stößt
Wie eine breite dunkle Mauer an die rote Fröhlichkeit
   der Sandsteinkirche.

Am Abend, wenn die Fabriken schließen,
   ist die große Straße mit Menschen gefüllt.
Sie gehen langsam
   oder bleiben mitten auf der Gasse stehn.
Sie sind geschwärzt von Arbeit und Maschinenruß.
   Aber ihre Augen tragen
Noch Scholle, zähe Kraft des Bodens
   und das feierliche Licht der Felder.

Sommer

MEIN Herz steht bis zum Hals in gelbem Erntelicht
   wie unter Sommerhimmeln schnittbereites Land.
Bald läutet durch die Ebenen Sichelsang:

roofs lean the hills, over which the vines climb and gleam in the sun
with their bright poles. Above that the pinewood closes in; it stands
out like a broad dark wall against the red gaiety of the sandstone
church.

In the evening, when the factories close, the high-street is filled
with people. They walk slowly, or stop in the middle of the road.
They are blackened with labour and engine soot. But their eyes
still carry the soil, the ground's tough strength, and the solemn
light of the fields.

Summer

MY heart stands neck-high in yellow harvest light, like land ready
for reaping under summer skies. Soon the song of sickles will ring
across the plain:/my blood listens, deeply saturated with happiness,

mein Blut lauscht tief mit Glück gesättigt in den
  Mittagsbrand.
Kornkammern meines Lebens, lang verödet,
  alle eure Tore sollen nun wie Schleusenflügel offen
  stehn,
Uber euern Grund wird wie Meer die goldne Flut der
  Garben gehn.

Form ist Wollust

FORM und Riegel mußten erst zerspringen,
Welt durch aufgeschloßne Röhren dringen:
Form ist Wollust, Friede, himmlisches Genügen,
Doch mich reißt es, Ackerschollen umzupflügen.
Form will mich verschnüren und verengen,
Doch ich will mein Sein in alle Weiten drängen –
Form ist klare Härte ohn' Erbarmen,
Doch mich treibt es zu den Dumpfen, zu den Armen,
Und in grenzenlosem Michverschenken
Will mich Leben mit Erfüllung tränken.

into the midday heat. Granaries of my life, long desolate, all your
gates shall stand open like lock-gates, over your floors the golden
tide of the sheaves shall go like the sea.

Form is Joy

FIRST mould and bolt had to burst, and world press through
opened conduits: form is joy, peace, heavenly content, but my urge
is to plough up the clods of the field. Form seeks to strangle and to
cramp me, but I desire to force my being into all distances – form is
clear hardness without pity, but I am driven to the dull, the poor,
and as I give myself limitlessly away life will quench my thirst with
fulfilment.

OSKAR LOERKE

Sommernachts über Land

Von Rüstern schauert die hängende
Ernte der Traurigkeit:
Schon steigt aus Wurzeln die drängende,
Die untere Ewigkeit.

Aus Brunnen krümmt sich der tastende
Verwesende Nebel und klimmt.
Aus Löchern kommt das fastende
Grauen und nimmt und nimmt.

Hat der Horizont seine klagenden
Harfen zum Klagen gebracht?
Die Erde hat ach die tragenden
Schollen zu Wolken gemacht.

Die Nähe voll bitter steigender
Schluchzer wird ungewiß.
Der Himmel steht wie ein schweigender
Berg der Kümmernis.

Der Kümmernisberg steht gläsern still,
Vor alle Ziele gestellt.
Und wer in süßere Meilen nun will,
Dem steht er vor der Welt.

Summer Night over the Country

The hanging harvest of sadness trembles from elms; already the urgent subterranean eternity rises from roots.

The groping dissolving mist curves and climbs up from wells; hungry horror comes out of holes and grabs and grabs.

Has the horizon tuned its plaintive harps to lament? Alas, the earth has turned the supporting clods into clouds.

Nearness full of bitterly heaving sobs becomes hard to make out. The sky is like a silent mountain of care.

The mountain of care stands there glassily in front of every goal, and everyone who seeks happier regions finds it barring his way to the world.

Strom

Du rinnst wie melodische Zeit, entrückst mich den
    Zeiten,
Fern schlafen mir Fuß und Hand, sie schlafen an meinem
    Phantom.
Doch die Seele wächst hinab, beginnt schon zu gleiten,
Zu fahren, zu tragen, – und nun ist sie der Strom,
Beginnt schon im Grundsand, im grauen,
Zu tasten mit schwebend gedrängtem Gewicht,
Beginnt schon die Ufer, die auf sie schauen,
Spiegelnd zu haben und weiß es nicht.

In mir werden Eschen mit langen Haaren,
Voll mönchischer Windlitanei,
Und Felder mit Rindern, die sich paaren,
Und balzender Vögel Geschrei.
Und über Gehöft, Wiese, Baum
Ist viel hoher Raum;

Fische und Wasserratten und Lurche
Ziehn, seine Träume, durch ihn hin –.

River

You run like melodious time, you take me away from the times,
my foot and hand are asleep far away, they sleep on my phantom.
But the soul grows downwards, already begins to glide, to travel,
to carry – and already it *is* the river, begins to grope in the grey,
sandy bottom with hovering concentrated weight, begins to reflect
and have the banks which look down on it, and does not know.

    In me there arise ash-trees with long hair, full of the monkish
litany of the wind, and fields, with cattle mating, and the call of
courting birds. And above farm, meadow, and tree there is much
lofty space; fish and water-rats and frogs move about through it, its
dreams./Thus I rush by in the warming furrow of the earth, I
almost feel that I *am*:

So rausch ich in wärmender Erdenfurche,
Ich spüre schon fast, daß ich *bin*:
Wie messe ich, ohne zu messen, den Flug der Tauben,
So hoch und tief er blitzt, so tief und hoch mir ein!

Alles ist an ein Jenseits nur Glauben,
Und Du und Ich, gewiß und rein.
Zuletzt steigen Nebel- und Wolkenzinnen
In mir auf wie göttliche Kaiserpfalz.
Ich ahne, die Ewigkeit will beginnen
Mit einem Duft von Salz.

Spiel

Du neigst die sanfte Bildung deines Ohres,
Mein Auge streichelt es, denn ich erkor es.
Den heitren Klang der Welt hält es im Innern
Verwahrt wie im Verschlusse eines Tores.
Du sagst: Ist dir die gleiche Welt nicht offen?
Nicht diese! schlug mein Herz, sein Schlag beschwor es,
Von dir nur kann es diese Welt empfangen;

How can I measure, without measuring, the flight of the pigeons,
it flashes into me so high and deep, so deep and high! Everything is
only belief in a Beyond, and you and I, certain and pure.

Finally, turrets of mist and cloud arise in me like the divine emperor's palace. I can feel that eternity is about to begin with a tang
of salt.

Play

You bow the gentle moulding of your ear; my eye caresses it, for
I chose it. It keeps the tranquil sound of the world locked safely
away in it as with the closing of a gate. You say: Is not the same
world open to you? Not this one! my heart beat in reply, its pulse
implored; it can receive this world only from you./Once it went a

Es ging einst andren Weg, doch den verlor es
Und liegt vor dir, ein Tagedieb und Bettler.
Einst, wenn die Sommerfeuer brannten, fror es,
Nun ist ihm warm beim Fall des Winterflores.

GOTTFRIED BENN

Ein Wort, ein Satz –: aus Chiffern steigen
erkanntes Leben, jäher Sinn,
die Sonne steht, die Sphären schweigen
und alles ballt sich zu ihm hin.

Ein Wort-, ein Glanz, ein Flug, ein Feuer,
ein Flammenwurf, ein Sternenstrich –,
und wieder Dunkel, ungeheuer,
im leeren Raum um Welt und Ich.

Verlorenes Ich

Verlorenes Ich, zersprengt von Stratosphären,
Opfer des Ion –: Gamma-Strahlen-Lamm –,
Teilchen und Feld –: Unendlichkeitschimären
auf deinem grauen Stein von Notre-Dame.

---

different way, but lost it and now lies before you, a ne'erdowell and
a beggar. Before, when the fires of summer burnt, my heart was
always cold, now it is warm though the winter leaves fall.

A word, a sentence – out of ciphers arises perceived life, abrupt
sense, the sun stands still, the spheres are silent, and everything
converges round the word.
   A word – a gleam, a soaring flight, a fire, a cast of flame, a shoot-
ing star – and darkness again, vast and monstrous, in the empty
space round world and I.

Lost ego, disrupted by stratospheres, victim of the ion, lamb of
the gamma-rays, particle and field, chimaeras of infinity on your
grey stone of Notre-Dame.

Die Tage geh'n dir ohne Nacht und Morgen,
die Jahre halten ohne Schnee und Frucht
bedrohend das Unendliche verborgen –,
die Welt als Flucht.

Wo endest du, wo lagerst du, wo breiten
sich deine Sphären an –, Verlust, Gewinn –:
Ein Spiel von Bestien, Ewigkeiten,
an ihren Gittern fliehst du hin.

Der Bestienblick: die Sterne als Kaldaunen,
der Dschungeltod als Seins- und Schöpfungsgrund,
Mensch, Völkerschlachten, Katalaunen
hinab den Bestienschlund.

Die Welt zerdacht. Und Raum und Zeiten
Und was die Menschheit wob und wog,
Funktion nur von Unendlichkeiten –,
Die Mythe log.

Woher, wohin –, nicht Nacht, nicht Morgen
kein Evoë, kein Requiem,
du möchtest dir ein Stichwort borgen –,
allein bei wem?

The days pass for you without night and morning, the years
without snow and fruit bear infinity threateningly hidden – the
world as flight.

Where do you end, where do you camp, where do your spheres
extend – loss, gain – a game of beasts, eternities, you flee past their
bars.

The glance of the beast: the stars as tripes, death in the jungle as
reason of being and creation, man, Battles of the Nations, Cata-
launian Fields, down the beast's gullet.

The world thought to pieces. And space and time and what wove
and weighed mankind, only a function of eternities. The myth lied.

Where to? Where from? not night, not morning, no Evoe, no
requiem, what you want is a borrowed slogan – but borrowed from
whom?

Ach, als sich alle einer Mitte neigten
und auch die Denker nur den Gott gedacht,
sie sich den Hirten und dem Lamm verzweigten,
wenn aus dem Kelch das Blut sie rein gemacht,

und alle rannen aus der einen Wunde,
brachen das Brot, das jeglicher genoß –,
oh ferne zwingende erfüllte Stunde,
die einst auch das verlorne Ich umschloß.

Sieh die Sterne, die Fänge
Lichts und Himmel und Meer,
welche Hirtengesänge,
dämmernde, treiben sie her,
du auch, die Stimmen gerufen
und deinen Kreis durchdacht,
folge die schweigenden Stufen
abwärts dem Boten der Nacht.

Wenn du die Mythen und Worte
entleert hast, sollst du gehn,

Oh, when they all bowed towards one centre and even the
thinkers only thought the god, when they branched out to the
shepherds and the lamb, each time the blood from the chalice had
made them clean
  and all flowed from the one wound, all broke the bread that each
man ate – oh, distant compelling fulfilled hour, which once en-
folded even the lost ego.

Look, the stars, the fangs of light, and sky and sea, what pastoral
chants, dimming, they drive before them, you too, who have called
up voices and whose thoughts have measured out your circle, fol-
low the messenger of night down the silent steps.
  When you have emptied the myths and the words, you must go,

eine neue Götterkohorte
wirst du nicht mehr sehn,
nicht ihre Euphratthrone,
nicht ihre Schrift und Wand –,
gieße, Myrmidone,
den dunklen Wein ins Land.

Wie dann die Stunden auch hießen,
Qual und Tränen des Seins,
alles blüht im Verfließen
dieses nächtigen Weins,
schweigend strömt die Äone,
kaum noch von Ufern ein Stück –,
gib nun dem Boten die Krone,
Traum und Götter zurück.

GEORG TRAKL

Ein Winterabend

WENN der Schnee ans Fenster fällt,
Lang die Abendglocke läutet,
Vielen ist der Tisch bereitet
Und das Haus ist wohlbestellt.

you will not see another cohort of gods nor their throne on the Euphrates, nor their script and wall – pour out, Myrmidon, the dark wine over the land.

However the hours may have been called, agony and tears of being, everything blooms in the flowing away of this nocturnal wine, the aeon streams away silently, hardly a piece left of the shores: give back to the messenger the crown, your dream, and your gods.

A Winter Evening

WHEN the snow falls against the window, the evening bell rings a long peal, the table is prepared for many, and the house is well provided.

Mancher auf der Wanderschaft
Kommt ans Tor auf dunklen Pfaden.
Golden blüht der Baum der Gnaden
Aus der Erde kühlem Saft.

Wanderer tritt still herein;
Schmerz versteinerte die Schwelle.
Da erglänzt in reiner Helle
Auf dem Tische Brot und Wein.

Trompeten

UNTER verschnittenen Weiden, wo braune Kinder
    spielen
Und Blätter treiben, tönen Trompeten. Ein Kirchhofs-
    schauer.
Fahnen von Scharlach stürzen durch des Ahorns Trauer,
Reiter entlang an Roggenfeldern, leeren Mühlen.

Oder Hirten singen nachts und Hirsche treten
In den Kreis ihrer Feuer, des Hains uralte Trauer,
Tanzende heben sich von einer schwarzen Mauer;
Fahnen von Scharlach, Lachen, Wahnsinn, Trompeten.

Many on their wanderings come on dark paths to the gate. The
tree of grace blossoms golden out of the cool sap of the earth.

The Wanderer quietly steps inside; pain had petrified the thres-
hold. There in pure radiance bread and wine are glowing on the
table.

Trumpets

UNDER pollarded willows, where brown children are at play and
leaves are sprouting, trumpets sound. A churchyard shudder. Scar-
let banners whirl through the mourning of the maple-tree, riders
along fields of rye, empty mills.

Or shepherds sing at night and stags step into the light of their
fires, the ancient mourning of the wood, dancing figures stand out
before a black wall; banners of scarlet, laughter, madness, trumpets.

Abendländisches Lied

O DER Seele nächtlicher Flügelschlag:
Hirten gingen wir einst an dämmernden Wäldern hin
Und es folgte das rote Wild, die grüne Blume und der
  lallende Quell
Demutsvoll. O, der uralte Ton des Heimchens,
Blut blühend am Opferstein
Und der Schrei des einsamen Vogels über der grünen
  Stille des Teichs.

O, ihr Kreuzzüge und glühende Martern
Des Fleisches, Fallen purpurner Früchte
Im Abendgarten, wo vor Zeiten die frommen Jünger
  gegangen,
Kriegsleute nun, erwachend aus Wunden und Sternen-
  träumen.
O, das sanfte Zyanenbündel der Nacht.

O, ihr Zeiten der Stille und goldener Herbste,
Da wir friedliche Mönche die purpurne Traube gekeltert;
Und rings erglänzten Hügel und Wald.

Occidental Song

O THE nocturnal wing-beat of the soul: shepherds, we once went
by darkling forests and the red deer, the green flower and the
burbling spring humbly obeyed. O the ancient note of the cricket,
blood flowering on the altar stone and the cry of the lonely bird
above the green quiet of the pool.

O you crusades and glowing tortures of the flesh, the dropping
of purple fruits in the evening garden, where once the pious dis-
ciples walked, now soldiers awakening from wounds and dreams of
stars. O night's soft bunch of cornflowers.

O you times of quietness and golden autumns, when we peaceful
monks had pressed the purple grape; and round us hill and forest
gleamed. / O you hunts and castles; evening peace, when in his

O, ihr Jagden und Schlösser; Ruh des Abends,
Da in seiner Kammer der Mensch Gerechtes sann,
In stummem Gebet um Gottes lebendiges Haupt rang.

O, die bittere Stunde des Untergangs,
Da wir ein steinernes Antlitz in schwarzen Wassern
    beschaun.
Aber strahlend heben die silbernen Lider die Liebenden:
Ein Geschlecht. Weihrauch strömt von rosigen Kissen

Und der süße Gesang der Auferstandenen.

Gesang der Abgeschiedenen

Voll Harmonien ist der Flug der Vögel. Es haben die
    grünen Wälder
Am Abend sich zu stilleren Hütten versammelt;
Die kristallenen Weiden des Rehs.
Dunkles besänftigt das Plätschern des Bachs, die feuchten
    Schatten

Und die Blumen des Sommers, die schön im Winde
    läuten.
Schon dämmert die Stirne dem sinnenden Menschen.

chamber man thought justice, wrestled in silent prayer for the living
head of God.
    O the bitter hour of disaster, when we look on a stony face in
black waters. But radiant, lovers raise their silver lids; one flesh.
Incense flows from rosy pillows and the sweet song of the risen
ones.

Song of the Departed

The flight of birds is full of harmonies. The green forests have
gathered themselves into quieter dwellings this evening; the crystal
pastures of the deer. The plash of the brook appeases a dark some-
thing, the damp shadows
    and the summer flowers that ring gloriously in the wind. Already
Man feels dusk gather round his forehead as he contemplates.

Und es leuchtet ein Lämpchen, das Gute, in seinem
    Herzen
Und der Frieden des Mahls; denn geheiligt ist Brot und
    Wein
Von Gottes Händen, und es schaut aus nächtigen Augen
Stille der Bruder dich an, daß er ruhe von dorniger
    Wanderschaft.
O das Wohnen in der beseelten Bläue der Nacht.

Liebend auch umfängt das Schweigen im Zimmer die
    Schatten der Alten,
Die purpurnen Martern, Klage eines großen Geschlechts,
Das fromm nun hingeht im einsamen Enkel.

Denn strahlender immer erwacht aus schwarzen Minuten
    des Wahnsinns
Der Duldende an versteinerter Schwelle
Und es umfängt ihn gewaltig die kühle Bläue und die
    leuchtende Neige des Herbstes,
Das stille Haus und die Sagen des Waldes,
Maß und Gesetz und die mondenen Pfade der Abgeschie-
    denen.

And a little lamp – goodness – lights up in his heart and the peace
of the meal; for bread and wine are consecrated by the hands of
God, and out of nocturnal eyes a brother looks quietly at you, so
that he can rest from his thorny wanderings. O living in the in-
spirited blue of the night.

The silence in the room enfolds lovingly the shadows of the old
too, the purple torments, the lament of a great family that now
humbly peters out in the lonely grandchild.

For out of black minutes of madness the patient sufferer always
awakes more radiant at the petrified threshold; and the cool blue-
ness and the glowing turn of autumn, the quiet house and the
legends of the woods, measure and law and the moonpaths of the
departed take him in powerful embrace.

Grodek

Am Abend tönen die herbstlichen Wälder
Von tödlichen Waffen, die goldnen Ebenen
Und blauen Seen, darüber die Sonne
Düster hinrollt; umfängt die Nacht
Sterbende Krieger, die wilde Klage
Ihrer zerbrochenen Münder.
Doch stille sammelt im Weidengrund
Rotes Gewölk, darin ein zürnender Gott wohnt,
Das vergoßne Blut sich, mondne Kühle;
Alle Straßen münden in schwarze Verwesung.
Unter goldnem Gezweig der Nacht und Sternen
Es schwankt der Schwester Schatten durch den schweigen-
    den Hain,
Zu grüßen die Geister der Helden, die blutenden Häupter;
Und leise tönen im Rohr die dunkeln Flöten des Herbstes.
O stolzere Trauer! ihr ehernen Altäre,
Die heiße Flamme des Geistes nährt heute ein gewaltiger
    Schmerz,
Die ungebornen Enkel.

Grodek

In the evening the autumnal forests resound with the noise of
deadly weapons, the golden plains and the blue lakes over which the
sinister sun rolls onward; night embraces dying warriors, the wild
lament of their shattered mouths. But silently, in the willow-grown
hollow there gathers a red cloud in which a wrathful god lives – the
shed blood, moonlike coolness; all roads end in black decay. Be-
neath the golden branches of night and stars my sister's shadow
wavers through the silent wood to greet the spirits of the heroes,
the bleeding heads; and in the reeds the dark flutes of autumn softly
sound. O prouder mourning! you brazen altars, today the hot
flame of the spirit is fed by a tremendous pain: the unborn grand-
children.

GEORG HEYM

Die Seefahrer

Die Stirnen der Länder, rot und edel wie Kronen,
Sahen wir schwinden dahin im versinkenden Tag,
Und die rauschenden Kränze der Wälder thronen
Unter des Feuers dröhnendem Flügelschlag.

Die zerflackenden Bäume mit Trauer zu schwärzen,
Brauste ein Sturm. Sie verbrannten wie Blut,
Untergehend, schon fern. Wie über sterbenden Herzen
Einmal noch hebt sich der Liebe verlodernde Glut.

Aber wir trieben dahin, hinaus in den Abend der Meere.
Unsere Hände brannten wie Kerzen an.
Und wir sahen die Adern darin, und das schwere
Blut vor der Sonne, das dumpf in den Fingern zerrann.

Nacht begann. Einer weinte im Dunkel. Wir schwammen
Trostlos mit schrägem Segel ins Weite hinaus.
Aber wir standen am Borde im Schweigen beisammen,
In das Finstre zu starren. Und das Licht ging uns aus.

The Seafarers

We saw the brows of the countries, red and noble like crowns, sink from us as the day sank, and the rustling tops of the forests enthroned beneath the roaring wing-beat of the fire.

A gale blew, to blacken the flickering trees with mourning. They burnt away like blood, going down to disaster, already distant. The fading glow of love rises just once more, as though above dying hearts.

But we drifted on, out into the ocean evening. Our hands caught alight like candles, and against the sun we saw the veins in them and the thick blood which dully flowed away in our fingers.

Night came on. Someone was crying in the dark. We drifted out comfortless with loose sails seawards. But we stood at the gunwale together in silence, staring into the dark. And our light faded out.

Eine Wolke nur stand in den Weiten noch lange,
Ehe die Nacht begann in dem ewigen Raum,
Purpurn schwebend im All, wie mit schönem Gesange
Über den klingenden Gründen der Seele ein Traum.

Der Krieg (1911)

AUFGESTANDEN ist er, welcher lange schlief,
Aufgestanden unten aus Gewölben tief.
In der Dämmrung steht er, groß und unbekannt,
Und den Mond zerdrückt er in der schwarzen Hand.

In den Abendlärm der Städte fällt es weit.
Frost und Schatten einer fremden Dunkelheit.
Und der Märkte runder Wirbel stockt zu Eis.
Es wird still. Sie sehn sich um. Und keiner weiß.

In den Gassen faßt es ihre Schulter leicht.
Eine Frage. Keine Antwort. Ein Gesicht erbleicht.
In der Ferne zittert ein Geläute dünn,
Und die Bärte zittern um ihr spitzes Kinn.

One last cloud stayed in the distance for some time, before night
began in eternal space, hovering purple in the universe like a dream
above the sounding depths of the soul.

War (1911)

HE that slept long has risen, risen from deep vaults far below. He
stands in the dusk, huge and unknown, and crushes the moon to
pulp in his black hands.

Into the evening noises of the cities there falls far away the frost
and shadow of an alien darkness. And the round whirl of the
markets stops and turns to ice. A growing silence. They look round.
And no one knows.

In the side-streets something takes them lightly by the shoulder. A
question. No answer. A face turns pale. In the distance the thin
sound of bells quivers, and the beards quiver round their pointed
chins.

Auf den Bergen hebt er schon zu tanzen an,
Und er schreit: Ihr Krieger alle, auf und an!
Und es schallet, wenn das schwarze Haupt er schwenkt,
Drum von tausend Schädeln laute Kette hängt.

Einem Turm gleich tritt er aus die letzte Glut,
Wo der Tag flieht, sind die Ströme schon voll Blut.
Zahllos sind die Leichen schon im Schilf gestreckt,
Von des Todes starken Vögeln weiß bedeckt.

In die Nacht er jagt das Feuer querfeldein,
Einen roten Hund mit wilder Mäuler Schrein.
Aus dem Dunkel springt der Nächte schwarze Welt,
Von Vulkanen furchtbar ist ihr Rand erhellt.

Und mit tausend hohen Zipfelmützen weit
Sind die finstren Ebnen flackend überstreut,
Und was unten auf den Straßen wimmelnd flieht,
Stößt er in die Feuerwälder, wo die Flamme brausend
zieht.

Already he has started to dance on the mountains, and he yells:
'All you warriors, up and at them!' And there is a rattling when he
shakes his black head, round which there hangs a sounding chain of
a thousand skulls.

Like a tower he stamps out the final glow, where the day is flee-
ing the rivers are already full of blood. Numberless the bodies are
laid out in the reeds, covered white with the strong birds of death.

In the night he hunts the fire across country, a red dog with the
shrieking of wild mouths. Out of the darkness the black world of
night leaps forth, its edge is horribly lit up by volcanoes.

And the plains are scattered over with a thousand tall, flickering,
pointed caps; and those who swarm and flee below on the roads he
pushes into the forests of fire where the flames roar and surge.

Und die Flammen fressen brennend Wald um Wald,
Gelbe Fledermäuse, zackig in das Laub gekrallt,
Seine Stange haut er wie ein Köhlerknecht
In die Bäume, daß das Feuer brause recht.

Eine große Stadt versank in gelbem Rauch,
Warf sich lautlos in des Abgrunds Bauch.
Aber riesig über glühnden Trümmern steht,
Der in wilde Himmel dreimal seine Fackel dreht

Über sturmzerfetzter Wolken Widerschein,
In des toten Dunkels kalten Wüstenein,
Daß er mit dem Brande weit die Nacht verdorr,
Pech und Feuer träufet unten auf Gomorrh.

FRANZ WERFEL

Lied vom Gezeichneten

Wenn dich der Tod berührt hat,
    Bist du nicht mehr beliebt,
Eh er dich abgeführt hat,
    Wirst du schon ausgesiebt.

And the flames, burning, eat up forest after forest, yellow bats jaggedly clawing on to the foliage; he strikes his poker like a charcoal-burner into the trees to make the fire roar properly.

A great city sank into yellow smoke, hurled itself without a sound into the belly of the abyss. But vast he stands above the glowing ruins and brandishes his torch three times into the wild heavens above the reflected glow of storm-torn clouds, into the cold deserts of dead darkness, to dry up the night afar with the conflagration, and he pours fire and brimstone down upon Gomorrha.

The Marked Man

When Death has touched you, no one likes you any more, by the time he takes you away you have already been separated out.

Du warst ein muntrer Kunde,
  Du spieltest schön Klavier.
Nun rückt die Freundesrunde
  Geheimnisvoll von dir.

Einst hat man dich gepriesen
  Wie standest du im Saft,
Jetzt wirst du streng verwiesen
  In deine Einzelhaft.

Die Wangen wurden kleiner,
  Die Augen wurden groß.
Vielleicht fragt Irgendeiner:
  Was ist mit dem nur los?

Bevor du wirst dich strecken,
  Zur letzten Nacht bereit,
Mußt du den Zwieback schmecken
  Der Ausgestoßenheit.

Und eh du darfst entsinken
  Dem leergewordnen Kreis,
Bekamst du längst zu trinken
  Des Weltraums Äther-Eis.

You used to be a happy fellow, you played the piano well, now
your circle of friends mysteriously withdraws from you.
  Once people used to praise the way you looked so vigorous, now
you are sternly sent into your solitary confinement.
  Your cheeks have grown smaller, your eyes have grown bigger.
Perhaps somebody asks: 'What *is* the matter with him?'
  Before you lie down ready for the last night you have to taste the
dry biscuit of ostracism.
  And before you can be allowed to disappear from the now empty
circle, you will long ago have had to drink the ether-ice of inter-
stellar space.

BERTOLT BRECHT

Vom armen B.B.

Iᴄʜ, Bertolt Brecht, bin aus den schwarzen Wäldern.
Meine Mutter trug mich in die Städte hinein
Als ich in ihrem Leib lag. Und die Kälte der Wälder
Wird in mir bis zu meinem Absterben sein.

In der Asphaltstadt bin ich daheim. Von allem Anfang
Versehen mit jedem Sterbsakrament:
Mit Zeitungen. Und Tabak. Und Branntwein.
Mißtrauisch und faul und zufrieden am End.

Ich bin zu den Leuten freundlich. Ich setze
Einen steifen Hut auf nach ihrem Brauch.
Ich sage: es sind ganz besonders riechende Tiere
Und ich sage: es macht nichts, ich bin es auch.

In meine leeren Schaukelstühle vormittags
Setze ich mir mitunter ein paar Frauen
Und ich betrachte sie sorglos und sage ihnen:
In mir habt ihr einen, auf den könnt ihr nicht bauen.

Poor B.B.

I, Bᴇʀᴛᴏʟᴛ Bʀᴇᴄʜᴛ, come from the black forests. My mother
took me into the towns while I was in her womb. And the chill of
the forests will be in me until I peter out.

I am at home in the asphalt city. From the very beginning
equipped with every sacrament for the dying: with newspapers,
and tobacco and liquor. Suspicious and idle and in the end con-
tented.

I am pleasant to people, I put on a bowler hat as their custom is.
I say: They are quite particularly smelly animals. And I say: It
doesn't matter, so am I.

In the morning I sometimes sit a few women in my empty rock-
ing-chairs and I look at them happily and say to them: I am the sort
of man you can't rely on.

Gegen abends versammle ich um mich Männer
Wir reden uns da mit «Gentleman» an
Sie haben ihre Füße auf meinen Tischen
Und sagen: es wird besser mit uns. Und ich frage nicht:
    wann.

Gegen Morgen in der grauen Frühe pissen die Tannen
Und ihr Ungeziefer, die Vögel, fängt an zu schrein.
Um die Stunde trinke ich mein Glas in der Stadt aus und
    schmeiße.
Den Tabaksstummel weg und schlafe beunruhigt ein.

Wir sind gesessen ein leichtes Geschlechte
In Häusern, die für unzerstörbare galten
(So haben wir gebaut die langen Gehäuse des Eilands
    Manhattan
Und die dünnen Antennen, die das Atlantische Meer
    unterhalten).

Von diesen Städten wird bleiben: der durch sie hin-
    durchging, der Wind!
Fröhlich machet das Haus den Esser: er leert es.
Wir wissen, daß wir Vorläufige sind
Und nach uns wird kommen: nichts Nennenswertes.

Towards evening I collect men round me. We address one an-
other as 'Gentlemen'. They sit with their feet on my tables and
say: Things will be better for us soon. And I never ask: When?

Towards morning in the grey dawn the pine-trees piddle and
the birds, their vermin, begin to cry. At that time I finish my glass
in the city and chuck my cigar end away and go to sleep, worried.

We have been living, a frivolous breed, in houses which were
supposed to be indestructible. (Thus we have built the long cells
of Manhattan Island and the tenuous antennas that talk to the
Atlantic.)

Of these cities there will remain what passes through them – the
wind! The house makes the eater cheerful – he empties it. We know
that we are only preliminary and that after us there will come –
nothing worth mentioning.

Bei den Erdbeben, die kommen werden, werde ich
   hoffentlich
Meine Virginia nicht ausgehen lassen durch Bitterkeit
Ich, Bertolt Brecht, in die Asphaltstädte verschlagen
Aus den schwarzen Wäldern in meiner Mutter in früher
   Zeit.

Der Pflaumenbaum

Im Hofe steht ein Pflaumenbaum,
Der ist klein, man glaubt es kaum.
Er hat ein Gitter drum,
So tritt ihn keiner um.

Der Kleine kann nicht größer wer'n.
Ja, größer wer'n, das möcht er gern;
's ist keine Red davon,
Er hat zu wenig Sonn.

Den Pflaumenbaum glaubt man ihm kaum,
Weil er nie eine Pflaume hat.
Doch er ist ein Pflaumenbaum,
Man kennt es an dem Blatt.

In the coming earthquakes I hope I shan't let my cigar go out for
bitterness – I, Bertolt Brecht, cast away into the asphalt cities out
of the black forests when I was in the womb in time long past.

The Plum-tree

There's a plum-tree stands in the yard, you'd hardly believe how
small it is. It has a fence round it, and that way no one tramples it
down.
   The poor little thing can't grow any bigger. It wants to grow, of
course, but there is no chance of that, it gets too little sun.
   It's hard to believe it's a plum-tree, because it never has a single
plum. But it *is* a plum-tree; you can tell by the leaf.

ELISABETH LANGGÄSSER

Frühling 1946

Holde Anemone,
Bist du wieder da
Und erscheinst mit heller Krone
Mir Geschundenem zum Lohne
Wie Nausikaa?

Windbewegtes Bücken,
Woge, Schaum und Licht!
Ach, welch sphärisches Entzücken
Nahm dem staubgebeugten Rücken
Endlich sein Gewicht?

Aus dem Reich der Kröte
Steige ich empor,
Unterm Lid noch Plutons Röte
Und des Totenführers Flöte
Gräßlich noch im Ohr.

Sah in Gorgos Auge
Eisenharten Glanz,

Spring 1946

[On reunion with the author's daughter, released from a
concentration camp]

So you are back again, gracious anemone, and coming up with
bright calyx to comfort me for my bruises, like Nausicaa!

Wind-stirred bowing, wave, spume, and light! Oh, what delight
from other spheres has cast the weight at last from my shoulders
that were bent with the burden of dust?

I rise out of the toad's domain, with the redness of Pluto still
under my lids and the pipe the guide of the dead played still sound-
ing horribly in my ears.

I saw the steely hard gleam in the gorgon's eye,/I heard lies'
squirted venom whisper that she could kill me utterly.

Ausgesprühte Lügenlauge
Hört ich flüstern, daß sie tauge
Mich zu töten ganz.

Anemone! Küssen
Laß mich dein Gesicht:
Ungespiegelt von den Flüssen
Styx und Lethe, ohne Wissen
Um das Nein und Nicht.

Ohne zu verführen,
Lebst und bist du da,
Still mein Herz zu rühren,
Ohne es zu schüren –
Kind Nausikaa!

CARL ZUCKMAYER

*An die Rotweinflecken auf dem Tischtuch in einem
französischen Restaurant* (1936)

Ich sehe euch mit ernster Freude an
Und schieb' den Teller weg, der euch verdeckt.
Mein erster Schluck dem unbekannten Mann,
Dem es vor mir an diesem Tisch geschmeckt!

Anemone! Let me kiss your face: unmirrored by the rivers of
Styx and Lethe, without knowledge of 'No' and 'Not'.
Uncorrupting, you are alive, you are here, in quietness to touch
my heart, not to stir its fires – child Nausikaa!

*To the Red Wine Stains on the Table-cloth in a French
Restaurant* (1936)

I look upon you with solemn joy and push away the plate that
hides you. My first mouthful of wine to the health of the unknown
man who enjoyed his meal before me at this table!

Aus euren lilablau zerlaufnen Rändern
Schaut ihr mit sanft verträumtem Trinkerblick,
Und gleicht dem Schattenriß von fremden Ländern,
Von Madagaskar oder Mozambique.

Noch ist mein Platz bestreut mit goldner Krume
Des Brots, das man bedächtig brach und aß.
Du Land voll Wohlklang und Burgunderblume,
Gleichst du noch immer jenem Königtume,
Das einst sein Fürst nach Fudern Weins bemaß?

Du spätes Land, bespielt von Abendstrahlen
Aus reifer Sprache buntem Prismenglas,
Wo Genien, Zaubrer, Zollbeamte malen,
Und wo selbst Gott sein Himmelreich vergaß!

Ich sah dich stahlzerfetzt und blutbegossen,
Ich lag an deinem Leib in Angst und Weh –
Vielleicht war der, der mich so schwer beschossen,
Der freundlich-wohlbeleibte Sommelier –?

From your lilac edges where the wine has run you peep out with
the gentle dreamy drinker's glance, and look like the silhouettes of
strange lands, of Madagascar or Mozambique.

My place is still strewn with golden crumbs from the bread that
someone slowly broke and ate. O country full of pleasant sound
and the aroma of burgundy, are you still like that kingdom which
its sovereign once assessed by tuns of wine?

You mature country, on which the evening light plays through
the many-coloured prism of ripe language, where geniuses, magi-
cians, customs officers paint and where even God forgot his Heaven!

I saw you torn with steel and drenched with blood, I lay on your
body in fear and agony – perhaps it was the friendly-portly wine-
waiter who was shooting so hard at me?

Und trank ich nicht aus deiner Tränenquelle,
Und litt ich nicht mit dir die Sterbenspein?
Ach, Schwesterland – ich knie an deiner Schwelle
Und küsse jeden Fleck von Blut und Wein!

Er schenkt mir ein. Es sprüht vom Flaschenmunde.
So trinke, Tischtuch! Trink die Libation!
Der Fremdling neigt sich deiner holden Stunde
Und macht sich nordwärts, nebelwärts, davon.

FRIEDRICH GEORG JÜNGER

Mit dem Saft der Maulbeere ...

(i)

MIT dem Saft der Maulbeere haben die Kinder
Ihre kleinen Gesichter beschmiert.
Näscher sind sie, Koster der Süßigkeit.
Sie tanzen in ihren geflickten Kleidern,
Und mit ihnen tanzt der Westwind,
Tanzt auf den Schnüren die Wäsche.
Es ist, als ob ein Hauch des wunderbaren Lebens
Die leeren Hüllen des Menschen fülle.

Didn't I drink at your well of tears, and didn't I suffer the pain of
dying with you? Ah, sister country, I kneel at your threshold and
kiss every stain of blood and wine!

He fills my glass. The wine comes sparkling from the mouth of
the bottle. Well, drink, table-cloth. Drink the libation! The
foreigner bows to your gracious hour and pushes off, bound for the
north and the fog.

THE children have smeared their little faces with the juice of the
mulberry. They are fruit-stealers, tasters of sweetness. They are
dancing in their patched clothes and the west wind dances with
them, the washing dances on the lines. It is as though a breath of
wonderful life is filling the empty husks of man./Ghosts, spirits,

Gespenster, Geister, Träume.
Eine Trommel rührt sich in den mittagshellen Dörfern,
Ein Wachtelruf, der Gesang des Neuntöters im Schlehen-
    busch.
Dieses alles ist einfach.
Zurückgekehrt bist du,
Zurückgekehrt an den Ausgang.
Du merkst, daß Wiege und Sarg sich ähneln.
Durchmessen der Kreis, das heißt:
Die Mitte gefunden.

(ii)

Ich steige nicht tiefer,
Als die Quelle gründet,
Das Feuer zündet,
Nicht tiefer hinab.

Von der Wurzel zur Krone
Steigen die Lieder,
Und abwärts wieder
Fällt der Gesang.

Ans Dunkle zu rühren
Und an das Lichte,
Das ist der Gedichte
Vollkommener Gang.

dreams. A drum sounds in the midday-bright villages, the call of a
quail, the cry of a shrike in the sloe-bush. All this is simple. You
have come back, come back to where you started. You realize that
cradle and coffin look alike. The circle is measured, that is, the
centre found.

I go no lower than where the well springs, where the fire kindles,
no deeper than that. From root to crown the songs rise, and down
again the chant falls. To touch what is dark and what is light, that
is the poems' perfect course.

Weil vom Wohllaut deiner Lieder

WEIL vom Wohllaut deiner Lieder
Selbst das Totenreich erbebte,
Kam's, daß die Geliebte wieder
In den lichten Äther schwebte.

Hättest du nur nicht so zweifelnd
Deinen Blick zurückgewendet,
Wäre ihr ein neues Leben
Durch des Liedes Kraft gespendet.

In der Unterwelt Gehäuse
Muß sich jeder Dichter wagen,
Um wie Orpheus Eurydiken
In das Licht emporzutragen.

Meines Weinbergs Hyazinthen,
Welche Muskatduft verhauchen,
Haben ohne Zweifel Wurzeln,
Die bis in den Hades tauchen.

BECAUSE even the kingdom of the dead trembled at the melody of
your songs, it came about that your beloved came up into the bright
air again.

If you had not turned your glance backward in such doubt, a
new life would have been given to her through the power of song.

Every poet must risk the journey into the catacombs of the
underworld to carry up, like Orpheus, Eurydice into the light.

There is no doubt that the hyacinths in my vineyard, which
breathe out a scent of musk, have roots which reach down into
Hades.

Dieser Duft ist wie ein Schlüssel
Zu den allerfernsten Räumen,
Wo die Geister aller Blumen
Ihre Liebesträume träumen.

Charons schwarzer Nachen kann nicht
Nach dem andern Ufer finden,
Ohne daß die lichten Horen
Hier ein Rosensträußchen winden.

Ultima Ratio

WIE der Titanenwitz
Hinweg nun siedet,
Wie alles rostig wird,
Was er geschmiedet.

Sie hofften töricht toll,
Daß es gelänge.
Nun brechen überall
Blech und Gestänge.

This scent is like a key to the most distant spaces, where the spirits of all flowers dream their dreams of love.

Charon's black boat cannot reach the other shore unless the bright Hours bind a garland of roses here.

Ultima Ratio

As the Titanic conceit now boils away, everything it forged grows rusty.

Foolishly mad, they hoped to succeed. Now everywhere the sheet metal and the couplings are breaking up.

Die Unform liegt umher
In rohen Haufen.
Geduld! Auch dieser Rest
Wird sich verlaufen.

Sie schafften stets ja mit,
Was sie vernichtet,
Und fallen mit der Last,
Die sie errichtet.

The shapeless lumber lies about in great dumps. Patience! This
remnant, too, will pass away.

All the time they were creating what has destroyed them, and
they fall with the burden which they set up.

Abschied vom Leser

Die Muse schweigt. Mit jungfräulichen Wangen,
Erröten im verschämten Angesicht,
Tritt sie vor dich, ihr Urteil zu empfangen;
Sie achtet es, doch fürchtet sie es nicht.
Des Guten Beifall wünscht sie zu erlangen,
Den Wahrheit rührt, den Flimmer nicht besticht.
Nur wem ein Herz empfänglich für das Schöne
Im Busen schlägt, ist wert, daß er sie kröne.

SCHILLER

Farewell to the Reader

The Muse has finished speaking; with maidenly cheeks, a blush
on her modest face, she comes before you to hear your judgement
on her; though she is not afraid of it, she respects it. She wishes to
earn the applause of the discerning, who are touched by truth and
not deceived by tinsel. Only the man whose heart in his breast is
receptive to beauty, is fit to hand her the palm.

INDEX OF TITLES
AND FIRST LINES

INDEX OF TITLES AND
FIRST LINES

453

MORE ABOUT PENGUINS

Penguinews, which appears every month, contains details of all the new books issued by Penguins as they are published. From time to time it is supplemented by *Penguins in Print*, which is a complete list of all available books published by Penguins. (There are well over three thousand of these.)

A specimen copy of *Penguinews* will be sent to you free on request, and you can become a subscriber for the price of the postage. For a year's issues (including the complete lists) please send 30p if you live in the United Kingdom, or 60p if you live elsewhere. Just write to Dept EP, Penguin Books Ltd, Harmondsworth, Middlesex, enclosing a cheque or postal order, and your name will be added to the mailing list.

Note: *Penguinews* and *Penguins in Print* are not available in the U.S.A. or Canada

THE PENGUIN POETS

Some Anthologies

9118